Before the Sun Fades

V. L. Bending

To Glenys

May your light never fade!

First published 2015

This work is licensed under a Creative Commons Attribution-NonCommercial-ShareAlike 4.0 International license.

ISBN: 978-1514189894

Printed by CreateSpace.

Also available in most ebook formats.

For Magnet and Tim

Without whom none of this would ever have been possible.

Acknowledgements

Many thanks to everyone who helped even tangentially with the writing and editing of Before the Sun Fades, including but not limited to: Magnet and Tim, readers, critics, and makers of that drink of gods, tea; Sparky, for all the writing over all the years; Richard, for reading, encouragement, and endless timed word wars; to the Open University's physics coffee club for your interest and comments; to the Milton Keynes NaNoWriMo writing group for all the companionship during the painful process of actually finishing something instead of spending my entire life trying to perfect it on the first draft; and to Alex and the crew of the Fortune, for always making everything more awesome.

Contents

Chapter 1: The Unseen Rift.................................1
Chapter 2: The Point of No Return.........................21
Chapter 3: Vardra...36
Chapter 4: Survivors in the Shadows.......................49
Chapter 5: What Can Be Done, Must.........................65
Chapter 6: Deeper into the Darkness.......................86
Chapter 7: The Temple of Forgotten Gods..................102
Chapter 8: A Stranger's Reflection.......................129
Chapter 9: Hunted..151
Chapter 10: The Shapes of Answers........................165
Chapter 11: The Price of Resistance......................192
Chapter 12: Sacrifice....................................205
Chapter 13: Brief and Fragile Peace......................232
Chapter 14: With the End in Sight........................256
Chapter 15: Palace of the Dead...........................276
Chapter 16: Waiting for a Saviour........................295
Chapter 17: The Strength of Desperation..................308
Chapter 18: Apart from Time and Consequence..............325
Chapter 19: Though All Things Fade.......................352

About the Author...374
Also by the Same Author..................................375
V. L. Bending Online.....................................376

CHAPTER 1
The Unseen Rift

The dark cliff cut a sharp line across the gently rolling green lands. In places it was smooth and sheer, in others fissured and cracked, its uneven edges softened by time save in the deeper crevasses, where the winds raced down from the land above, funnelled to a howling fury. Some of those fissures held paths, most barely more than goat trails that switched their way back and forth up the steep sides, clinging precariously to the cliff face in defiance of the wind. Few people made their way up them any longer, leaving them in desperately poor condition, in some places all but fallen away completely. There was nothing to be found at the end of those trails, if indeed there ever had been.

Atop the cliffs, the land continued on as smooth and flat as though the entire thing had once been a great column, sheared off by some unimaginable force. The winds that howled down the narrow fissures were gentler there, almost playful, though they were no less constant. In the cool, high air, the season of late summer, the entire mesa was alive with an ocean of green and gold. Ripples chased endlessly through it, the tall grasses bending and swaying in the ceaseless wind, and thin, dappled clouds mirrored them in the brilliantly blue sky above.

In places, darker patches could be seen amidst the sea of grass: a bush or low, stooped tree interrupting the pattern, the ripples breaking about it like a rock in a stream. Smaller than any of them, one dark shape stirred, began picking its path forward again. Travelling roughly eastward across the mesa, it was a horse and rider, twin figures that moved as one and left their own little wake through the waist-high grass. The wind that blew the grasses caught at the sandy-coated horse's dark mane and tail, tugged the rider's long braid into its endless dance. Though she'd begun moving again, she still gave little thought beyond the subconscious to it, letting her thoughts roam with the wind. Places such as that high mesa in the midday sun, open and unforested with unobstructed views in every direction, were kind to her. There could be no creeping menace awaiting a wrong turn, no shadows lurking to twist around her: there was nowhere for them to hide. Others might have felt exposed in such a place, but she found herself closer to being at peace there than she would almost anywhere else.

Looking up at the softly rippled sky, she let out a soft sigh, wishing idly that she could breathe her troubles, her dark memories, away with it. Atop the mesa, her thoughts were quieted, her constant alertness relaxed, but never quite quiescent. Somewhere, someday, she still held on to the hope that she would find true peace, that at long last her journey could finally end.

She was jolted from her musings by her mare's sudden stop, an irritated whinny signifying displeasure as she backed up a pace. Instantly, the traveller snapped back into full alertness, her senses focused on the landscape before her even as she rapidly regained her balance. At first glance, there was nothing out of the ordinary. The grass had grown thinner, the ground harder, and bare rock showed in many places through the firm soil. The barren patch continued for a short distance, rock clearly close to the surface, before the grass grew strong again further on. There was nothing strange visible ahead, and yet the horse had stopped as though there had been.

"What's wrong?" she asked softly, as much to herself as the horse. Her horse turned one ear back towards her, listening to the sound, and only the wind whistled in response. Had something simply spooked her? Or was it something more? Experimentally, the traveller nudged her horse forward again. If she'd taken offence to a stray shadow or tuft of grass while her rider's attention was elsewhere, it would be a simple matter to continue on. If it was more serious than that, on the other hand...

As she'd half feared, the mare took only a single step before snorting, turning abruptly to the right, almost perpendicular to the course they'd been on before, as though there were some invisible barrier in her path. She let her continue on for a short time before bringing her to a halt with the lightest shift of her weight, surveying the land to the left again before trying to turn her once more. Had they passed it, whatever it was?

She was quickly answered with a no as her horse turned a full hundred and eighty degrees, heading back along her own hoofprints. There was something there, something invisible to the human eye that she simply would not go past, as surely as though there were a wall in the way that, search though she might, the mare could not find a way around. Again, a light shift of her weight stopped her easily in her tracks, and the rider secured the reins to the saddle before dismounting. She moved with an easy grace born of long practice, the movement one repeated countless times over her life. Patting the horse on the shoulder, she looked around slowly, scrutinising every detail of the landscape with care. The sky above was marked only by peaceful ripples of cloud, no unusual edges or boundaries in it to signify anything amiss, nothing even remotely unusual there. Ahead, the bare rock and soil quickly gave way to luxuriant grasses again, subtle differences in colour and shape hinting at different varieties amongst what at first glance would seem a uniform sea: again, she could see nothing unusual there, nor in the distance out to the foreshortened horizon. Below her, the ground looked at first glance unremarkable, rocky and sandyish, largely lifeless, marred only by a single long crack. Head tilted to one side, she gazed down at it, alert to danger from all directions, though her mare didn't actually seem particularly unsettled, not in any way that she would if she'd sensed an actual threat nearby.

The traveller drew a dagger from her belt, extending it carefully towards the air above the crack. If there were a magical ward there, she would expect to feel it, but there was no resistance, not even the faintest tingle of warning. Something, though, was definitely wrong: though the crack traced a wavery, drunken path along the ground, it did so as far as she could make out in either direction, and in no place could she see anything, even a grain of loose soil, bridging the two sides. There should have been caught tufts of grass, earthworm castings, pebbles, *something* — but there was not. Not only that: as she studied it closely, she realised that the ground on the other side was a fractionally different colour, the rock discontinuous in places. Slowly, straining her every sense to its limit, the traveller knelt beside it, keeping her dagger in the air above. Still nothing changed, still she felt nothing. Other than on the ground itself, it seemed that there was no difference there at all. Slow, every muscle tense to spring away if need be, she lowered the dagger still further until its tip touched the stone on the other side.

Instantly, her horse whinnied and bolted, and the traveller all but threw herself back in instinctive reaction, landing on her feet with the dagger gripped ready in her left hand, her right on the hilt of the shortsword she carried. Her keen brown eyes flicked over every inch of the landscape, but other than the crack, she could see nothing there. If she had felt anything, it had been lost in her surprise, and she still could not see what was wrong beyond that the ground on the two sides did not quite match. Glancing over her shoulder, she saw the horse stopped again, now observing from what she evidently considered a safe distance, and looked back, frowning, to the crack. She had felt nothing out of the ordinary that she had noticed in her moment of surprise, and that could only mean one of two things: either there was no magic present, which seemed more and more unlikely, or it was old, deep and subtle, far beyond her skill and likely her comprehension. She would be the first to admit that she was no great mage, what little skill she had in the art hard-won and at great cost, but she knew that even she could tell when she encountered most crude or particularly powerful magics. The fact that she had felt nothing, or nothing that had not been hidden by the mare's reaction, gave her pause.

Straightening slightly from her fighting stance, she

lifted the dagger, held it before her, studying it closely. Nothing had happened to it, no damage or dirt marring the slim steel blade, a wavery sliver of her own face looking back at her in reflection. There was no clue to be found there, and she returned it to its sheath. She still had one more way to investigate this unknown magic, though it was difficult for her to use, and all too likely to leave her head spinning. Before she began, she took several paces back, stopping only once she was on the other side of the line of hoofprints that ran parallel to the crack. Though what she did would put her in no more danger than she was already in, there was a chance that whatever she revealed might prove unpleasant or disturbing.

Standing in place, she opened a small, padded pouch at her belt and withdrew an unusual lens, overlarge and oddly shaped. The padded metal frame at its edges was contoured to fit around a human left eye, and from it hung a narrow strap with a sliding buckle, allowing it to be tightened at will. Closing her left eye, she fitted it to her face and settled the strap into place, pulling it as tight as she could. Only once it was secure, the fingers of her left hand resting on four slim, ridged wheels that ranged in a diagonal pattern across the metal upper surface of its frame, did she risk cracking open her eye once more. The moment she did so, the whole world seemed to change.

The lens that she now wore over her eye was a construct of magery, a far more delicate and complex work than she could ever have managed herself. Such devices were designed and created by master mages for themselves and their students, to allow those who could not spare the concentration to separate out and view the many planes of existence without expending more effort than was necessary to set up and maintain the alignments of the tuning wheels. The planes became ever more difficult to tune to the further removed they were from the physical world, and the traveller knew that, even if she tried, she would never have the skill to view more than a handful of the nearest regardless of how desperately she wished to. She was lucky to have obtained the lens at all, never intended for one such as her, let alone to have learnt to attune it as far as she could.

Freshly positioned, the lens was as yet completely unattuned, and though the view from her right eye remained the same, her newly opened left now saw the world in an incredible array of prismatic colours, here washing together, there splintering apart. A hundred landscapes overlaid one another in those disparate colours, none matching or meshing together, drifting in different directions across one another in a discordant flurry of coloured shards and swirling shades. Everywhere their lines collided, it set up a storm of splinters, clouded ribbons of power that only added further confusion to an already senseless scene. Hissing quietly through her teeth, the traveller rotated the wheels, one colour slowly shading towards another, the patterns and images changing and fading away towards a smaller, more manageable number. As they did, her vision cleared correspondingly: though it was still awash with myriad small conflicts, the general large-scale contours of the landscape were now visible through them. Only once she had got that far could she even begin to attune it further, shutting out the unwanted planes and realms, even those of magic and spirit, intending to strip all away but the true world beneath, the bare plane of earth that not even its own inhabitants could see purely.

As her focus narrowed towards the physical realm alone, so the world before her changed. Though the land on which she stood was just as it had been, a vast chasm yawned before her in place of the simple crack she had seen before, oddly dark as though the sunlight that fell so brightly across the plain were barred from reaching within, filled with a mist so thick that she suspected she would not have seen to the bottom however bright it had been. The view from her right eye confirmed that its near edge followed the line of the crack, the far side too far away to make it out in any but the broadest of detail. There was definitely magic there, then: powerful, yet so subtle that her senses had not registered it on even a subconscious level, and almost certainly far beyond her comprehension.

The traveller studied the chasm intently for a short while, hoping to make something out below the level of the barely-moving mist, but not a single swirl stirred it, even a little. She suspected that however long she looked, it would remain all but motionless, revealing nothing. All the physical realm could show her was what was truly there. To find out why — how — it was hidden, she would need to look away. Slowly, carefully, she moved the wheels once more, altering what she saw to bring the realm of magic into focus, tracing the landscape in lambent, hidden colour. At once, there it was, shown to her now as a wide expanse of thick, deep blue-purple, calm and all but unstirring. Even more obscuring than the mist, no hint could be seen of what lay even a hand's breadth below the lip of the chasm:

whatever magic burned there — illusion and something else, she suspected — had been laid by a person or force of incredible skill, power, and control. It seemed non-hostile, though, simply a thing that was, doing no more than merely existing in all its calm majesty. She had never seen anything quite like it, and despite her wariness, she found herself intrigued. What had laid that magic in its place, and for what purpose? What lay beyond it, beyond the illusion that sealed the depths below? The chasm was undoubtedly real: when she had seen it, all but the bare physical realm had been closed away and all she had been able to see was what was truly there, stripped of all artifice of enhancement or concealment.

After studying the realm of magic for a little longer, unable ever to discern the fine weave of the spell, to make out even some sense of what had gone into it beyond its purpose, she shifted back to blocking out all but the realm of earth, and once again the mist-filled chasm was spread before her. She gazed at it a moment longer, then looked from side to side. It went on in both directions, far longer than it was wide, further than she could easily make out, the edges weaving back and forth — maybe even to the clearly foreshortened southern horizon, the closest edge of the mesa. It might have been the perspective, a trick of distance, but she thought the canyon narrowed perceptibly off to her left, to the north. Making her decision, she called her horse with a sharp whistle, pulling off the lens once more as the mare obediently trotted back to her.

"You could see it, couldn't you?" she said, stroking her briefly. "That's why you didn't want to go on."

Animals were often more sensitive to such things than humans. She didn't know why, had rarely had both time and inclination to concentrate on anything much beyond the present moment. Hers had been an existence whose demands she found yet again obtruding into her life. Even so, it was not entirely unwelcome. Seasoned traveller though she was, jaded by experience though she might have been, a part of her still sought out danger despite her desire to slow down and one day stop. It was a fact whose irony she'd reflected on before, that she of all people could no longer find peace in anything but the very adventures she sought to escape. In truth, it had been her only way of life for so long that she no longer knew another way to live.

"Let's go around. Maybe we'll learn something, too."

She tucked the lens back in its pouch, securing it firmly and double-checking that it was buckled securely with practised fingers. After that, she climbed easily back into the saddle and turned the mare to travel along the rift, once more appearing to her as only the slightest crack in the dusty, rocky ground. She kept it to their right, travelling north and letting the mare pick her own way along its edge, knowing that she was much more aware of it than her human rider could ever be without the lens. Even with it, she would have to keep one hand on it almost constantly, adjusting the wheels as both the planes and the lens' focus drifted about one another. It would be better by far to simply trust the horse and let her find her own way, knowing as she now did that her mount would not willingly cross the crack.

The day wore on as they rode at a walk, following the crack both visibly and as evidenced by the mare's refusal to ever turn towards it. Her unwillingness to approach an edge that she could clearly sense was the best guide of all. For the most part it ran through clear and open soil or rock, as might be expected from the worn ground at a cliff's edge, and however much the traveller studied it from her horseback perch, it was never once broken or interrupted. She kept her eyes on it more often than not, following its wavering line, but occasionally she did still glance up and ahead. It was in one of those infrequent glances that she sighted something, a glint of light on the ground as of the sun reflected off water or metal. Intrigued, she urged her horse into a trot, not quite willing to go any faster along the edge of what she knew was a cliff, even if she had thought she felt at least solidity on the other side. If there was water ahead, water that had not found its way further along, then it might have found an entrance into the chasm below.

It was not long before she reached the source of the glint, proving her guess correct: it was water, and not only that, but a stream. It seemed to sink tracelessly into the ground, and, she saw as she rode closer, the crack ended in the same place. It was not just an entrance to the chasm, but perhaps its very beginning. Keeping a short distance from it, she halted her horse and dismounted, securing the reins.

"Wait there, Dawn," she said, once again taking the magical lens from its pouch and strapping it on. Too much time had passed since her last use of it for it to have remained even remotely attuned, and she flinched slightly as she opened her left eye to the violently conflicting realm of shifting colours that it showed her. Despite the headache it threatened to engender, however, she kept her hand steady upon the wheels, gently turning them one or several at a time until the colours calmed and the landscape settled. Only then could she make the last final, subtle adjustments that would focus her firmly onto the plane of earth. As she did, and her vision cleared, she saw the chasm once more spread before her — only not, this time, as a chasm. Instead, it appeared as a shallow dip into which the stream flowed without the slightest hint of interruption, deepening further on into a valley whose steep sides became cliffs and whose rocky, sharply descending ground became quickly lost in mist. It seemed to be a larger, foggier twin of any of the cracks and defiles that bordered the mesa's edge, though the mist thickened with distance, preventing her from seeing as far as she would have liked. She gazed into its oddly dark, forbidding interior for a little before recognising something that she had seen without noticing, snapping her eyes back down to the streambank. She was not deceived. Alongside it ran a stone path, wide enough to be a road, flagged in places and cut into the bare rock in others. It bore signs of both use and disuse, the stones worn, but also shifted and twisted out of true, now higher, now lower than the next. Though it had been well-travelled once, it was clear that it had long since been left to decay.

Her eyes followed the road as it ran towards her, saw a sharp discontinuity in its character where the valley's seemingly reasonless shadow ended and the sunlight began. On one side it was still clearly a road, but on the other, if it remained there at all, it was hidden beneath the relatively short grass that marked out her side of the stream. That in itself, she thought, was also odd, given that most of the mesa was covered in waist- or even shoulder-height grass elsewhere, including near the stream. It spoke of something lying only just beneath the surface, an unyielding barrier through which the grass struggled to find what it needed to grow to such heights. Dropping to one knee, still alert to any danger, she dug the fingers of her right hand into the roots, rewarded instantly as they hit stone, finding it covered by little more than a hair's breadth of trapped soil. So, the road did continue on.

The traveller stood once more, wiping her right hand off absently even as she took the lens from her head with the left, tucking it carefully back in its pouch. It would be little more help to her now that she knew what lay beyond. Other than that, however, she wasn't completely sure what she should do. Thinking on it, she turned, crossed back to the mare, who had wandered over to drink from the stream. Should she stay? Risk herself in the unknown and all its dangers? Or should she journey on, and leave whatever this was behind her?

"What do you think?"

The horse pricked her ears and snorted, and her rider petted her, smiling faintly. Loyal and obedient though Dawn might have been, she certainly couldn't respond to that. The decision was hers alone. She turned slowly, thoughtfully, eyes drifting across the landscape — and abruptly froze. Standing stock-still, she lifted her left hand to her face in case she had somehow left the lens on after all, but it was gone, and all she felt was the contours of her own face. Scarcely believing her eyes, she stared ahead into the dark, foggy valley. Was the illusion incomplete? She slowly leant from side to side, testing it, seeing the valley one moment, no more than a crack in the ground the next. So, there was a narrow window from which she could see the land ahead as it really was, unconcealed by magic. If that was so, she wondered, might there also be as simple a way in? She started forward, moving slowly, careful to keep her head in the region that allowed her to see into the valley. It seemed to grow easier as she approached, the area from which she could see it growing steadily wider until she was standing on the very border between the sunlit grass and the dark, exposed stone of the road within. Her hand lifted experimentally, almost hesitantly, stopping as she felt the faintest of resistances, even less than that which a bubble might put up to her questing fingertips if it did not burst on contact. Very carefully, she raised her hand further, keeping it in contact with the barrier, then extended it. It passed through with no more resistance than her touch had met, and she could see her hand and arm clearly on the other side. Daring, she leant forward, feeling the barrier break around her forehead, then her whole face, until her entire head was through. She looked around, able to see the valley ahead, the mesa to either side, and herself if she looked down. The barrier was no more visible from the inside than the out.

After a little time of looking around, the traveller stepped back, passing back through the barrier with no more resistance than she had encountered penetrating it. So, she could get in — but should she?

A reflective sigh escaped her as she crossed back to the horse, who had remained quite unconcerned throughout her exploration of the barrier. She could move on, leave the unknown depths of the steep-sided valley behind, and if she were lucky, if fate favoured her for once, it would not be a decision that would return to haunt her. Whatever lay within, perhaps it would be wisest to leave it undisturbed. Yet, could she leave it behind her, not knowing? The seal that lay across the valley was old and powerful: good reason to leave it, but also perhaps good reason to see what it hid. What might await at the end of that long-unused road? Where had it run from, and where to, and why had it been closed off? If a shadow lurked within, then sooner or later, someone would have to face it, or see it unleashed on an unsuspecting world.

She pressed the heel of her hand to her forehead, feeling an echo of a coldly burning pain beneath her blue bandanna. If any were to challenge the shadow that lay over the valley, she knew that, however she might wish it, there was unlikely to be another who could face it better. Only three people had survived what she had been through, and they had scattered, for all she knew to the ends of the earth, unlikely ever to meet again. Though they had once been brothers in arms, none of them, she knew, truly wished to encounter the others again. For the remainder of their lives, they, as she, would stand alone.

That, she knew with simple finality, left her. She was the only one to pass that way, an instrument the gods had used and put aside, perhaps to be taken up again, perhaps to be left, broken. Whether it was fate or simple fortune, she had found the shadowed valley. She was the one who would have to learn what lay within. She could not in good conscience leave it... if it were not her business, nor her problem, then whose? The burdens of the world could not be so easily sidestepped.

If she were to admit it to herself, it called to her: both the puzzle and the danger of what lay beyond. Her life had been that of an isolated wanderer for too long, and a mercenary before that. If she was not a warrior against shadow, in her own way, then she was nothing. She had long since lost sight of any other way to live.

Tilting her head back for one last, long look at the sky, the traveller sighed, her mind already made up before she had even done thinking, and knowing with a sense of inevitability that it could not have been any other way. She patted her horse's neck, and set about unbuckling one of the two larger saddlebags, lifting it free. She usually travelled light, carrying no more food than she would need to last her a few days and supplementing or replacing it with whatever she could hunt and forage, and always packed such that she could transfer one or both of the two bigger packs to her back without needing to rearrange anything within. Walking around to the mare's other side, she followed suit with the second, unstrapped her tightly-rolled cloak from the saddle, and stepped away to sit cross-legged on the grassy ground beside the stream. There she worked quickly and methodically, clipping them together and reworking the overlong and sometimes unnecessary-seeming straps into a shoulder harness that would cross over her chest, running from the top of the uppermost pack to the bottom of the lower. Between them, her carefully-rolled cloak buckled snugly into place. When finished, she stood, taking bow and quiver momentarily from their positions and letting them lie on the grass. She would not have her access to them restricted even a fraction. Quickly shrugging on the packs, she adjusted the straps, tested her range of movement, secured the harness firmly to her belt and gave a slight nod to no-one but herself. Only then could she pick up bow and quiver again, attaching them to the new straps and anchors now available to her. If she alone were to be considered, she would already be ready to enter. However, she still had her horse and other equipment to deal with.

The rock lay close to the surface all across the mesa, and particularly so beside the stream, which, she suspected, had etched its way into the side of the buried road beneath her feet. She stepped in cautiously, finding it to be deceptively deep — enough so that she suspected the water would rise above her knee-high boots in the centre. Retrieving a water-worn rock from its bed, large and heavy, she carried it out with a little difficulty to set it down several metres upstream and as far from it as she could get without leaving the short grass. Again and again she repeated the procedure, arranging the rocks in a square with a couple of additional piles within, taking care that they would all be more or less the same height. Leaving them to dry in the sun and the wind, she crossed to her horse once again, unfastening her tent pack from the saddle and spreading it out on the ground. It would be no use where she was going, too heavy and bulky to carry, but it could serve her in other ways. The tent poles went together quickly, and she set them to one side, positioning the remainder of her bedroll in the centre of the sturdy, waterproofed tent fabric.

Leaving her things there, she returned again to the horse, who was watching calmly with only mild curiosity, used to her rider's antics. This time it was the saddle itself she unfastened, unbuckling the girth on one side before walking around to lift the entire saddle off from the other. She couldn't leave Dawn tacked up when she expected to be away for several days at the very least. Hooking it over her left arm, she took the reins and led the mare across to where her tent lay spread out on the ground. She let Dawn stand there for a few moments after that, patiently waiting while the traveller rolled up the saddle blanket and stacked it atop the bedroll, placing the saddle carefully over both. It was a reasonable fit, as she'd known it would be, and she quickly took the headcollar from one of the smaller saddlebags, turning back to her horse.

Dawn seemed pleased as her rider removed the bridle and replaced it with the much freer headcollar, buckling it carefully in place. She stepped back a few paces when she was done, checking her horse over carefully. She was in good condition, and the open spaces of the mesa would provide her with food, little danger anywhere visible. She would be fine. A nod affirmed it as the traveller stepped forward one last time to pat the horse's neck.

"All right, Dawn. Off you go. I'm going to be gone for a while."

A snort was her only response, and she smiled a little before turning away to rinse the bridle quickly in the stream. Her horse would be fine alone until she returned, able to find food and outrun danger. It was unlikely that anything more would happen to her than ever had. Drying the wet parts of the bridle off in the crook of her elbow so that they would not stay wet and invite rot while she was gone, she walked back to tuck it under the saddle, together with everything else she was leaving behind. Finally, she could finish, wrapping the whole lot in the waterproof tent and tying the resulting compact bundle up with one of the guy ropes. Her things would be as safe from whatever might befall them as she could manage.

Next, she turned to the tent poles, wedging them firmly into her piles of rock to make the basic framework of a platform, on which she put the tent-wrapped bundle of her belongings. Leaving them on the ground would be asking for damp and rot to attack; the low platform might not have been much, but it gave it some clearance, and that was all she needed. Stepping back, she viewed her handiwork for a minute, carefully judging its worth, then turned away to begin gathering yet more stones.

A couple of hours later, she'd successfully constructed a low cairn over her things. They would be safe there from predators, from rain — from anything she could reasonably expect, other than other people, and the mesa was a lonely place. Though she'd picked up a few fragments of legend that said there had once been trade routes over or onto it, listening here and there to scraps of rumour about the direction she'd chosen for herself, there were certainly none now. Nobody but her would be likely to find themselves atop the mesa, or in the precise spot she had... and even if they did, anything they took she would be able to replace in time. Until then, she would simply have to go on without it, something that she knew she could do if needed.

At long last, the traveller turned back towards the stream, running a hand across the top of her forehead, just above the line of her bandanna. She hesitated a moment, glancing at the sun: it had grown late into the afternoon while she worked, but now was as good a time as any, particularly with her tent already packed away. The little tiredness she felt from carrying the rocks would vanish quickly, and it wouldn't affect her ability to fight or run as need be. Following the short grass and the buried path it marked, she made her way back to the place where the stream seemed to vanish, watching the landscape ahead as she did, seeing the angle she could see the hidden valley from grow steadily wider as she drew closer to it.

Standing before it once again, she paused for a moment, thoughts focused, every sense alert. Then, squaring her shoulders, she took a quick breath and stepped through. To her, there was no change, save the faintest feel of magic breaking over her — but to the world outside, she simply vanished with an odd twisting of the air.

CHAPTER 2

The Point of No Return

Standing at last within the hidden valley, the traveller looked around again, gazing across it with a keen eye. Though it began smoothly, it quickly fell away, shallow defile deepening into a sharp-cut canyon with rough, rocky walls. The old road she stood on followed the stream at first, only to veer away to the right as the ground grew steeper and the sides further apart. She could see little further than that, a gentle mist hazing the distance into obscurity, revealing nothing. Deeper in, she knew, it would become the same fog she had viewed from above, thick and impenetrable. In addition to the mist, the ground was oddly shadowed, though the sun still fell on her face, threatening to dazzle her as she looked up towards it. She paused then, closing her eyes almost completely, taking in the feel of it one last time in the still, almost motionless air.

A moment later, her eyes snapped open again. She had been on the mesa for some time, and the winds had shown no sign of ceasing. Within the magical barrier, all was silent, though they should have been funnelled down the valley as surely as they had every other crack and canyon in the mesa's edge. Behind and to either side of her, the grass continued to bend and sway, dancing to a force she could no longer feel, proving beyond doubt that the winds had not stopped. What, she wondered, was she about to walk into?

Whatever it was, she was already committed. There would only be one way to find out, and her decision had already been made. If danger lay ahead, as the silent valley's ominous nature suggested, she would have to find and face it. Better by far another dark battle than to leave an unknown shadow sleeping, only to unleash itself later on the unsuspecting and unprepared world beyond. She would do all in her power to prevent that, with her dying breath if need be. Though it was true that her own actions might wake an evil that even she could not fight, if she couldn't, who could? She had found the valley, found the way in. She couldn't tell if it were chance or something more, and she could not now turn her back. Picking her steps carefully, alert to both the possibility of danger from ahead and the unknown nature of the worn road beneath her feet, she started forward once more.

The slope was gentle at first, but quickly grew steeper as she began to make her way along the road, enough so that she was still beside the stream when her head dropped below the canyon's edge and the light of the sun sharply faded away. She gasped, frozen in shock, eyes darting across the landscape before her in the sudden gloom. Nothing appeared to have changed: it in itself seemed almost lighter than before, if anything, perhaps because the sun was no longer in her eyes. Slowly, she tilted her head back, looking for whatever cast the shadow that lay across the valley. The moment she did so, the moment she brought her gaze above the top of the steep walls, her eyes rebelled, and she stumbled back, half-falling into an instinctive crouch with a gasp. It had been so close, just above her head, something impossible so near her face had nearly brushed it —

Placing a steadying hand on the damp cobbles

beneath her, she mentally braced herself before looking up again. It was easier a second time, perhaps because she was further away from it, but her eyes still felt almost as though they were trying to look in opposite directions. Above her, from what she could bring herself to make out, appeared to be a solid rock ceiling, with no more than a single narrow opening letting a little light filter through from the world above. She pressed the fingertips of her free hand between her eyebrows and tried to focus, only to find that she couldn't even seem to define a distance between her and the rock, couldn't find anything to focus on despite how detailed it gave the impression of being. Her eyes wanted to skate away, to look at something, anything, else, and the strain was already giving her a headache. Resigned, she looked away, cautiously standing back up, her posture instinctively slightly stooped. Whatever was above her, could she touch it?

  She raised her right arm slowly, exploring the cool, still air above her head. Her fingers touched chill, wet rock, rough and bumpy, feeling real in every aspect. There was none of the strange, disconcerting feeling that had been so readily apparent to her eyes. Experimentally, she pressed against it, but it would not give. Was this strange barrier what had blocked the light from the entire valley? And what did it mean for her chances of return?

  Slowly, keeping her hand on the rock ceiling above and her eyes cast down slightly below the horizontal, she turned around. As she'd half expected, she saw it continue towards the mouth of the valley, becoming no more than a dark, low space between the walls in the end, through which a stream somehow filtered. There was no sign of an opening from where she stood, and she wondered if the barrier could only be passed through in one direction, just as the rock — whatever it truly was — above her head had become solid the moment she had stepped below its level. If that were the case, the only way out would be to go forward. Her decision on the open plains had, it seemed, become irreversible.

Despite the entrance's appearance, she tried anyway, keeping one hand flat to the rock ceiling above her and walking back along the road, quickly forced to stoop, then kneel. There she stopped, and for an instant her breath caught with the chill certainty that she was trapped underground, with no way to return to the daylit surface above. Deliberately, slowly, she forced herself to let it out again. There would be another means of escape, perhaps further in, perhaps at the other end. There had to be. She refused to let herself think of the consequences if there were not.

She turned in place, a little awkward in the constricted space, and made her way out again. There was no use dwelling on her situation: she had to go on. If nothing else, the stream came in, and if it had no way out then the valley would have flooded long ago. When she'd found out why the valley had been hidden, perhaps it would provide her with a means of escape, just as it had let her in. Picking her way carefully along the uneven, slippery road, she continued onward and down, alert and ready for any danger — yet at first, at the least, none came.

She followed the road as it traced the stream's edge, and continued along it even when it veered away from the tumbling waters, tracing what must once have been the safest and easiest path down the valley's steep sides. Glancing at the walls, which in places had turned to sheer rock, the traveller wondered if nature or magic had carved their unforgiving lines. There was no easy way to tell. Though they were a match for any of the smaller cracks on the mesa's edge, that meant little: sufficiently powerful magic could have riven the rock as easily as a natural flaw.

The further she went, the further apart the valley's sides grew, a thin mist beginning to turn the air between the near and far hazy, making it difficult to judge the true distance. Thicker wisps collected in hollows and sheltered edges, a grey blanket clinging to the holes in things, softening sharp rock and adding to the thin film of moisture that coated everything. As she reached a hairpin bend, turning nearly a hundred and eighty degrees to continue on down the valley's steep side, she looked back to the entrance, only to find it lost in the mist that cloaked the distance. There was only her, alone on a road that had by all appearances gone unused for generations. She doubted any feet would tread its worn stones again, for who could live in such a place as the shadowed, mist-filled valley? Though the road itself was proof enough that people once had passed through in great numbers, it was also proof, as if it was needed, that they did no longer.

Tracing her hand across a worn boulder at the road's side, she wondered about the people who had once passed that way, whose footsteps she was unknowingly tracing. What, in the past, might such a rock have seen of the ancient road? Why had it been built, and where had its builders gone? In the end, had it seen them flee? Had it seen them killed? But if the cool stone beneath her hand held any such memories, it would not give them up to her, and she was no great mage to tease them from it. As her hand left it, trailing drops from its slick surface, only her mind's eye played out the scenes it might have seen. The road was more than wide enough for carts and carriages even where its edges had eroded, and so they must have passed through, perhaps laden down with trade goods or bearing people to destinations far across the mesa. There would have been travellers on foot too; there always were, and riders as well. Though there was no sign of such a presence on the part of the mesa she had crossed, beyond the odd worn marker stone or tumbled low wall, there must once have been, matching the handful of tales she'd heard told of lands beyond that had long since drawn inward and fallen silent, or turned their trade to easier-to-reach destinations. The mesa had not always been the impassable barrier it was seen as when she had arrived at its base.

Then, one day, something had happened, though she knew not what. Whether it came suddenly or slowly, obvious and openly or creeping and hidden, something had seen the valley sealed, and she had no doubt that it was dark. Beyond her own, no feet would walk the formerly well-travelled road again, nor seek whatever lay at its end. If anyone had come the way she did, they had left no trace of their passage, and could never have returned the way they had come. Anyone who had would have to have either left at the other end, unable to return to their homeland, or died somewhere within the valley. She preferred to think the former.

Even so, she paused to take her bow from her back and string it. One of the few things of genuine value that she owned, she had had it custom-made for her and her alone. Spelled to resist the ravages of weather and battle, of the everyday abuses that even the most careful traveller's belongings might go through, it would take more than a few days of exposure to the mist to harm it. The mage who had set that particular enchantment had assured her it would last unharmed on the bed of a lake for a month, though needless to say, she had never actively tested his word quite that extensively. Perfectly shaped and balanced, imbued with other enchantments that would add power to her arrows at her command, it rested in her hands like a natural extension of her body. So armed, she would be able to make any attacker pause in its tracks, if not kill it outright. Cautiously, she continued her journey ever downwards along the trail.

Despite her wariness, nothing seemed to happen. The valley was silent, save for the odd drip and the scuff of her boots on stone, and even those were oddly deadened by the fog. Rather than calming her, the absence of sound only made her more uneasy, knowing as she did that it spoke of something wrong, something out of place. There were no birds, nor animals, nor even a breath of wind to feather her hair and murmur in her ear, or stroke whispers from the rocks. She found herself reflexively stepping down hard, or sliding her feet a fraction as they landed: anything to break the silence and affirm again that she, at least, still lived in the midst of the seemingly endless mist. In concert with the silence, the fog thickened as she descended, not quite far enough to render her bow useless, but still trapping her in a dully grey cocoon, lit by whatever light filtered through from the hidden ceiling above. Several times, her hand strayed to one of her belt pouches, felt at it and checked itself there, as if affirming the presence of something held within and consciously holding back from drawing it out.

It seemed like an age before the faint sound of running water began to intrude into her awareness again, and she unconsciously quickened her pace towards it until she had reached a second hairpin bend that swung the road down in the direction of the centre of the valley. The stream that had led her into the valley had become a natural waterfall some distance ahead, feeding a man-made pond that might once have provided a watering hole at the broad, roughly flat corner before tumbling on down a further series of rapids, away from the road and out of her sight once more. She found herself lingering at its side a moment, unwilling to relinquish her only companion, however inanimate, in the silence — then she caught herself, and shook her head. There was no choice but to go on: to follow the stream would risk a broken neck even without the film of water coating every hard surface. Once again, she would have to leave it behind.

As she went on, the road veered further from the valley wall, its incline decreasing further as the ground levelled out at last. Eventually, it turned to the right to run along what she suspected was the rough line of the valley's centre, and as she rounded that last bend, she saw a dim shape looming in the fog. Its hard angles spoke of a man-made structure, even softened by mist as they were: vertical walls, a shallow-sloped peaked roof with a flat base below, mist gathering inside with less darkness than might be expected for an enclosed space. Intrigued, the traveller picked up her pace towards it, and whatever signs of its vanished people it might conceal.

Her approach revealed it as open at both ends, a little longer than the length of a horse, plainly ornamented and with no sign of walls to either side, nor gates within. It served no defensive purpose, then, and indeed would have been in a poor place for it compared with the head of the trail, where there had been nothing but rock walls and the open road: whoever had lived here had not feared attack from the mesa above. As she neared it, she slowed again, then stopped, looking at the two stone walls. Mould and the inevitable residue of water covered them, but unless her eyes deceived her in the weak, shadowless light, there were carvings of some form at eye level. Moving slowly, she lifted her hand to touch them, as much feeling their lines as trying to brush away the accumulated slime of years. Beneath it, timeworn symbols lay marginally better revealed, probably as old as the structure itself, and she bent closer to squint at them. They appeared to be letters, but so aged that she could only make a few of them out. Whatever the inscription might once have said, it had become lost to the ages.

She hesitated a moment longer before stepping under the arch, caution in her movements. If it held magic, as the entrance to the valley had, there was no way of telling what she might be about to walk into. This time, however, despite her caution, nothing untoward seemed to happen at all. Other than the occasional drip of water from the ancient stone, and the sound of her own breathing, the valley remained unchanged, fog-blanketed, as still and silent as the grave. Emerging from the other side, she looked around again, with the same result. There had been no sense of a barrier broken, no tell-tale shimmer or transition, no new twist to her vision — all was as it had been before. She glanced behind herself in a further test, seeing only the road down which she had come, and turned back to the path to continue once more.

As she moved on, the land to either side began to look more and more familiar. Even in the mist, she realised with a heavy certainty that she knew the patterns she was seeing: overgrown fields and the withered frames of rotten trees, hemmed in by tumbling walls. It would have been farmland, once. Long ago, the sun must have shone into the valley, the mists absent and the land flourishing, but it didn't seem as though much light had made its way down there in a very long time. It was no more now than a ghost of what had been.

With a quiet sigh, the traveller turned her gaze forward again. The road wound on before her, losing itself in the mist, only unknowns ahead. She would follow it, however long it took, and learn what awaited at its end.

* * *

She had walked for almost an hour, passing the occasional ruined farmhouse on her way, when the fog in front of her began to take on a slightly darker quality. At first, she barely even noticed: though the thickest layer seemed to be a little distance above her head, like a low-lying cloud, it was still relatively thick at the ground where she walked, and the landscape was everywhere shaded and edged in muted grey. Only as she grew close did she realise that the darkness ahead was a looming wall, disappearing swiftly into mist above, a lighter arched gap with oddly angled sides suggesting a great gateway. The gates must once have been proud, but as details began to resolve through the mist, she saw that they were old and rotten, hanging at an angle from their rusted hinges and scored with what appeared to be the marks of large blades, wielded with a strength that sent a warning chill down her spine. War had come to the valley in its last days, then — one that the inhabitants had likely not survived. Fully open, the gates would have let two carts pass easily side by side, but no such luxury would have been afforded those fleeing the city in its final hours. The exodus she had pictured before would have been a panicked flight of the lucky few, with terror behind lending them speed.

The traveller walked slowly up to the gates, distant screams echoing whisper-thin in the back of her mind. She lifted a slow hand, calloused fingers resting across the wide score left by some ancient blade. The wood was dank and moist, needing only a little encouragement to peel away, despite the care it must once have received. The gates towered above her, but they had fallen to ruin... as had the rest of the city. Through the thick mist, she could see the gutted shells of buildings, some more intact than others, windows and doorways in many places no more than gaping holes. Water dripped from somewhere, the oddly muted sound all that was audible in the silent, smothered desolation. It felt almost unreal, in a sense, a ghost city long since dead. Letting her hand slip from the gate, the traveller stepped through.

The main street ran straight as an arrow into the fog, buildings crowded together on either side. The remnants of signs hung at crazed angles from some, the skeletal frame of an awning catching her eye for an instant before she realised what it had once been. Windowboxes on the higher floors that might once have held flowers now hosted only pale and uninviting fungi, glistening slightly in the permanent damp, a pattern repeated in the gutters above. Empty and cold, there was no welcome left in the city, barely even the promise of shelter. The only way on, however, was through.

Slowly, she began to make her way along the ancient road, ready to react at a moment's notice, though no sound reached her ear, nor motion caught her eye. She glanced down each side street before passing it, straining her eyes to pierce the thick fog that cloaked the city, but finding nothing each time. Even so, her eyes were never still, alighting on broken windows or hollow doorways, on debris in the street that would never be cleared away. It was clear enough that the buildings to either side had been largely shops, and if she was any judge, the floors above would have housed their owners. Nothing had been sold in the city for decades at the least, though, and her guess would have placed it closer to centuries had the wood not still remained. Broken windows with their shutters ripped askew, rotten doors hanging open or torn from their hinges, the occasional gouge still visible amidst the decay to remind her of the ones on the gate — it all spoke of slaughter. Yet there were no bodies, or if there were, they were hidden from her view. The traveller didn't know whether to thank fate for that small mercy or curse it for the doubts and fears that it raised. Perhaps the people had fled; perhaps some had returned later to bury their dead, or else the invaders themselves had. Alternatively, they could have taken the inhabitants prisoner to kill them in some more terrible fashion later... or worst of all, perhaps their remains still roamed the empty city, shuffling and lurching through its alleys, blindly seeking the living who were no more.

With such thoughts on her mind, the fog began to seem thicker, darker, and it was a short while before she realised that it was more than just her imagination. Could it truly have grown so late while she walked? Outside the valley, could the sun be setting? She looked up into the mist, seeking some clue as to its position, but found nothing. The fog above was a featureless, oppressive grey, seeming to hang over her head like the roof of a cave. For an instant, she had to fight the feeling that it would smother her, too, into lifelessness, looking down and shaking her head to clear it and re-establish herself. Even if a hostile presence lurked above, it would not take her without a fight: bitter experience had left her well-prepared. Until such time as it showed itself, she had to concentrate on the immediate moment, not let her thoughts be swayed by fear. If the sky outside truly was already darkening, then she would need to find shelter, and quickly. It would need to be at least of reasonable quality, too, the more intact the better. Not only would she be protected overnight, but it would give her somewhere to return to if need be as she explored the city. There was no doubt that that would take her some time, even if all she did was find another way out.

Seeking the best location while the dim light held, she made her way further along the road, listening to the eerie silence all about her. Pockets of thicker fog hung in corners, still and ghostly, and other than her soft footsteps, the only sound was the muted drip and splash of water running from roof and gutter to pool in the empty streets. Softened by mist, the puddles blurred into the worn cobblestones surrounding them, featureless grey on grey. In the motionless air, there was no whistle of wind to complete the ghostly, haunting effect, and somehow that made it all the more unsettling.

Seeing a somewhat lighter patch ahead, the traveller picked up her pace towards it. The road opened up into a wide market square, a raised pool in its centre. Though the fountain that stood at its heart had long since ceased flowing, it was still full of water, a perfectly flat surface mirroring the grey fog above. She looked down into it, her reflection dark against the fog, indistinct in the low light despite the calm of the water. How many other people had done that, once, when the pool was alive with ripples from the fountain at its heart? She could picture faceless strangers sitting on the broad, flat lip at the edge, the eerily silent square buzzing with the sounds of countless people. Lifting her head to look around, she considered the square, the old wreckage at the foot of the walls. It had, perhaps, been a market: stalls would have lined the edges and been scattered through the open spaces, completing the image in her mind.

Now, however, all was dark, broken and wreathed in fog. Gazing into the shifting mists in the dimming light, the traveller found she could barely make out the roads leading away from the square. Not far beyond, it became too indistinct to see at all, outlines fading away to nothing. Thoughtful, she shifted her weight to one leg, regarding the landscape. The buildings around the square were large and open, pressed together oddly. For a campsite, she would need something smaller and more defensible: windows narrow, entrances limited. She'd take the smallest road, then, she decided, more likely to lead to such a place than the broad avenue she'd entered by.

As she was about to turn and step away around the pool, a sound drifted to her ears, muted by the mist and yet standing out for the simple fact that it was something other than the fog-blanketed silence and the muffled drips that were the only noise beyond her own that she'd heard for hours. It had sounded almost like tearing cloth, and had come from a side street that opened onto the square where she stood!

"Who's there?" she demanded, automatically snapping her right hand back for an arrow. There was a definite gasp, and a figure shot up, a quick flash of movement half-hidden by the corner of a building to her left, springing back around it. Unwilling to let the only living being she'd seen get away from her now, the traveller chased after it at a run. Whoever, whatever it was, she wouldn't let it escape.

CHAPTER 3
Vardra

Knelt beside a wall, a thin young man in ragged clothing surveyed the square ahead. Open spaces were dangerous, but the pool there was one of the best sources of untainted water for some distance around, and that made it a risk worth taking despite how late it had grown. Dark eyes surveyed it slowly, leaving no edge or shadow overlooked — and stopped just moments after sweeping past the fountain. There was a figure in the square, standing right by the very pool itself! He froze instinctively, pressing himself flat to the wall and soundlessly praying not to be seen... and indeed, it seemed he wasn't. For another day, his luck had held.

Thoughts catching up a moment behind his ingrained reflexes, he looked again at the dark figure, its edges blurred into the mist. Slim, upright, bulked out by what might have been the outlines of some form of backpack, it seemed... human. He breathed out noiselessly in a silent sigh of relief. Though it was foolish to stand out in the open so plainly, the shape was not vardran, and that meant that it was safe. He watched it move slightly as if surveying the square, still unsure whether it was a man or a woman in the fading light. Either way, he needed water, and it was always worth trading news. Cautiously, he began to get to his feet, feeling a slight tug in the fabric of his tattered jacket and stopping a moment too late. It ripped, the sound of tearing cloth quiet but still, apparently, audible.

"Who's there?" the figure snapped, a woman's voice, strong, commanding, and far too loud. He gasped in surprise, jumping to his feet and reflexively springing back. Footsteps started after him at once, and he heard the stranger's voice again.

"Wait!"

She'd shouted that time, and he spun around, running. A sound like that would carry too far, too well! It wasn't likely it would have gone unheard, and soon enough something would come to investigate, violent and hungry, hoping for prey. The practice of a lifetime kept his footsteps soft on the cobbled street even at that speed, but behind him he could hear another, louder set. Risking a look over his shoulder, he saw the woman from the square, slightly closer than she had been — she, too, must have realised the mistake she'd made. The nearest safehouse wasn't far away, not too far unless the vardra were close. With luck they'd make it, slam the shutters on the outside world and wait out the night, wait out the vardra as long as they had to. Panting, he shot around a corner and into a narrow alley, the second set of footsteps now close behind him. It wasn't far now, not far at all.

Just as he was thinking they'd make it, a weight slammed into him from behind! For once, he cried out, terrified, knowing in that moment that he was going to die. They'd caught up, cut them off, and now...

There was no pain, he realised dully, drawing a constricted breath he hadn't expected to be able to take. It had him pinned, but other than where it had hit him, where he'd hit the floor, he wasn't hurt — what was it waiting for? Even as he thought that, it moved, and he flinched, unable to protect himself or even really struggle as the hard line across his shoulder blades moved somewhat, his captor repositioning itself. This was it, had to be, a killing strike. There was nothing he could do.

"I won't hurt you."

For a moment, he was unable to comprehend what was happening. The voice was the woman from the square, coming from just above him, and he couldn't make sense of anything. What was she doing there, sounding so calm? How could it be possible? Had she knocked him down to prevent him running into some danger ahead that she'd seen and he had not?

"Let me up," he managed, almost stumbling over the whispered words. He felt the woman's weight shift slightly again, a long, brown braid falling to the ground and barely missing his nose, as though it had just slipped from her shoulder.

"Only if you'll stop running away from me," she said, more quietly, and he blinked. She'd thought he was running from *her?* "Do we have a deal?"

"I... I wasn't running from you," he responded, not quite sure what he could say, keeping his voice all but silent. Why would he run from her? Who — what — was she? He tried to look up, but her position made it impossible for him to see more than the very edge of her head, then not even that as she sat up, keeping one hand pressed between his shoulders to keep him pinned. There was nothing for it but to hope she'd had a reason. "What did you see?"

"Nothing," she murmured back, voice calm yet growing urgent. "What's out there?"

"Vardra, what else — we have to keep going! The

safehouse is just around the corner!"

She got up, half-pulling him to his feet by his ragged collar, and he felt something give in the stitching.

"Lead the way."

He nodded and shot off ahead, pausing at the mouth of the alley to glance up, left, right, then dashing around the corner to the safehouse he knew waited for them ahead, the door firmly shut, windows either too small or boarded, a single loose shutter allowing someone to slip inside. "There, in there!"

The stranger followed him closely as he scrambled inside, slamming the warped shutter closed behind her and plunging them into pitch blackness. Unable to see, he began to edge slowly away from the window, feeling his way carefully on silent feet. His heart still raced, and he wasn't sure whether she was moving or not. Still, they'd made it. For the moment, they were safe. His straining ears caught what sounded like a clink of metal, and he half-turned back towards the sound and the window, listening. It was followed by a slight rustle of cloth, and suddenly, a ray of soft, white light shone into the room, bright as the fogbound light in the middle of the day. It was emanating from an oddly angled something in the woman's hand, something that proved to be a small, flattened sphere as the remainder of the cloth covering it slipped away, leaving the room lit in its soft glow. Taken aback, wonder pushing back lingering fear, he could only stare.

The two looked at each other for a little, able to see one another's features clearly for the first time. The traveller saw a dark-haired, dark-eyed young man with shockingly pale, almost white skin, his layers of ragged clothes almost falling apart from the constant damp. For his part, he saw a woman in plain but fully intact clothing and battered leathers, tense expression looking somehow weary, a strip of blue cloth bound across her forehead above rich brown eyes, and her skin — it was an almost unbelievable colour to someone who had never seen the sun, tanned as it was from a lifetime spent outdoors. Who was she? Where could she be from?

He was still staring when she spoke, voice calm, less demanding than it had been.

"Who are you?"

"Tei," he managed, finding his voice a moment late. "Uh, I'm Tei."

"My name's Rakariel," she responded. "I'm-"

A scraping sound from the street outside cut her off, and she whirled to face the shuttered window, stance abruptly poised and ready. Tei backed off towards the far wall, for what little good it would do him if the house's defences failed.

"What was that?"

"A vardra," Tei hissed. "They're here!"

Rakariel drew the sword that hung at her side, stepping back a couple of paces to cover both the door and the window at once. Outside, they could hear something heavy moving, sniffing, something that abruptly slammed against the jammed door with a splintering sound, jarring the entire frame. Tei flinched at the impact, but Rakariel remained motionless, lightly poised, attention focused on the door. She watched as something jerked it, then hit it again, a hard core within the damp wood still resisting its attacker. A final yank rattled the rusted bolts and threatened to pull the entire thing free. Neither she nor Tei made a single sound as the scraping noises resumed, moving around as though something was looking for another way in and eventually, finally, backing off with a frustrated howl that made Tei's hair stand on end before at last falling silent. Still, she waited a further short while before lowering her blade and backing up to stand closer to him, still keeping an eye on the door.

"What are they?" she asked, keeping her voice low, barely above a whisper. Tei broke his gaze from the door with something of an effort, turning his head to look at her, lit by the light shining from her left hand.

"What do you mean?" His own voice matched hers, slightly quieter if anything. Nobody really knew much about them, beyond when they came, how to avoid them.

"What do they look like?" she answered. "Where do they come from?"

"Where do they come from?" he echoed, blankly. Nobody knew the answer to that question. They came from the fogbound night, from above or from just around a corner, hunting silently across the rooftops for their prey. They roamed the ancient city just as its people did, and had done since beyond living memory. The stories said that they had come when the valley closed forever, that they hadn't existed before that time, when the mythical sun still shone. He wasn't entirely sure what a sun was, beyond that it had to be something powerful. The stories said that it glowed brightly, cutting through the fog...

His thoughts paused, mind stopping in its tracks. It couldn't be, could it? No, it wasn't possible — was it?

"Yes, where do they come from?" Rakariel asked

again, the pointed question insisting on an answer. "Is there a cave? A building? A particular part of this valley?" He wondered why she was so insistent on pinning down the shadows, and more importantly, unbelievably, how it was that she didn't already know.

"I... I don't know." No matter how strongly her tone insisted he look at her and answer, his eyes and thoughts kept being drawn back to the stone, shining in the dark. "There are more around the palace, I guess, but they just come to sound. Especially in the dark. Where are you from, how — how don't you know?" He couldn't hold the question back. It wasn't the one he wanted to ask most, but it was close to it, and he didn't — quite — dare.

"I'm from outside this valley," came the calm response, and Tei could only stare. It wasn't possible, and yet...

"I found my way in along the path of the river, up on the mesa." She gestured in the direction of the valley's unseen head, somewhere far away through the wall and the fog. "I wanted to find out what was wrong here, why it had been hidden."

"Hidden?" he asked, not really capable of anything more sensible or coherent. It wasn't possible, and yet her movements, her confidence, the alien way she looked, so very different to the thin, pale people he knew — all of that, and the light she held...

"This valley is hidden by some kind of old, powerful magic," she told him. "From the outside, it doesn't look like it's here at all. I only found it because my horse has sharper senses than I do. When I found the stream that flows down here, I managed to follow it in along the path. It comes down through a square gateway before passing through farmland and the city gates. Have you ever been out there?"

Tei slowly shook his head. "It's too dangerous in the open, and I don't think there's any way out up there." He paused, still disbelieving, wanting to hear the impossible confirmation again. "Are you really from outside?"

She nodded. "I am."

Finally daring, he asked the question that had waited on his lips almost since the first moment her light had shone into the room. "Is that... a sun?"

"A sun?" Rakariel repeated, and it was her turn to look at him blankly. "Is what the sun?"

"That," he answered, pointing at it. "The... glowing circle."

"*This?*" Her voice softened suddenly. "No, this is just a travellers' lightstone." She held it out to him, a pale, glowing stone resting in the palm of her hand, bathing the room in its cool radiance. "Have you never seen the sun?"

"No," Tei admitted. "I don't really know what it is." He knew the stories, but they rarely spoke of what it was — only that it had always been, until one day it was not.

"Well, it's..." She paused, looking for the words. "It's golden, and it hangs in the sky, far above this mist. The light that comes from it is much brighter and more powerful than my lightstone, and it's warm, too. It's so bright you can't look at it, but there's nothing like turning your face towards it and feeling the light wash over you." Her sudden, brief smile was almost shy. "Perhaps one day you'll see it for yourself."

Tei didn't know how that could be possible, but he

didn't question her. To him, she was something other, almost alien, incredible and awe-inspiring and in a way, almost frightening. Her presence, her very existence was impossible in the darkened world he knew — what was one more impossibility on top of that?

"Now," Rakariel continued, solemn once more, though still with a certain soft element to her voice, "tell me everything you know about these monsters and the history of this place. Even if it's only stories. Everything."

"Long ago," Tei began, and hesitated, thinking of how to go on. "...Long ago, there were no vardra. Generations ago. There's no-one alive who still remembers it. There was a sun... there was no mist..."

* * *

The valley had basked in the sun's radiance, its people prosperous and content. Settled firmly in a deep fault in the mesa, it was a peaceful kingdom, its influence spreading both up onto the highlands at its head and, at its foot, out onto the lowlands on the other side. It had doubtless been one of the best routes from the mesa's top to the lands around it, and, sheltered by its steep sides, it had been green and fertile. By and large, its kings had been good, or at least not bad: the people remembered them kindly, particularly the last. Tei spoke his name with a certain amount of reverence: King Sariven, the man who had battled the curse falling over his valley until the very end.

Nobody had known what had brought it on, nor how to stop it. It began slowly, almost unnoticed at first, as the priests began to lose their power. Though Tei didn't know what they had been, he had always been told that the blessings that had been granted to the people slowly began to fade. No longer able to communicate with the source of their powers, the priests could not say what had befallen them, like men struck blind. People tried to appease the gods, but it could not be done.

Even in those darkening times, King Sariven had stood tall to protect his people. No-one had worked harder than he to stave off the oncoming darkness. Even as terrible monsters began to appear and the valley's top closed in above its people's heads, he had spent all the magic at his command in an effort to delay the inevitable. Yet not even he could fight forever. The numbers of monsters steadily grew no matter how many were killed, the ranks of the army and the guardsmen steadily thinned until only the King's Guard were left... and eventually, even they fell. King Sariven vanished, doubtless to his death, and the palace, forever under attack, became a home for the creatures that the frightened citizens had named vardra. Even more than the city streets, it was now a place of danger and death.

* * *

"The palace," Rakariel mused as Tei finished relating his tale. "Hmm." She fell silent, one calloused finger angled up her cheek, the rest curled before her mouth, chin resting on her thumb. After a time, greatly daring, Tei ventured a question. She seemed so deep in thought...

"What about the palace?"

She frowned, focusing on him again. "They focused on it even early on?" His nod was enough, and she continued before he could manage any other answer. "There must have been something there that called them. It could be one part of the curse this valley is under." Her eyes flicked off to the middle distance, focused somewhere through the walls to the right of Tei's head, but she kept speaking, laying out her thoughts for him. "Another part may be the temples. If the priests began losing the powers the gods granted them, something must have either angered the gods, or stepped between them and their followers. Either way, there may be a clue there." There was another pause then, and her gaze swung back to him, disconcertingly intent. "How many people still live here in the valley?"

Tei blinked. "Uh. I last heard my grandfather say... around twelvescore. Do, uh... do you know how many that is?" Not many people could really comprehend a number that high. Tei and his family had been well-taught by their predecessors, but few others ever needed to care much for numbers beyond a couple of dozen.

"Yes," Rakariel said sadly. "Almost none, for a city this size. But from what you say, it's good that anyone has survived at all. Do you know how they did?"

Tei shrugged. "You have to be careful. Very careful. The first thing anyone learns is to never make a sound. Stay apart from each other, never in large groups. It's easier to find food that way, too, where there aren't too many people who all need it — it's difficult to find enough for a family. You have to remember where the best water is, too, like the pool where I saw you. It's open there, though, so it's more risky. I wanted to get some for my sister or I wouldn't have been there."

"You have a sister?" she asked, her voice softening again.

"Uh-huh. She's three years younger than me. We don't really get sick most of the time, since we're careful. Lots of other people aren't as lucky." Tei looked down at his hands, pale against dark clothes. "My family's always careful. That's why we've done so well. My grandfather's the mayor because of it, because we're the best at surviving."

Rakariel looked at the ragged young man in front of her again. "The mayor?"

"Uh, yes. I don't think the mayor from back then survived, but my family took over early on, when there were still more people. They needed someone to lead them, and we were the best then, too. I suppose my father will be mayor next." He paused for a moment. "I should take you to them — they'll want to meet you."

"I'd like to meet them, too," she said. "I'll need their advice, if they'll give it to me. And I should tell them what I intend to do, before I set out. Is it safe to go now?"

Slipping across the room to peer out of a crack at the edge of one of the warped shutters, Tei fell silent for a little before shaking his head. "It's dark now. We should stay here a while longer anyway even if it wasn't, until they forget we were here." He turned back to her, questioning, and she realised he was looking to her for guidance, for leadership. Would he go, she wondered, if she asked him?

"Then that's what we'll do. Is this house a safe place to sleep?"

"It's the safest place on this road," he answered. "I don't really think we should move to anywhere else."

Rakariel nodded in response. "Then let's get some rest. I'd like to meet the mayor tomorrow, and after that, I'll start looking into the curse. From what you've said, I think I should start with the temples." She was moving as she spoke, shedding the oddly-linked twin packs from her back, hissing under her breath as her braid caught momentarily in one of the straps. Thick and looking slightly faded in the lightstone's glow, it swung as she moved, hanging over her right shoulder again as she unfastened the roll of cloth that had been tied between the packs, shaking it out to reveal it as a dusky green and brown cloak, heavily waterproofed on the outside, lined on the inside for warmth. Swirling it about her shoulders, she fastened the strap that held it closed, pulling it close about her before simply sitting down against the wall, one leg bent, one almost straight. Tei remained where he was, watching her, until her head lifted and she shot him a quick smile.

"Rest, Tei. You should take the chance whenever you can."

Abashed, he looked away. Hadn't he been told that a hundred times? Walking past her with a last curious glance for the lightstone, still lying where she'd placed it on a half-rotten table, he experimentally poked a collection of rags left lying in the corner furthest from the door, then curled up on them. Most safehouses had somewhere set up for a person to sleep, and awe-inspiring though the stranger was to him, she was also a little terrifying. Watching her through half-closed eyes in the lightstone's pale glow, he found his thoughts chasing in circles for a long time before he finally drifted, unknowing, into sleep.

CHAPTER 4

Survivors in the Shadows

Tei awoke the next day unsure of how much of the one before had been a dream, reluctant to open his eyes and learn the truth either way. Could he really have met a stranger who claimed to come from beyond the edges of the world, one who claimed she would set herself a task of which he could barely conceive? One who bore a light brighter than any candle flame and claimed to have seen the mythical sun, to know a world without mist as was spoken of in stories and legends of a time lost before any living man was born, whose skin was a light brown utterly foreign to him? That stranger in her unusual clothes that had never known the damp, with her worn, serious expression that had shown an unexpected light, had she been real? Or only a dream...?

There was only one way to know. Bracing himself against the answer either way, the disappointment if she wasn't and shock if she was, Tei cracked open his eyes. Even before he had properly focused on anything, he could see the room washed in a cool white light that shone from something small on a table, right where he remembered the mysterious lightstone being the day before, too steady and bright for any candle. It was true?

Hardly daring to breathe, he pushed himself up quietly into a sitting position, feet tucked under him. Against the far wall, the strange, almost unbelievable woman still sat... Rakariel. Even her name sounded odd, like none he'd ever heard before. Leaning forward against her raised leg, she seemed to be asleep. Moving as silently as he was able, which was almost completely so after the long years of practice the valley had forced on all its people, he rose cautiously to his feet and crept towards her, not wanting to wake her. The hood of her cloak was down, having fallen off sometime during the night, and her bowed head rested against her knee. Even so, he could see much of her face clearly, relaxed in sleep, loose wisps of hair pinned beneath the strip of cloth she wore across her forehead. It was true — she was real. Real, and unlike anyone he had ever seen.

He sat still a little longer, watching her, before beginning to rise. His clothes made a faint rustle of cloth as he stood less carefully than he had knelt, and at once Rakariel's head snapped up, her eyes suddenly open, automatically pressing herself back against the wall even as her left hand shot up in reflexive guard, the right moving lightning-quick to the dagger at her belt. Tei stumbled back, staring at her half-frozen, and for a moment her eyes were as chill as if he were a vardra himself... then she blinked, recognising him, and slowly held up her empty hands in response to the fright in his face.

"I'm sorry."

Tei spoke at the same time, almost stammering, stumbling over his words. "I'm sorry, I — I didn't mean anything, I just-"

Rakariel cut him off, her voice soft, sounding almost tired despite the sleep she'd had. "It's not your fault. I'm... not used to being near other people. If anything comes near me, I have to assume it's dangerous." She shook her head slowly. "I'm sorry."

Arms still spread, she rose, the cloak pushed aside by her position. Tei took the opportunity to back off another couple of steps, watching her as she brought her hands back together to undo the clasp, taking the cloak from her shoulders and spreading it on the floor to fold and roll it up into the tight bundle it had been the day before. She worked with a quiet intensity, focused on what she was doing, and he didn't dare to interrupt. Until it was folded and secured in its place between the two packs, it seemed he wasn't even there in her world.

He crossed to the window instead, listening carefully at the crack in the shutter before gingerly easing it open. The ever-present fog hung in the street outside, thin and almost still. Droplets of water fell from rooftops and guttering to land with a muffled plink and splish on the street below, but that muted, constant sound was all that he could hear. The dim, grey light that filtered down from above didn't even outshine Rakariel's lightstone this early in the day, though there would have been little else to see even if it were brighter: the streets and buildings had been stained an almost uniform colour by centuries of neglect and abandonment. There was no sign of danger anywhere.

"Tei?"

He turned at the sound of her voice, looking back towards her. Once again, she was ready to travel, her things packed and the packs on her back. Only the lightstone remained, still shining its unwavering light from its position on the table.

"Are you ready to leave?" she asked, and he nodded. He was hungry, but there was no point in dwelling on that, and she hadn't eaten any more than he had. When they got back, his family would be able to spare them something. He didn't expect to be able to find enough for a single meal for them both while leading her there.

"Then please, lead on," she said quietly, picking up the lightstone to wrap it in a black cloth and slip it into a pouch. Tearing his eyes away from it as it vanished from sight, Tei turned back to the shutter and opened it wider, climbing out of the resulting opening. Rakariel followed, a little less quiet, but relatively agile and light on her feet despite everything that she carried. He turned back and watched her as she crossed to the door that had so nearly been forced open the night before. She ran her hand over the fresh gouges in the old, slowly decaying wood, deep, long lines that could almost have been made by a blade. A shiver ran down Tei's spine at just how deep they had struck, and when she was done he turned away with a small measure of relief. Looking around carefully, he set off down the street, avoiding the puddles where his steps might splash, placing each foot carefully on the slick cobbles. His gaze alternated between the ground ahead and the rooftops above, always alert for danger, noting each possible bolthole and avenue of escape that he passed in case anything were to happen. He'd always been taught, and seen for himself all too recently, that to grow careless was to be killed. Behind him, he could hear a second set of footsteps, matching his own and keeping quiet, though louder than he'd expect from anyone he knew. But perhaps, if she'd come from the mythical world outside, there was less to be afraid of where she was from...

They reached an intersection, and Tei paused by the wall, considering his choices. He hadn't actually managed to get water on the previous day, but then, he had Rakariel to escort. Was it worth turning back?

"What is it?" she whispered at his shoulder, her voice barely audible.

"The square," he whispered back, equally quiet. "I didn't get any water."

"We can go back," she said. "I wouldn't take from your family."

He thought about it a moment longer. They'd been attacked the previous night and the frustrated vardra could still be in the area, though it wasn't as likely to be hunting during the day. Still, there was a risk, one of many that he'd had to weigh up before. His family could do without a single trip's worth, but he'd done similar things and got away with it before, too. An uneasy feeling pressured him to turn away, and Tei, as always, bowed to his instincts, subconsciously honed through years of survival.

"No," he murmured, shaking his head. "I don't like it. We'll just go home."

She nodded, following him as he started moving again, slipping across the street and around the corner into a narrower one. He hadn't walked this particular road for a while, but he knew the layout of most of the city well, taking them on a compromise route that balanced speed with safety. A few old windowboxes jutted out from the walls, the plants they had held long since decayed away, now home only to moist, pale fungi. Tei cast an evaluating glance over them as he passed, stopping at each to pick two or three of the most mature, vaguely aware of Rakariel watching him curiously as he stuffed them into his various pockets. As they passed the last box, he held one out to her, its twin in his other hand. For a moment, he thought she wasn't going to take it, but she did, examining it closely with her head slightly tilted as if not sure of what he wanted her to do.

"It's fine, you can eat it," he whispered. No-one would begrudge any passer-by a meal. Far enough from their home not to draw attention to it, his family grew crops in that area much of the time, always keeping them dispersed. Acting on his own words, he bit into the one he still held, eating quietly. Rakariel watched him for a few seconds before slowly following suit.

"Thank you," she said in a matching whisper. "Are these common here?"

"Of course," he answered, almost bemused. "We grow them wherever we can. Don't you have them... outside?" He paused before he said it. It still seemed mystical, unreal. He had never even heard of a person who lived anywhere outside the city — and yet, everything she said and did told him that she was from somewhere unimaginably different.

"We do," she said, "but not everyone eats them. A lot of people don't know what's safe."

"What else do you eat?" The conversation remained at a whisper, and they were both still walking, but even so, Tei's surprise was plain. Some of the little yellow plants were good for seasoning, and of course rats and fish were fine when you could catch them, but the main food everyone ate were the mushrooms that sprouted all over the moist, shadowed city. What else was there?

"All sorts of things." She spread her hands in a

shrug. "Most plants may not be able to grow well in this fog, but outside, there are so many you can eat. Animals, too."

"There are rats," Tei offered. "They're good."

Rakariel's faint smile was sad, somehow, and he wondered why. "I didn't mean rats."

They fell silent after that, picking their way through the puddled streets, their surroundings still quiet save for the constant, irregular dripping of the water continually settling out from the fog that filled the valley. Mist drifted in idle eddies, swirling around them as they moved through it, a slow and ill-defined tracer of their passage. One turn followed another as they wound their way through the empty roads, Tei always leading the way, though Rakariel had discerned his overall direction early on. He picked a few more mushrooms when he found them along a side path, sharing with his strange companion. Though she might not have been used to it, she didn't object, seeming quietly grateful as she took them from him. After some time of this slow, silent travel, they stopped outside a stone building with heavily boarded windows, a slightly arched passage cutting through on the ground level to what might once have been an interior garden.

"It's here," Tei whispered, slipping into the passageway and pausing at its end to glance around and up before stepping out, Rakariel following. The space beyond had probably once been well-tended, but only the black, rotting skeleton of a small tree remained as a sad reminder of what it had once been. The flagstones cut across the dark, moist soil in a gently curving path, crossing the old garden to a door that looked as firmly boarded as the windows next to it. She stayed close behind as Tei turned away from the door, moving along the wall to another narrow window a little further along. The shutter over it was reinforced with a heavy board, one that looked surprisingly sturdy considering that the centuries he'd told her had passed should have seen it rot away. She noticed that the line of the hinges was clear as he stopped before it, slipping his fingers through a hand-sized opening in the shutter's edge and doing something on the other side, perhaps unfastening some sort of catch or bolt. She thought she heard a faint grating sound before he withdrew slightly, hooked his fingers around the hole, and opened the shutter without resistance to reveal a narrow window beyond, a rectangular opening into blackness.

Rakariel eyed it dubiously, pushing away a heartbeat's flicker of dread. It would only lead to safety — if she could get in. Small and narrow, she would have to edge through it sideways, and without her packs. Shrugging them off, she gestured silently for Tei to go first. He understood at once, nodding and climbing through in a clearly practised move: first one leg, then the other, and last his body. Moments later, his thin, dirty hand reappeared through the dark opening, and she handed him her packs. He pulled them in, twisting his hand as the bottom pack stuck and shaking his somewhat unwieldy burden a couple of times until it turned sideways and finally slipped through. Rakariel waited for a few moments to be sure he was out of her way before following, getting her right leg through first and finding the floor — wooden, she thought, and noticeably higher than the ground outside — before somewhat awkwardly shifting her weight to it and ducking through as he had.

Inside, it was pitch black, and as she straightened she was sure she could sense the ceiling just barely above her head. She stuck out her arm, hitting a wall almost immediately and scraping her fingers against it, repeating the move with more care on the other side. Whatever room this had been, it was so narrow that with her back to the window she could feel both walls without even straightening her arms fully, and for an instant she had to push back the choking feeling of being trapped, one hand dropping to the pouch that held her lightstone.

"Now what?" she whispered, welcoming the sound of another voice as the equally quiet response came from just ahead.

"Close the entrance!"

She nodded automatically, whether or not he could actually see her, and turned back to the window, crouching and leaning out into the grey light one last time. Holding onto the windowframe with her left hand, she gripped the shutter with her right and slowly pulled it closed, moving her hand to the same little hole Tei had used in order to close it against the angled stone. A heavy metal bolt on the inside, just below the hole, slotted into place — and it was done, and she and Tei were alone in the dark.

"Just wait a moment," he whispered. "There are candles..." He trailed off as she brought out the lightstone again, finally able to use it without alerting the creatures outside. Cool white light washed through the room, proving that she was crouching on a wide wooden bench around knee-height from the actual floor, where Tei stood. Looking around the tiny room, its single door just beyond him, she realised she was almost certainly in what had once been an indoor privy, her 'bench' a simple cover over its seat, and her hesitation of the moments before almost seemed faintly ridiculous. Almost.

"It's all right," she responded, keeping her voice low as he had. Glancing from the lightstone to the door, Tei hesitated before handing her packs back to her and opening it as she stepped down from the privy seat and pulled them back on.

"Grandfather?" he murmured, his voice sounding louder than it should have in the silence of the dark hallway. "It's me, Tei. Grandfather?" He waited a short while for a response, glancing back at Rakariel just moments before she heard the shuffling sound of quiet but uneven footsteps on the floor outside. Instinctively, she tensed, hand dropping to the sword at her side as Tei stuck his head out of the doorway.

"Fayel?"

"Tei!" The voice was quiet, but fairly high: most likely a young woman's. Rakariel let out a breath, allowing some of her tension to fade away. "...Is the door open?" the girl continued, doubtless confused by the strange light.

Tei glanced at Rakariel before looking back out and shaking his head. "No, it's something else, something — do you know where Grandfather is?"

"Of course," she said, curious and puzzled. "What's happened? What's wrong?"

"Nothing's wrong, I — I brought someone back here."

"Really?" Tei's excitement was plain, and it clearly made the girl even more curious. "Well, all right — I'll go right now and bring him!" The shuffling footsteps began again, making their way back down the corridor and fading quickly into the distance.

"Who was that?" Rakariel asked.

"My sister." Tei couldn't help but smile somewhat as he said it, clearly fond of her. "She'll fetch Grandfather. Uh... you should come through to the meeting room. He'll be there soon."

"All right," she said, following him as he stepped through into the hallway. Another door opened into what might once have been a small drawing room, windows heavily boarded, furniture old and a little musty, but still apparently solid. As if proving the point, Tei sat down on one of the stiff chairs, eliciting something of a creak from it. Following his example, Rakariel perched on the edge of another, reluctant as yet to remove her packs. Doing so would mean that she was intending to stay, to herself if no-one else, and she wouldn't rest easy with that idea until her welcome was explicitly assured.

A short while later, she heard the shuffling footsteps return, together with another, more even set. A young woman entered the room first: fourteen, maybe fifteen, Rakariel thought. Like Tei, she was incredibly pale, and somewhat on the thin side. One of her legs was splinted and braced, causing the shuffle, her hair as dark and scruffy as Tei's. She stopped in the doorway, staring at the traveller in amazement until a hand touched her shoulder and she stepped inside.

The man who followed her was old, but not in the least infirm. Rakariel couldn't guess his age beyond that his face was lined and hair that had probably once been the same raven black as that of the other two was now grey: he stood straight and tall, unbowed by time.

His bearing was such that even without knowing his position, she would have been tempted to react to him as a leader, and she stood.

"You must be the mayor," she said, inclining her head somewhat in a brief show of respect. "My name is Rakariel."

"Mine is Jan," he responded politely, though she could see the curiosity in his dark eyes. "Please, sit."

She waited to do so until both he and the girl, Fayel, had, then resettled herself on the edge of her chair. "Mayor Jan," she began. "I'm a traveller from a land far from here, outside your valley. Your grandson Tei brought me to you at my request." Seeing him hold up his hand, she stopped there, ready for the inevitable questioning.

"Outside the valley?" His look pinned her with a surprising intensity, and she nodded. "How can that be so?"

"The valley is sealed, and cloaked by illusion well enough that I would never have seen it on my own. My horse found it, not I, and I managed to follow the river in, though a rock ceiling seemed to form above me the moment I had." She held up the lightstone, bright in her hand, the room lit without the aid of candlelight. "Tei tells me that he has never seen anything like this before. I hope it will serve as some proof to you."

"What is it?" Rising from his chair, the mayor crossed to her, his hand held out. Rakariel placed the lightstone in his palm, letting him take it from her and examine it despite the faint uneasiness she felt at its being out of her possession. "...I have never seen such a thing." He held it closer to her face, looking closely at her; she sat still and permitted the inspection, knowing how outlandish she must appear to the thin, pale people of the sunless valley. "And you bear no resemblance to any person I have known."

"She doesn't fear the vardra," Tei chipped in. "She didn't know about them 'til I told her."

"From what he says, it's lucky that I met him before I was attacked," Rakariel agreed. "I might have been able to fight them off, or not, I don't know."

"Not, I think," the mayor told her gently. "There are those among us who try to fight the vardra, but it is an immense endeavour to devise a trap certain of bringing one down, and an even greater one to do so without injury." With his eyes on her, Rakariel felt sure that he was evaluating her reactions as another way of testing the truth of her words, plain though her foreign origins were to the eye. She was, after all, a stranger, and he the guardian of his people.

"Perhaps so," she agreed. "Tei tells me that they hunt by stealth; I would not have been fully prepared."

"Even prepared," he said, "how would you fight them alone?" The question seemed sincere rather than rhetorical, and Rakariel responded in kind.

"I have a bow," she told him, "one that will not suffer from the damp here. It bears some enchantments, and I have a little magic of my own. I have fought such creatures before, though not specifically your vardra." She paused for a moment, lightly tapping a finger in thought, and resisting the desire to take her lightstone back from him. It was close by and in her sight: that was enough. "The fog here doesn't allow me to shoot far. The vardra seem large?" A nod was enough to confirm it, and she continued almost without a break. "I'd seek shelter inside, where their movement would be more restricted than mine, and where I would know there to be nothing that could attack me from behind. There I would have to stand my ground." Another moment's pause. "Your people have neither bows nor magic, do they?" Without magic, they could certainly never maintain any form of archery in such a place, and from what Tei had told her, it seemed clear enough that magic was no longer a part of their lives, if it ever had been.

"No," the mayor said. "Those things we know only from legend. But those legends tell us that our lord King Sariven tried and failed to stop the darkness even with all the power at his command, and all of our army and guardsmen died in battle."

Rakariel's eyebrows lifted. "*All* of them?" That couldn't be true. There were always deserters, for whatever reasons they had, always those who could not face the onslaught, from those who had retreated and fled to protect individuals rather than an entire city that was falling away before them to those whose nerve had simply broken. Some would have — or should have — survived.

"All of them," Mayor Jan confirmed. "What my people know of fighting the vardra, we have had to teach ourselves. And you... where did you learn these skills?"

Rakariel sighed, quietly. If she could only do so, she would forget the past that had made her what she was, but that would never be an option. "My people learn archery as children, and many of us leave to seek our fortune in other lands. I was one of those: I became a mercenary, and a good one. But..." She looked down, falling silent, then up again and shook her head as if dispelling a memory. "The band I joined was one of the best. I learned most of my skills during my time with them. In the end, when we contracted to deal with a 'small' problem that proved the seat of a great evil, I was one of the only survivors — both from my band and from those others who also heeded the call." She pressed the fingertips of her right hand to her forehead wearily. "We won, in the end. That darkness was defeated, and I hope never to see its like again." Looking up again, meeting the mayor's dark eyes, she gave a long, slow sigh. "To be honest, I didn't ask to be what I am. Or if I did, I was a fool. But I can't turn away now, even if I could leave. This is why I came to you — I want to try and lift the shadow that hangs over this valley, and undo whatever may have seen it sealed." She paused, knowing she had to tell him all the possible consequences, though doubtless he was already aware of the worse. "It may be dangerous for you. Anything I do to disturb these creatures, these vardra, could incite them to attack more than they already do. But if I die, they will forget me in time... and if I succeed, your people will be free." Rakariel lifted her hand to clasp it around his, around the lightstone resting in it, sending thick-barred shadows across the wall from her fingers. "Tei does not know what the sun is, except as a legend. What safety is. I want to give that back to your people."

Mayor Jan blinked at her, taken by surprise once again. "Why? How do you think you can do such a thing?"

"I can't be certain that I can," she admitted softly. "But I know that I must try."

"Do you truly understand how dangerous this is?"

he asked her, gently opening his hand and relinquishing the lightstone, letting her take it from his open palm. "For you even more than us?"

"I saw the claw-marks on the door of the building I stayed in last night," she answered. "I heard them attack it, seeking a way in. I don't expect it to be easy. But I have faced things like this before, and I must try."

Slowly, he nodded. "I will warn my people. You must let me do that first. We will give you what help we can."

"Thank you," Rakariel said quietly.

"No, he replied. "Thank you."

CHAPTER 5

What Can Be Done, Must

After a few moments of silence, Mayor Jan turned his attention to his grandchildren. Despite his experience and authority, his gaze continued to flick occasionally to Rakariel, sitting erect and still with the lightstone resting on her lap.

"We will need to call the people to meet, so we can warn them if nothing else. Fayel, will you prepare the call markers, please. Tei, you can start setting them out until the others return. I think the lady traveller and I still have much to talk about."

Rakariel said nothing, and both Fayel and Tei nodded, rising. Tei offered his sister his arm, but she took no heed, choosing to make her slow, careful way across the room without his aid. Only in the doorway did she pause, looking back at Rakariel for a long moment with curiosity and still slightly sceptical wonder intermingled in her expression. Then she turned once again, and, trailed by her brother, left.

Settling down in one of the chairs once more, Jan smiled faintly. "I am lucky to have those two, I think." He looked into her eyes, serious again. "So, Traveller Rakariel. Tell me of the world outside."

Rakariel frowned in thought. How could she explain the world she knew to those who knew only the chill, dark valley, shaded in drab greys and browns? How to describe a pleasure as simple as a crisp breeze to one who knew only the still air of the valley, smelling of underground damp and heavy with fog?

What likenesses could she possibly draw on?

"It's... bright, I suppose," she said eventually, searching for words. "In the day, the sun shines in the sky, so bright that no-one can bear to look at it for more than a few moments. It's golden, and it's warm: even with your eyes closed, you can feel it shining on your skin, like being near to a fire. Plants grow everywhere in its light, even on bare rock, in every shade of green, and their flowers can be any colour and scent you can imagine." She was smiling, faintly but fondly, the care of past years partially lifted from her face as she looked within herself to the memories others might have called everyday, but she still treasured so dearly. "There's no fog, except now and again, and from any high point you can see for miles. Birds fly everywhere, carried on the wind, and there are many more animals than can live here: everything from mice and rats to creatures bigger than you and I." She looked down with a sigh. "It isn't without its dangers... or its monsters. There are places of great evil, even in the light of day. Yet, it's... to me, this mist might be normal for a day or two. For it to be like this, never breaking, never changing, feels dark and wrong. It feels wrong to me that so little can grow here, that I can't hear animals and birds calling, or feel the wind on my face. To me, it feels as though this place is waiting somewhere between life and death." She shook her head, slowly. "I hope this makes sense to you. I honestly don't know how to tell you about it." A rueful smile escaped her. "I never was much good with words, and I'm no mage to capture images in crystal to show you. I would, if I could."

The mayor was silent for a moment, taking in all she had said, before speaking softly. "That is all right.

Your words are enough." He paused. "Our stories tell of such things, from the time before the valley closed and the mist and vardra came upon us. There's no way for us to know if they were ever true, though the city itself tells us that something must have changed greatly since it was built. But you... you give me hope. Do you really believe that you can learn what has made our city this way — and that you can set it right where our people have failed?"

"I believe that I can try," she answered quietly, "and that I must. Everything I do is a risk, and I know that one day, something will kill me. Until that day, I face it as best I can — what else is there to do?"

"A brave man's words, I think," he said, seeming quietly approving. "You could simply run."

"There's nowhere to run to," Rakariel said, her voice soft, words a simple statement of fact, at least as she saw it. The mayor fell silent, studying her with a considering expression. Lost in the distances of her own mind, she didn't react, though she was vaguely aware of it. Many people had watched and evaluated her in the same way over the years. Where their eventual opinions fell varied, but there was little she could do to change them once they had been formed. What was, would be: she was what she was, and though she could change the world around her with bow and sword, the people in it were not so mutable, or perhaps far, far too much so. She knew how to battle a physical foe, but less so how to change even a single person's mind once it was made up, with little ability to convince or cajole, and no will to dissemble. Her experiences set her too far apart.

They sat in silence for a while longer, Mayor Jan

apparently contemplating her words, Rakariel's mind drifting between past and present. In the end, it was the sound of softly shuffling footsteps that broke their respective reveries. The distinctive walk told Rakariel at once who it was: Tei's younger sister. It was confirmed moments later as Fayel stepped into the doorway, pausing there with one hand on its frame. She gazed at Rakariel for a few moments before speaking quietly.

"Grandfather? May I come in?"

He looked around at her, unsurprised, clearly as aware of her entrance as Rakariel had been. "Of course."

Taking her habitual small, shuffling steps, Fayel made her way across the room and sat on a chair with a look of faint relief.

"Tei has left with some of the markers. He said he'd try and be back quickly." She hesitated there, looking again at the stranger who had so suddenly, even impossibly, come to her home, searching for a sentence that never formed, and finding herself with nothing but silence.

"What is it?" Rakariel asked, taking pity on her.

"Who are you?" Fayel blurted, and flushed, the colour vivid against her pale skin.

Rakariel sighed. Poorly worded though it was, she knew what the girl had meant. Though she'd known it was coming even before the words had been spoken, it was a question she did not want to answer, one that meant so much more than her name.

"I'm a traveller, a fighter," she began, seeing no choice but to be honest. "I left my home long ago... to seek adventure, I suppose. It seems rather foolish, now.

I sought danger and found more than I bargained for, but in the end I survived." She looked away slightly as she remembered, glancing down and to one side. "I have been called Shadow-Bearer for the darkness I've touched, and at the same time hailed for my part in defeating it. I travel, now, as I have for years, and I stop where I feel I might be needed. I wield some small magic, but I'm no mage, for what little I know I was forced to learn to survive." She paused, looking up again. "Does that answer your question?"

Fayel gave a small nod. "I — I think so. Thank you."

Rakariel shifted uncomfortably in her seat, watching both of them. She was the closest there was to what they and their people needed, but she wasn't someone who was always welcome, even where her aid could be used. She'd felt the sting of closed doors before, seen it in suddenly opaque eyes when she could offer no more than what she was, what she had become. At the same time, she knew that she could not ask for trust from people who knew nothing about her, who saw her refuse to answer the questions they asked. Before the two strangers' silence, she felt again as though she balanced on a knife edge, caught between two worlds as surely as she had been when standing with one foot either side of the barrier at the valley's edge. Eventually, she herself broke the silence, as much to hear someone speak again as anything else, though with another goal in mind.

"Fayel, what happened to you?"

The girl blinked, looking up at her. "I... I was careless," she said self-consciously. "I heard something coming when I was up on a roof. I tried to run to safety, but I slipped and fell off. I... would probably have been killed if Father hadn't been there. He carried me inside just in time." She rubbed her leg. "It's getting better, slowly. I think I'll still be able to go outside."

Rakariel nodded. "I hope so." She hesitated for a moment. "...I might be able to help you, a little."

Both Fayel and Jan looked at her questioningly, as though to ask how.

"I told you I'm not a true mage," Rakariel continued, "but I do know a little magic. Healing other people is a lot harder than yourself, but... I've been able to do it before." She gazed across the room into startled dark eyes, her own expression still calmly serious. "I don't think I'll be able to put everything right, but it could speed your healing, help you recover faster. If you'll permit me to."

"Of — of course! You can really do that?"

"I think so. As I said, it won't heal everything, but it will help." She stood, a little stiffly, at last removing her packs to drop them on the floor beside her chair. Crossing to Fayel, she knelt before her, looking up into her excited, anxious face. She was peripherally aware of the mayor watching, his expression a much more subdued and controlled version of his granddaughter's. "Try to relax, if you can. Close your eyes and think of something you like, or somewhere safe."

Fayel's dark eyes obediently closed. As close as she was, aided by the lightstone she placed beside her, Rakariel could see that they weren't quite black, but rather a deep and smoky grey. She rested her hands gently on the young woman's injured leg, running them slowly along to feel the line of it beneath the bandages and splints. It had been set well, at least as far as she could tell, the bone seeming straight and true under its thin covering of cloth and flesh. She closed her own eyes, picturing a leather-bound book opening against a backdrop of unrelieved blackness. The strange lettering of the spell she pictured on the page struggled against her memory, but she held it in place, forcing herself to recall every last detail. Only when each letter was still and solid with certainty did she begin to speak the words, her voice low and soft, weighted with a power beyond the ages. Each symbol of magery was a single syllable or linking mark, even its pitch defined: in such manner were all spells written, for those who knew enough to read them. Half spoken, half sung, they could work miracles indeed in the hands of a master mage. Though she had little affinity for the power and had struggled desperately hard to master what magic she did know, Rakariel still felt their value and import deep in her bones.

The spell she spoke was all too general, she knew. A good healer would have learnt how to tailor and adapt it to the situation she faced, and a master healer would find that knowledge instinctive. By contrast, Rakariel was almost completely unable to tailor any of her spells to any task, beyond simply controlling how much power she gave them. Despite the spell's generality, she felt strength leave her with each syllable she spoke, an inner fire powering the magic with all she dared give it until at last it was loosed. For a single lingering moment, she felt it woven around Fayel's life force as it sank into the girl's being.

As that moment of magical power faded away, the toll it had taken on her made itself felt. Rakariel found herself as exhausted in spirit as though she had gone without sleep for days, for all that her body was as strong as it had been before. Fayel opened her eyes slowly at her healer's worn sigh, clearly amazed at the feeling of magic settling over her and leaving her refreshed in both body and spirit. Rakariel saw her twitch her toes experimentally, felt the muscles under her hands temporarily tense as if to stand.

"It works," Fayel breathed, awed. "I feel so much better."

"Keep your leg bound for now," Rakariel cautioned. "You'll feel better than you truly are for a while, so don't make any judgements until at least tomorrow."

"What happens if I do?"

"You could over-exert yourself," she said, settling back into a sitting position and drawing her knees up, one hand on the timeworn wood floor. "You'll think you're all right, until you try to do more than you can actually stand. I've seen it happen before... I've even done it myself. In the end, you'll only make your injury worse, maybe even more so than it was before it was healed. So be careful, at least for a day or two."

Fayel nodded, understanding clear in her dark eyes. "I will. Thank you — thank you so much."

Rakariel gave her a tired, sincere smile. "I'm glad I could help you. I'm little good as a healer, but it's a power I prefer to use when I can."

"It's a wonderful power." She hesitated, an idea occurring to her. "Could... could you teach it to someone else? To me?"

"Perhaps," Rakariel answered honestly. "If you have a gift for it, it will feel natural to you, and you'll learn fast. If not, you'll have to struggle every step of the way, but it can still be learnt." She pressed the fingertips of her free hand to her forehead again, the cloth bound across it soft beneath them. Could she teach this girl in the time she had before her lightstone faded and gave out completely? It would only last so long without sunlight, and when it gave out she would be plunged into darkness. Walking into the valley had been different: she had known that it was with her, ready to be pulled free at a moment's notice and chase the shadows from her surroundings. Once its light was gone, it would not return unless she could place it in the sun again to let it soak up and store the precious light it gave back to her in darkness. Without it, she would be alone and helpless, a prisoner in a shadowed realm.

"Is something wrong?" Fayel asked.

"Ah... no," she managed, shaking her head. "I was just trying to decide if I would have time to teach you before my lightstone ran out."

"Ran out? But it's so miraculous... how could it run out?"

"The same way a candle burns down," Rakariel replied. "It's not eternal. If it doesn't see the sunlight again in nine days, its light will fade and die." She kept her fear hidden as she spoke, fear of the darkness and what lurked within it. She could only fight what she could see to pin down. She never wanted to be trapped helpless in the dark again.

"Does it have to be... sunlight?" Fayel hesitated over the last word, almost savouring it, mythical to her rather than real. Rakariel nodded.

"It's the only thing bright enough. The full moon will give it about as much light as it uses, so it will never die in full moonlight, but only the sun is bright enough to actually give power back to it. A mage might be able to do it without the sun — a better one than me."

"You need this lightstone?" Mayor Jan asked worriedly.

"Yes," she replied. "I can't do anything without it. I can't fight if I can't see."

"Hmm." He stood up to pace across the room, unbowed despite his age. "It will take time for my people to gather here, even with the best of luck and with all things in our favour. I was intending to present you to the representatives at our meeting and let you explain again to them." He turned to face her again, hands behind his back. "Teach my granddaughter your magic if you can, for then we will have something even should you fail. In when you leave, I will have to let your judgement guide you."

"Thank you, sir." Slowly getting back to her feet, Rakariel frowned slightly, pensive. How long would it take her to cross the city? How hard would it be to find the heart of the seal on the valley? When she eventually found it, how hard would it be to destroy? Could she possibly do it even in the full nine days? Perhaps — but it all depended upon so much. Though weariness still dragged at her thoughts, it didn't affect her body, and she found her movements almost snappy as she took her own turn to pace. How best would she be able to do it? What would she need? Supplies, for one thing: she never carried that much under normal circumstances, and she would have to, because there would be no hunting and likely no returning to the mayor's house until and if she succeeded. Though she could forage along the way for the fungi Tei had gathered before, she had no way of knowing which would be poisonous to her and which would not, unable to rely on them being the same as those of her distant homeland. She had little idea of what qualities would make one place safer than another against the creatures Tei's people called vardra, though she could ask, and guess if she needed to. Worse, she didn't know in which direction anything lay, would be forced to find her way using only her innate sense of direction, navigating the city by luck and guesswork. What she needed... and she stopped, pressing her hand to her head again as it came to her. The answer was not one she wanted to think. What she needed was a native guide, a resident of the city, to help her — and anyone who travelled by her side was all too likely to die.

Pushing those thoughts aside, she dropped her hand and turned sharply back to Fayel, meeting her eyes once again. "I won't be able to teach you much in what's left of today. If you have a good memory and a gift for magic, I might be able to teach you the healing spell I used on you, but that will be all."

Fayel nodded. "That's all right. If you could teach me that — if you could teach me anything at all —"

Rakariel smiled faintly at the eagerness in the young woman's voice, recognising it in a way. "Is there somewhere quiet and secluded we can study, where we can make a reasonable amount of sound if we need to?"

"Use the cellar," Jan suggested. "It's underground and covers sound well. When the children were young, it was where they lived."

"Thank you," Rakariel said, before turning her attention back to Fayel. "Are you ready?"

"Of course!"

Picking up her packs as the girl got to her feet, Rakariel followed her unexpected student out of the room and left along the hallway, which turned right at its end towards an old kitchen. Judging from the cleanliness of the surfaces and the faint smell of food, it even still saw use, though probably not as often as it once had. At the end furthest from the door, she saw a wooden trapdoor set into the stone floor. An iron ring clearly showed how it was meant to open, and she quickly stepped forward to do the task before Fayel could attempt it. Hands on the ring, she hesitated for an instant. It had never used to bother her, but she hated the underground now, the enclosed spaces with any amount of rock and earth between herself and the free, fresh air. The world above might not have always been safe, but it was not the place of horror that the underground had become. She kept her reaction from her face, however, refusing to let it affect her more than she had to, determined not to let Fayel see it. Instead, she simply braced herself and tugged the trapdoor up, revealing steep wooden steps that led into the darkness below. Gesturing for Fayel to go first, she held it for her before beginning her own descent, steeling herself against the all too final sound of the trapdoor closing as she shut it behind them.

Lit by the lightstone, the cellar appeared to be a reasonably comfortable place. Although it still housed wine racks and unmarked boxes against its rear wall, the near end had seen quite a different use, with rugs and furniture brought down and beds made up on the floor. Below ground though it was, it was almost slightly warmer than the chill of the shadowed valley, and the still air was fresh enough to tell her it was used regularly. Though it felt to her like a prison, Rakariel could still see that it made a comfortable living space.

Picking one of the mismatched chairs, she pulled up a small table and sat down facing towards the stairs, putting her packs on the floor and the lightstone on the table. Fayel chose another and followed her lead, sitting at right angles to her.

"What do we do?"

Rakariel was quiet for a moment, thinking of how best to explain something she knew all too little about herself.

"A mage once told me that magic was all about patterns," she said slowly. "Every spell is like a pattern made of words. Mages have their own language to describe those patterns. I don't have time to teach you much, but I'll try to show you what I can. Can you sing?"

"Sing?" Fayel looked surprised. "I have to sing?"

"Not really. I was told it helps. You have to know *how* to say what you're saying. Otherwise, well, it won't do anything. If you already sing, that makes it a bit easier."

"Oh. Well..." She hesitated almost as if embarrassed. "I used to, a little, down here."

"It's better than nothing. So let me show you, ah..."

Rakariel leaned over to delve into one of her packs, coming out with a creased roll of paper bound with a plain offcut of spare fabric. She slipped a sheet from the inside of the roll and spread it out on the once-polished table, the paper crackling as she pressed it flat with her hand in a largely futile attempt to stop it from curling up again. A little further searching produced a battered quill pen, snapped in half at some stage of her travels, and a tightly stoppered bottle of ink. She shook it a couple of times before opening it and dipping her pen in to draw an unusual symbol on the paper. It was angular, yet flowing, with three smaller marks near or attached to the main body.

"Symbols of magic usually look like this. They tell you the exact sound, and how it has to be said. This one is... *cey*." She paused for a moment before she said it, drawing an extra breath and perfecting the intonation. A minute touch of strength left her with the sound, the faintest hint of magic hanging about her for a second before fading away into nothingness. "If you say it correctly, you should feel a little strength leave you with it."

Fayel nodded, frowning, and tried to repeat the syllable. She had to try a good seven times, corrected occasionally by Rakariel's example, but on the eighth it worked. Even if Rakariel hadn't been close enough to hear the faint resonance of magic in her voice, she would have been able to tell from the girl's surprised expression.

"I — I felt it, I felt something!" she stammered. "Does that mean I can do it?"

Rakariel gave her a faint smile. "Yes, you can do it. There are only three elements to casting a spell you know: how well you can speak the language of magic, how well you can stand losing the strength it takes from you, and if you don't have the spell in front of you, whether or not you can remember it. Now, let me show you the next one."

They worked for some time, Fayel learning the spell syllable by syllable, picking some up almost instantly, but struggling over others more foreign to her. Determination as much as anything else made her a relatively quick student, for all that she had likely never before had to remember sounds so precisely. Rakariel could see that she was intent on memorising as much as possible before her tutor had to leave.

Despite the girl's focus, they were still only part of the way through before a sound from above broke Rakariel's concentration. She jumped and snapped her head up towards it, fast enough to catch the trapdoor lifting before someone set foot on the steep steps. She watched keenly as the person descended, proving to be Tei as he got low enough to close the trapdoor over his head and look at them quizzically.

"Tei?" Fayel said, a question in her voice.

"Fayel? Grandfather told me you were down here — learning magic?" Curiosity and a little awe were apparent in his voice, for all that Rakariel could tell he was trying not to sound too eager. A thought crossed his mind, and his eyes shifted across to her. "Uh, is it all right for me to be here?"

"Yes," she replied calmly. "Don't worry." There wasn't much Tei could do to interrupt the workings, and even less, she suspected, that he would.

"Good." He smiled brightly, pleased. "I can bring you both something to eat, if you want?"

"Maybe in a little," Rakariel said. "I'd like to keep going for now."

Tei nodded, finding himself a seat a little further away and watching as she and Fayel returned to their work. Both of them were sounding the strange syllables out so carefully, and he could hear a strange resonance in his sister's voice when she got it right, a sound that matched that echoing in Rakariel's own soft demonstrations. It was strange to listen to, stranger still to think what it might do — he'd never so much as heard its like. He couldn't help but wonder what it would be like to try it for himself, if he could hear his own voice echo with that odd resonance as though the empty air were repeating his words as he spoke them, but to try even once would be to distract Fayel and Rakariel. Instead, he leaned forward to get a better view of the symbols that Rakariel was slowly setting down, utterly foreign to him for all that he could usually read most things he found. Every now and again his eyes were drawn back to the lightstone, resting in the centre of the table and casting its pale radiance across the room. For all that he'd seen it several times, it still gave him a feeling of wonder to look upon it, so different to the dim grey mist and hoarded candlelight that were all he'd ever known. She'd said the sun was brighter yet, but he found that hard to even imagine, the lightstone's glow already stronger by far than any flame he had ever dared light. What would a light like that be like? How could anyone even open their eyes in such brilliance?

She'd said it was in the sky, shining down over the world just as the legends agreed. He closed his eyes, trying to picture it as the slow and sometimes halting words of magic washed over him, filling the room he'd known since he was a child with possibilities unknown. What would it be like to stand beneath the sun? Would the fog around him glow as it did in a fire, be touched golden as by a candle's light? He wanted to ask, but he knew that he couldn't, not in the middle of something as important as the magic he was listening to his sister learn.

It seemed dreamlike, almost unearthly, that his little sister would be learning something so strange. He found himself wondering if it were true, if he might somehow just be dreaming, asleep and safe somewhere as fragments of legend wove themselves into a new tale in his mind. Yet he could hear it, something no legend he knew had ever spoken of, a strange reverberation of power in both their voices, as much felt as heard and yet barely either, an echo on the edge of awareness that somehow caught at the world around them. He had been told of Rakariel's warning that some of Fayel's recovery would be illusory, for all that he had also been told that she felt much better, and why would a dream include something like that? No, he had never known magic, nor seen or felt it used: this, even more than the distant sun, was part of a world far beyond his experience.

In the end, he didn't know how long he listened, how long he watched them, though his legs grew stiff and he had to change position more than once. When Rakariel finally spoke other than in guidance, it barely even registered on his awareness, his thoughts broken only when he realised that he could hear no more of the magic words and his mind scrambled to process the sentence he had almost missed.

"If you think you can do it now, you should try."

Tei blinked, focusing on her in surprise and disbelief even as his sister responded.

"Are you sure? Uh — how? On what? Can I just say it?"

Rakariel shrugged. "This spell is very simple, very... general, I suppose. You can use it on anyone who's injured, even yourself, although it'll make you feel weaker instead of stronger, and won't be as effective as one intended for such use. You can use it on me if you want, although since I'm not injured, you won't be able to see any effect."

"I think I see," Fayel said, a little slowly. Tei unintentionally cut over her, excited.

"You could try it on me! If... if that would be all right, of course."

"Are you hurt?" Rakariel asked, looking at him for the first time since he had entered.

"Not really. A little scraped, but it's not anything serious." He didn't mention that it was from when she'd knocked him to the ground as he ran to safety. "I'd just like to feel it."

She smiled faintly. "That will do. It'll be a good demonstration. Stand next to Fayel and show her."

Tei did as he was told, standing and crossing to Fayel's chair, one scraped hand held out to show her. She looked at it, then back at Rakariel, unsure and seeking further advice.

"Just touch him and recite the spell, concentrating on him and on what you want to do. Don't let yourself put too much into it — he doesn't need much healing, and you don't want to tire yourself. There's a certain amount of strength that the spell will always take from you, but beyond that, you can decide on its power at least somewhat. Don't put too much of yourself into it." She hesitated, thinking. "That's all I can really tell you. Just try it. And remember, timing is also important. Don't wait too long, or go too fast."

"What will happen if I get it wrong?"

"Almost certainly nothing," was Rakariel's answer. "There aren't many ways healing spells can go badly, so I think you'll be all right. Just remember what I told you, and focus on the spell."

Fayel nodded. "Should... should I start, then?"

"Of course."

Touching the fingertips of her right hand lightly to Tei's palm, Fayel picked up the paper in her left hand and began to slowly pronounce the unfamiliar sounds she had so carefully memorised. Tei listened, awed, feeling power building gently around her, hearing the faint resonance grow fractionally as the words built on one another. Once he heard her almost falter, saw Rakariel sharply mouth the next phrase, and it seemed to be enough of a reminder for her to continue in time, magic's subtle echo still underlying her words.

The spell was surprisingly short, he realised as she completed it and fell silent, an anxious expression on her face. Just a heartbeat later he felt it settle over him like a soft blanket of warm air, one that settled into his very being, leaving him feeling reinvigorated, almost more alive than before. Awed beyond immediate words, he looked down at his scabbed hand and experimentally flexed it. There was no pain or even stiffness, and as he experimentally poked at it with his other hand, the scabs fell away as though he'd had more than a week to heal, nothing but slightly pink skin underneath.

"Wow..." he breathed, amazed. If he hadn't both felt and seen it for himself, he would barely have believed such a thing to be possible, but it had to be. The world beyond the valley had to be amazing indeed, an unimaginably different and distant place he was barely even beginning to comprehend — and it did exist, for it had to: nothing like what he had just seen had ever been possible in his experience, or his father's or grandfather's, trapped in a world whose limitations had always been simply how things were. He looked at Rakariel again, human in shape and build and the weariness in her brown eyes, but so very different from him and anyone he knew in manner and appearance and worn, matter-of-fact daring. Those who thought to fight the vardra thought only of killing one or two, unquestioned rulers of the mist that they were; no-one had tried to take a challenge to their lair and ever been heard of again. No-one did such a thing save for those determined to die, who for whatever reason had given up their claim on life and sought only to attempt to wreak vengeance with their last breath. Rakariel was nothing like that, as far as he could tell: she seemed determined to live and to fight for the living despite the dangers her path would encompass.

"It worked," she said quietly, cutting into his thoughts as she looked at his hand. "I'm glad." There was a short pause, and her tone became more instructive once again. "Now. Practice the spell in parts whenever you have a chance. If you're to remember it long enough for it to do your people any good, the sounds and symbols have to be ingrained into your memory. You'll have to do that alone... I doubt I'll have time to help you much longer." At a quizzical look from Tei, she continued, explaining again what she'd told the other two before.

"If it doesn't see sunlight again, then around seven or eight days from now, my lightstone will fade and die." Again, she hid her fear from them, fear of what would happen if it did fail her and left her trapped in the dark, with no way to escape. "After that, I... won't be able to help you. I can't fight what I can't see."

Tei nodded slowly, understanding the import of her words. Whatever she did, whatever she might be able to do for them, it would have to be done quickly. It was no wonder that she hadn't felt able to spend much time teaching Fayel. With so little time...

"Do you think you can really do it?" he asked without thinking. "Whatever you have to do, do you think you can make it in time?"

Her response, when it came, wasn't the most reassuring.

"I have to."

CHAPTER 6

Deeper into the Darkness

Absorbed in the lessons of magic, not even Rakariel had noticed quite how late it had become while she was teaching Fayel the healing spell. By the time the younger woman had gained enough mastery of it to attempt her relatively feeble healing of Tei, midnight had already passed them by, and all three had grown more tired than they realised. After Rakariel's less than reassuring words regarding her own survival, they had eaten largely in silence, a small meal of assorted fungus and a dried meat that was almost certainly rat. Sleep had followed almost immediately, Rakariel given a room to herself with a comfortable bed already made up in it and falling quickly into slumber despite her many reservations.

She awoke with a start, a stifling blackness bearing down on her, pinning her so that for an instant she couldn't move or even breathe, heartbeat racing impossibly loud in her ears. Rakariel lashed out blindly in an instinctive attempt to throw back the shadow that she couldn't fight, and in the same instant the suffocating darkness was torn away, cool air flooding in across her face like a breath of precious wind and a steady, unflickering illumination picking sharp-edged shadows across her field of vision. She gasped, tense and still, and forced herself to focus despite the fear that kept her breath ragged, heart still pounding. All at once, the curves and lines made sense: she was lying on her back, looking up at a mould-spotted and somewhat damaged ceiling of moulded plaster. At once luxurious and prosaic, it bore little resemblance to the vaulted stone arches and claustrophobic passages of her nightmares.

Resolutely slowing her breath, Rakariel tilted her head from side to side, looking around the largely empty room. Her lightstone glowed from atop a wooden dresser, its varnish dulled by years. Heavy planks covered what must once have been a window, and she stilled an instinctive urge to tear them aside, remembering at last where she was and why, and what danger lay beyond. Drawing in her arms, she slowly sat up, realising belatedly that the heap of blankets at her feet must have been what had caused the stifling darkness that had mingled so easily with the nightmares that still plagued her sleeping mind, pulled over her head until she awoke and threw them off. Such a simple explanation, and once again, she could force the darkness to recede back into her past.

She wondered what time of day it was. Regardless, it wasn't likely that she'd find sleep again until the next night. Standing up, she stretched, feet cold on the chill wood of the floor, long braid falling down her back and trailing wisps of loose hair. The mirror on the dressing table reflected her image back to herself, marred by spots of tarnish. One happened to cover her forehead as she looked consideringly at the reflection, and she turned aside, lifting her hand to slip two fingers under her bandanna and brush them across the scar it hid from view, an echo of old horrors catching at her heart. Rakariel let her hand fall, firmly shaking her head as if to deny darker thoughts any hold within it, then bent to pick up the outer clothes she had left on a chair the day before and dress.

Clad once again in her close-fitting leathers, subtly spelled for strength and resistance, she took up packs, bow, and sword, and retrieved her dagger from its hiding place under the flat cushion that had passed for a pillow. Looking again at the bed, she realised with some surprise that it had been made up using what were likely to be the best blankets the valley-dwellers had to offer, worn but still soft, patterns relatively bright and few darns or patches to be seen anywhere. She felt unexpected gratitude at the realisation, mingled with the more sobering reminder of Tei and Fayel's awe, the pedestal she feared they might put her on. She might be more skilled than they, but not better, and that skill had come at a great price.

Glancing about the room one last time, Rakariel picked up the lightstone and headed for the door. It opened silently, latch and hinges well-oiled, and she shut it quietly behind her. The landing she found herself on was unlit save by the lightstone, some doors open, others closed. Beyond the banisters further along, the stairs descended into blackness.

Lightstone in hand, she made her way to the top of the stairs and looked down, then descended quietly, drawing the layout of the building from memory and fixing it in her mind. Her light confirmed sketchy recollections, and she continued to the main room where she had spoken with Mayor Jan the day before. It was empty, left much as she'd last seen it, and she sat down in one of the more comfortable chairs, her weight eliciting a protesting creak from the aged wood. Leaning forward slightly, she gazed at the light held in her hands, focusing on the future and the new task before her rather than the immutable past.

She hadn't been there long when she heard a noise, looking up sharply to see Tei framed in the doorway, a candle in his hand. Though his eyes went to the lightstone, he kept it lit.

"Tei?" she said, taken aback. She hadn't expected to see him so early. From the look of his expression, he hadn't expected to see her, either.

"Uh, hello," he managed, slightly late.

"It's all right, you're not disturbing me." Her thoughts hadn't been getting her anywhere in any case. "I just didn't expect anyone else to be awake yet."

Tei shrugged a touch self-consciously, blowing his candle out and walking into the room. "I couldn't sleep." That despite how late she knew he'd gone to bed. It didn't really surprise her. "Do you always wake up before the light?"

"Sometimes," she said, watching as he sat down on another of the chairs. Some days she woke before the sun, others, with it. Only when she was particularly tired would she oversleep. After the night she'd just had, she was glad to wake early, to simply sit and stare into space; glad again of Tei's interruption that kept her mind from wandering down darker paths. "I'd like to leave as soon as possible, to give myself as much time as I can."

Tei frowned, all too clearly thinking of something she herself had thought and not wanted to admit. "Won't it take you a while to find your way? I mean... wouldn't it be easier if you had someone with you who already knew their way around?"

"Yes," she acknowledged reluctantly, "but I can't. Taking anyone with me would put them in danger, and worse. I don't even know what I'll have to face — I can't protect someone else as well as myself."

"But you have magic," Tei countered. "You used it on Fayel, and taught it to her. Even if something did happen to someone, wouldn't you be able to heal them?"

"I can't bring back the dead!" she snapped. "I couldn't even heal your sister's leg fully! I'm not a mage: I know just enough magic to keep myself alive, and that's all. I can't defend someone else, I can't help someone else, not in battle. I'd only be leading them into danger."

"What if they thought it was worth it?" he pressed. "You said yourself that you did."

"*No!* No-one goes with me. No-one."

"Why not?"

Rakariel stopped herself before she answered, forcing herself to take a deep breath and letting it out in a long, slow sigh. The truth was that she was afraid. She didn't want anyone else to face what she had, to have to become what she had. More than that, she feared that, though she would do anything in her power to stop any companions from dying, it wouldn't be enough. However far the curse on the valley went, she was afraid it would prove far too far for anyone with her.

"Because I won't be able to save them."

"Maybe you should let them worry about that," came a new voice from the doorway. Both Rakariel and Tei looked over, startled. "If what Father told me about your lightstone is true, then you will need someone to go with you, someone who knows the way. Maybe even someone who knows enough to get *you* back here if it goes out."

Rakariel fought to hide her instinctive flinch at that thought, but something of her reaction still escaped, at least enough for the man at the door to notice. To his credit, he didn't mention it, but she could see he'd seen her fear.

"If you really are from the world outside, then you're a stranger here," he continued. "You don't know how, where, or when to hide, when to move, where to go. Going alone would be suicide, plain and simple." He folded his arms, staring her down with the dark eyes that seemed common to Tei's entire family, features of a similar enough cast to be related. For once, Rakariel was the first to look away. "You told my father that you wanted to give us light. That you thought it was worth the risk of stirring up the vardra against you and us if you could get rid of them for good. If you go alone, that won't happen."

She thought about pointing out that she'd fought before, but decided reluctantly against it, for all that it was true. She had fought any amount of horrors, but that alone would not be enough to save her, was never enough to save anyone. She knew her limitations now. She had to. Those who hadn't learnt theirs in time had died. Forced to reluctantly concede the stranger's point, she simply bowed her head, her mind still rebelling against the necessity. There had to be another way. These people had already helped her: let that be their role, not following alongside as she went into dangers any sensible person should run from.

"Let me go with you," Tei abruptly volunteered, his words coming out in a sudden rush. The others turned to look at him as one, and he shifted in his seat, but went on anyway. "I know most of the city, I went on the long walk most recently of all of us! It has to be one of us, right? So why not me?"

He managed not to add that he'd met her first. A childish claim like that wouldn't help to lend any validity to his argument. The truth was that he wanted to go, unreservedly if he didn't think too hard about the dangers of it, and even if he did consider them he still wasn't content to remain in safety while she left. Rakariel was a miracle, bringing a hope as impossible and bright as the light from her stone, the quiet and matter-of-fact words she'd spoken making the inconceivable sound almost possible simply by virtue of the calm way she approached it. There had been what she'd said to him at the very first, her talk of the world above, her determination to save his world before he had even entirely believed that hers was real. There had been the moment when she'd spoken of the sun, and seemed suddenly more than the tired, battle-weary warrior whose demeanour she largely bore. There had been her determination to protect him even in the face of impending death as she stood between him and the door that could have broken under the vardra's assault. All of Tei's family who had so far met her had been swayed by her words to a greater or lesser extent, but without proof, who could not feel at least a twinge of doubt? More than anyone else, Tei had seen that she stood by what she had said. If it was possible, he believed that she might actually be able to do it — and if she went without him and failed, if she died, it would haunt him for the rest of his life.

He didn't know if she could read his expression, but she let her head drop again, not meeting his eyes for more than a few moments. "No. Not you. I can't." Something in her resigned tone, her weary posture, told him he had her.

"Who else will you take?" he asked. "It has to be one of the family. Grandfather's too old, you said Fayel still wouldn't be completely better, and out of the rest of us who're even here, I'm the only one you've really met." He took a quick breath. "I know my way around the city, like I said before, and I believe you can do this. I believe we should help you, I should help you." He was running headlong into it now, he knew. There was no turning back. It felt like jumping from a roof without even looking down to know if he would land well or die as Fayel so nearly had. "Uncle Ves is right, someone has to go with you. So take me."

Rakariel sighed, defeated. She could tell she wouldn't be able to fight the determination in that voice, not without more time than she had, and even then she still didn't think she had a chance. He'd follow her, she feared, whether she was willing to let him or not, and out of her sight he'd be in even more danger than in it. Instead, she fell back to the only position she had left short of acceptance, passing the choice to someone else in the desperate hope that they, as well as she, would refuse him.

"It's not my decision. It's the mayor's. You should talk to him."

That said, she turned her head away slightly. He might be largely a stranger, but she still didn't want to put Tei in danger, even if she did have no choice but to take someone with her. He was young, she guessed a good ten years younger than she herself if not more, easily awed by the traveller from outside and by the magic she bore. She knew she must seem even more marvellous to him than the warriors of her own people had seemed to her when she was a child. She had looked up to them, respected them, emulated them and followed in their footsteps when she came of age, setting out for adventure. That she'd lived was all she typically felt like saying for herself. The cost of all she'd done had been greater than she could ever have expected as a child. How could Tei understand what he might have to face?

Unaware of her thoughts, Tei stood up, his quick movement sinking her further into gloom. In truth, it was more fear than enthusiasm that kept his motion rapid, the fear that he would falter if he once stopped to rethink what he had said. How could he do that before someone so determined, so calm even in the face of death? How could he do any less than try to live up to that example?

"I'll ask him, then," he said, trying to keep trepidation from his voice. Still without giving himself pause to reflect too deeply, Tei left the room, followed by his uncle. With them gone, Rakariel was once again alone.

It was at once too long and too short a time before anything else caught her attention. Rakariel found her thoughts travelling aimlessly from place to place, all too often shadow to shadow. There might be little use in reflecting on the past, but it was forever at her heels, and Tei's brave, foolhardy insistence had not helped. She saw him just as she had once been, convinced of her own immortality, not fearing death because she didn't really believe it would come. She'd travelled the land as part of a band of mercenary adventurers, one arguably more successful than most, a handful of small dangers falling to her arrows and only bolstering her confidence. She had won, they had won; she had never then paused to think on what would happen if they did not until it was too late. Out of them all, only three had been left standing in the end, and they had long since gone their separate ways. For all she knew, she could be the last... and Tei's confidence, his innocence and youthful invulnerability, would be shattered as hers had. In all likelihood, he would die.

The more Tei thought about his suggestion, even just during the short walk from room to room, the more afraid he was. Living his life with the spectre of death around every corner, he knew what it was like to just barely escape its jaws — and now he intended to walk calmly into them. Yet each time fear threatened him, he thought of Rakariel's calm if careworn demeanour, her measured responses, her acceptance of the possibility of her death with no sign of the paralysis fear of it could bring. That spoke of a courage beyond anything he had ever seen, far removed from the desperate dash in the heat of the moment to snatch someone else from danger or the foolhardy overconfidence that he knew still saw people killed from time to time. It was something far greater than either of those. She knew her measure and held it up against her unknown foe, accepting that if she fell short then it would be the end of her, yet still doing what she felt had to be done. How, now that he had seen that courage in her, could he let himself falter? How could he step back from trying to do the same in her aid, or stand aside when he knew that his help could prove the difference between victory and defeat as she fought not only the vardra but the steadily fraying thread of time?

Arriving at his grandfather's door, Tei took a deep breath and knocked, heart still racing in his chest. She had probably been right that he should ask him first... but it was already taking longer than he would have liked.

Downstairs, Rakariel stared blankly at nothing, her eyes fixed on a point just short of the far wall as she brooded over Tei's intent. She was so deep in thought that her gaze automatically snapped to the door almost before the sound she'd heard from it even registered on her conscious awareness. Light footsteps were making their way closer, and closer still, until she saw a woman probably a little older than her pass by with candle in hand, not looking in and so not seeing the traveller sat slumped in her chair. The rest of the building was clearly beginning to wake up, and it occurred to her that it would be a better idea to find something to eat before she left, as well as anything that she might be able to take with her, rather than let her thoughts chase themselves in circles over Tei. His grandfather would doubtless refuse him in any case, greater experience teaching him how little Tei knew of what he stood to lose. Surely he would have to.

* * *

Breakfast proved a welcome distraction, as she had hoped. The other woman, who she learned was named Misa, Tei's aunt, seemed somewhat intimidated by her at first, but quickly plucked up the courage to ask about the lands outside, about the sun she had never known. Despite the shadows that weighed on her mind, Rakariel found her spirit somewhat lifted by the simple talk, describing the memories she cherished so dearly to others who, for once, truly understood their value. Even so, she ate quickly, itching to set out. The limited life of her lightstone was ever-present in the back of her mind, urging her on, its force added to by the thought that if she left at once she could be gone before anyone could follow. Only her reluctant acceptance that it was foolish kept her in the house, distracting herself with talk of daylight and the calm and peaceful land beyond the valley.

After a while, she made her excuses and returned to the main room, pacing restlessly. What was keeping the mayor so long? Surely refusing Tei could not have taken that much time. She was almost tempted to go and find them herself, to ask what was wrong, but it was not her place to intrude. Only if she had to wait for hours would she grow that impatient.

It wasn't particularly long before her concerns were silenced. Her own footsteps drowned out the others until they were actually at the door, and she stopped as, turning to face it, she saw Fayel, Tei, and their grandfather, his lined face unreadable. Tei looked oddly nervous and edgy, and Fayel was quiet and solemn, her eyes occasionally flickering to her brother, her stance still somewhat lopsided, though less so than it had been. Casting her gaze across them as they entered, Rakariel wasn't instantly sure what the decision had been. Tei looked far too serious and worried to have been given the permission to adventure she'd believed him to be seeking, but Fayel seemed far too solemn for her brother to be staying in safety with her. Or was someone else close to them, such as their uncle — Rakariel had learned from the breakfast table that their parents were away elsewhere in the city as part of their duties — going to be sent with her instead?

After a few moments, the mayor broke the silence. "Rakariel," he began, calling her wandering attention back to him and him alone. "It is clear you must have someone to accompany you, and Tei has argued that he should be that person." That much she knew: she waited, on edge, to hear what he would say next. "I have agreed with him that he may go... indeed, that he may be the best choice to go."

At that, she could do no more than stare. What choice had he made, sending Tei with her after all? How could he have let him go so easily? Her eyes flicked back to the young man, standing quietly, resolve and... was that fear, in his dark eyes? She couldn't be certain, but she thought it might be, though there was no telling what of. If he had any sense at all it would be of what he had agreed to, but for all she knew, it could simply be of her own reaction to the news. Her last hope of keeping him from danger gone, all she could do was sigh, and bow her head, and accept it. There would be no changing this now. Even if she could, she didn't have the time. She couldn't refuse to set out, or argue her case more convincingly than she had.

"Very well," she said, slowly. "But you must understand... he may never come back."

"I know," Tei himself said quietly, trepidation in his voice. Rakariel glanced at him again, his reaction not the one she had half expected. That was not the sound of the cocksure young woman she had been at his age: did he know, truly know, something of what he faced? What he could be forced to see, and to endure? There was no time to consider it, though, nor much point in doing so. She — and he, however much she might wish it were otherwise — had to set out as soon as possible.

"You should pack, then," she said. "Bring whatever you think we'll need, but travel as light as you can. Don't account for me for more than seven days." She looked reflexively to the lightstone in her hand, still steady and bright for now, but all too soon to fade. Despite that, she found herself reluctant to take it up and bind it into its place on her forehead, because that would mean that she truly was descending into darkness once again. Yet, however much she might want to, there was no time left to turn away from her fears: she had to face them. Looking back at Tei, and without taking her eyes off him, she lowered one hand to retrieve the metal and leather framework that would hold the stone, clipped it into its place in the centre of its harness, and smoothly fastened the whole thing across her brow, padded by the bandanna that served as a cushion against its pressure. Snugly fit to her head, it wouldn't move easily, casting light wherever she chose to look.

"Go on," she said. "Go."

Tei nodded suddenly, almost startled, and left without a word.

Once he was out of sight, Rakariel looked to the others, finding her speech suddenly hesitant. "Have you... have you said your goodbyes?" She hadn't known family ties for a long time, whether her own by blood or even the looser bonds of camaraderie and shared experience that had held the mercenary group together. Now she was breaking someone else's.

It looked for a moment as though Fayel would say something to go with her quick nod, but she simply closed her mouth again, looking down slightly as as her grandfather spoke.

"Yes, we have." He paused for a moment as though searching for words, his tone measured and thoughtful. "I thank you for being concerned for him, and for us. It gives me still greater reason to believe in your intentions and your cause. But I think that perhaps you underestimate him. Much though I want to keep my grandchildren here in safety, he has argued that he should go with you, and I find that I cannot deny him. Watch over him if you can, but I think that, in a way, I'm glad he has chosen what he has, for the reasons he has." He shook his head, very slowly. "All I can do now is wish you both luck. I dearly hope you will succeed."

Rakariel dipped her head, saying the only thing she could, hopelessly inadequate though it was. "I'll do everything I can."

Silence fell across the room. Rakariel saw Fayel studying her through her eyelashes, and wondered what the girl was thinking. She wasn't sure she wanted to know. Awkward, but feeling unable to pace as she usually would, she waited uneasily for Tei's return.

It wasn't all that long before he reappeared in the doorway, his voice quiet, tense. "I'm ready."

Rakariel looked him over. He'd found himself several additional packs and pouches to complement his ragged outfit, each one narrow, held so closely to the contours of his body that it was difficult to see where they added any bulk at all to his slight frame. Even a cursory glance was enough to tell her just how suited it was to his life, unlikely to hinder him in the slightest wherever he found himself needing to scramble and hide. Other than that, his worn and patched layers of clothing looked much the same; she even recognised his jacket. She shook her head and sighed. There was no time to put it off, not any longer. With no way back to the light, she already had precious little of it.

"We should go." She shrugged her shoulders to check the fit of her packs, tightened a couple of straps and twisted side to side to be sure that everything was settled, then pulled a fold of cloth down over the lightstone to prevent it from alerting the creatures that waited in the fog. An air of worn readiness settled across her, an easy balance in her economical movements as she walked to the door. Only as she was about to step through did she pause, looking over her shoulder.

"Thank you — all of you."

With that, she was gone, and after one last glance back, so was Tei.

CHAPTER 7

The Temple of Forgotten Gods

As they left the house, latching the old privy window shut behind them, Rakariel led the way towards the street outside, stopping in the dubious shelter afforded by the slightly arched passage that led out onto the wide road. Her ragged companion stopped beside her, glancing around, and she suspected his wary pose was one he habitually adopted when forced to stand outdoors. She held back a sigh, looking at him, his expression clear this close even in the shadows. She didn't see the overconfidence she'd expected to find in his eyes, though, rather a mixture of determination and trepidation. That, at least, was for the best, though it almost felt wrong somehow, clashing with her expectations on a level she didn't even consciously register.

"I'm going to the temple first," Rakariel whispered, keeping her voice as low as possible, aware this time of the danger that stalked the dimly-lit valley, of how she could all too easily become the hunted. "Whichever was the most important. Which way is it?" In a city this size, she would have been shocked indeed to find only one temple, whatever gods the inhabitants had worshipped in the past. There would, however, always be one considered the most important, the most grand, where a majority — however small — of the people's major rituals were held.

Tei glanced up and around before replying, the motion instinctive despite already knowing exactly where he was. "This way," he murmured almost soundlessly, slipping around the corner and left into the road. His motions were irregular, footfalls perfectly placed to make almost no sound at all, and what little he did make simply blending in with the uneven dripping that sounded dully throughout the city. Rakariel followed him, keeping as quiet as she could: it was silent enough for most purposes, but still louder than Tei. Like him, she kept her movements irregular, hiding the sounds of her passage amongst the splash of falling drips, the occasional creak and tick of tired, rotten wood and eroded stone. The muffled silence of the all-enveloping fog made small, minor sounds simultaneously dead and loud, echoes muted, yet each drip the only sound to enter her awareness outside of her own breathing, her own soft steps. She couldn't help but think that it felt like a ghost world, captured in the transition between life and death, as she had said to the mayor the day before.

She quickly lost track of how long they'd been walking, of precisely what route they'd taken through the unnerving fog-bound city. Even accustomed as she was to keeping a reasonably accurate mental map of her surroundings, it was difficult to follow the faded, looming landmarks that were lost as quickly as they came, the junctions which, by and large, looked much the same as one another in their misty ruin. There was nothing she could use to orient herself by beyond her own sense of where north lay, and while she thought she could set a bearing in the rough direction of Tei's home, she would all too likely fail to find it, end up wandering lost in the fog. Much though she would have preferred not to admit it, she found she was already glad to have a companion, for that reason if no other. If once she became lost, and failed to find her way, her time would run out before she had even begun.

Buildings passed them by, sometimes low, more often high. Tei stopped at odd moments, listening to the silence of the city, to sounds — if there were any — that Rakariel could never have identified herself. Occasionally he would turn aside, creep down alleys to avoid open spaces; at other times he would flit across broad squares like a shadow. Rakariel followed, keeping her silence: even if he could tell her what he heard or saw or simply sensed, she would be unlikely to learn in so short a time. Eventually, as a shape even higher than the others all around began to loom dimly from the mists before them, Tei stopped, ducking down beside a low wall. A wide road ran across their path at a right angle, and on its other side a wall somewhat taller than a man, broken only by a pair of arched gates that had once been finely wrought.

"This is it," he whispered, just moments before Rakariel could ask him.

"The temple?"

He nodded, looking over his shoulder at her where she crouched behind him. "Those are the main gates. There are others, but some of them are rusted shut, and these are the closest." She saw him glance forward again, hesitation in his motions.

"Are you sure you want to do this?" she asked, keeping her voice at a whisper to match his own, barely a sound at all. Tei nodded fractionally, quickly.

"I'm sure."

Though he was out in the open, exposed and vulnerable, the thoughts that crowded his head ran much as they had even before they'd left the safety of the mayor's home. Despite the fear he felt — which, at the moment, was only somewhat stronger than the everyday backdrop of wariness that made up his life — he had to go. He couldn't do less after seeing what Rakariel was, what she was prepared to face, or after hearing the words she had spoken of the world beyond. If it was possible, then it was worth risking his life for.

Rakariel stood first, leading the way across the road in a quick, broken stride. The gates stood partially open, and he watched her as she rested her hand against the rusted iron bars and ornamentation. She stood there for a long moment before stepping inside, and, keeping low to the ground, Tei followed. He stopped as he entered the gates, looking around while still within the dubious shelter of their archway. He'd rarely been inside the temple grounds, for all that it was fairly close to the area he considered home. Wild and choked with dead, overgrown plants, it was full of a ragged kind of cover that he wasn't used to, one that he couldn't trust to protect him from anything but a cursory glance, and making betraying sounds if he tried to move within it. Like any sensible person, he'd habitually avoided it in favour of narrow-windowed buildings on which the doors had long ago been barred, or which he could at the worst bar himself, if it came to it. As his glance came back forward again, he realised that Rakariel was already moving on again, and he hurried to catch up, keeping just slightly behind her. In the unfamiliar surroundings, he was even more tense and alert than usual, even without the knowledge of what they were risking to spur him to additional care.

Before him, Rakariel slowed, peering upwards as

though she were trying to make out the true shape of the tall, fog-cloaked temple. Faint streamers of thicker and thinner fog drifted lazily across it, moving on a breeze lighter even than a simple breath, and curled gently about the long-dead plants and the stained, mould-covered statues that lined the broad stone-flagged path. Tei paid each one a sharp glance as he approached, checking instinctively that their shapes were as they should be, concealing no dark and vicious hunter in their meagre shelter. He noticed his companion doing the same, her alertness almost a match for his own, strong and skilled presence at least somewhat reassuring.

The distance to the front of the temple was only short, but it seemed much longer to Tei, forced into the open and on unfamiliar ground. Though the temple doors were smaller than the gates that stood forever open, it was not by as much of a margin as he always expected: the building was no house, not even a grand one, and was built to an altogether different scale. The thick wooden doors were closed, as they always had been, almost certainly barred from the inside, though Tei doubted that anyone still living knew for sure. Rakariel tried pulling, then pushing them while he was still looking up at the arching doors and the sheer wall above, but all she managed to do was cause a faint creak from the old wood as she threw her weight into it, a sound that made him jump regardless of how slight it had been. She gave up on that means of entrance almost the moment it proved closed to her, and turned to Tei once again.

"Where now?" she whispered softly. There had to be another way in somewhere, one that would be easier than forcing these strangely sturdy doors. It was a pattern she had been noticing throughout the city: that the old wood, though partially rotten, was far less decayed than she would expect — after the generations Tei's family attested to had passed, anything not cared for or magically braced should have fallen apart long ago.

Tei glanced around as she thought, knowing that he had to find another way into the temple, and quickly. Even the faint sound Rakariel had made trying to open the doors might have been enough to call a vardra, though if there had been one that close by it would have attacked already. He searched his memory, but came up with nothing: no-one had ever sought to enter the place that he knew of, keeping a respectful and wary distance from the interior just as he himself always had.

"We'll have to go around," she muttered under her breath, while he was still thinking. Tei refocused on her just in time to see her gesture to one side, then the other, a silent question in her expression as she asked him wordlessly which way to go. Knowing as little as he did, he could only shrug, to which she responded with a nod and turned to the right, walking up to the broad path's edge.

"Has anyone ever been inside?" she whispered to him, and he shook his head.

"No."

Their voices were barely audible, little more than shapes swirled out into the mist. As Rakariel stepped from the path, her slow footsteps squished quietly in the waterlogged soil, Tei's making much the same sound a moment later as he followed her. On such ground, he could for once be no quieter than she. In places, pools of standing water were vaguely visible as mirror-smooth patches of grey or brown-black, and the two avoided them by unspoken consent while keeping close to the tall, moisture-slicked temple wall. They had almost reached the corner when the air was split by a strange, ululating cry from somewhere in the distance, a cross between a roar and a scream. The inhuman noise was only slightly out of the range of sounds a human could conceivably make, adding an extra dimension of eeriness above and beyond the fog-deadened strangeness of a howl in the silent city. Tei froze in place the moment he heard it, barely moving more than his eyes as his gaze flicked about in a quick and jerky fashion, what few movements he made tense to the point of begrudging each instant spent in motion as he searched frantically for cover or danger. Rakariel, too, had halted at the noise, and she twisted to face its source, hands automatically reaching to bow and arrows, but closing on neither as she watched Tei and his reactions, took her lead from him. Instead, she slowly leant towards him, turning her head to face him but keeping her gaze fixed outward in the impenetrable mist.

"That was them?" she breathed, already knowing the answer. "How far?"

"Not here," came the near-silent response, Tei's voice trembling ever so slightly on the words. "Someone else." As he always did at that distant sound, he felt both relief and fear intermingled: relief for himself, that he was not the prey, and fear, sympathy, even horror for the unknown stranger who was. It could all too easily have been him who had sparked that hunting call, who was now desperately having to run in the few seconds that were all too likely to be the last in that person's life. He hoped that they escaped even as he was selfishly glad that it had once again been someone other than him.

"How far, though?" Rakariel persisted. She needed to know where that noise was coming from, how distant it was. She needed as much knowledge as Tei could give her about what those sounds meant, what they were up against.

"Maybe... a minute, half a minute?" he whispered back. Rakariel's eyebrows lifted in surprise at the time. If her guess at the distance was even roughly right, the creatures were *fast.*

"Then keep moving!"

True to her own words, she picked up the pace at once, now with bow in her left hand and an arrow held lightly between the first and second fingers of her right. Still stepping as lightly as she could in the clinging soil, she paused at the corner, leaned out slightly so that only the side of her head showed around it, then stepped out when she saw no danger waiting there. If the areas of light and dark in the mist were any clue, she thought the temple had to bulge out further along the side, and made her way towards the dimly-seen shape. Its outlines grew clearer as she and Tei closed, proving that, indeed, a wing of the temple swept out to the side ahead of them, its roof sinking to a lower level than that of the main building. The darker shapes of windows and doors were beginning to resolve when the roar they had heard before sounded again, unmistakable frustration and anger in its tones — and, moments later, was taken up by another of the eerie, inhuman voices. Tei paled, his heart racing. Anybody with any sense would be in hiding after that. Their quarry escaped after the hunt was announced, the vardra would be angry, and searching all the harder for a kill.

"Hurry!" he urged, voice gaining a touch of sound as his caution was almost overtaken by the desperation to find a place to hide. Responding to the urgency in his tense, strained voice, as well as her own feelings about the howls in the dimness, Rakariel broke into a run, stopping short at the first of the darker shapes: a narrow, wooden side door. She twisted the latch, shook it back and forth, but it held, locked in place as securely as the main entrance, for all that there was no keyhole visible in either. Wasting no more time in frustration, she moved quickly along, feeling the outlines of a narrow, paned window. Might they be able to gain entry there? She placed her head almost next to it before lifting the cloth over her lightstone the slightest fraction. Light spilled from it, reflecting from the thick-paned glass, enough making its way through to show her only dark, close-grained wood on the other side. The window had been boarded from within! Doubtless that was also the reason the lockless doors wouldn't open, unsurprising given how the city had fallen, but worse than useless to her and Tei where they stood outside. She tugged the fold of cloth down again, cutting out the revealing light, and almost pushed herself away from the window to move swiftly to the next, searching for some omission or mishap, anything that might give them a way in. Just as with the first, it was barricaded from the inside, and she mentally braced herself for a fight. If there was no way in, she and Tei would be forced to stand their ground.

"Rakariel!" came a hissed call from somewhere

behind her, and she turned to see Tei standing several paces back, peering up into the fog. "Look!"

She stepped away from the wall and tilted her head back to follow his gaze. Dark, regular shapes above them were windows — and one showed a ragged centre, even darker than the glass around it, mist lazily curling into the hole. The window was broken, and would be a perfect way in if they could only reach it!

Even as she began to evaluate how they might be able to get up there, Tei was moving again. Almost fumbling in his haste, he reached under his ragged jacket, lifting it to expose a coil of rope seemingly looped around his waist. Hooked at the small of his back rather than actually coiled around *him*, it came loose easily, and he kept it in one hand as his other delved quickly in a pouch, retrieving a slightly rusted three-pronged hook that he tied securely onto the end of the rope. Rakariel watched with surprised approval as he tugged on it, testing the knot, then backed up a little further, eyeing the broken window high above. The glass in it still gave him pause, potentially able to fray and cut the rope, and he hesitated.

Rakariel, too, had realised what he had. She edged out still further, passing him and finding the edge of a largely-hidden paved path that had once led through what must have been well-cultivated grounds. In the damp and mud, it was easy for her to simply pry up a cobblestone and heft it, looking back at Tei. Realising what she intended, he swallowed and nodded, nervous but agreeing. They had to get inside, even at the cost of making sound on the way, because if they were only indoors they could find a room to barricade themselves in for as long as they had to until the danger went away.

Outside they could still be killed at a moment's notice, whether they made a noise or not, even whether they moved or not. Once a vardra saw them, that would be the end.

Stepping up beside him, bow and arrow replaced on her back in favour of a cobblestone held in each hand, Rakariel took aim, carefully gauging the distance. She was still for several seconds — then, suddenly, she moved, poised, coiled power unleashed in a single throw. The stone soared high and true, smashing through the ancient glass with what seemed to be a tremendous, rending crash after so long spent in the city's silence. The glass shattered and fell, the delicate leading that held it buckling, shorn of its support. Without waiting for the sound to die or the glass to even finish falling, Rakariel switched her second stone to her right hand and threw again. It flew as straight and true as the first, smashing through what little was left of the window at its base and completing its destruction. Almost in time with the impact, the twin roars came again, wavering eerily, rising and falling out of tune with one another. She jumped back as Tei, hands trembling with tension and fear, swung his hook before releasing it, watched it sail up to the window almost as if in slow motion, his senses and thoughts racing in time with his almost painfully accelerated heartbeat. The hook vanished through the gaping hole, and he heard it hit something within, bounce, and stop. He tugged gently on the rope, not daring to pull any faster as it slid across the room's unseen interior until, wonder of wonders, it caught on something somewhere within. He dared then to pull harder, even to yank on it with all his strength, and it gave only slightly in time to a strange, sliding creak, then held motionless.

At once he dashed to the wall, splashing in the waterlogged soil, and shot up it as fast as he knew how, feet finding footholds he was barely even aware of seeing. Once, he slipped, swung for a terrifying instant, then caught himself and scrambled further, finally reaching the edge and hauling himself over it. The roars sounded again, deathly close, and for an instant he froze still on hands and knees on the floor, paralysed by terror.

The sudden jerk of the rope through his hands brought him back to his senses, forcing him to let go of it and reminding him of what else, besides the vardra, was out there. Standing, he turned and looked down: Rakariel was clinging to the rope, climbing determinedly but all too slowly up the wall. She couldn't possibly make it in time!

He couldn't afterwards have said what it was he was thinking in that moment, acting entirely on instinct, and conflicting instinct at that: a part of him wanted to run, but another part couldn't, wouldn't leave her there in so much danger and so close to safety. He found he knew what to do, was doing it almost before his conscious mind, still half-paralysed by fear, could even catch up to the decision. Tei grabbed hold of the rope again, bracing himself against the uneven floorboards and hauling it up with all his might, tugging hand over hand with a desperate strength he hadn't known he had. Rakariel's head and hands appeared over the windowsill, letting go of the rope to grip it instead and boost herself inside, tumbling to the floor and rolling back to her feet with bow already in hand. Tei hauled the remainder of his rope up into a messy loop about his arm — the hook detaching from the table it had caught on as he did so — and saw a dark shape fall through the open space outside just moments later, terrifying him into a small and surprisingly high-pitched yelp.

"Run!" Rakariel yelled, snatching the fold of cloth from her lightstone and unintentionally whipping the entire bandanna from her head, leaving it to hang from the back of the lightstone's circlet. The room suddenly blazed with light, almost blinding after so long spent in the mist, and Tei gasped, bolting at last for the doorway. The door itself lay in the corridor, split and almost shattered by some long-ago force, but he ran anyway, not daring to do anything else. Backing up more slowly, Rakariel followed, pausing in the doorway to loose an arrow that gave rise to a terrible scream of rage and pain, a sound that only an injured vardra could make. He shot a glance over his shoulder to see her turn and run after him, then whirl again to move backwards, fast and sure. Her controlled intent lent him the strength to regain a touch of control, to look around rather than simply run through the curving corridor in headlong flight, but each door on either side hung open at a crazed angle, the few that were closed remaining stubbornly so even when he ran full-tilt into one. It gave only slightly, otherwise held stiff and fast by whatever had reinforced it from the other side.

"I can't get in!" he shouted, half screamed, turning back to see a terrible dark shape beyond the small, glowing silhouette that was Rakariel, her feet firmly planted in the middle of the corridor, stance as unyielding as stone itself. She loosed another arrow, one that only seemed to enrage the vardra further, then another and another, snatching them from her quiver almost without pause. As it stumbled back, she suddenly turned and ran towards him, her expression something savage yet determined, reined in by chill experience, any fear buried deep.

"Keep going!"

He spun, dashed away, his own breath loud and harsh in his ears. Rakariel followed almost directly behind him, increasing the distance as fast as she could before the monster behind regained its composure enough to follow. She'd seen its shape in the corridor as she paused to face it: dark and hulking, naturally armoured, its figure humanoid but twisted and bent, what would have been hands replaced by long, black blades of what she assumed was probably nail or bone. It was too large to be able to match their headlong dash in the confines of the corridor, hemmed in by walls and ceiling designed for creatures smaller and slimmer than such a beast; if she and Tei could find somewhere to hide, they would be safe.

Or would they? The thought nearly brought her up short, caused her to falter for the briefest of instants. No, they wouldn't, couldn't be. They would only be trapped. Her first instinct had been right, it had to be. While they had the advantage of terrain, she had to fight, or even if they lived they could remain prisoners until her light ran out.

She stopped, spun around with an arrow nocked, aiming just past the near wall of the gently curving corridor. The creature was already out of sight, but she knew it would show itself quickly, and she would be ready when it did. She had chosen her ground — now it was time to defend it.

Hearing her quick footsteps stop, Tei halted as well, turning to look back and seeing nothing but Rakariel and an empty corridor.

"What are you doing?!" Even his silence had given way to sound now, with no point left in trying to conceal his all too obvious position. What was she thinking? Standing still was suicide!

"We have to kill them. Here and now." Her every word fairly hummed with determination, with a kind of controlled tension that would propel her through any battle until, at the last, her body had nothing left to give. Eyes fixed on the curve of the corridor, she waited, as patient as a predator preparing to spring. There was no other way: this was how it had to be done.

Disbelieving, Tei took up station behind her in a half-crouch, his own hands betrayingly empty until he snatched the knife from his belt. Though it would be next to useless when — if — the vardra reached him, it was comforting beyond words to grip even that pitiful weapon, allowing him to take refuge in the shelter of Rakariel's impossible determination.

The dark horror loped awkwardly around the corner just moments later, its gait a kind of trotting run in the narrow confines of the corridor. With a howl of hideous anticipation, it raised one bladed arm to strike, the other held close to its chest in an almost protective pose — and an arrow snapped from Rakariel's bow, flying straight and true to strike the creature in its armoured head and only narrowly missing an eye. The vardra stumbled with a grunt, rocking back on its haunches as it caught itself, then skidded, rearing further back and giving her a clear shot at the target she had so painstakingly sought. Her second arrow flew at once, embedding itself deep in the vardra's exposed throat, and it stumbled again before collapsing with a hideous, rattling groan, its spasmodic movements quickly dying away as its blood began to pool on the wooden floor.

Heart still thudding in his ears, Tei only then realised that he was holding his breath, forced himself to let it out in a long, slow sigh of utter disbelief. Was it truly possible? The vardra had fallen to Rakariel's strange weapon, even though she was alone save for him, even though she was making her plans anew with each passing moment! It was dead, it truly was, and he took a slow pace forward — only to realise that Rakariel hadn't relaxed, that she still stood in place with that same tight-wound determination, her only movement that which she needed to ready another arrow.

The light shining from the stone on her brow showed nothing but the fallen vardra, the blood still pooling at its throat, arrows snapped and whole protruding from a couple of joints where they had previously found hold. For a breathless moment, all was still, and the living as motionless as the dead. It was then, in that silence, that she heard it: the second set of those oddly loping steps, growing swiftly closer. Behind her, Tei froze into complete immobility, but she had known this was coming, remembered the second howl taken up so quickly after the first. There were at least two of the creatures hunting them, potentially more depending on how many had been drawn to investigate and had come swiftly enough to follow. Rakariel could only wait, tense, for the next to appear.

It wasn't long at all before it came into view, but it felt to both Rakariel and Tei like a lifetime. This time, she knew how to catch them off-guard, knew where to aim: her first arrow shot high, striking the vardra's plated head and causing it, like its fallen companion, to stop for an instant. Dark eyes squinted towards the light, seeking a target through the unaccustomed glare, but she was still. For a moment, it was, too. Then she loosed her next arrow, and the world moved again all at once, the vardra howling as the arrow struck deep into a joint and Rakariel snatched out another and hesitated. This vardra had hunched over rather than rearing back, and its hulking form presented no obvious targets. She shifted her balance subtly just as it launched itself towards her in as fast a run as it could manage, the motion close enough to a human gait to be disturbingly uncanny. Still she held her ground, letting it draw close, and as it bounded over the corpse of its fellow, raising bladed arms in the process, she finally saw the chance she had been looking for — and let fly. Just as with the first of the creatures, her arrow pierced its throat, and what would have been a heavy but agile landing became a stumbling crash. It rolled once with the momentum of its run, and lay still.

Still Rakariel waited, straining her senses for the faintest of sounds even as the fallen vardra's dying motions ceased, waited until it became clear that, for the time being, there were no more. At last she allowed herself to relax slightly, even permitting a faint sigh as some of the tension and poise left her body, putting away the arrow she had held ready and returning her bow to its place against the side of her packs, where she could snatch it up in an instant.

Tei straightened a little after, this time following her lead. She had brought down both of the vardra that had come to hunt them, though she had stood alone and unsheltered. She had succeeded, and they were still alive. He watched as Rakariel walked forward, hesitantly trailing along behind, though staying somewhat further back from the bodies as she retrieved those arrows that were still intact from them, wiping them clean quickly before returning them to her quiver with the others. The vardran corpses, lifeless, sprawled grotesquely across the floor, only moving when she placed her booted foot on them to tug the arrows free. Curious, she paused over one, shoving it onto its back and examining it. The proportions were wrong, the build wiry in some places and stocky in others, but it still followed the same basic body plan as that of a person, other than the bladed hands, the tough, armour-like skin. She noted a couple of stubby fingers sticking out at the base of each blade, probably useless for most tasks requiring much dexterity, but strong-looking, naked and lined like a monkey's. She had never seen creatures quite like the vardra before.

Straightening, she left the bodies to their final rest. Tei watched her come back towards him, absently wiping off her bloodied hands as she walked. Their blood was red, he noted with an oddly detached clarity. Just like his own.

"We should keep going," she said quietly. "I think this passage will lead back to the main part of the temple. We've come most of the way around already."

Still almost in shock from the battle, and trusting her judgement, Tei simply nodded, letting her lead the way onward. When she paused to look into one of the rooms, he did the same, and realised suddenly that he was trembling. All he could do was look at his shaking hands even as Rakariel studied the room beyond. It had been a single-person bedroom with table and chair in its centre, a narrow cot against one wall with a couple of shelves on the wall opposite. The shutters were firmly closed, but the mouldering mattress had been ripped and torn long ago, a wide, dark stain marring both it and the floorboards below. That and the other damage — mostly to the table, its chair flung across the room — only served to add further weight to the suspicions she held, though she couldn't yet be certain. Turning away from the wreckage, she made to leave and paused, looking at Tei where he leant against the doorframe, still staring at his trembling hands. After a moment's hesitation, she lifted her hand to touch his shoulder, recognising what he had to be feeling.

"It will pass. You survived."

Startled, Tei looked up at her, into unexpectedly compassionate brown eyes, a little difficult to see below the glow of the lightstone. She tightened her hand on his shoulder for a moment, then let go. Drawing a little strength from it, Tei took a deep breath and, with some effort, forced himself to straighten up. Rakariel gave him a fractional, approving nod, coupled with the faintest of smiles.

"Come on. It's better to keep moving. Don't let yourself stop."

Though her words were terse, her tone was almost soft. He managed a quick, jerky nod in response, and followed her as she stepped away to continue on down the gently turning corridor, absently tucking her bandanna back beneath the lightstone's circlet.

They didn't have far to go before the end came into sight, an arched door set into a wall at the passage's end. Rakariel stood next to it for a moment, barely breathing as she listened to the silence beyond, before gently lifting the simple latch that held it closed. The door creaked alarmingly as she swung it slowly open into the cavernous space beyond, and both she and Tei froze, but no other sound disturbed the still air. As she'd thought, they were alone in the temple. Slowly, still moving with silent care, she slipped through.

The view beyond was impressive, made all the more so by the lightstone's inability to fully illuminate all of it, painting the distance in half-seen shades of grey. They were on a balcony at least a floor up, looking out and down across a vaulted hall, the sphere of light that the lightstone cast dwindling so quickly to shadow in the vast space that both ends of the hall disappeared into darkness. Rakariel fought back a moment of hollow dread, unconsciously gripping the ornate stone railing that stood between her and the rest of the shadowed temple. A sound beside her touched her awareness a moment late: Tei, breathing out slowly in a quiet sound of amazement. It broke her thoughts, and she shook her head.

"We need to get down to the floor," she whispered to him. Though it had been fairly quiet, even that whisper raised the slightest of echoes in the chill, empty space, so different to the fog-deadened world outside. Tei looked around fearfully; in that strange place, the unfamiliar sound seemed as though it could be nothing but the mocking voices of distant, angry spirits — but Rakariel caught his arm and dragged him along with her as she moved off to their left. As she'd told him not long before, motion was the key. She wouldn't let either of them stop.

As luck would have it, she'd chosen the right direction: they hadn't gone far before she saw an opening in the wall that gave way to a spiral staircase, winding both up and down. Peering both ways before setting foot on it, the movement of her head throwing shadows this way and that, Rakariel headed down with Tei trailing behind her. She tried to push thoughts of other descents from her mind. That had been long ago, in a land now far distant, and it had no bearing on what was happening to Tei's people in their hidden valley.

They descended three full revolutions before reaching the ground, stepping out through another doorless arch and back into the hall. It seemed even larger from that new perspective, vaulting ceiling lost to the cloak of shadow. Both looked around, Rakariel's innate sense of direction telling her that the main entrance had to be to the left, and she turned right, headed deeper into the temple.

"What are we looking for?" Tei whispered as he followed, still seeking purpose to distract him from the battle they had fought above, and feeling both aimless and almost incompetent as he compared himself to her quick, purposeful stride.

"An altar, maybe," Rakariel whispered back. "Holy books, maybe a record chamber somewhere beyond that. Anything that might tell us something more about what happened here, what your priests saw."

Tei nodded and fell silent, his gaze drifting in search of both danger and anything useful, even if he still had little more idea of what that might encompass.

They passed alcoves in the walls, some dimly set with windows that gave little to no light, some contaning statues that, from their poses, looked to commemorate heroes of times long past. Dank lines of cloth on the otherwise stone floor gave somewhat when they stood on them, rows of ancient cushions that had doubtless once supported worshippers as they sat or knelt in prayer before their gods.

"Tell me more of the gods your people followed," Rakariel murmured, her voice still raising strange echoes in the empty hall. "Your grandfather told me that they once gave blessings to the people, that they were just and fair."

"I guess," Tei replied doubtfully, part of him still listening to the echoes his own near-silent voice raised. He'd heard those tales since he was small, just like anyone else. But how could it be just to leave his people, abandon them to the vardra and their fallen city?

"Gods have their own rules," Rakariel whispered, his tone and expression giving her some clue as to his thoughts, "and they're different for each. They do not often change their nature. There are only three things I can think of that could have happened here, if they once responded to you as your grandfather said: your people angered them greatly in some way, something evil came between you and them... or they were changed, corrupted, by another power. I dearly hope it is not the last, for all our sakes."

"What if it was?" Tei found himself asking. Since she had come, a traveller from the almost mythical world beyond, he no longer knew what was possible and what was not.

"Then we find a way to escape them, if we can," she replied softly. "We find a way to leave the valley. There would almost certainly be no other way, and even that probably wouldn't work. You should hope that whatever happened, it is not that. Only then do we have some hope."

Tei swallowed. "Right."

"So tell me," Rakariel persisted. "What do you know?"

"What anyone knows, I suppose," he said, slowly. "It's said everyone would pray to them. Sometimes, you could ask the priests to talk to them on your behalf, and if your wish was strong enough, your heart true enough, and you were willing to give up something of equal value in return, they would grant a blessing. King Sariven carried a great many: the gods and our people both loved him. But there are no priests now, and no king, and the gods speak to no-one."

"There are no priests?" she asked

"None survived."

Rakariel frowned. "How many people in the city?"

"About twelvescore?" He wasn't sure what she was getting at. There had never been any priests, not even in his grandfather's lifetime.

"And there would have been more. Yet there were no priests among them?"

"I don't know. I guess not. People always say that none of them survived. That we wouldn't know how to speak to the gods even if they came back."

"Why were there no priests?" She was talking to herself as much as him, but he answered anyway.

"I don't know."

Something killed them deliberately, Rakariel

thought, it must have! Survival against undirected monsters was a matter of sheer chance for anyone untrained in combat; unless these priests had deliberately gone into battle to defend their followers — unlikely given the way that the temple was barricaded, given the lack of any even remotely martial adornments save the statues in their alcoves — then a small number of them should have survived. Which meant that they had died for a reason. It gave them a chance of greater hope, but also implied a greater foe to fear.

"We need to go back," she decided suddenly. Tei looked at her in confusion, and she quickly elaborated. "When we're done here, I want to see those rooms again. If we don't find answers here, we might find something there. We might learn how they died."

Tei remembered the old stain, the violently torn mattress. "Vardra killed them, didn't they?"

"*All* of them?" Rakariel asked, and he could find no answer. What would have killed them other than the vardra? But it was possible...

They had stopped as they spoke, and as Rakariel started forward again she realised that the hall narrowed not far ahead, the walls curving inward as the floor she walked became a gentle upward incline before levelling out once more, creating a smaller platform somewhat above the worshippers' endless rows of cushioning where she expected the priests would have conducted their rituals. In the centre of the space, a pool of water was surrounded by a simple rim of plain, smooth stone, looking almost black in the dimness. Behind it sat an ornate altar holding two triple candelabras, one at either end, and between them a small pedestal held a large, mildewed book, open to perhaps a quarter of the way through. A closed door at the very back presumably offered the priests a way to enter and leave without walking through their congregation. Though it was the book that immediately caught her attention, Rakariel nonetheless stopped at the pool first, looking down into the perfectly still water. It was incredibly clear, but she could see only a long, smooth-sided shaft extending down until her light lost it in darkness — that and, superimposed over the top of it, her own worn reflection, as perfect as though she were looking into a mirror, the lightstone's bright reflection largely hiding her features. Satisfied there was nothing to see there, at least for the moment, she stepped back and walked around to stand behind the altar, looking at the book. Rot and mildew had rendered the open pages unreadable, but it hadn't completely decayed.

"Did you feel that?" Tei hissed nervously, still standing by the pool. Rakariel looked up, instantly alert, and shook her head. She'd felt nothing.

"What was it?" she whispered back.

"I think it was a cold wind." He shivered slightly, afraid and looking to her for reassurance. "There it is again."

"How strong?"

"A breath, maybe... just enough to feel cold."

Rakariel looked around, alert, but could neither see nor feel anything. "There's probably another opening in the temple somewhere," she decided. "Come around here." If it was something more, then she'd prefer to have him by her side, where she could defend him.

Tei did as he was told, hands gripping his elbows. The mysterious wind had chilled him to the bone. He watched, slightly awed and largely nervous, as Rakariel turned a fair-sized chunk of ancient pages at once, rewarded with a billow of dust, paper flakes, and text that was, at least in the middle of the page, largely readable. She traced the words with a finger held just above the page, mouth forming quick, silent shapes as though she spoke them aloud, and he peered past her shoulder in an attempt to read along with her. He'd only ever mastered the basics of reading, and still struggled somewhat with the skill, since he had little immediate use for it. She was faster than him, though he realised to his surprise that both his parents and grandparents were faster and better than she was. Even so, he'd only just managed to make out a couple of paragraphs dedicated to Megthi, goddess of the harvest, before she reached the bottom and began carefully unsticking the next page from its fellows.

Rakariel read intently, focused on her task as she skipped back and forth through the book in an attempt to find something useful. Unwilling to break her concentration with speech, Tei stepped softly away after a little while, turning to look around the hall again. The deep, seemingly bottomless pool was the only nearby feature other than the ornately wrought pillars that lined the walls, and he crossed back to it on silent feet, sitting down on the shallow lip. Just enough light reached it from Rakariel's bent head to allow him to look into its depths, though he couldn't see far at all. Mostly visible was his own reflection staring back at him, its raggedly-cut black hair falling up towards him around its near-white face in a mirror of the way his own fell towards the pool. The chill came again, and he shivered, then steadied. Rakariel was right, it would be a breeze from elsewhere finding its way in, and while it couldn't possibly be safe to be where they were, it would be even less safe to wander off alone. Not only that, but with answers potentially so close, leaving would be, in effect, worse than useless, however cold the temple was. With an inaudible sigh, Tei turned his attention back to the pool — and stopped, staring in disbelief, because the face looking back was no longer his own.

CHAPTER 8

A Stranger's Reflection

Looking back from the pool, a strange face regarded Tei inscrutably, almost as oddly brown as Rakariel's and showing none of the thinness that characterised Tei's features, though it shared his dark hair and eyes, his face's general shape. Stunned, he barely managed to stop himself from falling into the pool in shock, and almost threw himself back from it instead in violent overreaction, landing flat on his back. Rakariel's head snapped up at the sound, and she dashed to him before the echoes had even had time to die away, instinctively drawing the shortsword she kept at her side for close-quarters combat.

"What happened?" she demanded, forgetting to keep her voice down, the whole formerly silent temple reverberating to its echoes.

"A face — there's a face in the water!" Tei stammered. Cautiously, blade held out before her, Rakariel edged over on light feet, ready to jump back at any moment... but when she peered in, she could see nothing but her own reflection, half-obscured by the lightstone's bright glow.

"I don't see it." Her tone wasn't disbelieving, but merely a statement: whatever Tei had seen in the waters, it was gone. Slowly, encouraged by her matter-of-fact response and the fact that she didn't simply dismiss what he'd seen as his imagination, he got back to his feet.

"I was just looking at my reflection and I started to

think about something else. When I looked back at it again, it wasn't my face any more!" He tried to keep his voice as calm as hers, tried and failed, but it only shook a little, and his fear, though audible, remained under control. He'd heard stories, of course, tales of faces in the mists, of lost spirits seeking a home or a victim — and like everyone else he'd felt it the preserve solely of stories told to children and things half-seen by those whose senses were already so tired and overwrought that they could see anything in even the most normal of things. After seeing his own reflection change so, he would doubt them no longer. "Its skin was dark, too, like yours."

Rakariel felt a faint twinge of surprise at that. Although tanned from a lifetime spent on the road, she was naturally only a little darker-skinned than Tei himself — but of course, he'd never seen the sun, or even met people who had. "How dark?"

"Just like you." He paused, trying to keep fear under control and bring the changed reflection back into his mind when most of what he'd registered about it was shock that it wasn't his own. "Um. It had dark eyes, I think. Dark hair." He looked to her for approval, but she was too busy staring into the pool.

"...Come here," she said, after a few moments' thought. "Tell me if you see anything."

Warily, he stepped back to the pool, encouraged somewhat by Rakariel's alert, watchful presence. Still, even with her beside him it took courage to lean over, to angle his head above the water until he could once again see the reflection that should have been his — and see once again that it was not his own. Instinctively, he jumped back, Rakariel looking at him in surprise.

"There it was again — didn't you see it? It wasn't my reflection!"

"I only saw you."

They stared at each other in silence for a moment, Tei disbelieving, Rakariel rapidly thinking through the possibilities.

"Whatever it is," she said, "only you can see it for some reason." The only other choice was that Tei was lying, and she didn't believe that at all. Nor did she think that his imagination had shown it to him, not a face so different to his own and certainly not twice, the second time with another person looking on. That meant, however little she liked the thought, that it had to be true. "Maybe because I'm not from this valley. Stand close to me — as close as you can."

Tei obeyed, edging closer until he was barely millimetres from brushing her arm, so close that he could almost feel the faint heat of her body. Still poised with sword in hand, she withdrew something from a pouch at her belt: some kind of lens on a strap. His eyes followed her movements as she pulled it on one-handed, struggling for a moment to get it in place past the lightstone's circlet, setting the lens over her left eye and running her fingers expertly over a set of relatively inconspicuous little wheels set into its top. Whatever she was doing, he trusted her implicitly, nervously watching what she did.

Rakariel kept her sword up and ready, most of her concentration focused on the view seen from her left eye as she slowly made progress in attuning the lens. It was even more difficult than usual, or so she felt, as though the swirling planes were refusing to be pinned down, but gradually, a second world began to take shape before her. It was the spiritual plane she had chosen this time, cloaking both herself and Tei in shimmering white and her sword in a striking tracery of light grey, the whole temple delineated in very faint shades of off-white as it resonated still with the last echoes of the power that had once inhabited it, the pool itself startlingly bright. To her newly enhanced vision, the apparition Tei had seen in the water was clear, if not quite where he had seen it, and she took a pace back, sweeping Tei with her with her elbow as her hand remained on the lens, sword pointed directly at the figure.

"I see you, spirit," she warned, noticing without heeding the way that Tei looked at her in surprise and some awe as she spoke to empty air. The spirit 'sat' cross-legged on the flawless surface of the pool, its appearance that of a young man between her and Tei in age and wearing clothes that matched neither one in style, delineated in a dull and faded shade that would once have been the same vibrant, shimmering white that cloaked Tei. It — he — looked at her in shock and flew to his feet, lifting several inches off the surface of the water in the process without seeming to notice, and all without disturbing its serene surface even the slightest fraction. After a moment, his mouth moved as if in speech, but she heard nothing.

"Don't come any closer," she said. There was a pause before she spoke again, warily. "What do you want?" From its admittedly few actions so far, there was a chance that this particular spirit might still be at least partially sane. It was a fine line that the dead walked, from what little she knew and the few others that she had encountered. Those left trapped in the world, unwilling or unable to take the path laid out by their chosen beliefs, often succumbed to madness over time. Sane or not, though, the spirit might know something useful, if it could only be convinced to reveal it.

The spirit slowly lifted his open hands as if to demonstrate that he held no weapons, a gesture that would have held rather more meaning in life. He tried soundlessly to speak again, and looked frustrated as it became evident that she couldn't hear his words. He pointed to Tei, then the pool, then himself, looking frustrated again at her continued incomprehension.

"I wish to restore light to this land, spirit," she said slowly. "Do you understand that?"

The spirit gave a vigorous nod, its whole expression lighting up as any living man's might have on hearing and believing such news. He 'stepped' forward, still slightly above the pool, looked at her sword, and hastily retreated once more.

"You lived here once," Rakariel said, her statement met by another nod. "Was it before the darkness fell?"

Again, the spirit nodded. He hesitated a moment before lifting his hands above his head, as far apart as they would go, and slowly moving them closer until they touched. Rakariel watched, uncertain as to what he was doing and letting it show in a somewhat questioning look. The spirit repeated the motion, looking up at his hands, then dropped them to turn and step to one side, miming reaching a wall, feeling it for a moment before giving up and bowing his head. Facing her again, now drifting above the stone floor rather than the pool, he looked at her hopefully. Rakariel thought quickly.

"...There's a barrier?" she asked, and he nodded sharply. "You can't get out. Something above you closed, and you can't get out?"

A particularly vigorous nod followed that question, the spirit seeming pleased to have got his message across. Tei touched her arm lightly, and she glanced at him just in time to hear him whisper.

"The valley closed..."

"The-" she started, only to see the spirit already nodding in confirmation. "...You were alive then?" she asked instead.

He shook his head, then nodded.

"What do you mean, no and yes?"

Her only answer was an exasperated shrug. Then, after a few moments, he tried something else, holding his right hand out on its side, fingertips pointed towards her. With his free hand, he pointed to it, made a quick version of the 'closing' gesture he had used before, then put it back in its place. Beside it, so close that they almost touched, he put his other hand in the same position. Rakariel frowned.

"Close to then — to when the valley closed. You were alive close to then?"

Another nod greeted her question.

"How close?"

The spirit held up thumb and forefinger, almost touching one another so that she could barely see through them.

"Almost exactly then... before or after? I mean," she continued, realising that he wouldn't be able to easily answer that, "were you alive before it?" A yes or no question would be much easier to answer silently.

He nodded once more, rested his head on his hands as if in sleep, then repeated the 'closing' gesture.

"You died just before it?" A new tone had entered her voice, a kind of wary hope. If it wasn't insane, if it could be trusted, the spirit might hold some clue to the fate of the valley, far better than anything she was likely to find by searching books! His nod confirmed it, and she paused again, trying to work out how she could possibly phrase the questions she wanted, needed to ask.

"Do you know what caused it?" she tried.

He shook his head.

"Any ideas?"

A shrug. Nothing.

"That's helpful."

The spirit had the decency to look slightly chagrined at that, mouthing something she guessed was an apology.

"Will you help us?" she tried. This time, the response was another enthusiastic nod, and she slowly lowered her blade, keeping it clear that she could be back in fighting stance within a heartbeat if provoked. The spirit, however, showed no inclination to so much as drift slightly closer.

"What's happening?" Tei whispered. Unable to see the spirit, he could only be aware of Rakariel's side of their 'conversation', such as it was.

"The spirit you saw is real," she murmured. "He seems to want to help us. I don't know how much he knows, but he was there when the valley was sealed. I can't hear him speak, so it's hard to work out what he's trying to tell me."

"Why... why was he in my reflection?"

Rakariel shrugged at that, looking to the spirit to provide an answer. At once he walked — if still slightly above the ground — back to the pool and knelt more or less on its edge, one intangible hand reaching down into the water. It seemed to brighten fractionally in the spirit realm as he touched it.

"He's reaching into the pool," she told Tei, then turned her words back to the spirit. "Is there something down there?"

The spirit shook his head in response, beckoning them with his free hand.

"No, she said, answering her own question for Tei's benefit. "He wants us to go to it."

Slowly, very warily, she advanced towards the pool, Tei still staying close by her side, glancing from the still water to her eyes and back to try and guess where she was looking, hard though it was past her raised hand and the lens over her left eye. Not being able to see whatever she was focused on made him even more nervous than he would already have been.

Rakariel peered into the pool, once again seeing nothing more than her own reflection, then looked sharply up again at the spirit, still knelt on its far side. "What do you want?"

The spirit pointed to Tei, beckoned him, touched the pool with an exaggerated motion.

"You want Tei to put his hand in the pool?"

The spirit glanced up at Tei, who shrank behind her slightly at her words, and nodded, looking concerned.

"That's what he wants," she confirmed. Suspicion was plain in her expression, in her voice. Though the spirit didn't look as though he meant any harm, he could be deceiving them for his own ends: she had no way of knowing what the spiritually strong pool might do, and even if it were only water it was very, very deep. Sanity alone didn't make a person harmless, alive or dead.

"If you mean him any harm, I'll destroy you," she warned, voice hard. "You can see my sword can do that."

The spirit flinched slightly, giving her a nervous look, but didn't otherwise move, expression nervous, but hopeful, and faintly pleading. Unable to see it and not quite willing to look in the pool, Tei looked up at Rakariel instead, searching for guidance. Looking back after a few moments, one eye seeing the skinny boy in his drab, ragged clothes, the other seeing him lit in the shimmering white of his spirit, she found herself forced to speak again.

"I can't be certain what will happen," she began, taking what refuge she could in honesty from that look that asked her to tell him everything would be all right. She couldn't do that. All she could give him was the truth. "This spirit could know what happened, but we don't have the time to even try and be certain that he won't hurt us." From the corner of her left eye, she saw the spirit shake his head vehemently, denying it, and ignored him. "He seems to want to help, but it could still be a trick. On the other hand, he's weak — I can fight him if I have to. If you try it, I'll keep hold of you." Her voice turned slightly threatening again. "And at the first sign of anything going wrong..."

Tei nodded, glancing nervously from her to the far side of the pool where it seemed that the unseen ghost waited. In the end, his gaze turned back to Rakariel.

Did he trust her? He found that the answer was yes almost before he'd even realised he was asking the question, and all the more so for her honesty. What he'd said before was still true. To help her, he was going to have to take risks, even ones he'd never before envisaged.

"All right," he said, softly. Rakariel lowered her left hand from her face and gripped his right wrist firmly as he knelt on the pool's rim, his hand closing on her own, reassured by the strong and solid feel of her grip. She wasn't going to let anything go wrong. Taking a deep breath, he looked into the pool, seeing once more the strange reflection that was not his own. This time, he found he could study it more carefully, take it in more clearly. The dark-haired, dark-eyed man looked back, somewhat older than Tei himself. Was it, he wondered, the same as the ghost she saw — in the pool's strange reflections, was he seeing what she had? Slowly, hesitantly, he reached his free hand towards the pool, hesitating just before the surface. The reflection moved exactly as he did, just as his own should have. If he touched the water, he would touch it, whatever it was. Taking a deep breath and resisting the urge to glance back at Rakariel, his right hand unconsciously tightening on her wrist, Tei dipped his left into the water, ripples finally disturbing the still surface. At once his mind became a jumble of feelings and confused impressions, and he froze, unable to pull away.

He was there for long minutes, the plane of spirit beginning to drift slowly out of focus with the lens unattended, touches of others beginning to creep into Rakariel's vision as distracting swirls of colour and movement. She was about to pull him back, for all that he and the spirit both seemed motionless, each with one hand in the spiritually charged pool, when he suddenly gasped and spoke.

"He says — he says his name is Avin." Rakariel listened as he went on, words broken and distant, struggling through confusion. "He died here before the city fell. Before the vardra came. He's tried to watch over us. But he can't go far alone. He says he wants to help us. Anything that's in his power." A pause, in which his eyes widened, and Rakariel watched like a hawk despite the prismatic splitting of her vision for anything that might be wrong. "He says we're family. Me and him. That's why I could see him in the pool." Another pause. "He didn't know the first mayor was called Avin, too. All my family have been mayors since the city fell. He says that must have been his son. He never knew him." Tei's voice was sad, and Rakariel could see a stronger version of the same sorrow in the spirit's expression. "...He says you should ask him questions while you can."

"All right," Rakariel said, quietly. "What happened when the city fell?"

Tei was silent for a few moments, then began to speak, slow and distant as if repeating something he was hearing, or perhaps seeing — or both. "He says it started slowly. It was after he died, but not long. People began to come to the priests, asking why things seemed wrong. He says he was trapped here, then. He didn't know how to leave until much later."

"He died here? In the temple?"

"Yes. He says..." Tei shook his head, searching for words he couldn't find. "He just wanted his family to be safe. He doesn't want to — the king? King Sariven? But I thought-" A pause, ending in a sigh. "He doesn't want to talk about it. It's over and done with. Everyone from those days is dead."

"What happened to the king?" Rakariel pressed.

"Nothing. I mean..." There was another long pause. "He says he had to give his life for the king to gain another blessing. In return he was promised his family would be protected. He says he supposes that doesn't mean very much now. He, ah..."

"He had to give his life?" she cut in. "Why?"

"That's what the price was, he says. He says it had to be him because everyone else was... was almost in love with the king? That's not right, but... Anyway, he says that was the price."

"Hm. Is that why he hasn't passed on?"

"He says he doesn't know. He died, but he was still here. He doesn't know why. He says at first he could talk to one of the priestesses, but not properly. Then she left. He doesn't know what happened to her, and he says after that all he could do was watch. Eventually the monsters, the vardra, came here. Some of the priests had left by then. He says he doesn't know what happened or where they went, but the others kept talking about it, they didn't know either. Some of them went with the guard and most of them just vanished. By then they'd stopped being able to talk with the gods. He says they almost seemed afraid to try. They talked about how the top of the valley was closing in. Some of them said they were going to run away, but he doesn't know if they managed to. Then, he says, the monsters he'd started hearing about, the vardra, attacked the temple for the first time. Some of the priests who were left barricaded themselves in, but the vardra got in from somewhere anyway. They were all killed, he thinks. He says he didn't want to watch." Tei swallowed. Avin's ghost remembered the temple echoing with screams. "But he was trapped here. He says he's tried to leave, but he gets too weak. He has to come back before he goes too far. Even here, he..." Tei's voice trailed off, and then suddenly rang out in a shocked exclamation that, though relatively quiet, still set the hall resonating once again with its echoes. "What do you mean, you can get strength from me? -Yes, but-" He fell silent again, glaring at whatever he saw in the water, and Rakariel could only keep hold of him and watch, alert to any change, but there was none.

A short while passed, in which Tei's expression slowly, unwillingly relaxed. Eventually he sighed and went on, voice back to its customary near-whisper. "He says he can take strength from me. When I thought I felt a breeze, that's what he was doing. He says it wasn't much, only enough for him to appear in the pool — he's been too weak even to do that. That's why he can't leave the temple any more. He says he tried recently, and it nearly killed him." Tei blinked, aware of how strange that sounded, and tried to think of a way to phrase in words what he was being told in unspoken thought. "He says if he dies here, if he runs out of strength completely, he thinks he'll be dead forever. His spirit will die too."

"I know," Rakariel said quietly. "Even spirits can die a second death, if they cannot move on to the next world. Whatever's keeping him here, it won't let him go yet, and he won't be safe until it does." Mortal death was terror enough, but at least something would live on: the spiritual death was final and irreversible. Nothing of Avin would survive.

Without looking up from the pool, Avin's spirit gave a slow nod. Rakariel winced as the motion set a wave of swirling colour rippling through her vision, intensifying the growing headache that came from using the lens misaligned. Slowly, very slowly, she loosened her hold on Tei's wrist, finally letting go completely. Neither he nor the spirit made any move as she lifted her hand to her face, adjusting the lens slowly back towards focus on the plane of spirit, and that alone. The dancing ribbons of colour slowly thinned out and faded as she found that focus, and she breathed a silent sigh of relief.

"He says he wants to help us," Tei continued slowly, before she'd quite finished. "But the only person he can talk to away from the pool is me, and he doesn't know how well he can do that. He wants to come with us, but..." He trailed off, but Rakariel knew what the rest had to be in any case. The only way a spirit so weak could accompany them would be by staying close to, and drawing strength from, his youthful descendant. "He says... but we can't," Tei said, cutting himself off to respond to Avin aloud. "We can't come back here, we don't have the time." He fell silent again, staring into the pool, and finally, slowly, nodded.

"No!" Rakariel snapped, knowing instinctively what he was up to, what he had to be agreeing to. "I won't allow it!"

"You need my help. You need *our* help." Tei's voice had become a lot less distant. "Avin knows things about how the city used to be — I can almost see it! He was there when it fell, he knows what happened. We might need his help again and we don't have time to come back here, not if we have to cross the city every time, you said so yourself! He won't hurt me, he'd rather die first. All he wants is to help us, to protect us."

"If he wanted to protect you, he wouldn't have suggested taking your strength so easily," Rakariel said sharply.

"He didn't," came Tei's response, unexpected enough to shock. "I did."

"*What?*"

He pulled his hand back from the pool, droplets falling back towards its surface to cause ripples upon ripples. Avin's spirit watched them in ghostly silence as Tei stood up and stepped back from the pool, turning to face Rakariel with fear and determination mingled in his expression.

"I'm scared. Everything he knows says he won't hurt me, but I still don't like it. But... I have to do it anyway. It's like you said about helping us. I have to help you, any way I can. I didn't even feel it when he did whatever he did before, I thought it was just a cold wind. I'll be fine, and we need him."

"Some spirits feed off the living, Tei," she warned. "They go mad, or just get to like it. Either way, they're deadly."

"Yes, but — he won't. I don't think."

"I can't let you take that risk!"

"Would you do it?"

She stopped, moments away from speaking, unable to respond for an instant.

"If he could help you?" Tei pressed. "If you felt his mind like I just did — that's what the pool lets you do, that's why it's here. Would you do it, if you knew he could help you?"

The silence stretched out for a second that felt like forever. Then Rakariel moved, sheathing her sword and angrily unfastening the leather bracer on her left arm. Even as she knelt, she yanked up her sleeve, leaning forward to plunge her arm up to the elbow in the cold, still water. Across the pool, Avin's eyes widened in surprise — and so did hers.

At first it was a feeling beyond confusion: a jumble of images, senses, even feelings flooded through her mind, overwhelming her to the extent that she could neither move nor pull away, nor even think clearly. Slowly, though, the contact steadied, and she found herself beginning to understand the mind of what had once been a young man named Avin. He cared deeply for his lost family even now, had little sense of how much time had passed beyond that it had been long indeed. He feared for her and Tei, but Tei especially, his young descendant dear to him despite the fact that he had never known him. He would do anything rather than endanger them, but how could he help from the confines of the temple? He approved of her, she realised, and found to her shock that just as she had been assessing him, so he, too, had been taking her measure: that each could see what lay at the surface of the other's mind.

'Stop it!' she thought intensely, concentrating as hard as she could on that thought and that alone. Startled and rebuffed, Avin's contact jerked away in a fashion that she could feel, but not describe, suddenly growing more distant. Relieved, she nonetheless remained mentally watchful. Her mind was no place she was willing to allow others into, her thoughts hers

alone to keep: she could no longer tolerate that kind of intrusion, however well-meant.

Despite the new distance between them, she could vaguely sense an apologetic feeling radiating from Avin's spirit, and she relented enough to direct a further thought at him, as plain and untainted by the rest of her mind as she could make it.

'Better.'

It was as much a feeling as a word, but it seemed to serve its purpose. After a moment, she focused on another.

'Tei.'

Unlike her, Avin deliberately let his guard down, allowing the feelings that the thought evoked to brush her mind without asking anything in return. There was surprise there, and pride in this unexpected young relative with his deep courage; sorrow for what had become of them combined with joy that they had lived at all; wonder and amazement that his once-poor family had become what they had. He cared for them, however distant, though he had never known them save as glimpses from Tei's mind: for Fayel; for their ever-active parents who travelled the city as the mayor's representatives; for their sometimes stern, experienced grandfather. No, he would never let any harm befall Tei if he could possibly help it, wanted him to live a long, long life and die the peaceful death that age would eventually bring. But he wanted so much for him to live in the sun, in the world he had known; for Tei to know some other life than that of shadow and fear, of mushrooms and rats and half-blind fish and the monsters that stalked in the dark. He wanted him to know the city as it had been, full of life and largely at peace, despite the odd feeling he had occasionally felt in the air towards the end. No, he wouldn't harm Tei even at the cost of his life, but there had to be some way that he could help them, some way for him to do something more than tell his brief tale before they left! There had to be more that he could do...

Rakariel snatched her arm back, almost blue from the chill water. Even though the contact between them had been almost one-way save for the very beginning, she didn't like it. Her mind was, had to be her own, and it held far, far too much that she did not want anyone else to know. She didn't want to know what was in Avin's, either, didn't want to feel what he did. She didn't want to have to know that Tei's words had been true, to have to agree to risk his life even more than she already had. It would be so much simpler not to trust the spirit, to be suspicious of him as she'd learned to be of so much, to walk away and find another way and keep Tei as safe as she could. It would be simpler still if she could just rely on herself alone, as she had in the years since she had left the last of her mercenary companions behind, with no-one to care about — no-one to lose. No-one more for whom she would have to know, as she always knew, that if she had done something different then they might still be alive.

She gave a shaky sigh, shook her head and unstrapped the lens impatiently with cold-stiffened fingers as the sharp movement made the whole world swirl and spark around her. Tei watched, looking worried.

"Fine," she snapped. "I trust him. I don't have a choice. But be careful." She whirled away, jamming the lens back into its pouch and crossing back to the altar with sharp, choppy movements, pulling her sleeve back down as she did. Both Tei and Avin's unseen spirit watched in silence as she stood before it, buckling her bracer back on before turning a few more pages of the ancient book and eventually leaving it open at the same unreadable location as she had found it.

"And he'd better be able to tell us of his gods. Now, is there anything else here we can use?"

Tei began to turn back towards the pool, only to stop in surprise before he'd even completed the movement. He frowned in concentration, then spoke, almost to himself, in a soft murmur.

"I can hear him. Like a very faint whisper. But it's so cold." He shook his head, voice returning to whispered clarity. "He can tell you what he knows. He wasn't a priest, though. As... as for the rest of the temple, everyone here either died or left before the monsters came. Their spirits are gone."

"Where'd they go?" she asked. "The ones who left."

There was a pause as Tei listened, head cocked, to a voice that only he could hear.

"He doesn't really know. Some of them were asked to go to the palace by the King's Guard. They mostly didn't come back. Some just stopped appearing, he never knew what happened to them. The King's Guard came before the last attack and tried to get everyone to go with them, but a lot of them refused."

"How did the others react to the ones who disappeared?"

"They were all scared," Tei replied. "He doesn't think they knew where they'd gone. The gods were leaving them by then, though. They talked around it, never actually about it, but he says it was all they could think of."

"What of the king?"

"He didn't come to the temple again. He had his own shrine in the palace anyway. He only came here for show." There was a slight pause, and Tei went on, this time addressing someone other than Rakariel. "You... didn't like him much, did you?"

"What's he saying?" Rakariel demanded as Tei listened silently to whatever it was that only he could hear.

"Sorry. Uh, he says he supposes he was a good enough king. But he didn't really like him. I always thought everyone loved him..." Tei trailed off again, frowning at some unheard response.

"What? What is it?"

"They did," he said, clearly quoting Avin's words of moments before directly. "That was the problem."

Rakariel frowned. "What do you mean?" she asked, slowly. Some rulers were good, many indifferent, a few bad. How could a king be too loved by his people?

"Uh." Tei hesitated, listening, trying to understand what he heard before he relayed it. "He says they loved him too much. That it didn't feel right. He didn't really care one way or the other, but everyone else thought the king was incredible. He didn't do anything bad... but he says he didn't do anything amazing, either. He just... was there. And yet everyone loved him for it." Another pause. "He says it doesn't matter now. King Sariven told him that the kingdom needed a strong king, someone who could stand for it no matter what happened. He... says maybe he should have been more willing to help. But in the end, it wasn't enough anyway." This time, he turned, looking at the empty air where the spirit had to be. "But we're still here. We survived. It... it's not so bad." He struggled for words, found none. He couldn't find a way to say what he wanted to. His life was dark and full of danger, yes, but that was the way it had always been, and it had its bright points, the comforts of home and family. The thought of another life was dreamlike, unreal, even told in Rakariel's soft words or Avin's faded yet bright memories. How could things be other than they always had been? He had never known the loss of all that made Avin so sad.

'Not so bad?' He heard the spirit's voice as though on the edge of hearing, sorrowful and more than a touch bitter. The memories that to Tei were distant dreams had once been real, and he knew why he felt so, yet he couldn't really feel it himself. It was too far away: he had never known anything of that long-vanished world.

"You did survive," Rakariel said, her voice soft, guessing the nature of what Avin had said from Tei's tone, for all that she was unable to hear his words. "His people did survive. There's no point now in thinking about how much that has cost: thoughts like that will get us nowhere. We have to keep moving on if we're to have a chance of returning the light to this valley, and to your people." Thinking of light, she half-turned to glance at the high, circular window set into the wall behind her. The lightstone's illumination made it seem still dimmer than it would already have been, but she wasn't sure that night's blackness hadn't started to fall over the valley once again. At the very least, she felt that it was getting later, whether the limited light was quite beginning to fade or not.

"For now, that means finding somewhere safe to rest. After that... I think we should go to the palace." She went on after a moment, explaining herself before Tei, or Avin through him, could protest. "We know that some of the priests went there, or were taken there. We know that King Sariven fought to the last, and probably made his last stand either there or somewhere nearby. We still don't know where the curse came from or why, but that seems like the next place where there are most likely to be clues. Also, if it is where the monsters dwell, then I may be able to find out how they came here, and perhaps even stop them." She paused, fixed Tei with a hard stare that almost pinned him to the spot. "When I do that, you are *not* coming with me."

Tei said nothing. The mere thought of walking, not just into danger, but into the vardra's very lair, terrified him more than almost anything else. Yet, with Rakariel alongside, if it turned out that he would be able to help, then he was all too afraid that he might find that he had to go. Against her quiet courage and determination, the relief he felt at her words seemed almost as much shameful as sensible.

"Come on," Rakariel said after a moment. "We should find somewhere safe."

He nodded. They could get out the way they had come, and that would do just as well as any other route. Rakariel quickly caught up to him as he set off towards the steps they had come down from the floor above, walking directly down the centre of the hall. It was time to seek shelter, and to leave the temple behind them.

CHAPTER 9
Hunted

As Tei veered off towards the stairs, Rakariel kept to her straight path down the centre of the hall, bringing him back after her, though he wasn't sure where she was going. Only when she stopped before the front doors did he realise. They had been hastily barred and barricaded, one long beam placed through brackets that might actually have been intentionally placed when the door was made, miscellaneous furniture piled up against both doors in clear desperation. Though that barricade had clearly worked, it hadn't saved its makers.

Rakariel pulled a table away from the doors, as carefully and quietly as possible. Within a relatively short time, she had the left-hand one clear, save for the bar that held it — and that, with some effort, she managed to lift up on her shoulder, pushing it far enough through the other bracket that it would no longer hold the door closed. Finally, she threw the rusted bolts that had been sunk into the floor, and gave the door a shove. Long-unused hinges creaked and groaned in protest as it opened just far enough to let her out, and she slipped through, pulling a fold of cloth over the lightstone as she did, darting along the path to the dubious shelter of the archway into the grounds with Tei right beside her. They stayed there, sheltering against its sides, for a short while, but no shapes emerged from the gathering dusk, no hunting cries sounded in the distance. Slowly, Tei looked out across the street. Rakariel followed his lead as he shot across the wide road and vanished into a house through a broken window. She didn't have time to do more than glance about the wrecked rooms as Tei quickly wove through the building, slipping out of the back into a small garden, through a broken fence and straight into another house, getting as far away as he could while coming into the open as little as possible.

They were several streets away before he slowed, began looking around for somewhere they could rest along the fog-shrouded roads as the light continued to fade. Pausing to think for a moment, he crouched in a doorway, Rakariel beside him — and heard a horrific sound that chilled his blood to ice. Indubitably made by the vardra, it was a long, drawn-out sound that went on and on, enough to freeze anything that heard it with terror, and taken up by other inhuman voices from all directions. Tei had heard that sound less than a handful of times in his life, and he knew that if they were found, it would mean terrible, bloody revenge. Almost panicked, he made a mad dash to the best hiding place within his restricted vision, a narrow-windowed building with a barred door, fumbling with the shutters in desperate haste and diving through the glassless window without thought or care for what might lie beyond. It was only luck that ensured there was nothing in his way beyond the floor, which he hit, rolled, and came back to his feet, looking around. Rakariel followed more cautiously, quickly closing the shutters behind her and tucking the fold of cloth back behind the lightstone to let its light fill the room. Tei looked back at her, afraid.

"What does it mean?" she asked, quietly. That had

been nothing like the hunting call she had heard before.

"They- they know what we did," he stammered, voice shaking. "They won't rest until they find who it was."

"So they've found the bodies of the two we killed." She sighed, settling cross-legged on the floor. "There's little we could do to prevent that. We couldn't have hidden them." She ran a hand over her hair, a few loose strands winding through her fingers. "If they don't find us, will they forget?" She hoped so. Monsters such as those could have any level of intelligence: perhaps they were mere dumb beasts, slave to the nature their dark creator had given them; perhaps they reasoned and thought and took sadistic joy in the chase. The latter she hated with a passion far beyond her calm disgust at the former. Though the end result was often the same, at least a creature with no more brain than a cow had no choice to act other than as its instincts demanded.

"I doubt it," Tei said dubiously. Though vardra rarely watched the same place for long under normal circumstances, moving on unless they sensed a weakness in a known hiding place — in which case they would attack it with brutal ferocity, and woe betide anyone who was there when they found a way in — on the very few occasions when someone had managed to kill one of them, the implacable pursuits had been known to last for weeks, and almost always ended in at least one death. "I — I should check — this place is safe."

Rakariel nodded, rising slowly. "I'll go with you." Tei would be unable to see well without her light, and she could not give it to him. There was no way she could wait in complete darkness while danger lurked outside, potentially capable of finding its way in while she was defenceless. The mere thought was enough to bring the shadows of old terror back to claw at the edges of her mind.

Unaware of her fears, Tei simply nodded quickly. He was as glad to hear the offer as she was to see him accept it. With the vardra enraged and hunting outside, the last thing he wanted was to be alone.

Together, the two of them searched the building, the city's silence irregularly punctuated by the awful, eerie howls of the vardra. Like many others, it had once been a house, and probably quite a comfortable one to live in. Long years of abandonment had left it cold, damp, and musty, but the shutters were intact and most of the windows boarded from the inside, and Tei suspected it had served as a safehouse before, as a great many buildings in the city had through the generations. Everyone knew that danger could strike at any time, and the nearest bolt-hole had to be already reinforced if it were to offer much hope of keeping a hunting vardra out for long. The topmost floor had a trapdoor in its ceiling that led into the unknown loft space above, but though Tei eyed it dubiously, it was firmly bolted shut and had several additional planks nailed across it. For all that they sported an intricate relief pattern and had probably once been part of some piece of furniture, they looked relatively sturdy. As far as he could tell, the building was about as secure as it was easily possible for it to be.

"All right," he whispered eventually, glancing at the trapdoor one last time. "I think it's safe."

The howling continued as they made their way

quietly back down the aged staircase and into the room from which they had entered, seeming to come from all directions, as though the vardra in every quarter of the city had taken up the call. It was impossible to tell how many were now hunting in the dark of the night, the sounds shifting and changing from moment to moment as one fell silent and others began, echoes rippling back and forth through the deadening fog. Tense, but unable to run or hide any better than they already had, Tei paced nervously, his feet noiseless on the stone-flagged floor. Rakariel perched on the edge of a still-intact chair, trying to remain outwardly calm as her inner tension ratcheted higher and higher. If the vardra's vengeance call was meant to spook their quarry, it was succeeding all too well.

All at once, the vardra fell silent, not a single noise breaking the sudden stillness. Tei froze halfway through a step, one foot still in the air; Rakariel shot to her feet with one hand automatically reaching for her bow. Something had happened, but what? What were the creatures doing? The sudden absence of sound was almost more eerie than the howls that had come before, and neither she nor Tei broke the silence as they strained their senses to the limit. Had they been found, somehow? What did that silence mean? Was something coming for them even now? Each faint and muted drip from the outside now held an echo of threat, a sound that had to be tested for danger, every half-heard breath begrudged for how it might hide something else beneath it.

Tei jumped suddenly, startled, eyes wide and hands sharply held to his mouth in an instinctive guard against making any sound. Rakariel saw his motion from the corner of her eye and whirled to face him, though she herself had heard nothing. Settling slowly, he nodded to something unseen and unheard before shivering convulsively as if gripped by frost. Rakariel crossed the distance between them in three quick, light steps, her whisper barely a sound at all, one that could have gone unheard if they hadn't both been so tense.

"What happened? Are you all right?"

Tei nodded, the motion still slightly shaky. "Avin went to watch them for us. He needed my strength." Another violent shudder ran through his thin frame. "It's so cold." Seeing the worry on her face, he tried belatedly to reassure her. "It's only cold. I'll be all right."

A little awkwardly, Rakariel put a hand on his shoulder, watching his reactions, though he did no more than glance at her. Even through his clothing, how cold he felt shocked her, though she tried not to show it, and she gently pushed him down into a sitting position. He obeyed readily enough, still trembling for all that he seemed to be trying not to, and she sat beside him, tentatively putting an arm around his shoulders in an effort to help warm him up. Though she could see his surprise, he seemed to realise what she was doing, and made no objection, nor attempt to pull away. Still keeping a watchful eye on the window and listening hard to the empty silence of the city, she held him close, warming him in the only way that she could. For all its radiance, the lightstone was as chill as any unenchanted rock, and fire was denied them even if they had had its makings. Tei leaned against her, unresisting despite the tension they both felt, and she waited as he slowly began to feel warmer once more.

Tei's shivers had only just died away when they both heard a muted thud from above, looking up and springing to their feet in almost the same motion, turning to face the door to the hallway, with its staircase and, two floors above, the trapdoor to the attic. The way they had been sitting left Tei slightly in front of Rakariel, and she gripped his shoulders to push him behind her before quickly readying her bow and edging cautiously out into the hall, aiming up the stairs, though she could see nothing there — yet. Her range was terribly limited in the confines of the house, but she knew from the vardra's build that they would be far too strong for her, that if she attempted to fight one with her sword she would be all too likely to die despite the enchantments it held. Her lightweight armour, even enhanced as it was, simply would not be able to confer enough protection, and the strength of her arm would not be enough to prevent her from being forced back in a clash of blades even if she could otherwise block every strike.

With nothing immediately in sight, she crept slowly up the staircase, keeping to the wall where the old floorboards would be marginally less likely to creak beneath her weight, pausing momentarily on every step to listen. Nothing leapt from the shadows to attack her, and, keeping an eye on the next set of stairs, she moved slowly on to check each of the first-floor rooms in turn, alert and watchful. As she turned to leave the first, she saw a shape in the doorway, automatically bringing her bow to bear in an instant and only just able to prevent herself from loosing the arrow as she recognised Tei, looking at her wide-eyed.

"What are you doing?" she hissed, annoyed at both

him and herself, frightened by what she could so easily have done. She hadn't heard him follow her up the steps, had had no idea he was behind her — she could have killed him! Tei slipped into the room, chastened and afraid, but still clearly more frightened of what lurked outside.

"I — I'm sorry. I just — if there's something — at least here I can see it. And — if they get past you, they'll find me anyway."

Rakariel paused before nodding. He was probably right: directly behind her was the safest place for him to be. She of all people could hardly fault him for being unable to wait in the dark while unknown dangers stalked outside and potentially within, when it was something that she could barely even bring herself to contemplate.

"Stay close behind me," was all she said, moving on again as silently as she could in the old, decaying building. Tei followed, obediently sticking close, immeasurably relieved to be in the dubious shelter her protection offered. She checked each room on the first floor before moving quietly and very cautiously up to the second, noting with relief that the trapdoor was still in place and apparently undamaged. Despite that, she went through all of the rooms, checking the windows, looking for any sign that anything, anywhere, had been forced open to allow danger in. Behind her, Tei looked about every bit as warily, his movements even quieter than hers, until both were finally satisfied that nothing had entered. They were alone in the building, and whatever had made that sound, it had come from somewhere outside.

"There's nothing here," Rakariel murmured softly

as she made her way back to the room they had originally entered by. "We're safe." Another sound from above caught her attention, and she paused mid-step, looking up sharply before forcing herself to ignore it. The vardra were on the roof, and that was all: their forcing an entry would have been louder, splintering and crashing. Whether or not they had some idea that the prey they hunted might be hiding almost directly beneath them, such suspicions clearly weren't enough to prompt an attempt to break in. Even so, she stayed still and silent, unavoidably tense, for a short time — until a startled twitch from Tei caused her to jump slightly, reflexively lifting the arrow she still held even as he spoke.

"Avin?" he whispered, and she slowly relaxed again.

"What's he saying?"

Tei listened to the spirit's silent voice for a few moments before telling her. "They're everywhere. They're on the roofs all over. He says it's as though they're searching for something." Try though he might to keep his voice from shaking, and quiet though it might have been, Rakariel could still hear a slight tremor in it. "They're looking for us."

"They won't find us," she whispered back, sounding more confident than she felt. "This building is well-sealed. Just... come here."

He edged towards her obediently, standing beside her once again as she finally returned bow and arrow to their place on her back.

"I'm going to cover the lightstone," she warned softly. "That way, they won't be able to see anything even if there's a crack in the shutters." Her left hand gripped his shoulder, a move intended as a gesture of reassurance, but tightening unbidden at the thought of what she was about to do. The last thing she wanted was to hide her light, knowing that she was not only in darkness but surrounded by foes. Though it would remain at her fingertips, ready to blaze forth once more the moment she revealed it, the thought of plunging herself into darkness again was not one she welcomed, however necessarily. "We'll stay still and silent until they're gone."

Tei nodded mutely. For all that he didn't want to lose the light, he knew the sense in her words. If that many vardra were to find them, surely not even Rakariel would be able to hold her own against the weight of numbers, and he... with her gone, and nothing that he could do to defend himself alone, he would die almost immediately afterwards. He watched as Rakariel lifted her free hand to her forehead, tugging out several folds of the strip of cloth that covered her forehead and pulling them down over the stone. Pitch blackness fell across them, not even the slightest trace of light escaping through the thickly folded material. Despite herself, Rakariel's hand tightened still further, and Tei reflexively edged closer, seeking the reassurance of contact. To his surprise, the experienced, unbelievably brave traveller seemed to welcome it almost as much as he himself as they waited together in the dark.

Neither Rakariel nor Tei could have said how long they waited in blackness, each afraid and trying not to let it show. Occasionally a sound would filter down from the roof, making Rakariel tense as if to reach for her lightstone, Tei flinch and wish that he could flee. As time wore on, they both gradually began to relax fractionally, accepting that the danger outside was passing them by, that the sounds were only that and the old house truly was a place of safety. Eventually, the irregular sounds of passage on the roof above stopped altogether, though neither initially realised it.

A short while later, their unseen guardian returned. Tei stirred with the faintest hiss of breath at some unheard sound, glancing first at Rakariel before belatedly realising what it had been: Avin's voice, or what passed for one.

'They're gone,' he heard the ghost whisper. *'The search has gone outwards, past you. There are still some at the temple, but you should be safe now.'*

"Avin says they're gone," Tei breathed, his voice still no more than a whisper as he relayed the message. "He says it's safe here now."

Rakariel slowly lifted her right hand to remove the cloth that covered her lightstone, her motion smooth and slow to avoid dazzling herself in the sudden light. All was quiet and still, the room just as she had seen it last: old, dusty, and sealed against the outside world. It was only then that she realised with a shock just how tired she was, wondered how long it had been since the previous night, though she hadn't slept much then either. If they truly were safe, she could rest... with luck, dreamlessly. The tension and exhaustion of times such as these often served to drive her dreams away temporarily, though it was only ever that, and she knew that the nightmares among them would be stronger and more frequent for some time afterwards. It was an odd contradiction that only while she walked in shadow was her sleep free of it.

Before either could rest, though, she knew that

there was one more thing they ought to do. She didn't feel much like eating, and knew that Tei would likely want to even less, but she also knew that they both had to keep up their strength regardless of their feelings. Letting the tension rule them would only result in one or both wearing out far earlier than they should have at a time when they most needed to remain strong.

"You should try and eat, if you can," she told him quietly. "You'll need your strength for when we move on."

Tei nodded rather unenthusiastically, seeing the sense in her words for all that he didn't really feel like it. Looking in one of his packs, he retrieved some strips of dried meat, offering some to his companion. Rakariel took them with a quiet murmur of thanks, and watched as Tei began nibbling at the edge of one he'd kept. She set her own on her knee in order to take off her linked packs, thinking for a moment before looking in the uppermost. Near to the top was a cloth-wrapped chunk of heavy wayfarers' bread, good for travel and little else as far as most people were concerned. She took it out and unwrapped it, setting the cloth on the floor with the bread on top. Tei looked on, curious, venturing a question after a few moments.

"What is that?"

"Travellers' bread," she whispered back. "It doesn't taste great, but it keeps well, and it's filling. I always have some with me."

Tei reached out hesitantly, made bolder by her nod, and broke off a small piece from the edge. He sniffed it before trying a cautious bite, and Rakariel watched his expression as he did so see how he would react — which seemed to be with surprise.

"That's really good. I've never had anything like it before."

She smiled. "I have another half a loaf, so have some more if you like." She was already breaking a piece off even as she spoke, estimating the amount she could allow them both with each meal while still leaving enough for the remaining days. Once her light was gone, it would no longer matter whether she had food or not: either she would have won, regaining the sunlight, or died. "There," she said quietly, handing it to him. "That's for you."

Tei took it, watching as she broke another, similar-sized piece for herself before wrapping the remainder up again and putting it back in her pack. He nibbled the edge of his piece again, marvelling at the strange new taste. It was like nothing he'd ever eaten.

Though to Rakariel her food was simply the plain, tough travellers' bread she used to supplement her foraging, its main attraction how well it kept on the trail, she could see what Tei saw in it. If his diet consisted of little more than fungus, fish, and rats...

Shaking her head slightly, she set to eating, making something of a sandwich from her bread and the dried meat Tei had given her. It wasn't the best meal she had ever had, but it was a long way from the worst, and in far better surroundings — and the point was more to eat than to enjoy it in any case. With the food so dry, both had to take fairly frequent sips from their respective waterskins, and she wondered how long it would be before they needed refilling. Water was hardly difficult to find in the fogbound city, but she wasn't sure how much of it she could trust.

It didn't take either one long to finish, no trace left

of their meal but a few breadcrumbs. They sat in silence for a little while afterwards, each thinking their own thoughts, listening to the silence of the city outside. Rakariel was the first to break it, the whisper she was quickly growing used to beginning to sound more like a normal volume than she had expected, so that if she spoke normally she almost felt it would seem like shouting.

"We should try and rest now. It's safe here, and we need to sleep."

Tei nodded, again seeing the sense in her words. She was right, it was safe: they hadn't heard any sounds from above for a while, and Avin had reported the same thing. He stood obediently, moving on silent feet to the pile of musty rags in the corner and giving them an experimental poke with his foot to check that nothing unexpected hid within. All that emerged was a little dust, and he knelt, separating out a couple of the larger pieces to pull over himself as he lay down, curled up on his side. Unrolling her cloak and donning it as she had two nights before, Rakariel settled down almost beside him, her back to the wall. She watched quietly until he lay still, then pulled her hood up and a fold of her bandanna down over her lightstone. Darkness descended over the room once again, one less little thing to risk betraying their presence with, and she bowed her head, letting it rest against her raised knee as her eyes closed.

CHAPTER 10
The Shapes of Answers

Tired as they were, both Rakariel and Tei slept through the eerily silent night. Tei was the first to awaken, his eyes flicking open in time with a sudden, soft breath, remaining motionless at first in the darkness as he remembered where he was, and all of the impossible things that had happened the day before. His eyes fixed on a dim shaft of dawn's first greyish light filtering in through a crack in one of the shutters, lending the faintest of dark tones to the room around it so that, as he focused, he began to make out shapes of black on blackness. It was barely enough to discern even vague shapes, let alone make out precisely what and where things were, but nothing moved. Overlaying what he saw with the memory of the room as it had been the day before, Tei breathed a slow, silent sigh of relief. The night had passed, and they were still alive — alive, and safe.

He sat up slowly, holding onto the rags he'd pulled across himself for warmth as he did, letting them down gently so that they wouldn't make a sound. He'd already seen for himself how easily Rakariel could be woken, how fast she would snap into instant, defensive wakefulness at even the slightest of motions too close to her. As it was, he could just about hear her slow, steady breathing, and guessed she still sat slumped against the wall much as she had been when he'd last seen her. The lightstone would be on her brow, hidden still by the fold of cloth she covered it with, its brilliant light concealed to protect them in the night. Hidden in shadows, they had remained safe.

Resettling himself quietly to get more comfortable, facing out into the room, Tei moved his lips in time to an unspoken thought, wondering if the ghost could hear the sound that was no more than a shaped breath.

"Avin?"

Somewhat to his surprise, he felt a presence at his right shoulder, a chill he was fast coming to recognise touching him for a bare moment as Avin regained a small fraction of his failing strength. He twisted towards the sensation, though he knew he would see nothing.

'They're still at the temple.'

Avin's inaudible voice felt to Tei as though it had whispered from just beside him, and in the darkness, he fancied he could see the strange, brown-skinned face that had looked back at him from the pool in the temple, the reflection that had been so unlike his own. Despite the chill he'd felt, most of his fear of the spirit was gone: their contact through the pool had been far too long for him not to know what he could believe. He knew almost as surely as he knew his own mind that Avin meant neither of them any harm. Thoughts of what Rakariel had said the spirit could be capable of did scare him a little, if he dwelt on them, but the long meeting of their minds had allowed him to trust that Avin would never use such power against him even if he knew how.

'And they're probably still searching,' Avin continued. *'They seemed very intent. I... wouldn't have expected monsters to act like this.'*

"We killed one of them," Tei murmured

soundlessly. "Didn't they do this before — when you saw them come?"

He pictured Avin shaking his head, an unseen motion in the blackness. *'No. But there were less of them then. After the temple was attacked, I didn't — couldn't — see them any more. I've never been able to leave for long.'* He hesitated, something Tei could feel as surely as if he really could see and hear him. *'I'm sorry I wasn't able to help before. If I could, I...'*

"I know," Tei whispered. "But you couldn't leave the temple." He paused for a moment, a thought occurring to him. "Rakariel said you were kept here, didn't she? Was it to help us?"

'I don't think so,' came the silent response. *'I would have chosen that, if I could — but I can't. I don't even know how to move on. If it was why I'm here, it wasn't by my choice. I hope I can help you, I want to, more than anything. But if that is why I'm here, someone else chose it for me before I could. Does that make sense?'*

Tei frowned, thinking it through, and eventually nodded. "I think so." He was quiet for a little, glancing back to the shapeless figure of black on black that hid Rakariel, draped in her heavy cloak. "What was it like, back then? In the city?"

He'd seen some of it in the ghost's mind, caught glimpses and flashes of memory, regret and sorrow for that the things and people that had been lost.. Yet even with those images, it remained a world away, as distant and unreal as Rakariel's tale of a land beyond the valley where the legendary sun still shone. As her tale had sparked in him a longing to see it, to see all those things that could be so precious to one such as her, so Avin's memories had done the same. Now he wanted to learn more, to hear Avin's words of his lost land if the spirit would tell him.

There was a long silence, long enough for Tei to begin to wonder if he shouldn't have asked, before Avin finally, slowly, answered.

'How can I describe it? The city was bright. There were people everywhere, filling the streets. There was always the sound of it, a thousand and more people talking and working and walking, everywhere. Fog only came at times, at night... until the valley closed.' He seemed to sigh. *'You could see it, then. And I can still feel it above me.'*

"What can you feel?" Tei asked, curious. He had never seen the distant valley roof, though he pictured it much like the stone ceilings he had seen in cellars. He certainly wasn't aware of being able to feel it.

'It's like a locked door above my head. Even though I can't see that far as a spirit, I can feel it above me. It affects the shape of everything.' He paused, thinking, and when he 'spoke' again it was with a reflective tone. *'You see the world differently... like this. Everything is a kind of haze that you feel as much as see. Walls, floors, dead things like wood and stone hardly exist outside the temple, but life is so bright —— proper life.'* Tei could picture his shudder, the strange sight of Avin in the pool still conjured up by his mind in the darkness before him, moving and reacting as he felt the spirit was. *'I see the monsters and they look wrong. They're twisted somehow. The worst thing is that in a way they look almost similar to you and Rakariel, but what should be bright is dark, and forced into a shape that doesn't fit, like squeezed clay. The world around*

them doesn't want to touch them, it pulls away from them. I don't see them the way you do — I've never known quite what they look like to the living until I saw them through you, in the pool. But they scare me.'

"They scare everyone," Tei said, still as silently as before. "Rakariel's the only person who isn't afraid of them. I've never met anyone like her before."

'She is afraid,' Avin corrected. *'Don't think she's not. I don't know her, I wasn't welcome in her mind, but I think she would tell you the same thing. Not being afraid is the action of a fool. She's afraid. She knows what she faces, I'm sure of that. I shouldn't speak of her, for her, you should ask her yourself — but true courage is knowing what you face, and going on anyway.'*

Tei nodded, quiet. Was Rakariel really every bit as scared as he was? Was the difference between them really only a matter of the way that she reacted to it? Could she really face the vardra alone, knowing the same fear that until now had sent him fleeing to whatever bolt-hole he could find? But then, he thought, she could fight them. Her weapons were like nothing he had even seen before, almost mystical in their own right: the handful of blades his people had seen either old and worn through centuries of care, or pitted and rusted to uselessness; her bow, as she called it, like nothing he had ever known save as a word from legend. If he could use that incredible weapon, would he dare to fight as well? He had already stood before them once, pitiful though his defence would have been, when they had come at Rakariel in the temple. Perhaps, if he were by her side, he could fight. She had already proved that possible. But to be the person that she was, the one who stood before certain death alone...

"Mm..."

Tei startled at the faint sound, looking over to the shapeless mass that hid her, its dark-smoothed, uncertain outlines shifting and moving as she lifted her head. He made out her arm raising just moments before a bright light shone out, and he flinched, hastily shutting eyes that had moments before been adapted to the room's previous pitch blackness.

"Tei?" came her voice, quietly concerned for him. "Are you all right?"

"Uh-huh," he responded, nodding without opening his eyes. "It's just bright." Very slowly, holding a hand over his face, Tei cracked open his eyes once more, peering through eyelashes and fingers into the now dimly-illuminated room, less than a third of the lightstone visible. Watching him as he slowly lifted his hand from his face and opened his eyes fully, Rakariel lifted the cloth further, then tucked it back behind the lightstone's circlet once again. The room was just as she'd seen it the night before, to her relief: nothing had changed while she slept.

"Is Avin here?" she murmured.

Tei nodded again. "I was just talking to him. He says some of the vardra are still at the temple, and he thinks the others are probably still searching. He said they seemed very intent... now they've found we killed one of them, I don't think they'll give up for a long time."

Rakariel sighed. "Then it's as I feared."

"What do you mean?"

"Animals mostly don't understand revenge the way people do. They don't often hunt down the one that killed another of their kind. If the vardra continue to search so intently, I have to assume that they're intelligent... like us." She bowed her head, shadows all around the room moving with the lightstone. "I hate creatures of evil that can think. An animal is just an animal: it has no choice other than to do what its instincts tell it. Something with a mind has a *choice*. It has a choice, and it chooses to do evil, and takes pride in what it does..."

The thought, phrased that way, troubled Tei as well, on a different level to any the vardra had before. They had always been a fact of life: he had never thought of them other than as terrors that stalked in the fog, nightmares that came to sound and lay in ambush for the unwary. What Rakariel had said was terrible indeed.

Again, she sighed, breaking Tei's thoughts as well as her own as she lifted her head, returning to the present and the matter at hand. "If they're intelligent, we'll have to be doubly careful. Avin will have to keep scouting for us, if he can. If they think we're still in the area, they might set a trap for us." She paused. "If they can think like us, then you have to think of what you would do if you were them — because there's a good chance they will do it."

Tei swallowed, and nodded. She was right. Remembering something else from before, he hesitated for a moment before speaking, his low voice slow and unsure. "Avin said he doesn't see like we do."

"No," Rakariel said. "He's a spirit — he can probably only see in the plane of spirit. But why?" She seemed understandably puzzled at his apparent change of subject, but she let him carry on, waiting for a reason. Tei paused in thought, then went on. He didn't, couldn't know for certain: he knew nothing at all of other planes, whatever they were, but he trusted her knowledge, and what Avin had said sounded enough like what she had told him that he thought it might serve as confirmation.

"He said that to him, they looked like us, but twisted and wrong. He said they were dark instead of bright, and twisted into a shape that didn't fit."

To his surprise, Rakariel shot to her feet, her cloak billowing out behind her as she began to pace the room with fast, snappy steps. "Was that *exactly* what he said?" she hissed, all intent and focus.

"Well... I think so. Avin?" A part of him felt some small surprise at how easily he'd come to accept calling on the spirit for help, but he was already doing so much that should have been impossible, or insane, or both. What was one more oddity against that? He could hear Avin's responses even if Rakariel could not, and they had both felt his mind through the temple's pool. Spirit or not, he was definitely there.

'Yes. That's what I said. They look twisted, like clay that's been pressed into the wrong shape. They're dark, and the world pulls away from them.'

"He says that's what he said," Tei confirmed. "That they look like clay that's been pressed into the wrong shape." He knew what clay was. It lined some sections of the riverbank, slippery but mouldable, a toy for children and useful material for adults on the occasions someone risked bringing it back, or traded some across the city for food, or shelter, or any of the thousand little things a person needed. "They're dark, and the world pulls away from them. That's what he said."

He heard a sharp hiss of breath from her, and she stopped dead, cloak dropping to hang in folds around her once again. "And they look like us?"

'Yes,' Avin said, though she couldn't hear him. *'I think so. If they weren't so dark and twisted...'*

"He thinks so, if they weren't so dark and twisted," Tei relayed. "Why...?"

"Because if he can see that... then they may once have been people. Just like you and I."

At that, Tei could only stare at her in shock.

Slowly, moving with almost exaggerated-looking care, Rakariel began to unfasten the clasp of her cloak, holding it close around her for a moment before swirling it off with an understated, economical movement. Kneeling to fold and re-roll it, she began talking again, her voice still low.

"They have to be stopped. They have to die. This has to end." Her back was to him, but he could picture the cold expression on her face that went with the flat finality of her voice, something even beyond determination. Every word spoken in that chill, measured tone fell into place with such finality that he found himself believing without question that not only was it true, but that she could, and would, do it, regardless of what it would take. "Their suffering has to stop."

There was nothing he could say in the face of her words, no agreement that seemed worth voicing without the strength behind it that he could not put there. She rolled and packed her cloak in silence, strapping it securely back in place between the twin packs before fastening them back on, tightening a couple of the straps a notch.

"We need to start moving," she said. "Avin will go ahead of us as a scout. He should start now, and check that the route to the next safe house is clear before we leave. We'll move from one to the next — it's the safest way, now that they're looking for us." She stretched, rotating her arms, testing her range of movement to make sure she was unencumbered. "Avin, go now. Move as fast as you can."

'Uh — yes,' came the silent response. Tei couldn't help shivering again as the spirit drew on his strength once more before fleeing to carry out the search.

"He said yes," he told Rakariel.

"Then all we can do is wait until he gets back." Noting the shiver, she shot him a direct, assessing look that flicked after a few moments to the shuttered window, tense with a restless energy and needing somewhere to channel it. Unable to move on until Avin returned, she turned on a heel to pace again just as Tei spoke, halting her.

"Rakariel?"

She spun sharply back to face him, expression softening after a moment: the tension she felt was neither because of nor directed at him. "What?"

"Can you teach me magic? Like Fayel?"

His question was met with a blink, and a surprised look that settled swiftly into one almost of weariness. "We don't have time."

"Maybe not for all of it." *This is it,* he thought. Maybe — just maybe — there was a chance he could be of more use to her than as a simple guide, unable to defend himself, needing her complete protection. Though he didn't know if he would be able to do it, he had to try. "But if we're going to keep stopping like this while Avin scouts ahead, there'll be moments everywhere. Like now." He paused, added "I remember some of what you told her, I think." Resolved despite his doubts and fears, he met her eyes, only hesitating for a moment. "Se..." It started wrong, and he faltered, but forced himself to focus and try again, concentrating on the memory of that strange, unreal night until he could all but hear it once more, Rakariel's slow syllables resonating in his bones. He'd missed the first part, but he'd seen with every word that they each held a strange power, even without the rest of the spell around them. "*Sar... thae...*"

A strange feeling shot through him, his own words resonating just as hers had days before, drawing power from somewhere within him and hanging in the air for an instant before fading. Tei couldn't keep the expression of surprise from his face: saying it was something different again to hearing it, like nothing he had ever felt before. Rakariel looked at him in silence for a long, long moment, her expression unreadable.

"All right," she said eventually. "But I'm no mage. Even if I manage to teach you a spell, that's all I'll be able to do."

"That's all I need," he replied. He wasn't even sure what else there could be to learn beyond those strange words, every syllable so carefully shaped. "Just teach me... something that will let me fight."

Again, she blinked at him, and he went on before she could so much as open her mouth to rebuff him.

"I'm only a problem for you if they find us again, aren't I? I can't use a weapon like yours. I've never even seen one before. But I... I'm no use to you if I die.

And maybe I can help you somehow." He knew she had to be able to see the fear in his eyes, hear it in his voice. There was no way that he could hide it: the thought of standing before a vardra again, even in Rakariel's strong and determined shelter, was terrifying. Avin had said that she was afraid as well, but even so, surely it would only be weakness in her eyes.

Rakariel saw his fear, and through it, determination. He was older, more mature than she'd thought, in mind if not in body. He knew what he faced: she could see him remembering how he'd stood beside her as the creatures charged them, unable to fight but not quite letting himself run. She could see he knew that if he learned to fight from her, he'd have to stand again and risk their lives on his own actions. He didn't want to be helpless beside her again, though the mere act of having the knowledge would force him to use it when his every instinct screamed at him to run. He would have to knowingly offer his life to the things he feared the most.

After a long, long silence, she took a deep breath, her voice quiet even for the whisper she was growing accustomed to. "Very well."

Coming back to the wall, she sat cross-legged, taking off her packs again to find paper and the battered quill she'd used before, then shrugging the packs back on. Tei came to sit beside her, watching quietly as she dipped the pen into the ink, tested it once, and began to lay out a careful symbol on the curled and crumpled sheet, similar to the ones he'd seen before, yet different. When it was finished, Rakariel twisted it to face him, looking up from the paper into his eyes.

"The spell I'm going to teach you," she said softly,

"will let you use lightning as a weapon in battle. You must be very careful with it: battle magic is short and fast, and it's all too easy to make a dangerous mistake, one that could hurt or even kill either of us, just by mispronouncing one syllable. Do you understand?"

Tei nodded, expression grave, though also faintly quizzical. After a few moments, he ventured "What's lightning?"

Rakariel blinked. "You've never seen lightning?" She looked up at the ceiling, and through it to the unseen rock above, cloaked in fog. "...I suppose you wouldn't have. It's a bright power that strikes from the sky during a storm, setting whatever is in its path ablaze and blasting it apart. It happens in a flash, so it's almost impossible to dodge or counter if you don't recognise the spell being cast. The spell that I know isn't as powerful as storm lightning, but it serves."

Again, Tei nodded, wide-eyed. He tried to picture it, found he wasn't sure how, beyond a flash of light, though the way she spoke made it seem more than that. Could he really master such a weapon as that? One even further beyond his imagination than her bow would have been just a few days before?

"Now," she continued, calling his mind back to what lay before him. "This symbol is *karr*."

A little hesitant, he repeated it, matching her intonation on the third try and feeling the magic echo once again in his bones.

"Again," she said, though he'd already succeeded once. Tei did as he was told, trying once more.

* * *

Rakariel coached him carefully and intensively, making him repeat the syllables over and over, with the result that he'd only learnt another two when he felt Avin's presence return, looked up from the paper a moment before the spirit 'spoke'.

'I've found you another safe-house,' he said. *'The path to it is clear for now, but they're still around — I found some hiding that I almost didn't notice. You'll have to be careful.'*

Rakariel had noticed Tei's sudden distraction, and didn't chide him for his silence, rewarded moments later when Tei relayed the message almost word for word, his voice at once back to the whisper he'd had to abandon for the sake of magical practice. She listened in silence, cleaning the quill on a corner of the paper, which she then rolled tightly and folded in half, shoving quill, paper, and stoppered ink into a pouch on her belt. "We will be. He should tell you the way, then go back to scouting for us."

Tei listened for a short while, then nodded slightly. "He says he will." He glanced to the shuttered window, gathering his courage. "Let's go."

Rakariel nodded, getting to her feet and crossing to it in silence. Easing the shutters quietly open, she leaned out slightly, looking first up, then to the sides. As Avin had promised, the street was clear as far as she could see, empty of all but fog. Moving slowly, she slipped out, a little awkward with her packs in the confined space of the window, but managing it almost noiselessly nonetheless. Behind her, Tei followed more gracefully with an ease born of long practice, closing the shutters gently behind them. He spent a few moments looking around before cautiously starting down the street on silent feet, sticking close to the walls. Once again, Rakariel followed, glancing from side to side as she did. She was beginning to notice differences and even landmarks in the misty streets: not just that some were wider or narrower than others, but also the quality and nature of the buildings that lined them, and how it changed as they moved from one place to the next. In the eerily deadened, fog-blanketed silence, the foreign city landscape, it was reassuring indeed to at last begin to understand something more of where she was than simply which direction she was facing.

Tei stopped dead suddenly, listening to the silence of the city, to Avin's soundless words, and Rakariel paused as well, following his lead quietly and without question. She knew almost as well as he that a sound, any sound, could see them hunted, and though they might not die, the chase and battle would waste far too much of their limited time — particularly since the vardra would all converge on their location if they were once found, making it almost impossible to move on again.

He started forward again after a few moments, ducking into a narrow side alley that cut between a couple of buildings. Rakariel followed, listening to the irregular drips, to the silence of Tei's footsteps and the faint sound of her own, alert to any betraying noise that might mean they were about to come under attack. The alley curved gently as they followed it, as many of the streets did, and it was a few corners before Rakariel could be confident that they were on a detour, looping towards their original destination again. She found herself unexpectedly glad of Avin's unseen presence, of the warning he provided. Whatever trap they had avoided, she couldn't say for certain that they might not simply have walked straight into its jaws had it not been for him.

The detour ended at what proved to be another safe house, Tei letting himself in without hesitation. Rakariel followed, closing the old but reinforced shutters behind her and bolting them securely before lifting the cloth from her lightstone. White light spilled into the room before them, illuminating dull, damp-stained walls that might once have been brightly painted, for all that the house itself was small and poky. Looking up, she saw the damp continuing onto the once-white ceiling, heavily mould-streaked paint flaking away in patches from slightly warped plaster. Yet, for all the superficial damage, once again the place seemed intact, at least as far as she could tell — despite the fact that a ceiling left like that should have caved in long before. Why it had not she could only wonder... what power was keeping the remains of the city alive? Though they had to keep moving beyond all else, it was another question to add to the mystery, potentially one more that needed to be answered, and potentially a favourable one at that. If something was preserving the city, it was unlikely that its motives were hostile. Like the faint and faded spirit, something still remained to protect it, somehow. Resolving to try and find out, Rakariel asked

"Has Avin sensed anything out there besides us and the vardra?"

Tei listened for a moment before shaking his head. "Nothing important, he says. He can see things like mould, moss, fungus... all those things. But nothing else."

She nodded. "I see. In that case, he should go

ahead again and look for another house. We need to get as far as we can, as fast as we can."

Tei nodded, and Rakariel saw a shudder grip him, his arms folding tightly before he straightened again, shaking his head as though to tell her he was all right. "He says he's going now. He'll come back as soon as he can."

"Hm." Though she knew how he'd respond, she asked him anyway. "Are you all right?"

Just as she'd expected him to, Tei nodded again. "I'm fine. He was just a bit weak — it really only feels cold for a bit. Not like the first time he went out to search for us. I think he's stayed stronger since then."

"That's good," she said, thinking *I hope so.* But no, she'd seen Avin's thoughts, felt them. She knew what was in his mind, or at least had done for that brief space of time. He had no intention of harming either Tei or Rakariel herself; it was her ingrained mistrust of anything or anyone that appeared to injure someone she considered an ally making her feel that way. Even knowing what she did about him, all she had seen and done made it difficult to entirely trust a being she could actually see drawing strength from her young and inexperienced companion.

"Will you teach me more?" Tei asked, whispered words breaking into her train of thought.

"In a moment," she murmured in response, dropping a hand to her belt. "I want to look for something first."

Tei watched curiously as she took out the lens. The only time he had seen her use it was to look for Avin, and he wondered what she was expecting to see. She fitted it over her eye, tightening the strap and resting her fingers on the wheels, flinching slightly as though something about it hurt her head. What was she seeing? Avin had told him he saw nothing out of the ordinary: what was she looking for?

Aligning the wheels carefully, Rakariel slowly closed on the plane of magic, shutting all else out. The real world around her faded away with her free eye closed, the interior of the house retraced in hidden colour. The faint spark of magic innate to life and nature was clear enough, the dull glow that lit within stone or wood present, the faintest pale blue wash suffusing the room the residual magic of still air. Her arm showed strong and solid, the subtle protective spells woven through the hardened leather of her armour making it more opaque than anything else in the room. And there, just faintly...

She stepped closer to the wall, her free hand held out before her in case there were some obstacle she couldn't see, unlikely though that would be. Almost everything in the world held at least a faint touch of magic, weak though it might be: it was a part of nature, woven through all things. Leaning close, she peered at it, hand shifting to cover the lightstone and hide the power that radiated from it. In the traceries of stone, there was the faintest hint of another colour: faded wisps of preservation's amber shade. It wasn't subtle, only old, and worn thin. She couldn't attune the lens anything like as finely as she would need to in order to perceive only spells of such nature, and so instead held the colour in her mind, turning slowly. It was difficult to see, but she thought that it lined just about everything in the building, shoring it up, holding it together in an unsubtle but effective weave. Or mostly effective. The house was stained by damp; many things in the city were rotten, at least on the outside. Either the spell was failing, or it had been set some time after the city's fall, fixing all things as they had been at that moment. Though Tei's people knew no magic, and surely could not have worked a spell that would cover the entire city in such fashion, she still wondered. Could it have been one of their vanished gods, a last benediction for the people who had somehow lost their blessing? It was possible, and yet it held none of the strong, ancient subtlety of the seal over the valley.

"What do you see?" Tei ventured hesitantly.

"I'm not sure," she replied, taking the lens from her head and stowing it back in its pouch. "This house is being preserved by magic. I think the whole city must be, but I don't know what could have placed it, or why."

"Preserved by magic?" he echoed. Magic was a thing for stories and fables, all but forgotten until Rakariel had arrived, with no-one so much as certain which of the tales were true and which were false. How could his entire home be preserved by it, and no-one have ever known?

"Yes. It's holding the walls together, stopping the ceiling from falling in. I've been thinking that something wasn't right for a while. Your doors and shutters are still in one piece, but they shouldn't be, not after this long."

Tei blinked. "Shouldn't they?"

Rakariel looked surprised for a moment before realisation dawned. Of course... he'd never known anything different. How could he?

"No," she said. "They should have fallen apart

after a few decades. Doors, shutters, floorboards — your city would be full of fallen stone; these houses should be empty shells if they stayed standing at all. Something is stopping the wood from rotting, the mortar from dissolving. Someone cast a very strong spell on this city, long ago."

"Can you tell who? Why?" Tei breathed, awed. He'd never even thought about it: to him, things were simply as they had been for his entire life, and his parents' and grandparents' lives before him. Using the lens that had let her see Avin's spirit before, Rakariel could somehow see this magic, an awe-inspiring impossibility that, if she was right, had infused his life without his ever being aware of it. But she shook her head.

"All the lens shows me is what's around me. I can see the magic, but all I can tell you about it is that someone or something wanted to preserve this city." She frowned slightly. "And that the spell isn't subtle, and it's faded. It's the opposite of the seal on the valley."

"What does that mean?" he asked, feeling slightly foolish. Rakariel took the question as seriously as any other, however.

"The valley is hidden by old, powerful, incredibly subtle magic. Think of it as... like the weave of my shirt. You have to look quite closely to see how the strands fit together; from any distance, it seems like one thing. And it's very strong, like my armour — it would be very difficult to break even for a master mage, impossible for me. It's old, but it hasn't been changed by time. The spell here, on the other hand, has faded with time, and even when it was newly cast, it was as obvious to someone who could see it as the planks of wood in a barricade. But it must have been cast by someone very powerful, or a group of powerful people, to cover the entire city, and to last as long as it must have."

Tei was quiet for a few moments. "King Sariven?" he ventured. Could the legendary king have done it in his battle to save the city?

"Perhaps," Rakariel said noncommittally. "Was he that powerful?"

"They say he was stronger than the others, the ones from other places, much stronger. That the gods gave him that power as a blessing, and he used it to fight the vardra until he died."

"Hm." She thought briefly. Legends had a way of growing and changing in the telling, and Avin, trapped in the temple as he had been, was unlikely to be able to say what the truth was. But if any single power had done it, one granted as a blessing to the valley's king was at least slightly more likely to be believable. Except...

"So the king kept his blessing when the rest of your people were already losing theirs?"

Tei frowned. "I guess. That means he must have been a good king, doesn't it?"

"Hopefully." That, or he'd gained the power from another source altogether. But then, what of the resistance Tei had told her of, the refusal to flee? How could he have carried out the ritual Avin had spoken of before all his priests, and none of them felt anything amiss? No... she just didn't know enough, not yet. Not enough to be sure. She sighed, shook her head. Perhaps more would come to her as they travelled. "But it's not the only possibility. I'll think on it while we travel — if you really want to learn the spell I was teaching you, we should carry on with that for now."

Tei nodded at once, still determined despite lingering trepidation, his awe at the thought of learning any magic, however little, just as strong as before. Rakariel settled on the floor, drawing out her pen and crumpled paper as Tei sat down beside her. Voices just barely above a whisper, they went over the syllables of magic for a short while longer before Avin returned, his unheard voice making Tei start.

'I've found another safehouse, I think, but you'll have to go the long way around. There are more of those monsters moving around out there. I'll need to guide you if you want to leave now.'

Tei swallowed, relaying the spirit's words to Rakariel and looking to her for approval. She thought for a moment, then nodded.

"We have to take the risk. We're moving too slowly." Folding the paper up again, Rakariel wiped off the nib of her pen and tucked them both away before continuing. "Let's go."

Once more, she was the first to leave, Tei climbing out after her and gently closing the shutters, a part of him wondering as he did about the magic she said ran through them, a mystery beneath his very fingertips. Pulling his thoughts from it, he turned away, slipping down the street under the guidance of his own instincts and Avin's silent warnings. He flitted from shadow to shadow as though he were one himself, pausing anywhere that would shelter him from above, flinching occasionally at the unexpected drips that struck his head or trickled cold down his neck. Rakariel followed behind him, gait uneven to hide the faint sound of her footsteps in the silent city, darting from one piece of dubious cover to the next. Stopping when he stopped, waiting when he waited, she crossed narrow streets and ducked down alleys behind him, until finally, they reached a broad avenue that cut directly across their path. Tei stood at its edge, looking up and down in the dull fog, and all she could do was look at him questioningly — until he abruptly shot out into it, as if someone had shouted at him to go, and just as suddenly stopped dead by the opposite wall, Rakariel almost slamming into him. For a moment, there was complete silence, and she wasn't even sure that he was breathing — then he whirled and bolted, and she chased him without question through an open door, slamming it shut behind them. From outside came a rending, unnatural howl, so horrifyingly close as to be on almost the same building as the one they had run into, a vardra deprived of its prey. Tei shot backwards into the shadows of the house as Rakariel pushed the cloth from her lightstone and set an arrow to her bow. All at once, the hall was lit in its bright, pale light, only Rakariel's shadow streaming out behind her in unrelieved blackness as she backed up, getting as far from the door as she could without breaking her line of sight.

"'S not safe-" Tei managed in a rapid, shaky whisper. "-Windows!"

Rakariel glanced to them and realised at once what he had meant. Like those she'd seen around it, the house they'd been forced to take shelter in had larger windows than any Tei had used for hiding in before. A vardra would almost certainly fit through them with only a little struggle, and it didn't look as though the lightweight shutters had been touched by anything but water and mould since the city's fall.

"No choice!" she snapped back, knowing as well as he did that there was almost certainly no time to run. In almost that same instant, something slammed against one of the windows, splintering the thin wood that protected them and shattering the ancient glass. Rakariel saw a curved black blade pull back through the torn hole, and just moments later the vardra threw itself bodily at the window, crashing through and rolling to a crouch in a hideous parody of a warrior's battle-readiness. She loosed her arrow at once, another following immediately after, and a roar of pain split the air as the creature was rocked backwards. Whatever she had struck had not been vital, though: the vardra recovered itself enough to get to its feet and begin a slightly off-balance charge. Tei pressed himself against the far wall as Rakariel screamed a wordless battlecry in challenge and defiance, her lightstone throwing every detail of her foe into sharp relief as she hit it once again, making it stumble barely two paces before it reached her. In the space of barely a heartbeat, she'd flung her bow toward Tei and snatched out her sword, darting up to the faltering vardra before it could right itself, swinging herself up and around its shoulder with her left hand and landing hard on its back, driving it back to the floor even as she drove her blade into the back of its neck. It jerked once and was still, its spine half-severed by the strike, red blood dripping from the sword's exposed tip to pool on the stone-flagged floor below. Bracing herself, she yanked the blade free and jumped off, ignoring the spray of blood across her armour, glancing quickly to the shattered window before her fierce eyes lighted on Tei and she snatched her bow back from him.

"Go! Run! Now!"

He scarcely needed prompting, dashing at once through the house and out of a back door into what might once have been a pleasant garden, Rakariel hot on his heels. The house they had just left erupted into a crescendo of howls and the sound of furious violence against anything, however small or inanimate, that barred the vardra's way as they searched the house for the creature that had dared to kill another of their own kind. Tei leapt a decaying fence to reach the dubious shelter offered by another house's gaping back window, scrambling in and dashing through to the front — and stopped dead just before the firmly bolted door.

"Stop!" he hissed, tension in every line of his body, and Rakariel only barely managed to obey in time to avoid slamming into him. "Avin says stop! They came to the sound — they're outside — can't go on —" He turned as he spoke, face even whiter than usual in the lightstone's glow, seeking help... help, he suddenly realised, that she could not give. The warrior stood on the edge of a precipice, no way forward or back, and he could see in her eyes that she was bracing herself for what could prove to be the last fight of her life. Though he was frozen, his mind raced. She would do everything in her power, even though it might not be enough — he *had* to do the same! Then it came to him.

"The cellar!" he gasped. "House is big — have to be a cellar — underground somewhere —" His voice scattered and jumped through the sentence, but he knew he was right, thanks partially to Rakariel knew more than that: that the reason a simple latch or bolt could defeat the vardra was that they didn't have the flexibility to manipulate small things, that they could only grip anything from one angle without the terrible black blades that were their claws stopping them altogether. "No hands — can't open it — find the cellar!"

She looked at him blankly for a moment before realising, and hope shone sudden and strong through the flat resolve in her eyes. "You're right — quickly!"

They nodded to one another in unison and shot apart, dashing into different rooms to search. Though he had only the dim light from the windows to guide it, it was Tei who found it. He hauled the sturdy trapdoor, braced with pitted and rusted iron, open and held it.

"Rakariel!" His voice was as loud as he dared to make it, but the sounds of frenzied destruction from across the gardens and the converging howls from all around gave him hope that, for once, it would go unheard. It proved loud enough to call her to him, at least: she appeared in the doorway just moments later, took one look at him holding up the trapdoor and dashed over to grab the heavy iron ring herself.

"You first!"

There was no time to argue. Obedient, Tei let go at once, looking briefly down to see steep, wet-looking wooden steps leading into the darkness and into safety. Far faster than he should have, he began to scramble down, thinking of no more than escaping the vardra in time for both him and Rakariel to reach shelter. He wasn't even halfway when one of the stairs gave way, snapping beneath his foot. Tei yelled as his leg shot through into nothingness, as the rest of the staircase collapsed in a shower of soggily splintering wood and he fell into the hard, cold embrace of blackness.

"*Tei!*"

Rakariel stared in horror as Tei vanished into the darkness below with a cry and the sound of breaking wood. The air seemed to hang thicker and darker than ever in a deathly silence, and she called out again, afraid.

"Tei?"

No, no no no...

Without stopping to think, Rakariel threw herself around the trapdoor and into the hole, letting it fall closed behind her as she fell into the dark.

CHAPTER 11
The Price of Resistance

Rakariel felt the breath leave her as the lower of the two remaining steps struck her in the side and she fell around it, then just moments later felt herself hit something else with a blow like a fist to her leg even as the trapdoor slammed shut above her. She fell the last of the distance with her eyes closed, landing on her back in what felt like a pile of half-rotten wood. Winded and still trying to get her breath back, a deep pain burning in her right leg, she forced herself to open her eyes and sit up.

The lightstone cast odd, straight, hard-edged shadows every which way from the wreckage she sat in, damp and splintered wood that had failed to withstand the ravages of time even with the aid of the preservation spell that had been cast over the city. The light reflected oddly from the floor, almost seeming to move, and Rakariel had shot instinctively to her feet with her weight on her uninjured leg before she realised that it was only water, pooled across almost the entire floor. If that had been there since the city's fall, it was no wonder that the ladder had rotted, and she tried to put it aside. Even so, the motion she'd thought she'd seen, combined with all that had come before, kept her heart still racing in her chest as she turned slowly, surveying her surroundings with as much of her weight kept on her good leg as possible. More importantly than anything else, she was searching for Tei. He had to be there. He had to be alive.

Only as she'd almost completed her limping turn did she spot something that might have been him, a dark and uneven shape lying limp and motionless in the still-rippling water at the edge of the wreckage. With a sharp intake of breath, she dashed over, half-falling to catch herself in a kneel at his side as her shifting footing proved treacherous and landing with her hands in bone-cold water, but it didn't matter, not in that moment. Touching her fingertips to his neck, she was rewarded by a living warmth and a fast but steady pulse. He was alive; she hadn't yet caused his death — he was alive. She pulled him onto her knees and got her arms under him, forcing herself back to her feet despite the pain shooting through her leg and side, and her shoulder. She wondered for a moment what she had done to it, but it didn't matter: the most important thing was to take care of Tei, and if she left him in the cold water then he would die of it regardless of what else happened. Making her way painfully to the highest point of the wreckage pile, fighting to keep her footing as it shifted and snapped under her, Rakariel gently set him down... and started, nearly falling backwards, as his eyes, smoky grey to the point of blackness just as his sister's had been, blinked open and immediately shut again.

"Tei?" she whispered, watching him with concern. "Can you hear me?"

His dark eyes flickered open again, and stayed that way, though they were somewhat unfocused.

"R...kari...?" he mumbled, looking hazily up at her. Despite her various injuries, she smiled, though it was faint and still troubled. Her quest had not, yet, led him to his death.

"I'm all right," she said, and fell silent for a few moments while she looked him over, assessing what she could of his injuries through his several layers of ragged and now waterlogged clothing. Tei lay still, watching her dazedly, flinching once with a hiss of breath as she moved his arm. His clothes had only offered a little protection, and in addition to the bruises he'd gained in his fall, some of the cuts from the splintered wood had gone deep, though at least none were fatal.

Once she'd ascertained what she could without actually turning him over, Rakariel sat back. He'd taken quite the fall, but as far as she could tell, it was nothing that wouldn't heal with time, at least as long as he escaped infection. The only problem was that they didn't *have* time.

A sound from above caused her to freeze, then look slowly up, her eyes fixed on the heavy trapdoor. Something was moving above them — something large. Barely breathing, she strained her ears to listen to the dim sounds that filtered through to her. At first, they seemed restrained: movement and no more, but after a short while they began to change in nature, a frustrated growl making its way to her ears just moments before the crashing sounds of things breaking. Once, something heavy seemed to bounce directly off the trapdoor itself, and both she and Tei flinched, but nothing more came of it. It was some time before the sounds stopped altogether, and she listened for a few minutes longer before allowing herself a quiet sigh of relief.

His eyes clearer and more focused than they had been, Tei looked at her, and slowly, wincing, sat up. His back was injured as well, and Rakariel wondered once again just how close he had come to a truly serious injury, or even death.

"S...sorry," he whispered in response to the concern in her eyes. "I should have been more careful."

"We're still alive," was all she said in response, her voice a matching whisper, and he gave a faint, pained smile. It was true, they had lived, escaping once again from the very jaws of death, from vardra actively on the hunt for them. Whatever pain he might feel was a small price to pay for that! Slowly, he looked down at himself, already ragged clothes torn in new places — along with the skin beneath. Lifting his left arm to look at it, he flinched slightly on seeing the long gash scraped along almost half its length. He'd have to be careful and lucky if he wasn't to get too sick, but as long as he was still alive, he still had a chance. Reaching into one of his pockets for the cloth strips that would serve him as bandages, he found to his dismay that they, like he, were soaked through.

"Let me help," Rakariel whispered, and he nodded wordlessly, looking at her once again.

The next several minutes almost gave his cause to regret that assent, biting his lip to remain silent as she picked splinters of rotten wood from injuries he hadn't, in some cases, even known he had. She worked with the same quiet determination that she brought to any task, and for all that it hurt, he knew as well as she did that it was for the best. The rotten wood wouldn't help his chances at all if it were left alone. Eventually, her hands as bloodied as his ragged clothes, she sat back, studying him quietly for a moment.

"I think that's it," she said. "Hold still — I'm

going to try to heal you. Think of somewhere safe. It's easier for me if you're calm." *Or unconscious,* her mind added. Battle healers were frequently forced to knock their patients out, one way or another, before they could properly treat them. The mercenaries she'd travelled with had had just such a healer among their number... long dead, now.

Unaware of her thoughts, Tei nodded and obediently closed his eyes, head bowed. Rakariel took a moment to do the same, settling herself and focusing inwards before opening them again and resting a hand lightly on his injured arm. She could only deal with one or two wounds at a time, and to heal him fully would likely exhaust her. Still, she would do all that she could. Keeping her mind as clear as possible, she focused on the book that she always pictured her spells trapped in, making sure each symbol was firmly envisaged in its place upon the page and running through it once in her head before beginning the true spell out loud. Even quiet, her voice resonated slightly, as always, with the sound of magic, impossible to hide by its very nature. As the spell finished, Tei's arm twitched beneath her fingers, but to his credit he made no move, whether to pull away, to scratch it, or even simply to look at what she'd done. Rakariel sighed quietly, studying her handiwork. She had to keep some strength in reserve, couldn't afford to do everything, but the injury still looked to have had a week, perhaps slightly more, to heal.

"Stay still," she murmured, moving on to the next of his wounds and once again placing her hand across it, spread fingertips on opposite sides. About to look at his now-released arm, Tei instead did as he was told, closing his eyes again and thinking of the safety she had commanded he envisage. Though the image that his mind returned to was the cellar of his childhood home, it was not entirely as it had been in life: Rakariel sat in a chair near to the steps, her expression that one of calm, battleworn readiness that was already becoming so familiar, relaxed yet able to move in an instant, lightstone glowing coolly from its position on her head. Despite the short time he had known her, Tei found that he couldn't think of anywhere safer than in the presence of the quiet, oddly gentle warrior who was even now fighting for his people.

Magic built in time with the carefully-spoken words of the spell, settled into him like a warm breath of light as the words finished and their power was loosed. The wound beneath Rakariel's hand felt strange, a kind of creeping itch as though something were crawling across his skin and taking the pain with it as it passed, and he fought the almost irresistible urge to pull away or scratch it, preferably both. Then, as quickly as it had come, the sensation was gone.

She repeated the process another three times. The same feeling followed her touch, her spell each time — and with each cast, Rakariel grew progressively more tired. Finally, she ended with a fully general spell that would help ease more minor injuries, and sighed as the last of its magic faded away, allowing herself to slump. The amount of power she had needed to expend on him, combined with the fading stress of the earlier chase and its end, had left her drained, exhausted.

Tei, by contrast, felt better than he had even before they'd fallen into the cellar, completely revitalised to a degree he had rarely even experienced, buoyed up on the magical healing he had just received. He vaguely remembered what his sister had told him Rakariel had said to her, that not all of that feeling would last, but for the time being, at least, he felt incredible. Looking at his healed arm almost wonderingly, he was still for a few moments longer before it occurred to him to lift his head and turn to look for Rakariel. Worn out, head bent, she was still sat beside him where she had been to cast the previous two spells.

"Rakariel?" he whispered, concerned.

"I'm just tired," came the quiet response. In truth, she barely felt that she even had the strength to move, and Tei frowned, worried. He could hear it in her voice, see it in her posture, her unconscious readiness all but gone.

"Maybe you should sleep for a while," he suggested hesitantly, reluctant to so much as suggest such an obvious thought as that when she knew what she was doing so much better than he possibly could. Doubtless she was already well aware of that.

"Mm," was all she said, raising her head slowly. It only made him more concerned, able to read the exhaustion in her expression clearly for the first time. Eyes slightly unfocused, she slowly removed her twin packs, making sure they were somewhere relatively stable before detaching and wearily unrolling her cloak once again. "You, too. You're wet. Cold. Hurt." Her voice came from somewhere a long way away inside her, words almost slightly slurred, barely able to string them together enough to make sense.

Tei looked down at himself. He was, he supposed — wet, at least, and perhaps vaguely cold, if he thought about it. But he felt so good, it was hard to believe. "I feel fine."

"Magic," she said. "Magic. You... you think it's all right. Feel fine. But... you're cold and wet. Just can't feel it. Seen... seen people die that way. Stupid, but we all think we're fine. Had a good healer... feel fine until the cold kills you. ...'M not a good healer. You might notice first." Her brow furrowed as she continued struggling to piece the words together through the fog that filled her mind as thickly as its real counterpart filled the city streets, muffling her thoughts as surely as that did sound. "Other way around for me. Not hurt —" if she ignored the pain in her side, leg, and shoulder, still there and only worsening the mental fog "— but can't think. Too tired." Tei moved to help her as she slowly began to spread the cloak out, draping it over the wreckage. Thick and sturdy, it would provide both warmth and protection from the broken wood beneath when she lay down. The mere thought was so inviting... but she couldn't. Not yet. "Stay with me. Doesn't matter how... how you think you feel. Think about it hard — maybe you'll notice."

Tei frowned, focusing his attention inward as Rakariel awkwardly shifted position to sit on the cloak. He was a bit wet, maybe even a little cold, but it seemed so distant, so very far away from anything serious. He felt too good for it to possibly be a real problem. Yet, that was what she was trying to say, what she was telling him he would feel. Even though it felt incredibly unlikely that the faint chill could do him any harm, she was the experienced one, the one who knew magic. She said she'd seen people die that way, because their feelings were lying to them, and if she was right, his own were doing the same.

"I guess," he said slowly, sitting on the space she'd left beside her. "But it feels so... unimportant. Like if you've been running — it's cold, but you don't really notice."

"Mm. But it's not true. The magic... just makes you feel that way." She lay back slowly, with little care for the position she ended up in, and he could see her fighting against closing her eyes almost in the same moment that her head touched the cloak. "You have to warm up. Have to..."

Obedient, Tei lay down beside her, tugging the free remnant of the cloak as far across them both as he could. She was warm, he realised, oddly so — that, or he was as cold as she said, feeling her as unnaturally warm only because of the chill that remained settled into his bones. After a short while of thinking about it, in which Rakariel's quiet breathing had already fully drifted into the slow, even rhythm of sleep, he began to realise that she had almost certainly been right. He was still comfortable, and either he shouldn't have been so before, or he shouldn't be now, but not both. She didn't feel quite so warm any longer, either, closer to a natural body heat. It had to mean that he was warming up.

Gazing up at the ceiling above, still too full of energy from the magic's aftereffects to even seriously consider sleeping, Tei began to wonder what would come next. He was fairly sure that he and Rakariel could escape the cellar: he still had his rope and hook, and even if the two steps still hanging at the top weren't sturdy enough to carry them, there was easily enough wood in the cellar that they'd be able to find something long enough to push the trapdoor open with. That, in itself, was not a problem... it was what would come after that bothered him. How would they be able to continue evading the vardra all the way to the palace? They'd already been attacked twice, and the second time had happened even with Avin's invisible guidance. Could they really get past the rest of them, continue to escape if they were found?

Did they have another choice?

He sighed, mildly surprised to see the way his breath hung for a moment in the still cellar air. No wonder Rakariel had told him he was cold. Even as part of him wondered at that, another part felt much the same wonder at his own thoughts just moments before. There was always another choice: run and hide, the way of the survivor; keep their heads down and disappear. But he'd come to trust even more completely in Rakariel and her capabilities, in the strength and immediacy of her purpose. Whatever waited at their journey's end, whether at the palace or in the death of her lightstone, no part of him was seriously considering an alternative to the path she walked.

They had to leave the cellar, he mused, but they could only do that once the vardra were gone, and to be certain of that, they would need Avin. He wondered where his distant ancestor's spirit was, decided against attempting to speak to him with Rakariel so exhausted and so close by. Even if he were gone, Avin couldn't be hurt, and would come back to find them if his strength were flagging. It was most likely that he was watching over them, or the building they were in, at that very moment, and the thought was almost surprisingly cheering, certainly to a degree that would have shocked the Tei of just a week before, who thought ghosts the province of scary stories and nothing more, the product of stressed imaginations in the fogbound streets. Now, after their long contact in the temple's pool, he accepted Avin's existence and benign intent completely. With him to forewarn them of danger; having seen Rakariel fight and kill the vardra twice already; and knowing that he himself might soon be able to aid her with the spell she was teaching him, he no longer felt quite so terrified by what awaited them in the world beyond. He was still afraid, deathly so, there was no denying that — but when they opened the trapdoor and climbed out, it would be safe, and they would be ready, able to face the dangers ahead.

Thinking of that not-too-distant future, he began mentally going over the few syllables of magic Rakariel had taught him, doing his best, as she had instructed, to picture the sheet of paper she'd written on. Though it wasn't particularly reflected in the construction of the symbols, the lightning spell seemed to his ear almost harsh, jagged and spiked, where the healing spell had flowed like water. Silently, to avoid waking her, he mouthed what he could remember of both spells, doing his best to picture the symbols that went with each sound. Without his voice to give it power, there was no feeling or faint, resonant echo of magic, but even pretending to speak it aided his memory of the spell's shape. This sound was followed by that one, and that in its turn by another...

'Tei?' Avin's voice seemed to come from almost directly beside his ear, and he started reflexively, then glanced to his side — but, completely exhausted, Rakariel slept on undisturbed. Even in her sleep, her expression looked almost somehow protective. Tei looked back up at the ceiling, whispering as quietly as

he could.

"Avin?"

'Are you both all right?'

"I think so. She used magic to heal me... it wore her out." Another glance to the side confirmed what he could already feel: that she still hadn't moved. "She said she was just tired, but..."

'What happened?' Avin asked. *'I was watching the monsters. When I came back to warn you they were coming your way, you were already here, and you were unconscious. This is underground, isn't it...'*

Although it wasn't really a question, the fact that Avin seemed to feel the need to say it at all still surprised him, leaving him silent for a moment before he replied. "Yes, it's underground. It's a cellar. The stairs gave way." He flinched inwardly, remembering that awful falling moment, one that could only have lasted for an instant before the world went black in a burst of pain, but that had seemed to go on forever.

'But you're all right?'

"I am now," Tei whispered, trying to be at least a little reassuring in the face of Avin's evident concern. Talking to something — someone — he couldn't see was slightly unsettling: he kept finding his eyes searching the cellar in an effort to locate the voice his mind insisted was coming from right beside him.

'Good. The monsters haven't moved on yet, but I think they will, given time. I'll keep watching them.'

"Are you strong enough?"

Avin's 'voice' sounded as though he were smiling faintly as he replied. *'Yes. Besides, watching them doesn't take that much. I'll come back if I need to.'*

Tei gave a slight nod, unable to do much more

with his head in the position it was in. "Good. Be careful."

'I will.'

With that, Avin left, leaving Tei alone. He couldn't have said how, exactly, he knew that the spirit was gone and not just silent, but he did, or at least thought that he did. Left to himself, he began running through what he knew of the two spells, particularly the lightning one, until without realising it he slowly drifted into sleep.

CHAPTER 12
Sacrifice

Despite having been the last to fall asleep by some time, Tei was also the first to awaken, his eyes flickering open to the old cellar's curved stone ceiling. Half the room seemed to be obscured by shadow, and he wondered why, belatedly thinking to look to the light source for an answer. Immediately to his right, Rakariel lay on her side, facing towards him, the lightstone's glow sharply cut off by its own mounting and the shape of her head, and shining largely on his face. He had to squint just to see her through it, her expression not quite relaxed even in sleep. Though she looked at least somewhat less drained, she still seemed quite deeply asleep, and he experimentally edged away from her. She didn't so much as stir as he slowly got up and pulled the cloak further over her, the faint sounds of the rotten wood squishing beneath his feet the loudest noise he could hear.

Standing, Tei shivered a little. Protected by the waterproof cloak and warmed by Rakariel, he had largely dried out while he slept, but the cellar was still noticeably chill after the warmth he'd just left. The air, however, was still, and his breath being visible had as much to do with it being heavy with water as it did with the cool of the cellar. Still standing in the same spot, he took a long look around, observing the place properly for the first time.

It was largely waterlogged, still, dark water pooled on the stone floor. The damp, rotten wood beneath his feet that shifted worryingly at his slightest move must have been exposed to it for far too long, perhaps since even before the city had fallen. Would there have been water here, before? He wasn't sure. It didn't seem likely, but then, neither did many features of some buildings, so he couldn't be certain. Against the walls, shelves and barrels stood as mute reminders of the lives that must once have been lived in the house above, empty or useless now, any contents doubtless spoilt. The only thing of note on the ceiling was the trapdoor and its two remaining steps, the amount of weight they could hold decidedly uncertain. He considered testing them for an instant, but they were almost directly over where Rakariel had spread her cloak, at the pile of wreckage's highest point, and he wouldn't risk their falling onto her. Instead, he made his way to its edge, away from her, and paused again there to study his partially-healed arm, then glance back at Rakariel. She had worn herself out for no reason other than to heal him, though he was just Tei and she such an incredible figure from her almost unbelievable world. She had already killed three vardra, though most of those who saw them never lived to tell the tale; she had determined in almost the very moment that they met that she would bring back the light of the legendary sun or die trying, for the sake of the valley's scattered people. Yet she was also far more than 'just' a warrior, a person like any other, unexpected facets of her personality showing through at odd moments: her tone when she had spoken of the sun, her tension when they had sheltered together in the dark, her quiet concern after the first battle Tei had ever seen. She had healed him, just as she had his sister, and he was more grateful than he would likely ever manage to say. Still, he felt guilty for having placed such a demand on her, of all people, not to mention foolish for having let it happen at all. He'd been running for his life at the time, but even so, he should have taken just one moment to look...

He sighed. Thinking about it wasn't helping, and it wouldn't change anything. Padding lightly through the water — never more than ankle-deep: wherever it had come from, it either drained out again somehow or had gathered only incredibly slowly — he moved quietly over to the shelves. Though it might have been almost soundless, his tread sent ripples in every direction, shattering the dim reflections that had been visible in the still, dark water. Lit by the cool glow of the lightstone and the myriad sparkling reflections from the ripples, he began to search through the shelves, as much for the sake of having something to do as anything else. Some of the barrels were partially full, but he doubted they'd hold anything of much use. Soggy sacking split at his touch to reveal foodstuffs decayed beyond recognition, more like fungus-shot soil than anything else, and he absently rubbed the slime from his fingertips on his ragged trousers. There was nothing left that would be even slightly useful to them, and in the end he turned around again, leaning on a relatively sturdy-seeming set of shelves and looking across the cellar at nothing in particular.

Eyes caught by the smooth surface of the water, still now that he'd stopped moving through it, he leaned over a little, gazing into it. Only his own familiar reflection looked back, slightly more ragged than usual, paler than either Rakariel or Avin. Though he'd seen the spirit's reflection before in the temple pool, he couldn't now in this one even if he was there at all.

"Avin?" he whispered. Somewhat to his surprise, an answer came almost immediately. He'd half expected Avin to be outside, watching over them as they waited for Rakariel to awaken.

'What is it?'

"Nothing, really. I was just wondering if you were there." He tucked his hands into his sleeves to avoid the cellar's chill air, leaning back on the shelving again. While he doubted it would hold his entire weight, it was good enough for that, at least. "Will you tell me something?"

'Of course,' Avin replied instantly. *'What do you want to know?'*

"Well..." Tei hesitated. He hadn't thought that far ahead. What *should* he ask while Rakariel slept, and their time slowly drifted by? Something she'd said before came back to his mind, the comment that if Avin were to come with them, he'd better know about the gods. Tei, too, was curious about them. How could any once-benevolent beings have allowed the valley to fall as it had, from the world that Avin remembered and Rakariel had come from to the foggy ruin that was all he'd ever known?

"Can you tell me about the gods?"

There was a pause. *'I don't know much — not a lot more than anyone else, really. I was no priest.'* He sensed the ghost's rueful tone. *'I wasn't really much of anything, but apparently it was enough. The gods... it's hard to believe that you don't know about them. I know you don't, but it's still hard to believe.'*

Tei shrugged. "I can't see the city the way you did,

either. So... tell me about them?"
'All right. Where do I start? Let me think...'
* * *

Legend held that they and the world were in some ways almost as one, that they had come into being at its birth uncountable millennia before. They were distant and remote in some ways: the priests usually interpreted their will, and yet that will was also made evident in uncountable ways. Season followed season, peace and plenty granted to the valley and above all those who followed the gods' ways. An oath sworn before them was binding indeed, and even if no other person even knew about it, a severe penalty was inevitably exacted on one who broke such an oath. They governed the passage of life in the valley, of the sun and moon, laid down the laws of nature. Magic such as Rakariel wielded was, in a sense, outside of their domain, and was sometimes viewed with a little suspicion, rumoured in some places to bring ill fortune, though it was not then unheard-of within the valley or without. To those whose prayers were heartfelt and true, and who were willing to give up something in return for that which they sought, they would grant gifts: blessings of a magnitude to match whatever had been offered in return. So it was, Avin recounted with a sigh, that he had found himself knelt within the temple those long years before. For the sake of his young wife and unborn child, for all the protection and good fortune he had been promised they would find if he agreed, he had eventually consented to give up his life in exchange for the gift of a strong talent for magic within his king. His spirit had drifted, freed from his body, as the priests bestowed upon their king the blessing he had sought, one for which the price had been life itself.

"Why would he do that?" Tei asked. "Why would he do that to you?"

'He told me that the country needed a strong king to survive the strife beyond our borders. It needed those who represented it to bear all the power that they could. It didn't help, in the end.' A silent sigh. *'I agreed because he told me that my family's safety and prosperity would be ensured in return for my sacrifice, but he would make no such promises if I didn't agree to help him. But it didn't help. It doesn't mean anything.'*

"We've been safe," Tei whispered, trying with what very little he could to ease the ghost's heavy heart. "It's... not so bad. Not many people live as well as we do. We're careful, so we don't get caught, we don't often get sick — Grandfather is almost the oldest man in the city. That's why we've been mayors since the beginning."

'I suppose I should count my blessings,' Avin said wryly. *'If anyone had any any more.'* He was quiet for a moment. *'You know, Seivi told me before she left that they would be safe. She said no matter what happened, she was certain of it. She was just trying to comfort me — I couldn't leave the temple then — but it's good to know she was at least partly right.'*

"Seivi was the priestess you could talk to, wasn't she?"

'Yes. She was a little younger than me. Not many of them could hear me at all, but she was good at it, and she didn't try to avoid me or send me on to the next life.'

"I thought you couldn't go," Tei said, slightly

confused.

'I can't. Some of them tried it, but there was no power in the ritual. That was quite early on. After that, I only spoke to Seivi. The others were unsettled enough without me making it worse.'

"If she wasn't afraid of you, why were they?" he asked. He knew why *he'd* be afraid of Avin, if their minds hadn't met: a strange voice that only he could hear, sapping his strength, something he knew nothing about... but it had to have been different for the priests. Didn't it?

*'Because I shouldn't have been there. I should have moved on, but I couldn't, and they should have been able to send me on, but they couldn't. It scared them. It scared **me**. There wasn't anything I could do about it, though.'* Though he could see him, Tei was sure he felt the spirit smile in memory. *'She accepted that I couldn't go on and tried to work out why. We were friends, for a while.'* He gave another silent sigh, his lighter mood darkening again. *'Maybe that's what killed her.'*

"She died?"

'She vanished, and she would never have done that. She cared about the temple too much; she always believed in her duty as a priestess. Right before she left, she said she'd tried to tell the high priest something, but he wouldn't listen, so she was going to slip out and go to the palace. She didn't have time to tell me what it was, but she said she'd worked something out, and King Sariven had to know. By then he'd already issued the proclamation asking for the aid of anyone able to determine how to stop what was happening. All she said was that my family would be safe, no matter what

happened, and that she'd come back and explain, but she had to go at once, before things got any worse. When she didn't come back, I thought at first that it would just take a while, that she'd have to stay at the palace while they tried whatever it was she'd thought of. But by the time of the massacre... she had to be dead by then. The monsters must have killed her. Or worse.'

"Worse?" Tei echoed. What could be worse than death at the blades of the vardra?

'I don't know. But I said before that she wasn't the only one to vanish. For all I know, they all ended up like me.' Bitterness was evident in his words, and Tei's eyes widened as he realised what Avin had to mean.

"You can't mean that!"

"Mean what?" asked another soft voice. Tei jumped, looking over at the wreckage again, where Rakariel had sat up, her cloak still wrapped around her. Had he woken her? How long had she been awake?

"He, uh... Avin was talking to me about the gods, and the priests, and the one he could talk to, Seivi. He said she realised something that she thought the king had to know, so she left the temple to try and tell him, and never came back. He... said he wondered if she and the others who vanished or never came back ended up like he did."

Rakariel's eyes narrowed slightly. "Go on."

Tei glanced to the side, instinctively looking for Avin, though he was invisible.

'I don't know what would have happened,' he said. *'But he was willing to kill me. I don't know why he would have killed her, though, or the others. The high priest — Seivi wasn't sure, but she thought he was one of the first to lose the ability to commune with the gods.*

Without him, there wouldn't have been anyone to accept their offerings even if they had agreed to die. Only the highest in the priesthood could accept a life, and they were all at the temple. So they couldn't have done that.' It had been, for a while, the last slender hope he'd had for her life: that he knew, if she were forced to give it up, she'd have to return.

"Uh." Not for the first time, Tei wished that Avin and Rakariel could simply talk directly, the same way he could. Being the intermediary between them wasn't the easiest of tasks, not with a long and complex conversation like the one he'd just held to relay. "He says he doesn't know what would have happened, but since the king was willing to kill him, it wasn't impossible. Except, all of the priests who could accept someone's life were still in the temple. He says not many of them could do that."

"Accept someone's life?"

"Uh-huh. That's how he died, remember? He gave his life so that the king could receive a blessing of magical power." Tei sighed. "I always thought that King Sariven was magnificent. He was a hero — everyone knows how he fought to the last to save us all. Would someone like that really ask Avin to die for him?"

"Kings ask soldiers to die for them all the time," Rakariel said quietly. "But soldiers at least should know the risks they're taking when they sign up, unless they're conscripted." She paused for a moment. "Does he think that the king would have had him killed without the blessing?"

'No, I don't think so,' Avin responded. *'Why would he? I wasn't anyone important, I didn't do anything*

wrong. I was just unlucky.'

"He doesn't think so," Tei relayed. "He wasn't even anyone important."

"Was this Seivi someone important?"

'Not really. She was a young priestess. She didn't have any more influence than any of the other ex-acolytes in the temple, or in the rest of the city. There were lots of them... the only thing that made her different to anyone except me was that she thought she'd worked out was was happening.'

"Did she say what it was?" Rakariel asked, after Tei had finished paraphrasing Avin's words. She doubted it, or he would have told them back at the temple, but if she'd given him even a hint...

"No, he said earlier she just told him she'd figured it out but the high priest wouldn't listen, promised his family would be safe, and left."

Rakariel raised her eyebrows. "How could she promise that?"

'I don't know,' Avin said, soundlessly. *'I think she was just trying to reassure me. I was worried about them.'*

"He thinks she was just trying to reassure him. He couldn't leave the temple then, so he had no idea if they were all right. Anyway, she left to go to the palace and never came back. By the time the vardra got in and killed the rest of the priests, he knew she had to be dead."

"Hm. What, exactly, did she do before she left? If he can tell us anything, anything at all that was even slightly unusual, it might give us a clue to whatever it was she'd figured out."

After several moments of the spirit's silence, Tei

prompted him. "Avin?" The response, when it came, was only slow.

'I don't know. The last time she talked to me before it, we didn't talk about anything different or really important. We were... we were talking about how I died, and why. I remember she seemed to be thinking about something as she left to go to prayers, but I didn't follow her — it would just have unnerved the others. The time after that was the last I saw of her. She came to find me... she seemed very determined. She said she'd spoken to the high priest and he hadn't believed her, but she knew she was right, and her heart was telling her she was right. I believed her — maybe you had to have seen it, but I believed her. She was completely sure, even though none of them could talk to the gods any more. She said she had to see King Sariven and explain to him. She... I remember she promised me my family would be safe, that they would be protected. That was the last thing she ever said to me. She never came back.'

Tei took a deep breath before relaying what he'd just heard, adding bits here and there from all they'd said before. Rakariel listened quietly, intently, until he'd finished.

"How did she think she could see the king so easily?"

Tei was ready for that question. "He'd already said that anyone with any ideas about how to stop what was happening could go straight to him."

"Hm. And all they talked about the time before was how he died? That was all?"

There was a pause, as if Avin had reflexively nodded without realising that he had to say something, that not even Tei could see him.

'Yes. That's all we talked about, other than how we both were that day. Nothing special or really strange had happened that day, so that was it.'

"He says that's all they talked about, other than what had happened that day, and nothing strange had happened at all. Everything was the same as the other days before it."

Rakariel frowned, tapping the fingers of her left hand in a quick rhythm against her knee. "But after that, she seemed to be thinking about something. Had she been thinking before?"

'Not the same way, no,' Avin answered, and Tei shook his head.

"He said earlier she'd been trying to work out what was wrong for a while, but she wasn't thinking about anything in the same way before they talked that day, at least not that he could tell."

"Then maybe it was something to do with what they said," Rakariel said. "Either he's forgotten something, or it was something to do with what they talked about — with how he died."

'But how could it be?' Avin demanded. *'I did everything I had to! Everything!'*

"He wants to know how it could be," Tei said, a little slowly, surprised by the spirit's sudden outburst and yet understanding it in almost the same moment. "He says he did everything he had to... he really means it."

She sighed. "Maybe that's not the point. The point is, something to do with how or why he died let her work something out. Something that made her think things could be set right, something so important that she was willing to try and see the king over it even after she failed to convince her own high priest. His death *must* have been linked to what was happening in the valley, or at least she must have thought so, and how certain she was makes me think she must have been right." More likely to be right than she or Tei were, at any rate, both guessing blindly with far too little knowledge of what had happened those centuries before. "Whatever it was, she thought it was very important. Important enough that it might be the key to it all."

Tei nodded, slowly, thinking it over. What Rakariel said was true: something in her conversation with Avin must have prompted the long-dead priestess into the train of thought that had led to her answer, and if all they'd spoken of was his death, then only that could have been the link. Without all the knowledge Seivi must have had, it was their only real clue.

"Exactly how did he die?" Rakariel asked, while Tei was still thinking. He shrugged, looking slightly to the side to await Avin's response.

'I agreed to give up my life,' Avin related slowly. *'I accepted I was going to die, and I understood it. As long as my family were safe, that was all that mattered. Then I died. No-one touched me, no-one harmed me. I remember feeling that everything would be all right in the moment before my body hit the floor. Then I was just... confused.'*

"He agreed to give up his life, he says. He accepted it and understood it, and all that mattered was that his family were safe." Tei wasn't sure whether he'd be able to do that, either, facing down his inevitable fate and making his peace with it as calmly as it seemed

Avin had. Could he have agreed to the same thing? To protect someone else — his sister, his family? "He says he just died, then. No-one hurt him, no-one touched him. He remembers feeling that everything would be all right, just before... just before his body hit the floor. After that, he says, he was just confused." He paused, glancing aside again to speak to Avin. "Why confused?"

*'I **had** just died. There I was, still in the temple. It's not something I can even describe. I was **dead**.'*

"Oh. Because he was dead. Uh, sorry."

'It's all right. If there really is something about it that can help you, you can ask me anything. All I want is for this to be over... for you to all be free.'

To that, Tei could say nothing.

"That's understandable." Unable to tell he was speaking, Rakariel spoke before Avin had quite finished. "So he accepted that he was going to die. He gave up his life, and the gods must have accepted it, or he'd have lived. Yet he couldn't move on..." She paused, thinking. "...Why did he feel everything would be all right?"

Tei blinked. It seemed like an odd detail to catch on to.

'I don't know,' Avin told her. *'I held onto that feeling for a long time... but it was wrong. It was so strong, though... it let me carry on for so long. Sometimes I wonder why I didn't lose hope long ago.'*

"He doesn't know. He held onto the feeling for a long time, but it was wrong. It was strong enough to let him carry on all this time, though, he says."

"Avin," Rakariel asked, each word careful and deliberate, "why did you die?"

Tei thought he could sense Avin's confusion, something that was borne out by the tone of his voice, such as it was, heard only in his young descendant's head. *'I told you.'*

"He says he told you. He-"

'You know,' Avin mused, interrupting without realising as Tei fell silent to listen, *'Seivi asked me the same question. I told her it was because the gods took my life, just like Rakariel said. She said she knew, that it meant my sacrifice had been accepted, but she wanted to know **why**. That's when I told her what happened, what King Sariven really asked of me.'*

Tei hesitated, waiting, this time, to see if Avin would say anything more, but there was only silence.

"He says Seivi asked him the same question. He told her the gods took his life and she said she knew, that that meant the sacrifice had been accepted, just like you said, but she still wanted to know why. That was when he told her what King Sariven had really asked of him. Um... you know he said before that the king promised his family would be protected if he did. Die, I mean — for him."

"Yes..." Rakariel frowned again, fell silent, and Tei could only watch. Something in Avin's death had, must have given the priestess the clue she needed. Rakariel was no priestess even in her own homeland, so far away, and could certainly claim no knowledge of these people's half-forgotten gods; she had what Avin had, through Tei, told her to go on. He had given his life, but from all he had said, it had not been for either king or country save in name. And yet, it had been accepted, for he had died. Then there was that feeling he claimed to have had, about which she saw no reason to disbelieve him. Perhaps it had simply been a part of dying: though she was no stranger to death, she knew very little about it, about what awaited beyond the moment when a warrior's eyes closed for the last time, and the handful of revenants she had encountered before had been unwilling or unable to speak with her, lost to evil or to madness, or both. And there was Seivi's promise of the same thing, whether it had been an attempt at reassurance or something more: like that momentary feeling, it had made enough of an impact on Avin that he had remembered it across the centuries and thought to relate it to them. Even in his death, even waiting in the ruins of the temple for help that he could not expect to ever come, he had remembered, and had believed. It was almost as though the lost king's actions had barely mattered, save that they had cost Avin his life: he had neither spoken much of nor seemed to care much for anything beyond his family, and later Seivi; certainly not the man in whose name his life had been forfeited. His feelings about him were clearly mixed, conflicted: he had seemed to have his reservations before they met and certainly did after they had, though it was difficult to say how much his recollections had altered over the years with resentment. There was no way for her to really know, or to know if the implication were even true, particularly with every conversation filtered through Tei, but she wondered if, in those promises of good fortune, there might not also have been an implied threat: that if Avin helped, all would be well, but that if he did not, perhaps safety would have been the opposite of what he and his family would have found. Whether Avin had thought it then, or only now, or whether Rakariel herself was simply overthinking the whole matter and seeing menace where there had been none, she couldn't tell. The fact remained, however, that Avin was willing and able to entertain the fear that the king might have had the vanishing priests killed. Had he, then, been evil, and his subjects' adoration of him merely a glamour cast over them? Yet had it not been the gift of magic that Avin had died for? The king would have been unable to cast such a spell without it — and if he were evil, why would he have fought the oncoming darkness, rather than embracing it?

She shook her head. She was going too far. Still, one thing seemed clear: King Sariven had not been the unblemished hero Tei's people believed. A great many things could change and corrupt a man, she knew that all too well. Perhaps something of that nature had happened. If Avin had died by mortal hand, she would wonder even more whether his death had been but a sign of what was happening. Yet, if the young priestess had thought her king was turning to evil, she surely would not have gone to confront him alone, without even the power of her gods behind her. Was there more to it than that? Were the two things really as inextricably bound as she was beginning to wonder?

Had he made the wrong sacrifice?

Lifting her head a little, she met Tei's curious gaze and realised she would have to explain herself, though she wasn't entirely sure how. Her thoughts were still ill-formed and all too unclear, and she knew far too little about the valley and its history, but it would have to do. It was all she had.

"If Avin had died for his family, what would have happened?" she asked.

"Um. I... don't know," Tei said, frowning slightly in thought. He wished that he knew more, could be more useful than just relaying Avin's words to her. "You mean, if King Sariven hadn't been there at all?"

"Yes."

'I suppose they would have received what I'd have asked for. But all I would have asked was that they be safe.'

"He thinks they'd have got what he'd have asked for, but all he wanted was that they be safe."

Which was what he'd said he'd felt, what the priestess had said before she left: that they'd be safe, and more, that they'd be protected. It was what Tei had told her before, Avin only able to talk to him away from the pool because they were blood relations: that the first mayor of the fallen city had borne Avin's name, been the son he had never had a chance to know. Rakariel knew how unlikely it was that a child born to a woman alone in such desperate times would have lived at all, never mind come to hold the most important position among all the survivors. So many just like him must have died in the weeks, months, and years that had followed the sealing of the valley, and yet that boy had lived on, and his line beyond him. Tei had said that his family had continued to hold the title, such as it was ever since, because they so often escaped danger, so rarely fell sick. She might even have seen evidence of it with her own eyes, for Fayel had healed remarkably well even before Rakariel added her own magic to the healing, her bone set straight and true with no signs of infection or any lingering frailty beyond her obvious difficulty in walking. Was it all down to skill and good fortune, as they believed, or was there something else to it, something more?

"Tei, have your family ever tried to teach anyone else your skills? How you stay alive?"

Tei blinked. "Of course."

"And yet you still do much better than anyone else, don't you?"

"Well, yes." It was true, but then, he and his family had all grown up with it woven throughout their lives, whereas even with the best will in the world they could only teach anyone else for a fraction of that time. Was it any wonder they could never impart all their knowledge? They were skilled, and lucky, they always had been — and for the sake of themselves and everyone else, had to continue to be. "That's why my grandfather is still the mayor."

"He's quite old, isn't he? But he's not really weak or frail. His eyes are still good. He's not sick any more than the rest of you, either, is he?"

"Uh... no..."

"I think," she said, her voice still low, as it had been throughout the conversation, "that Seivi was right. Avin's family — your family — has been protected. I think he must have got what he wished for."

Tei blinked at her again, and he could sense Avin's shock as well, even stronger than his own.

'But how? I mean, that's what I wanted, but — but I didn't...'

Unable to think of much else to say, Tei simply repeated what he'd just 'heard' word for word, before he forgot it.

"He went before the gods and gave his life so that his family would be protected," Rakariel said, a little more firmly. It was fitting together, making sense. She was even beginning to question how she'd been so lucky as to meet Tei before a vardra — and him, grandson of the mayor, before anyone else. Had it been pure chance, or something more? It was only a half-formed speculation, though, and she kept it to herself. "From everything you've — he's — said, it sounds as though that's what would have happened without the king's interference."

'I suppose...' Avin said, and Tei repeated it for himself as well as the spirit.

"As for the king himself..." Rakariel paused, thinking again. "Perhaps something had already begun to change within him. If it was Avin's wish that was granted, then in the eyes of the gods, perhaps it was one more worthy. If he were turning away from them, even only a little, perhaps that was why. All gods are different, but... I cannot imagine those who valued a true heart would be as well-disposed to threats. The king may have angered them by asking Avin to do what he did... perhaps your priestess, Seivi, thought that she could explain something like that, and he would still hear her words."

Perhaps. There were too many maybes for her liking, but it was the best she had. She rarely had the luxury of certainty, often having to make decisions in instants that could prove to affect anything, and potentially never knowing for sure whether she had been right or wrong. She was struggling to understand what she could, but she had no way of knowing if her guesses were true. Still, it gave her, at the least, somewhere to start. If the valley's gods had grown angry with its ruler and withdrawn their protection from the land, it would have left it wide open to other evils, which could have wreaked any amount of havoc... and perhaps, if the young priestess had been able to persuade the king to atone, they could once again have been banished. Whether some evil had touched his darker side, or whether she had simply not been heard or believed, the consequences of Avin's death could have been the beginning of all that had eventually happened.

She caught Tei nodding slowly, eyes wide and expression thoughtful, as she tried to stand up, using her uninjured arm to push herself to her feet and catching her breath as the motion sent a wave of dull pain through her stiff leg. That would never do: how could she protect anyone, even herself, when she'd be lucky to manage a limping run, probably couldn't even properly draw her bow? She would have to spend yet more time on healing herself and recovering from the strength she would need to spend on it, time she could ill afford to lose. It had to be at least the beginning of the fifth day since she had entered the shadowed valley, leaving the sun behind, and given how much healing Tei had exhausted her, it was likely she had actually slept well past the sunrise. Nine days, she thought. Nine days in total, which left her with only four already, another of which she might now have to sacrifice on herself. Could she do it...?

"Are you all right?" Tei asked, concerned. Though her worn leathers looked largely undamaged, her stiff, awkward movements and her grimace as she got up made it clear that she was in pain — and that was without the expression of dread she had worn for the moment after...

"I'll be fine," Rakariel said, forcing her fears back

into the shadows of her mind. "I need to heal myself before we go on." Experimentally, she lightly pressed a hand to her injured leg, and had to force herself not to jerk it away. The bruise below must have gone deep, and remembering the impact, she knew she was lucky that it hadn't been worse.

"What happened?" He walked over as he spoke, quiet steps rippling the chill water until he stepped out onto a fallen plank, looking at her. She shrugged, passing it off.

"I had to jump down after you. I couldn't see where I'd be falling to, and I hit something."

"Is there anything I can do?" he asked. A faint smile crossed her face, lightening her expression a little.

"No. But thank you." Gritting her teeth slightly, she sat back down on her cloak, injured leg stretched out straight. Her left side still protested where she'd slammed into the steps on the way down, and her shoulder ached, though she still couldn't think what she'd done to it. She wasn't sure how much strength she'd have to use. There was a chance that she would only need to sit for a while afterwards: the spells she knew for healing herself were more complex and subtle than the two she'd used on Tei and Fayel, and would take less of her strength to produce the same effect. Slowly, focusing inward until everything else became an irrelevance she was only peripherally aware of, she pictured the heavy, leather-bound book in her mind as she always did, pinning the spell she wanted to its worn page, forcing each hard-earned symbol into clarity before she spoke.

Tei listened as Rakariel's voice echoed once again

with magic. It was different to the two healing spells she'd used on him, one of which she'd taught to Fayel, but it also seemed similar, many of the same rhythms and patterns appearing, possibly even the same 'phrases' in a couple of places. If that was right, and that was something that would be rather hard for him to test. It was longer, too, he thought, and almost seemed more intricate, somehow. Did that mean that she was better at it, or that it was a more powerful spell — or both? If she travelled alone, as it seemed she must, then perhaps that wasn't too surprising. Alone, she wouldn't need to heal anyone else nearly as often as she might herself.

When the spell ended, she sighed, pain replaced with weariness once again. Slowly, experimentally, she got to her feet, swaying slightly. No, it would be too unwise to leave like this, but also so, so very unwise to stay, the lightstone on her brow slowly but surely giving up its strength in her defence until, at the last, it would have spent its all. Without the sun, it would remain dark forever. Without even the hope of ever reaching the sun again, her light would be gone forever — and without her light, her life would end, another victim of all that waited in the dark.

"Rakariel?" Tei ventured, watching her. Something was wrong — had her healing failed? Her stance seemed improved, despite the swaying, but something about the way she stood and the dread that had touched her expression made him wonder what had gone wrong. "Did — did it work?"

"Hmm?" She forced the fear out of her voice with an effort of will. "Of course it worked. I'm just tired."

"Then what's wrong?" He was almost surprised at

his own daring, feeling foolish for asking even as she spoke. If he needed to know, she would surely tell him. But instead of growing angry or brushing his concern aside, she only sighed, replying softly.

"This is the fifth day. We have four more... four more before my light goes out." She didn't want to say it, to have to speak the words aloud and acknowledge them, and somehow the fact that she was whispering made it still worse. Still, she went on. "I have to rest before we leave again, and we're running out of time."

Tei swallowed. He wanted to tell her that it would be all right, somehow, to convince himself of the same thing. Without her miraculous light, she had already told him she would be helpless, and it was clear she feared its loss more than anything he had yet seen. Even if he could somehow save her from death in that moment, get them both to safety once again, what then? They wouldn't be able to go on, and he couldn't imagine her turning back, living the quiet, hidden life of his people. Nor could he be sure they would even make it back...

"...It will be all right," Rakariel said quietly, hoping that her words would prove true. "Four days is a long time. It may still be enough." She shook her head slightly in an attempt to dispel the dark thoughts clouding her mind, every shadow in the room jerking sharply back and forth in time to the motion. "See if you can recite the part of the spell I taught you. Don't let the magic build, though."

Tei nodded, looking up at the ceiling for a moment, then down again, closing his eyes. The bold strokes on the pale, creased paper were still sharp in his mind, the sounds that went with them still more so. He tried the first, only to find his pitch was off; settled himself internally and tried again, this time able to both hear and feel the faint, exhilarating reverberation of magic echoing in his quiet voice. The second followed easily, and it was an effort not to chain them together as felt only right, to let the power of each one fade before he spoke the next. He felt as though he was beginning to gain a sense of how the entire spell should feel, its structure building in his mind. The next few syllables dropped easily into place, continuing it for all that he was forced to leave each to fade unfulfilled, and he found himself smiling almost foolishly as the resonance of the sixth died away. He'd done it, he'd felt it — it had been working, each one right, each one in place. Rakariel raised her eyebrows slightly, but he didn't read condemnation in her look, and held her gaze.

"That was good," she said, keeping her voice neutral. In truth, she was more surprised than she wanted to show: she hadn't expect him to remember quite so well, the faint trip of his voice that would have linked the words of magic with a snap and a crack something she could never have taught him. Perhaps it had been luck, though most likely not, but either way, it wouldn't do to boost his confidence too far. If the caster grew overconfident, it was all too easy for disaster to result with any form of magic, but battle magic was worst of all. Pared down and finely tuned over countless generations of magical study, a single misspoken syllable could twist it into another form altogether. "How did it feel?"

Tei thought for a moment, a frown crossing his face. He could remember the feeling, but how could he express it, something unlike anything he'd ever felt before? Perhaps, he thought, he could at least talk around it. Even if he couldn't describe the sensation itself, perhaps Rakariel would understand what he'd felt. "It seemed to make sense, while I was saying it. I don't know what it meant, but it seemed to go together — it felt right. Does that make sense?"

She nodded. "Yes. That's good... it means you likely have some natural skill. But that also means you have to be even more careful." Her direct, intent gaze transfixed him, and he wondered if she spoke from experience, whether her own or that of someone else she had known. "Don't try to do anything other than recite the spell as you learned it. Anything. Just because it feels natural to change something doesn't mean that the end result won't kill you — it makes it *more* likely, when you end up loosing magic that you don't have the strength or skill to control. Do you understand?"

Tei swallowed. The tone of her voice left no room for doubt. "I understand."

"Good." She resettled herself on the wreckage with a quiet sigh, bowing her head for a moment. "I'll tell you the next part when we rest tonight. For now... I just need to wait a little longer."

"All right," Tei whispered. "Should I try to get the trapdoor open?"

Rakariel looked up, at the trapdoor and the two steps still hanging below it, supported by a pair of wooden posts, her light throwing them all into sharp relief. "If Avin says the coast is clear, it's probably a good idea. Wait until he's certain."

Tei nodded. "Avin?"

'I'm going now.' He felt a chill run through him, one caused from within his body rather than without,

and the spirit was gone.

"He's going to look," he told Rakariel, and seated himself on the wreckage with a sigh, rubbing his arms. It was surprisingly cold in the still, dark cellar — much colder than he'd thought, when he'd just been healed. A creak signified Rakariel shifting her weight, and he looked back at her to see her opening one of her packs and taking out some more of the strange travellers' bread she'd shared with him before. She broke off a portion about the same size as the previous one had been and held it out to him with a faint smile.

"Here. We both need to keep our strength up."

"Thanks," Tei whispered back, finding himself smiling in response. His own food had got as wet as everything else he was carrying, but it would probably still be good for a little while. He checked the pocket that held it and took out a few pieces of fish, rather wetter and softer than it had been — no bad thing, save that it would no longer keep half as well. Sorting it out into roughly equal portions, he offered one to Rakariel, which she took with quiet thanks. They ate in silence, and for a short time afterwards they could only wait. There was no way they could even tell how soon Avin would return.

CHAPTER 13
Brief and Fragile Peace

Not long after, something startled Tei into lifting his head. He tilted it slightly as he listened to a voice that only he could hear, and Rakariel watched, waiting to let him pass on what he'd been told in his own time.

"...They've moved on again," he said eventually. "They're further on — he thinks they don't think we stayed here. There are five of them gathered at the end of the street... we'll have to be careful when we leave." He was almost surprised by the equanimity with which he could speak of it. Though the thought of the vardra lying in wait to ambush them still scared him, as it should anyone with any sense, while he was closed in safety with Rakariel, dealing with them didn't seem impossible any longer. Somehow, it seemed as though it were merely a dangerous problem that they could find a way around, rather than the certain death he would have known it to be just days before. Perhaps it was her attitude rubbing off on him; she certainly nodded with a similar equanimity.

"Good. Avin, keep an eye on the street. Warn us if anything happens." She paused, looking up once again. "Do you think you can get up there on your own, Tei?"

"I think so," he answered. "If the steps hold. If they don't, I'll have to find something strong enough to push the trapdoor open with before we can get out, but I think I should be able to do it."

"Good," Rakariel said calmly, and he wondered what she would have said if it hadn't been possible.

With her calm air, with all that she'd done so far, he was sure she would have found another way, somehow. He watched as she slowly stood, testing her range of motion and seeming quietly pleased at her regained flexibility, with no sign of lingering pain. She picked up her cloak, draping it about her shoulders and lifting her packs with one hand before stepping slowly off the wreckage of the stairs and into the pool. Her steps caused the light's reflection to shimmer and waver on the walls as she made her way to the far end of the cellar, where a handful of flagstones still showed above the water, and turned around on that dubious patch of dryness to give him light and, perhaps, see what he did.

As he had back at the temple, Tei unhooked his coiled rope from its anchor around his waist, taking out the hook and tying it onto the end. He tested the knot, then took a couple of paces back from the stairs, gauging the distance, and flung it up. It sailed cleanly through the gap between the two remaining steps, hooking onto the back of the bottom one as he slowly pulled it back, and Rakariel noted abstractedly that he had quite a good aim with it, wondered how many uses it had in his strange, skulking life in the ruined city.

The stair creaked alarmingly as Tei leaned back, slowly entrusting more of his weight to the rope, then pulling on it. Despite the worrying sound, the old wood held, and he stepped closer, letting his rope hang vertically, looking up somewhat nervously for a moment before gripping it as high as he could reach and jumping up. The first moment was always the worst part, as he put his full weight on it for the first time, his feet off the floor: if his anchor gave way, he'd fall, and it could well land on him — but still it held as he trapped the rope between his feet and hung there for a moment, gently turning and swinging back and forth slightly. As long as he was quick and careful, it seemed as though it would be all right.

He was only still for a moment before beginning to climb. The longer he hung in place, he knew, the harder he would find it to move on. Pulling himself up, he lifted his left hand first, then snapped his right up to join it, finally bringing his feet up and trapping the rope between them once again. Moving as quickly as he could, it didn't take long for his reaching hand to touch the rough-grained wood of the step, and brought himself up as close as he could while still holding only the rope. The next part would be the hardest: he had to get high enough to reach over, while maintaining his grip. There was nothing he could brace his feet on to either side: all he had was the rope and the steps it was attached to. Tugging himself up in a quick move, he flung his right arm forward, managing to grab the back of the step, and reached up quickly with his left to grab the one above, the rope jerking beneath him as he pushed against it, his feet slipping slightly. It had worked, though: he was on the stairs! Gritting his teeth, he pushed himself up one last time, getting both hands to the back of the top step and his knees, at last, on the lower one. His head was pressed practically flat to the step to avoid hitting it on the trapdoor, but he was up there, and for a moment, could even relax.

Twisted a bit awkwardly, Tei looked at the trapdoor from the corner of his eye. There was no latch or bolt from this side, and he hadn't remembered any above, which meant all he needed to do was push. Slowly, carefully at first, he straightened his back a little, testing the resistance of the heavy, reinforced wood. It was difficult in the cramped space, and the trapdoor heavier than he remembered, but he could only push harder, reflexively tightening his grip on the back of the step. The stairs creaked again, and suddenly, with a jerk that made him think for a moment that he was about to fall, the trapdoor gave, snapping upward a fraction before sticking in place again. Encouraged, Tei put more of his limited strength into it, rewarded by the trapdoor lifting slowly further, accompanied by the sound of something heavy sliding in the room above. At first he froze, almost ducking back, before realising that there had to be something on it, something he was moving away; that that was why it was so much heavier than he remembered. Heart still beating a touch faster, he forced himself to straighten up the rest of the way, the trapdoor growing steadily easier to move the higher he lifted it until his head and shoulders were showing above the level of the floor, his arms straight. Determined, Tei gripped the stone-edged sides of the hole, and somewhat awkwardly crawled out, twisting as he did to catch the trapdoor before it could fall and make a sound.

He paused there for a moment to look around, his legs still inside the hole and the trapdoor resting on his lap as he sat on the kitchen floor. The dull grey daylight diffused in along with the fog, all the windows shattered, their glass scattered across the floor. Every stick of furniture had been smashed; the vardra had even made an effort to destroy the heavy kitchen counter, and half an upturned table rested at an angle across the trapdoor's hinges. Scrambling to his feet, he held the ring of the trapdoor with one hand and pushed the table the rest of the way off it, then leaned it back against the table's one remaining leg. Nudging a couple of shards of glass away with his foot, Tei knelt again, looking down into the cellar, where Rakariel had crossed back to the wreckage to look up at him from beneath the dangling rope, her light shining out into the kitchen.

"Can you climb up?" he whispered to her. The response was immediate, if not entirely certain.

"I think so."

She didn't know whether or not he'd be able to pull her up if she couldn't climb, and she was wary of the sense of physical well-being, coupled with lingering mental tiredness, that remained from her healing of herself. She couldn't wait, however: there was no choice but to try. The only other option would be to wait longer in the cellar, drawing ever nearer to the time at which her light would run out — ever nearer to the end. She reached up to the rope, lifting herself as she'd seen Tei do, momentarily relieved as the injuries she'd had failed to protest, only her leg twinging very slightly. That bothered her, but there wasn't time to dwell on it, particularly not partway up a rope. Hand over hand, she struggled to climb, fighting for every inch of height. Though she was stronger than Tei, he had skills she didn't share.

Looking down at her, Tei wondered if he should offer to pull her up, though she seemed to be making it, if slowly and struggling for every small step. He leaned into the hole, bracing himself with his left hand on the first step, and reached down towards her, right hand about level with the top of the rope. It was as far as he dared risk going without potentially falling in on top of her. As she came within reach, Rakariel grabbed his hand, and he fought to pull her up. It somehow seemed a lot harder than when she'd been on the end of his rope outside the temple, the mist-hidden vardra racing across the rooftops to attack them, even though he knew her weight couldn't possibly have changed since then.

With her free hand, Rakariel grabbed the bottom step, helping him by boosting herself up on it. Tei pulled with renewed effort, dragging her forwards and up until she, too, was kneeling on the bottom step, and he could finally relax. Right hand still gripping his wrist, Rakariel looked up at him.

"Thank you," she murmured, releasing him and straightening up. Her hand dropped below the step, finding the rusted hook by feel and freeing it to hand back to him. Even as he took it, she stood, stepping up and out of the cellar, leaving him free to stand and pull up his rope. He re-coiled it with practised ease, looping it over his arm to untie the knot that held the hook on and tucking it away before fixing the rope back into its position around his waist, where it would be ready within moments if he needed it. For a moment, he looked back into the blackness of the cellar — a moment that was cut off by Rakariel carefully lowering the trapdoor back into place.

"Now what do we do?" he found himself asking as she looked at him. With a quiet sigh, she crossed to the inside wall, her footsteps crunching slightly on broken glass.

"We give Avin a little more time to scout ahead, then move on." Hand on the wall, she frowned at the doorway that led to the rest of the house, a dark portal into the unknown with its door torn from its hinges by the vardra's murderous rage. A heartbeat later, she started towards it, moving cautiously. Something about her walk, about the way her fingertips trailed along the wall caught Tei's attention. It seemed almost out of place somehow, making her look more weary than she'd appeared from in front. He didn't comment on it, quietly following her through the dining room where they'd entered the house — as ruined as the kitchen had been — and back into the hall where yesterday, so long before, he'd run to the door only to be stopped dead by Avin's silent shout of warning.

Rakariel unfastened her loosely-rolled cloak and knelt on the floor to roll it up more tightly, strapping it securely into place while the packs were still on her back. It was clear she knew the routine so well she no longer even needed to be able to see to avoid bow and quiver or to use the buckles that held it in place, tightening them to their proper length automatically. That done, she frowned slightly, experimentally angling her shoulder back and forth again as if trying to decide whether the way she'd twisted had hurt or not. Her hand drifted to her left side, pressing lightly, then down to her right leg.

"I need to rest a little longer," she whispered in response to Tei's quizzical look. "The magic's still affecting me. I still don't know what I can really do." With a quiet sigh, she shifted into a sit, and Tei settled down on the floor as well. The lightstone showed a scene of devastation that he couldn't help but gaze across, worried by the frenzied destruction the vardra had wrought when they had once again failed to find their prey. If they managed to corner him and Rakariel... he didn't want to think about that. He focused on her instead as she pulled a fold of cloth from her bandanna down to half-cover the lightstone, cutting the amount of light that escaped into the hallway, potentially to betray them. Once again, he realised, she was ready in a way she hadn't quite been down in the cellar, an air of heightened awareness and easy poise settled across her. Her expression, too, was back to its usual set: not aggressive, but alert, aware, with no more sign of her thoughts than the faint tiredness that had always characterised it when they weren't actively fighting or running. It could have nothing to do with actual exhaustion; she'd looked that way from the first moment that he met her.

After a little, she stood again, stretching.

"That's as good as I'm going to get for now. Which way is the palace?"

"Uhh..." Tei hesitated for a moment, thinking. Which way *was* it? He wasn't even sure which way they were facing. Thinking back to the road they'd been on before the vardra had seen them, he placed himself relative to it, remembering the turns of their rush into and through the building, their flight across the gardens. He was in one of the several formerly rich districts, typically poor hiding places and largely avoided, and the palace was... "That way," he whispered, pointing. She looked at the angle of his hand and nodded.

"Let's go. Avin should notice when it looks like we're about to leave."

Tei returned the nod and crept ahead, down to the end of the hall. The door there had been ripped from its hinges, lying splintered but intact on the floor. Cautiously, he padded around it and up to the doorframe, glancing out under the shelter of the roofed porch as the last faint light from behind him winked out. Rakariel crept up behind him, keeping close to the wall, and for a moment they waited.

'You're moving on?' came Avin's voice, sounding as though it had come from a little way ahead of him. It was hard for Tei to remember that he wasn't actually hearing a sound.

"Avin's here," he whispered over his shoulder, then turned back to the unseen spirit, keeping his own voice to the shaped breath that seemed to be all Avin needed to hear him. "Yes, we are. We have to keep going to the palace. Is it safe?"

'For now.' Avin's tone sounded worried. *'I'll go ahead. Keep going as straight as you can, and don't follow the roads. They seem to be watching crossroads.'*

Tei nodded, twisting back to speak to Rakariel. "We'll have to keep cutting through buildings," he whispered. "He'll go ahead, but he said we should go as straight as we can, and keep off the roads. They seem to be watching crossroads."

"Like any good guardsman," Rakariel murmured blackly. It didn't surprise her, particularly now that she knew they were intelligent. The crossroads would be where they'd be able to see furthest, only the fog blocking their vision, and sound would be funnelled along the streets towards them in the city's deadened silence. Though the fog muffled it, it was so quiet in the empty valley that she didn't doubt for a moment anything too much louder than a whisper would carry at least far enough, just as Tei had warned her when they first met. "Let's keep going, then."

* * *

The next several hours were fraught with tension as Tei picked his way through ruined house after ruined house, sometimes having to turn back when he couldn't find an exit he couldn't be sure would be silent, other times warned off by Avin, having to detour around vardra lying in wait all too close. Though she knew the necessity of it, Rakariel subconsciously resented each step off their straight-line path, each moment passed in waiting for an answer: was it safe? Could they move? Need they turn back once again? She didn't speak of it, though, didn't let the additional tension show, and somehow, miraculously, they managed to continue avoiding the danger that awaited them until after all too short a time the light began to fade from the gently drifting mists.

"It's getting dark," Tei whispered to Rakariel, looking out from behind a ragged and half-rotten curtain onto a flooded road. "We should find somewhere to rest."

Though she was reluctant to agree, she nodded. He was right. They couldn't travel in pitch blackness, and with the lightstone lighting up the fog, they'd be an instant and obvious target for every vardra for miles around. Neither she nor Tei could hope to survive that.

"...You're right."

Noticing something in her tone, he glanced at her. Was that the same dread he'd heard before, some deeply buried fear? She looked troubled, but seemed to shake it off just moments after meeting his eyes, as if to tell him it was nothing.

"We'll keep going until we find somewhere secure," she said. "You should be the judge of that."

Tei nodded. He knew as well as she did that they

couldn't travel in the night, that they'd have to stop and wait for the dawn. But what was it that she'd said before: that they were on the fifth day? If that was true, and this was its end, then when they awoke it would be the sixth... and that would leave them with only three to go. Even Rakariel was beginning to grow worried, however she tried to hide it. Was it possible? Could she really do it?

Could her determination let either of them do otherwise?

Shaking his head, Tei left the room and slipped out of the warped, half-open front door, Rakariel following behind him. They'd reached a better area, at least to his way of thinking: one that had once been full of shops, small and close together with housing stacked two floors above them. There would be a safe-house nearby somewhere, if he could only remember where...

He crossed the street slowly, made his way along past a couple of shopfronts before finding one that looked as though they could slip through, wading through ankle-deep water in the fading light. Behind him, Rakariel struggled to move as quietly as he was, lifting her feet only slightly off the ground and moving them slowly through the water to avoid making it splash. She was repeatedly thrown, as even Tei himself occasionally was, by the way that the cobbled street had sunken and warped over the years, leaving the footing treacherous even without the slime that coated the underwater cobblestones. She wouldn't want to have to run on it even if it were out of water — even more than she ever wanted to run in general. To turn and run meant turning her back, and that meant giving all that lurked in the darkness a chance to catch up, a chance to strike. Eyes fixed on Tei in the gathering gloom, she followed him inside the building, its floors, too, flooded to the ankle, squishing softly underfoot. They made their way gingerly through and found themselves in a narrow alley, one that might once have been gravelled, but now seemed made of mud beneath the water. Rakariel suspected it had once been a combination of weeds and refuse, but all that really mattered was the way that it hindered their steps, sucking gently at them and drifting in lighter swirls on the dark surface of the water as they carefully edged through it.

Picking his way along the alley, Tei's expression brightened as he saw a set of steps, rising just high enough to be visible over the level of the water. A house with steps meant a raised floor, and this whole area was flooded — somewhere dry within it was bound to have been made safe at some point. He unconsciously picked up his pace slightly, feeling his way through the murky water with one balancing hand on the wall just in case, and Rakariel registered it almost before she'd actually realised which building they were headed for. It was a poky thing, squashed like an afterthought between two slightly broader ones, nothing remarkable about it to her eye until she, too, noticed the steps and realised that there was a chance it might actually be dry inside.

The single shutter looked to be closed tight as they drew level with it, as did the door. Creeping quietly to the window, Tei began feeling gingerly in the dimness for any hidden bolt or latch, tugging very gently at the shutter in case it was free and might swing open. Rakariel, meanwhile, checked the door: though heavy planks had been nailed across it, none seemed fastened to the wall, and she remembered again how impossible it was for the vardra to hold things, or perform delicate motions like turning a doorknob. They wouldn't be able to open a door or window towards themselves, short of getting their blade-like claws so firmly stuck in it that the effort of simply freeing themselves pulled it open. Testing, she gently turned the handle — recently-oiled, by the feel of it, and there was another clue — and gave it a light pull.

Despite the damp, the door swung quietly open, revealing a dark and empty space beyond that might once have been a shop's storeroom. Rakariel caught herself instinctively reaching for the lightstone, and stopped her hand before it could lift above her waist. No, not until they were safely inside, the door shut behind them. Avin would have warned Tei if there were any danger. She glanced over to him to see him already watching her, having heard the quiet sound of the door opening, seen it in his peripheral vision. With a quick, beckoning gesture, she stepped inside, holding it as he followed and gently closing it behind them. Darkness descended over the room, and at last she freed the lightstone, tucking the fold of cloth back behind it. Cool white light illuminated an empty room, a few old boxes piled in one corner. A single door led through to the other side of the building, just slightly ajar, only a thin line of blackness visible at the open edge to hint at space beyond. Turning, Rakariel saw the door to the outside world had been reinforced on the inside as well, a pair of heavy bolts making an additional defence. She slid them quietly closed before looking back at Tei, who had crossed to the other door and opened it to peer through. There was evidently no danger there, as he stepped in without hesitation, and she followed.

The front room had clearly been a shop, as she'd more than half expected. A sturdy counter ran along the wall to their left, a staircase in the corner behind it. The front windows and door were securely barred, and a few dust-covered objects still remained on the ancient shelves. Tei wandered along behind the counter, looking down at a fairly good-sized pile of cloth made up into a makeshift bed. It was in good shape, and he wondered how frequently the safehouse was used. The area was unpleasant to travel through, but not inhospitable; there were plenty of things that would thrive in the shallow water and the decay near it. Anyone trekking into it to forage would be able to stay here for the night, giving them two days to gather on their way in and out. Someone had clearly taken time and care over it, and he frowned a little, wondering who it was likely to be. There were three different families he knew of on the outskirts of the area; it could have been any or even all of them.

"Did someone live here?" Rakariel whispered, and he shook his head.

"I don't think so. But they probably come here often — there'll be fish in the water here, and other things." He sat down on the blankets, stretching his legs out. "I'd see what I could find if I had more time."

Rakariel nodded thoughtfully, taking her packs off and sitting beside him. Though he'd been eating it for several days running, she still noticed his eyes light up as she brought out her bread to share between them. Setting the piece she gave him in his lap, he checked his own food, pulling out a strip and sniffing it, then cautiously licking the edge.

"...It's still all right for now," came the whispered

verdict. He passed it on to her, and once again they shared the strange meal of waybread and dried rat, sheltered first by barred doors and windows and again by the old shop counter, lit by the unwavering glow of the lightstone.

Once they had eaten, Rakariel unfolded her cloak again, draping it around her shoulders as she settled against the wall, leaving the blankets to Tei. Though he looked too wakeful to easily sleep, he settled down readily enough once she had, lying on his side with the topmost blanket pulled over him.

"Rakariel?" he asked, just moments after she'd pulled the cloth over her lightstone, returning the room to darkness.

"Hm?" came the response, just barely above the edge of hearing.

"How much more is there to that spell — the one you were teaching me?"

Rakariel frowned for a moment, running through it in her mind. Though it was battle magic, condensed into the shortest possible form over centuries of use and refinement, and by the greatest sorcerers rather than simple warriors like herself, it was still longer than the six syllables they'd got through so far.

"You've almost half of it, if you remember all I've shown you." She paused for a moment before continuing, grudging approval in her voice. Though she was pleased and impressed by his success, she also feared it, or what it could lead to. Even if he spoke the spell correctly each time, if his newfound mastery of magic left him overconfident, made him think he could fight when in truth he could only run, she might not be able to save him. Yet he deserved some praise, good as he was proving to be. "You're learning quickly."

Tei smiled. Though she couldn't see the expression in the dark, she could hear its effects in his voice. "Really?"

"Yes. You have a strong focus and a good memory. But if you practice while I'm sleeping, remember... don't let the magic build. Not even a little."

He frowned. He knew he shouldn't risk casting the entire spell, but would chaining a couple of the syllables together really do so much harm? "Why not? It was all right when Fayel did."

"Yes," Rakariel agreed, "but Fayel was learning a healing spell, not battle magic. Every piece of that spell has been put together like any good weapon: to be as fast, effective, and easy to use as possible. Some parts of it could be partially effective even on their own: I don't know enough about even battle magic to tell you which parts are key and which aren't. All I've ever done is use the whole spell as I learnt it."

"Oh." He hesitated. "How did you learn?"

She sighed. "A long time ago. I... used to ride with a group of mercenaries: we sold our skills to anyone who needed good warriors quickly. It was a good life, for a while. One of our number was a battlemage. He taught me to read most of the symbols of magic, and helped me learn a few minor spells like the one I'm teaching you." Her mouth crooked upward momentarily in a quick, faint smile. "I was a very bad student until my life depended on it. I never really thought I'd need anything other than my bow... and as long as I was with the others, I didn't, really. We each had our own specialities."

"Why'd you leave?"

"I didn't." She closed her eyes, bowing her head again. "They died."

"I'm sorry," Tei said, softly. She shook her head.

"It's all right. You weren't to know."

Silence fell across the room, as blanketing as shadow. Rakariel leaned her head back against the wall, looking at the unseen ceiling above, subconsciously aware that the lightstone still glowed as bright as ever beneath its concealing cover. Though its light was at hand, the thoughts Tei had unintentionally raised still left her unwilling to sleep.

"I'll teach you a little more tonight if you want," she said eventually, the sound of her quiet voice louder in the silence than she had expected. Without waiting for a reply, she straightened up, lifting the cloth over the lightstone halfway and lighting up the room once more. She knew what his answer would be, and sure enough, the sudden light caught him already halfway through sitting up, blinking rapidly as his dazzled eyes adapted. He looked eager to learn, and not really tired — not surprising given how long they'd had to rest earlier. Tei's gaze followed her as she stood, retrieving the crumpled paper that bore the spell's symbols upon it and flattening it out on the countertop. He got to his feet, standing by her side to look at it, and Rakariel tapped the paper with a fingertip.

"So, can you read this now?" she asked.

"Sort of," Tei replied honestly. "They... the symbols represent the sounds you were teaching me, but they're not really how I think of it in my head."

A faint smile crossed her face again. It was about the answer she'd expected, and the feeling one she found familiar, one she'd struggled with herself. "Well, you'll just have to learn them anyway. When I was learning, I was told there wasn't a language in the world with enough precision to represent the sounds of magic properly. So read it for me. Start... here." She picked a syllable at random, pointing to it. Tei's hesitation was noticeable as he silently counted through the spell before saying the right one out loud, and her smile broadened wryly. He had a long way to go before he'd be able to actually read the spell that was in front of him. Still, given that she only knew a little magic and certainly didn't carry a physical spellbook, it was unlikely to make much difference. Neither of them had enough time to spare for her to teach him even all the basic symbols of magic, let alone the modifiers for things such as tone, length, or transition: the most important thing was making sure that he learned the spell itself.

"I won't teach you the full alphabet of magic. We don't have the time, and learning the spell is more important. But you do need to know the ones that make it up, so pay close attention."

Tei nodded, obedient and slightly chastened, though she knew he'd been paying far closer attention than she had when she first began to learn. "I'll try. They're just so different..."

"I know." She paused. "Well, tell me the spell so far, then. Don't forget to pause between the syllables — you can't let the power build."

His voice only just loud enough to speak the words truly, Tei did as she bade him, having to stop himself from speeding up more than once. It didn't feel right to pause when he was sure he could tell how the sounds had to fit together, sliding and snapping seamlessly into one another, the faint resonance of magic that imbued each syllable waiting to build... and fading denied as he paused before the next.

"Good," Rakariel said, a note of approval in her low voice. "The next part goes like this. Have a look, and tell me what you see." Pausing for a few moments to focus on the spell and bring its memory sharply back to her mind in its full clarity, she inscribed the next three syllables on the paper before turning it slightly towards Tei to allow him to see better.

He frowned, looking at it. What did she want him to look for? The three new symbols were as strange as the other six had been. Or — no, not all of them. Studying them, he realised one was the same as before, or nearly so, its main body the same, but some of the smaller markings different. Surprised, he pointed to it at once.

"That one's almost the same as this one here — *tah* — isn't it?"

Rakariel smiled, and he knew he'd done well. "That's right. It's the same basic syllable, but it's pronounced slightly differently. Things like that are why remembering these symbols is so important — even if you forget the precise inflection of the spell, the symbols will tell you, as long as you can read them. This mark means that it's held for slightly longer, and this one that you'll need to snap into the next syllable at the end. I'll read these for you... listen."

Looking at the paper in front of her, she quietly spoke each syllable in turn, hard-won knowledge keeping her true to the cast. Tei listened intently to her voice, humming with the faint but unmistakable resonance of magic, and tried to fix each sound in his mind as he had the ones before. It wasn't as hard as the first ones had been, each one following from the one that came before, leading into the one after, part of a spoken pattern, as if it were beginning to make sense.

"Your turn," she said quietly once she was done. "Just that part."

Frowning in concentration, he tried it. It took four attempts to get the first one right, and three for the second, but the third came easily, though it seemed that that had just been luck moments later, as he went through it a second time and finished only with the aid of a prompt from Rakariel. She coached him through the new section another five times before switching back to the whole spell, keeping it slow and broken to prevent either one of them from building up too much power. It went by surprisingly quickly, and Tei realised almost with shock how short the spell felt, as if he were already almost at its end, only a little more left to learn.

"What's the last part?" he asked, almost without thinking.

"You want to keep going?"

"There can't be more than three or four more syllables, right? It feels almost closed."

She blinked at him, uncertain of her response for a moment. "...Almost closed?" Even more surprising was that he was right: she'd taught him all but the very last fraction.

"Uh-huh." Tei frowned, trying to work out how to express what he felt about something he hadn't even really known existed until he'd met Rakariel, just a few days before. "It's a pattern. It's about to end soon... isn't it? It feels like it." His voice grew more uncertain as he realised what he was saying, and to who. How could he even know? But it felt right, somehow.

Wordlessly, she nodded, deepening Tei's surprise as he realised that he actually had been right, and wondering whether it even could be simple luck. He'd mastered what she'd taught him surprisingly quickly, and if he had that much of an innate sense for the magic, how much extra danger was she putting him in simply by teaching him? A natural mage with only a little training was more of a danger to both himself and others than either a trained or completely untrained one. With an instinctive feel for the patterns of spellcasting in whatever form he chose to use, but no real sense of either its limitations or of his own, he could all too easily end up experimenting with magic that could hurt or even kill him.

"All right," she said resignedly, Tei's expression quizzical at the resigned tone in her voice and the short silence she'd left as she thought. "This is the last of the spell."

Just as he'd said, she etched a final four syllables onto the paper, completing the lettering that she held in her mind. Wiping the battered quill dry, she tucked it and the ink away again before turning the paper slightly and pushing it a little towards him. "Here. But you can't test it. We're not safe enough here. Keep it as a last resort only — do you understand?"

He nodded silently, and she began on those last four, feeling the familiar sense of a little strength leaving her with each one she spoke, keeping them unconnected even though she knew that to speak them together would drain her slightly less up until the end. To do that, however, she would have to risk speaking almost the entire spell, and it was possible even that would be enough to set a part of it off. If they had been elsewhere, she would have demonstrated the full incantation, but though it was well-refined and surprisingly undemanding, the snap and crack of lightning would draw attention to them even if she managed to avoid setting fire to anything as it struck.

When Tei had at last repeated it all to her satisfaction several times, she sighed. "That's it. It's yours." She paused for a moment. "That last part chooses the target. It'll strike whatever your eyes focus on in the moment you complete the spell, so make sure you don't look at anything other than what you want hit. Understand?"

He nodded, more apprehensive than she might have expected, but less so than she would have liked. Well, she thought, it would do. It would have to.

"Can I practice the whole thing?" he asked, a little tentative.

"Yes," she said. "Just be careful. Don't complete it." She fixed him with a sharp look. "No matter how much you want to or how easy you think it would be."

Abashed, though he hadn't actually thought of it in the slightest, Tei nodded again. "I won't. I promise."

"Good." She pushed the paper gently towards him after a moment. "That's yours now. Be careful with it."

"I will." Taking the paper carefully from the counter, he scrutinised it closely, studying the angular yet flowing symbols inked onto it in Rakariel's slow, careful hand. She'd almost seemed to draw them rather than writing, as though copying from an image she held hidden in her memory. They were linked to the sounds, he knew, but the connection didn't seem instinctive for him, though she made it appear simple. If he could, he'd memorise it, taking to heart the importance of the words she'd spoken. The clear lettering, however foreign, would remind him of exactly what he was supposed to say if he could only understand it.

Rakariel moved back to the wall, settling down again with her head lifted, but her eyes half-closed, listening with half an ear to Tei's slow, not quite stumbling recitation. He was doing well, she thought once again. She still didn't know whether to be pleased by that, or afraid of it. Both knowing the spell and not knowing it could place his life in danger, just being with her put his life in danger far greater than he'd ever faced before, and yet she needed him. She didn't have a hope of succeeding without his guidance, and though she found she liked the companionship, better by far than fighting on alone, she still hated what she was doing — because she knew what it could cost him. She knew what it had cost her, and there was no guarantee Tei might not be forced to pay the same price if he lived at all. It was far too late to change it, though. She hadn't been able to from the start. Perhaps, just perhaps, Avin's legacy would protect him from the worst. She couldn't trust it, didn't dare, but she could hope.

Trying to banish the fruitless thoughts from her mind, she focused on his recitation of the spell again, staying quiet and still against the wall and listening to the resonance of magic, and occasionally its absence as he made a mistake. He went through the entire spell several times more before finally folding the paper carefully and tucking it away, settling back down onto the old bedding. Rakariel glanced briefly at him to make sure he was lying down, then pulled the cloth back against the lightstone, resting her head back against the wall.

"Sleep safe," Tei murmured in the darkness, his somewhat drowsy voice indicating it was from habit, pure and simple. Somehow, she found it oddly cheering.

"You too."

CHAPTER 14

With the End in Sight

Rakariel was the first to awaken as the next day dawned, her dreams unremembered, but leaving her restless and uneasy. She opened her eyes to blackness, forehead resting against her knees, but it didn't leave her even when she lifted her head.

Are you afraid of the dark?

"Mmph." The noise she made was faint, barely even a sound at all, just loud enough to hear: an edgy grumble to remind her that she was awake and alive and still in control, with nothing there other than her, her voice pushing imagination and memory back into the background where they belonged. The pressure against her forehead was no more than the lightstone's circlet, holding it securely in place. She raised her hand, feeling the stone's familiar bulge through the cloth that hid it, resting securely in its simple mounting. As long as it was there, she was safe.

Unless her light had run out...

Fighting back reasonless fear, she lifted the folds of her bandanna slowly, almost hesitantly. A ray of light shone out into the darkness, strong and steady, and she breathed a silent sigh of relief. The lightstone was still with her, cutting through the darkness that surrounded her, letting her go on. Without it, she would be helpless in the shadowed valley... without it, she would die.

Trying to avoid her darker thoughts, at least as much as she could, Rakariel tucked the folded cloth behind the lightstone's circlet once more. She was never without her bandanna now, something that served multiple purposes at once; it had been a part of her normal attire for years. Resisting the urge to scratch beneath it, she slowly surveyed her surroundings, the shadows turning in time to the motion of her head. Her roaming gaze lighted on little of interest: the counter, with empty shelves beneath it; the securely barred door and windows; the shelves along the wall that would once have held goods and now carried no more than a few dusty ornaments. Moving quietly to avoid waking Tei, she shifted to a kneel, pushing her hood back and unfastening her cloak's clasp. Smoothly and economically, almost automatically after all the years she had repeated just those motions each morning, she swung it off her shoulders and rolled it up again, strapping it back in place between her linked packs. Leaving them lying on the floor, she got to her feet, quietly stretching. Neither shoulder nor side pained her at all, and though her right leg protested with the lingering effects of her magic finally gone, it was only faintly, barely even an echo of the pain she'd felt before. Considering how the healing had tired her, she suspected the injury had been worse than she'd thought at the time — but as long as it was healed, that was unimportant. Keeping her steps smooth and quiet, she let herself out from behind the counter and walked around the room, letting the lingering stiffness fade.

One of the ornaments caught her eye, and she stopped by the shelf to look more closely, almost stepping back a moment later, her eyes widening in uncharacteristic surprise. Lifting her hand almost hesitantly, she rubbed dust from a small statuette, revealing the unmistakable sheen of metals and gems.

If it wasn't fake, something like that would be incredibly valuable — what was it doing covered in dust on a shelf of the run-down former shop? Her fingers traced over a necklace next to it, revealing time-dulled but intricately worked silver. It didn't make sense...

It was only after a little that she realised it did, that she shouldn't have been at all surprised. With so few people left alive, the city must have become a vast stockpile of unclaimed riches, the sealed valley preventing looters from ever finding them, the lack of trade rendering them useless to the few survivors. At some point, she mused, someone had evidently bothered to collect them, only to end up leaving their treasure trove on display as simple decoration, never to be touched again. The thick dust proved that no-one had even bothered to look at them for decades, perhaps longer, and a part of her was tempted to take a few of the smaller treasures even as another part hesitated to. She had some wealth of her own, enough to continue her travelling existence for some time, and it was easy enough for her to earn more if she needed to, leaving her with little need to steal from the long-dead collector, or the people who still used the house where he'd left his hoard. On the other hand, if life had taught her one thing, it was that she could never expect what might happen next. No-one would miss what she took, and it would cost her little to carry something so small, an unnoticeable weight compared to what she already bore.

"What're you looking at?" came a quiet, still faintly drowsy murmur from behind her, and she turned sharply in automatic reaction even as the voice registered as Tei's. He was sitting or kneeling, most likely the latter, his head visible above the counter as he looked at her.

"What's on these shelves," she said after a moment, beckoning him. "Come and look."

Tei got to his feet and, like her, let himself out quietly from behind the counter, walking on silent feet to stand beside her. He peered curiously at the dusty objects for a few moments before eventually asking a question.

"What about it?"

It didn't really surprise her, proof that the fairly obvious conclusion had been right. His people could have little use for gold and silver, and even less need to care about it.

"It's nothing special to you, then?"

Tei shook his head. "No. I mean, they're quite pretty, but that's all." He smiled. "Fayel and I got a lot as presents when we were little." He hesitated. "They're not magic, are they?"

"No, nothing like that," Rakariel told him. He looked up at her, puzzled.

"Then what?"

"Something like this would be very valuable outside the valley." She held up the necklace in illustration as she spoke, letting it swing freely from her fingers. "It's made of rare metals and jewels. Only rich people could afford to own something like this, the kind of people who would have lived in the bigger houses. Outside, you'd be able to trade something like this for a lot of food and other supplies, whatever you needed."

Tei blinked at it. "Really?"

"Really." She hesitated, still holding it. "Would

your people mind if I took some of these?"

The response was immediate as he shook his head again. "No, of course not. The big houses are full of them, like you said, and a lot of people have a few things like that. They're pretty, but... it's hard to believe they'd really be that useful."

"They are, though." She looped the necklace around her wrist, picking up a few more small objects she'd be able to carry easily: a pair of brooches, a bracelet, an ornate ring. "This will keep me travelling for a while, let me pay for places to rest, all sorts of things."

"Pay... for places to rest?"

"Yes, you know, rooms at inns and so on. I suppose you don't really have anything like that, do you? What do you do if you need to stay somewhere someone else lives?"

Tei shrugged. "They just let you in. It could be them next time. If you can, you should help them forage, or leave some of your supplies, things like that."

She nodded, understanding, and a faint smile crossed her face. "Right. I like that. It's sometimes not so different outside, really, but most of the time it's more convenient just to pay. Then later, whoever you paid can use the money to buy whatever they need." A brief pause. "Anyway, let's go."

He nodded, looking at the remaining items thoughtfully before dusting off and pocketing a couple. Though he still had no use for them, she'd given him something to think about. Could ornaments and children's toys really be so useful? Rakariel stepped back behind the counter to get her packs, and he watched as she disappeared from view for a few moments, perhaps taking something out, before standing and strapping them on once more. As she came back out from behind it, Tei crossed to the front door, finding a thick bar leant against the wall beside it that looked as though it would fit across the doorway, an additional reinforcement for the door. They could get out of both sides, then, as only made sense... but was it safe?

"Avin?" he whispered. As far as he knew, the spirit hadn't returned all night, which meant that they probably weren't being watched by the vardra. There was no response, as he'd half expected: Avin would be further away, keeping guard for them. They were almost certainly safe.

"He's not here," he murmured to Rakariel. "He must be keeping watch for us further away."

She gave a quick nod. "He'll see us moving on. Come on."

"Just a moment." Remembering something, Tei turned away, slipping quickly through into the back room. Rakariel watched him go uncomprehendingly: there'd been nothing in there, after all. Hurrying to the back door, Tei quietly slid the bolts back again, leaving it free to be opened from the outside by the next person who needed to enter. He noticed the faintly quizzical look on her face as he came back, and gestured behind himself as he was shutting the inside door.

"I had to unbolt the door so the next people to come here could get in."

She understood at once, realising how important that would be, and turned back to the front door. A simple latch held it shut, usable from both sides, and she carefully unfastened it, pushing it open. The street beyond was still flooded, but here and there she could see a cobblestone breaking the surface of the water; it had to be noticeably higher than the ground in the alley behind. Chill fog drifted above the surface of the water, making it reflect grey in the distance and seem to merge into the mist. Slowly, she walked down the steps, booted feet entering the water with barely a ripple. Tei followed behind, gently closing the door on his way out, leaving the safehouse as secure as they had found it. He paused beside Rakariel as she looked up and down the street.

"The palace is that way, isn't it?" she whispered, pointing through the buildings at something of an angle. Tei hesitated for a moment, checking their orientation against his mental map of the city, then nodded.

"Yes," he whispered back. "We should keep going straight, shouldn't we?"

Rakariel nodded quietly. The vardra had been watching the crossroads the day before, and doubtless still were. She didn't want to take any more risks than she had to.

Tei led her slowly across the road, careful to avoid splashing in the shallow water. Unlike the alley, it didn't even come over the top of his shoes, but it was still more than enough to make a betraying sound in if they weren't careful. As they reached the far wall, her hand touched his shoulder, and he stopped dead, almost biting his tongue in reflexive fright. Moments later, she was beside him again, holding out another piece of her strange bread, and he smiled in a combination of relief and gratitude. For an instant he'd feared she'd seen or heard something he had not, a vardra waiting in the fog to spring, but no. It was safe. He continued on after a moment, chewing on the bread as he walked, keeping close to the wall.

They cut diagonally through another two buildings, these ones built backing onto an open, muddy space that they were forced to skirt, before Avin returned. The first Tei knew of it was the sudden chill that gripped him, signifying the spirit borrowing his strength, as he paused for an instant to decide whether to enter another house or to keep moving on. Avin's voice sounded in his mind almost immediately afterwards, easier to hear than it had once been, and he wondered whether he was growing more used to it, or Avin was growing stronger — or both.

'You'll have to turn away from the palace a little to get around. They don't seem sure of where you are, but I think they must know which way you were going... there are a lot of them between here and the palace now.'

"How far will we have to go?" Tei whispered back, so quietly that he barely made any sound at all in the still air. Though he couldn't see him, he could have sworn he felt Avin shrug in response. It wasn't the first time he'd felt as though he had some idea of how his invisible companion was moving.

'I don't know,' he said. *'A few streets, I think. I doubt they can see much further than you can in this fog.'* Though he couldn't really perceive it himself, Avin had seen the fog as a constant throughout Tei's mind in their contact at the pool, knew the silent streets had to be filled with it even now.

It was subconsciously reassuring to hear that said. It had to be true, or Tei had always thought it did, but nonetheless, hearing it from Avin, who could see the vardra clearly, pared another thin layer from the supernatural mystique that surrounded them. They had plagued the city for longer than anyone could remember, and to many people they held the status of invincible, all but all-seeing demons, so far beyond the powers of a single ordinary person that once they caught wind of someone, they would be doomed if they couldn't find shelter in scant seconds. Almost superhuman though she herself sometimes seemed, Rakariel's actions had begun to strip away the mystery that shielded them, revealing them as mere monsters, with strengths and weaknesses. Though they were brutal, strong, and even horrifyingly intelligent, they were nonetheless mortal and fallible, avoided by stealth, slain by her weapons. Tei didn't doubt that she would continue to face them for as long as they stood in her way.

"What did Avin say?" she whispered from beside him. He'd stopped just before Avin had drawn his strength, and hadn't moved since, listening to his words.

"Avin says they seem to know which way we're going," he told her, "but he doesn't think they know where we are. We're going to have to go around another trap, and... probably more after that." Though Avin felt nothing, Tei was certain he sensed him nod. The danger ahead was great — but they could face it.

It was clear that Rakariel didn't like the prospect of another detour, let alone more, but after a pause, she was forced to nod. She had no choice but to agree. Even assuming they were alone, and thus possible to take out one at a time with well-aimed shots, the reduced visibility of the constant fog left her with no chance of seeing them without being seen herself, doubly so since she knew they would be on the rooftops, where height gave them an additional advantage. Once more, she was forced to follow Tei's lead as he picked a careful, circuitous path around the trap Avin had warned him of, turning her unwillingly away from what her sense of direction told her would have to be a faster route.

Tense and wary, they navigated the detour without incident, moving almost painfully slowly, waiting for Avin to scout and return and deviating far too far from any semblance of a straight path for her liking. They were running out of time...

Even worse, it happened again before they'd so much as come to the end of their detour, a warning from Avin all that stopped them from walking into another trap, set partway down a road where they might not have expected to find it. Whispered reports relayed through Tei told her just how many of them he was finding out there: group after group, each one two or three strong, wary and watchful — on guard. There was no mistaking it now, though there had been little enough chance before: they were intelligent, and not just intelligent, but malevolent, their usual dark satisfaction in the hunt doubtless enhanced a hundredfold by the burning drive to catch the prey that had been responsible for killing their kin. Rakariel had no illusions about what would happen if she and Tei were sighted even once. They were known to the vardra now without a doubt, perhaps by sight, quite possibly by scent, and definitely by intent. The odds were further from their favour than ever before, and because of it, she let Tei and Avin lead her ever further afield until it seemed almost as though they were spiralling slowly around the palace rather than really approaching it.

* * *

The mists were beginning to darken once again, Rakariel growing ever more tense at the fading light, when Avin returned a final time.

'The path is clear! I've found a clear path all the way to the palace!'

Eyes wide, Tei stopped dead, turning to Rakariel after a moment, his voice kept down by a lifetime of long habit despite the good news he'd begun to stop expecting would come.

"He's found us a clear path to the palace!"

A touch of relief washed across her face at his words, lightening an expression that had grown more strained with each hour the truncated day wore on. They had almost made it, and with another day to spare.

"Good."

Tei listened as Avin gave him directions, nodding once with the faintest murmur of acknowledgement, and led the way once more with what was almost a slight spring to his step, compared to the way he'd been moving before. Rakariel noticed, but couldn't find fault with it: she could feel the same slight uplift in her own. At long last, their journey through the city was all but complete, and if they could only face what lay ahead, it would be over.

Or would it? A frown furrowed her brow as the thought struck her that this might not be the end after all. The palace could prove not to be the true heart of the problem, though everything she'd been able to put together pointed to it, to the fallen king who had lived there. If it were not, then with her time limit now so close, it would all be over, as it would if she and Tei took too long in finding the source of the curse even if it was within it. If her lightstone failed then, she would be helpless in the heart of the vardra's lair. She would die, and Tei with her, and with them both the valley's scant hope of rescue until another traveller chanced to notice the crack across the mesa — and that assuming that the scant few score families still left alive had not all died by then. Gritting her teeth, Rakariel shook her head. She couldn't let herself think about things she could do nothing about. The problem would either be ahead of her, or it wouldn't, and she thought that it would. If not, well, she would face that darkness when she came to it, and until then force it aside, because to think of it would be to lure ever closer the shadows of fear that waited at the edge of her mind, clawing at her weaknesses. She could not afford to let them in.

Ahead of her, Tei knew none of her concerns. The heart of the curse was in the palace, whatever that might mean for them. Though every step he took left him wondering all the more what it would be, what might wait within. It could quite possibly be something even worse than the vardra, and he feared it all the more the closer they came, but he knew that, with Rakariel, he could venture in there. He'd help her to defeat it in whatever way he could, whatever form it took. He might even have to speak the spell she'd taught him, using the one weapon he had. That, at the least, he thought he could do, beginning to run silently through it in his mind as the larger part of his awareness picked a path under Avin's guidance. It kept him from thinking about what could lie ahead, from building his fear of the unknown. Knowing that their ethereal scout was watching over them helped, too, his ancestor's warning keeping them safe. As long as he and Rakariel kept their silence, all they had to do was go a little further, and they would be at the palace itself, where no-one had ever ventured within living memory.

The light had almost faded from the fog when they finally reached it, surrounded by extensive grounds bordered by a decorative shoulder-height wall that was draped with the blackened strands of long-dead plants. Barely daring to breathe, Tei slipped across the road and paused by the wall, peering over it. He couldn't see far in the growing dark, the open grounds fading away to fogbound blackness, but he knew from his family's carefully preserved maps of the city that they still had some way to go before reaching the palace itself. Rakariel joined him, resting one hand on the top of the wall, and he looked up at her.

"It's getting dark, but there won't be any safehouses this close. What... what should we do?"

Her lips tightened slightly for a moment as she thought. They'd have to cross the grounds in almost pitch blackness, the lightstone too much of a beacon to risk while they were still outside. Though it would soon be night, they were relatively well rested, and had all too little time.

"We go on," she whispered back. "We're too close to turn back now, or even to stop. Two days is all we have."

Tei nodded, though his skin prickled at the thought of crossing that much open space in the dark. Nobody with any sense travelled during the night... night, when the vardra hunted more actively than ever, and the slightest betraying sound would make them a target, unable even to see where to run to. But they had Avin, and Rakariel, with her weapons and her miraculous light. If she said they should go on, then they had to. He rested both hands on the wall, hesitated for a last moment, and boosted himself up. The vegetation under his hands squished unpleasantly, as though he'd just flattened a slug, but he had other concerns on his mind and ignored it. Getting his feet up, he paused, crouched on the top of the wall, still all but silent. Nothing happened, and he leaned cautiously over, looking down at the ground beyond. As he'd half feared, the other side was damp earth, no way of knowing in the gloom just how soggy, how treacherous it might be. Rakariel joined him atop the wall as he turned and slowly, carefully, lowered himself down, planting his feet as slowly and carefully as he could.

The soil he found himself standing on was more like that of his home than the waterlogged ground of the temple, his feet sinking only slightly and almost soundlessly as he lowered his full weight to the ground, keeping hold of the wall until he was sure of his balance. Letting go, he looked back up at Rakariel, crouched silent and still on the wall, and nodded silently to her. In the same cautious fashion, she followed his lead, letting herself carefully down to the ground with barely a sound. With an unknowable amount of open space ahead of them, it was more important than ever that they keep themselves from making even the slightest noise. If they were once noticed, they would have nowhere to run.

'Keep going.' Avin's voice came, unexpectedly but

encouragingly. *'I'll guide you if I think you're turning away from a straight line. I think I can see further than you can.'*

Tei nodded, feeling the spirit drain a touch of his strength again. Though he was invisible, once again Tei could have sworn he felt him go. Looking to Rakariel again, he pointed ahead, and she nodded in silence, ready to follow. Step by careful, torturous step, they began to make their slow way across the dead, decaying gardens.

It was hard going, harder than any terrain Tei had ever had to cover before. The ground was moist and uneven, and in some place, patches of loose gravel, perhaps once paths, almost gave them away. More than once, it was only Tei's strained senses and accurate reflexes that prevented it, feeling the slight wrongness underfoot and drawing back before resting any weight on it, then picking his path across even more carefully than before. In other places, long-dead plants blocked their way, the skeletal remnants of ancient bushes still hung in places with the black remains of leaves, and they were forced to go around. Even when they had to go quite some distance, Rakariel's sense of direction remained remarkably accurate, often letting them return to their previous heading without any help from Avin.

Making their way carefully between trees spotted with bulbous fungi in the deepening darkness, they almost walked straight into a half-hidden pond, its black water looking the same as the soil. One moment they were picking their way across ancient roots, the next Rakariel's arm had shot out across Tei's chest in the same instant as his leading foot began to slip in suddenly-softer mud, and he clung to it with a near-silent gasp of surprise, regaining his balance.

"Thanks," he whispered after a moment. She smiled faintly, the expression a little strained.

"I almost didn't see it. Look... it's too flat."

He looked ahead and swallowed, seeing what she meant. The 'ground' ahead was as smooth as glass, the reflections that should have betrayed it concealed by shadow and fog. While stepping into it probably wouldn't have been fatal, slipping and falling in, with the resulting splash, likely would have, at least indirectly. Rakariel looked from side to side before stepping around Tei to follow the shore to the right, unfalteringly leading the way around it until she could leave it behind and strike out in the direction they'd been going once more. Eventually, in almost pitch-blackness, they reached a looming wall, stretching up further than they could reach — which was the extent of their limited vision.

"Is this it?" Rakariel whispered softly, one hand on the wall. Tei nodded.

"It has to be." They were there. They'd done it.

After a shared moment of silence, both began to cautiously look around, feeling their way along the side of the building. As they'd found with the temple, reaching the place would be pointless if they couldn't find a way inside. They didn't have to go far, however, before finding that in this case, it would be much easier. In the lead again, Rakariel's hand found an area of smoothed stonework, then a sudden cutoff, a window or door, perhaps, recessed into the thick stone wall. Lifting the folded cloth the tiniest fraction to reveal a mere sliver of her lightstone, she shed the tiny ray of light into the darkness ahead, rewarded by the sight of a shattered window. Someone had attempted to fortify it once, in the long-distant past, but it was too wide to easily brace, and the ferocious attacks it must have received had simply torn the barricades apart. Damp, scored wood lay in pieces on the long-dead grass, half-rotted despite the preservation spell she had seen infusing the city. She looked at it for a moment longer, frowning, and cautiously knelt beside it. Uncertain, Tei leaned over as well, looking to see what she'd seen. The faint light escaping from the lightstone's cover showed him nothing overly unexpected.

Rakariel slowly reached out, lifting a section of broken planking in both hands. It gave slightly under her fingers with a damp squish, and she peered at it closely, tilting it from side to side to study the deep gouges left by the vardra's blades, then turned it over. On the other side, the wood was flat, or had once been before it had begun to rot. Still holding it, she remained motionless for a few moments in contemplation, until Tei leaned slightly further forward and into the edge of her field of vision. Catching sight of him, she looked over her shoulder, getting back to her feet and holding out the piece of wood in silent explanation. Tei looked at it uncertainly, still not sure what he was looking for until she let go with one hand to point at the gouges running across it, a silent, frightening reminder of the strength and fury of the vardra. Still uncertain, he looked up at her again, expression quizzical. Of course the wood was scarred: wasn't the way it had been thrown to the ground evidence enough of what had happened even without the splintered claw-marks? Only when she knelt again to place it back with the rest and indicate the deep scores that continued across them, then pointed up at the empty window, did he realise what she meant. All those gouges had been on the *inside*, before the barricade fell.

It reinforced the idea that at least some of the vardra must have come from inside the palace, at least, Rakariel mused, standing again and looking down at the broken barricade. It couldn't, however, tell her what lay in wait ahead. Even the fact that there were blade-marks in the wood didn't actually prove what had made them. Though whatever had done it had probably been the same kind of creature as the vardra, she couldn't be truly certain of anything beyond that they had used similar blades and had the same strength. With the wood so decayed, she couldn't even be sure that that *was* all there was to it, that there weren't other, shallower marks hidden by the ravages of time. Though Tei and his people only knew of the vardra, it wasn't impossible that other creatures existed, bound to remain somewhere within.

She shook her head fractionally. She could only deal with such things as she found them, if she did at all. She and Tei would simply have to be ready. Looking around for him, she saw him peering cautiously through the empty windowframe into the room beyond, and joined him at the low sill. As only made sense, the glass had fallen inside the room, but not far, giving way to the blows from within before the barricade itself had fallen, and there was no wood inside. Unaware that they were sealing themselves in with the menace, the frightened residents and their guardsmen must have tried to fortify the palace... until danger fell upon them from the direction they had least expected it. She and Tei were walking into that danger, and into the unknown. Alert and wary, she put her hands on the windowsill and scrambled inside.

The wreckage within gave little clue as to what the room had once been. It had once had a good view of the gardens, the large window illustrated that, but she could tell nothing about its actual purpose. Every last piece of furniture had been smashed to kindling. The thin ray of light that was all she could allow to escape concealed as much as it illuminated, showing the room in a ghostly grey half-light. A few darker stains marred walls and floor in one corner, but there was no telling whether they were patches of rot or something else, and no sign of any body. In her entire journey through the city, Rakariel still hadn't found a single corpse, not even scattered bones in the long-abandoned buildings they'd cut through. The thought made her wonder again where they could have gone, though it was most likely that the vardra had merely removed their kills to the heart of their lair. Tei had certainly never spoken of the dead walking, been shocked beyond words at encountering Avin's ghost. There was no sign that such a thing had ever happened here; the remains would simply be hidden, probably somewhere in the palace itself. Even if she found it, she doubted there would be much there beyond old bones. Tei's ragged people were too few, too careful to keep the levels of victims high.

As Tei clambered quietly through the window, Rakariel wondered idly what the vardra ate, besides people. Did they even need food? Just how long could they live without it if they did? Avin had reported just over thirty of them at one point, and there were doubtless more further away. That large a population couldn't survive on only the twelvescore or so people left alive in the city, even if they ate only once a month. That would mean that they didn't hunt for food, or at least that they didn't need to. They hunted for the thrill...

Tei looked to her for guidance, dark eyes wide and nervous, and she glanced from window to shattered door, hearing nothing in the silent night. Jerking her head to indicate he should follow her, she crossed the floor quietly and slipped through the doorway into the corridor beyond.

CHAPTER 15

Palace of the Dead

The hallway was, if anything, even darker than the room they had left, pitch black save for what little light escaped from the mostly-covered lightstone. Stepping along the wall so she was out of the direct line of sight of the window, Rakariel raised her hand and slowly lifted the cloth from it, tucking it back comfortably and securely behind her headpiece. From now until they left, she wouldn't hide it again. Beside her, Tei blinked in the sudden light, glancing warily up and down the corridor for any sign that anything might have seen them. She could see his lips moving slightly, soundlessly, and thought she recognised the careful shapings of magic. He was going through the spell again — and that wasn't a bad thing. Rakariel turned her head away, looking down the hall in the direction she guessed would be most likely to lead them deeper inside. Reaching back, she readied her bow, its familiar weight in her left hand granting a slight boost to her confidence. Danger of any kind could lurk around any corner, and though the walls were plastered and tiled, with delicate inlay in places, the damp, black mould, the mildew and the dank chill in the air, together with the enclosed space, amplified her sense of it a hundredfold. She and Tei could no longer hide or even hope to avoid danger: within the palace itself, they had only one chance.

An old, prepared tension in her every move, she walked slowly down the hall, an arrow nocked, ready to draw and loose in an instant. Tei followed, creeping on wary, soundless feet and still going over the spell even as a part of him wondered at the indefinable change in her attitude. He couldn't say what it was, but something was different even to the moments just outside as they forged on, deeper into the palace. Rakariel stopped at every corner with a degree of caution that not even Tei himself could match, pausing, then stepping sharply around with her bow drawn, ready to loose the arrow in an instant. The lightstone would alert anything still in the palace to her presence long before she herself stepped into view, so her best chance was to make the move as swiftly as possible, without giving whatever lay beyond a chance to react to the sight of her peering around the corner. All he could do was follow her lead, staying in shelter until she had satisfied herself that the path ahead was clear.

They passed ruined rooms whose purpose, like the first, could only now be guessed at, every stick of furniture within reduced to matchwood, glass shattered, stone toppled, metal rent. Rakariel paused at each doorway, stepping out sharply and checking each shadowed opening before moving on once more. It made their progress slow, but it had to be done. She could not risk leaving any danger to creep out and attack them from behind, the one direction she most rarely looked, though she did glance over her shoulder when she felt she could spare the time. Each swift movement of her head threw sharp, angular shadows across the wall, an effect she'd had to grow used to long before. The motion of the shadows was no more than a reflection of her own.

As they ventured further in, the ever-present signs

of the palace's ruin became yet more visible, from carpets sodden with decay to cracked and broken pillars, even tumbled statues of figures long forgotten. In places, the ceilings had caved in, spilling debris into the area below. All too soon forced to leave the hall behind, Rakariel crept from room to connected room, avoiding passing directly beneath the holes wherever she could and keeping close to the once-fine walls, staying as far away from windows as she could. Her light would shine out like a beacon, even mercifully dulled by fog, and if the vardra once noticed, she had no doubt they would call their brethren.

'Tei?' Avin's voice came suddenly as Tei waited for Rakariel to carefully skirt a hole in the ceiling, keeping her aim high in case anything waited above. He couldn't help but jump, more tense than he had ever been in his life.

"What? What is it?"

Rakariel glanced back, catching his motion from the corner of her eye, the faint edges of his whispered words in the otherwise silent palace. Seeing him looking into empty air, she realised after a moment that he had to be talking to Avin, and looked back up, edging further along.

'I'm not sure,' came the response, uncertain. *'I feel something in the distance here. Something... I don't know.'* Again, Tei could have sworn he sensed the spirit shake his head.

"Is it something bad, like the vardra?"

'I don't know. It feels like... tension, like a rope pulled too tight. It feels like the world is waiting. I don't know what it means. I'll go ahead, take a look — tell Rakariel.'

Tei nodded, and crept around the debris that had once been a chandelier and part of the ceiling, somewhat faster than Rakariel had since her actions had proved it safe. Knowing he'd have a message from Avin, she waited for him, bent slightly to let him whisper in her ear. To his surprise, she shook her head as he relayed the spirit's words.

"No," she hissed back, barely louder than Tei himself. "Avin stays with us now. We need his vision, and this place could be dangerous even to him. We don't know what happened here."

Avin hesitated, reluctant. *'...I suppose she's right,'* he admitted eventually. *'But how can I help you if I can't even tell you what it is?'* Tei relayed his words almost directly. It was still awkward, but he was getting somewhat used to being the conduit between Avin and Rakariel, and there was no other way for them to speak to each other.

"He can be our eyes," she said at once. "I can't see through walls, and nor can you. He can. He can tell if there's living danger waiting for us, he can tell us how near or how far we are from whatever he can feel, whether we're getting closer or further away. We need him with us now — and he needs to be here."

Though he couldn't see it, Tei sensed Avin's slow nod as he saw the sense in her words.

"All right," he told her. "He'll stay with us."

"Good. So, which way is the... tension he can feel?"

Without hesitation, Tei turned, pointing deeper into the heart of the palace, able almost to envision Avin performing the exact same motion just a moment before.

"I expected so," she murmured, so softly even Tei could barely hear it, and it might have been directed only to herself. "We have to press on."

Cautiously, navigating room by room, edging around obstacles, they continued on. The layout of the palace seemed to include a large number of central courtyards and interior gardens, a design that ensured that almost everywhere would, in better days, have been open to natural light. In the horror-filled night, it only served to turn it into a treacherous maze, open to danger from every side and with no way to be certain that anywhere was safe. At times, Avin warned them of a dark presence nearby, but his spiritual 'sight' was limited to things that were close, and though they could avoid the dangers he pointed out, the windows let Rakariel's light escape to potentially call them from far further than he could see. In some places, the rooms were less damaged: this one had been a reading room, books still strewn mouldering across the floor; that section likely a set of servants' quarters, though not enough for the entire palace by any means, perhaps the personal servants of someone who had lived on the floors above. Even with Avin keeping watch for them, forever pointing the way to what he had sensed, their stealthy progress was painfully slow, and both Tei and Rakariel began to lose track of time. Then, all of a sudden, he stopped.

'There's something else.'

Tei blinked, stopping dead. "What?"

'I don't know. It's so faint. But it's close. I can see it... over there.' Again, Tei felt him point, this time ahead and to the right, and was about to warn Rakariel when he saw that she had already, thankfully, stopped.

'I don't know what it is, it just seems to be all through the ground, but it's brighter — stronger — than anywhere else.'

"There's something brighter over there, he says," Tei whispered, dark eyes wide with tension and fear. "Faint, but brighter, all over the ground. He doesn't know what it is, but it's close."

Rakariel looked back at him, silent for a moment, lines of stress in her face that had not been there before they'd entered the palace. "We'll take a look," she decided. "We can't afford to miss anything. It could be a sign of what happened."

Tei nodded, understanding. They still knew all too little of what had happened in the palace, of how the vardra — creatures that Rakariel had said had likely once been people — had come to be or how they had gained entry, if they hadn't been monsters made from its occupants. He shuddered slightly at the thought. Terrible enough to know that they skulked outside waiting, a thousand times worse to fear that someone close to you, trapped inside with you, might somehow become one. That even you could...

He reflexively closed his eyes, only to open them in the same instant, not daring to render himself blind even for a moment. Rakariel frowned, concerned.

"Tei?"

"N-nothing," he said, whispered voice shaking. "I just — I just thought, if the vardra were people who lived here — how could it happen? Someone just changed-"

Listening to his whispered voice, looking into his dark eyes, Rakariel's expression softened slightly, though it lost none of the tension and strain. "I know," she said gently. "It's terrible. But you can't dwell on it, or it'll paralyse you. Just concentrate on what's happening now."

Tei nodded a little jerkily. She was right. He had to think of something else, to accept his fear, if he could, and put it aside. He had to go on. The only other option now was death.

"We'll see what Avin's found," she told him. "It might be nothing, but then again, it might tell us something. Stay close." She didn't need to add the words, but she did anyway, a little gesture of reassurance and concern. Whatever they found, she'd be watching over him. Grateful, Tei followed her like a shadow as she turned away and began to cautiously make her way onward.

A doorway to the right offered a chance to head towards Avin's mysterious 'brightness', even the frame splintered, the savaged remains of the door itself lying broken on the floor. Rakariel stepped carefully over the wreckage as she turned sharply to look into the room, its purpose unrecognisable, its wide window smashed. Beyond had to lie another internal courtyard.

"Is it there?" she whispered. Concentrating on the spirit, Tei relayed Avin's words almost as he spoke them.

'Yes, it's there — just through there. I can see shapes, I think.'

"What kind of shapes?"

'I don't know. They're all so close together, but they don't fit that way. I need to look closer.'

Rakariel nodded as Tei told her what he'd said, continuing on without waiting for him. Keeping to the left-hand wall, she edged up to the window, Tei only just behind her, stepped sharply sideways — and stopped, a faint sound catching in the back of her throat, the arrow almost slipping from her fingers. Beyond the window lay another internal courtyard... one that the cool white light showed filled with bones.

"Rakariel?" Tei whispered, but for once, she didn't answer. Unsure of what to do, unable to see why she'd frozen, he slowly risked reaching across to touch her arm. "Rakariel?"

Still she didn't move, and it only intensified his fear. He'd never seen anything quite like the look of distant, desolate horror on her face, as though a part of her were trapped in a nightmare far away. To see her, of all people, with such an expression, in the terrible confines of the palace, so soon after almost giving in to his own fears was almost more than he could bear.

"Rakariel!"

Abruptly, Avin was back at his side, his presence in that moment as welcome and reassuring as an old friend. *'It's bones,'* he said, shaken. *'What I could feel. It's all bones.'*

Tei bit his lip. "People's bones?"

'Yes. There are so many of them. I had... no idea there even could be...'

Paradoxically, Tei found himself almost reassured. Terrible though it was, though both Avin and Rakariel had seen it to be, it was no danger.

"Bones..." he whispered to himself, then looked up at Rakariel. "Just bones." Gathering his courage, he reached out and grabbed her arm, pulling her sideways, away from the window. She stumbled, then caught herself, having to take a couple of paces before regaining her balance. It was enough to take her out of the line of sight of the window, and together with the shock of the stumble, he could see the horror fading, that awful expression giving way to startlement and a more normal fear.

"Avin said it's just bones out there," he whispered. Rakariel looked down at him, focusing on his face a moment late.

"Yes. Just bones..."

She walked over to the corner, leaning her head into it for a moment, letting the lightstone shine brilliantly into the enclosed space her body created and give the momentary illusion of daylight. The memory of pain burned beneath it, and without thinking, she slipped a finger under the cloth of her bandanna, tracing the ridges of the old scar there. She'd seen so much, been forced to see so much, horrors she would never be able to banish from her mind. The courtyard of haphazardly piled bones, sudden and unexpected, had brought all those shadows howling back from the edges of her awareness to overwhelm her, reminding her of sights she could never forget however hard she tried.

"Are you all right?"

Tei's near-silent whisper broke into her thoughts, and she twisted to see out of her self-imposed prison, looking at him. "Yes. I... I'll be fine." Slowly, she let her hand fall, the arrow she was still holding tucked back along her arm. Tei was gazing at her with a combination of worry, concern, and fear, and for his sake as much as her own she fought to steady herself, to turn and lean back against the corner instead, tilting her head back to study the ceiling, then down again. "I'll be fine."

He glanced over his shoulder once at the shattered

window, then looked back at her. "Why...?"

Unsure what he meant by the hesitant question, Rakariel opted to answer the easiest one, though it might not have been what he intended. "The... the vardra must take their prey here. To eat."

Tei swallowed, his already pale face losing a fraction more colour. That certainly explained the numbers Avin had spoken of.

"We should get as far away from here as we can."

He nodded wordlessly. Not only was it a place of horror even without his seeing it for himself, it was somewhere the vardra would return to, somewhere close to the heart of their lair. Every moment he and Rakariel remained was another moment that could see one leaping down from above at the sight of her brilliant light, another moment that could see them discovered and hunted once again, through unknown territory and with no place to hide. They had to get away.

Brushing her hand along the wall as if in reminder of its reality, Rakariel led the way back out of the room, navigating with difficulty through the damaged halls. The first thought in her mind was to put more distance between them and the courtyard of bones, even orientation coming second to that urgency, though her pace remained set by her alertness, the need to be certain there was no danger ahead. A single mistake was all it could take to see them both killed. Tei followed unquestioningly, staying close, barely daring to breathe.

Eventually, they were far enough away that Rakariel decided they could stop, leaning against a wall with a silent sigh. The room they were in had just two doors and an intact ceiling, its shattered window small; it was as safe a place as they would be likely to find anywhere in the palace. Tei paused beside her, stressed almost to breaking point and desperately welcoming the chance to halt. He thought he felt Avin's presence drift further away from them, doubtless taking the opportunity to scout around.

"Does Avin think we can go wherever that tension was coming from without getting near the courtyard?" Rakariel murmured. Though she knew which direction they'd been travelling in before, she had no idea of how far they had to go. Tei looked around, wondering if he could call the drifting spirit back with only a whisper.

"Avin?"

After a few seconds, he responded — but not with the answer.

'I can see something else — someone else, a person, it's a little strange but I'm sure of it! It's very weak, but there's someone there!' Tei could almost feel him pointing, and was silent for a moment in sheer surprise before speaking, his voice still kept to a tense whisper, pointing diagonally up in the same direction he knew Avin had.

"He — he says he can see someone!"

Rakariel blinked, startled. "Someone? Not something?"

Tei nodded. "He was certain. He said they look very weak, though. There's something a bit strange about them, but it's definitely a person."

"Where's the thing he sensed before?"

Tei hesitated, making sense of Avin's somewhat distracted response. "That way, I think," he said, pointing again in a new direction. "He says it's still some way from us. He can't see it, just feel it."

Mentally lining herself up with the way she knew they'd come, Rakariel realised with relief that they would indeed be able to go around. The bones of the dead, though horrifying in their numbers, weren't that near to the source of the feeling of tension Avin had spoken of. As for the person, whoever or whatever they might prove to be, they were in a different direction altogether. She couldn't think of any reason for anyone alive to have entered the palace from the outside, when everything Tei and his people had told her agreed that such a venture would be suicide. The options she was left with, then, were a spirit like Avin himself... or some other once-human creature whose weakness of spirit was the only outward signifier of what had become of them. While she couldn't name one offhand, it was a possibility she felt was all too likely.

"It may not be a person," she said quietly. "We'll find out what it is, but I doubt it's alive. We'll need to be cautious. Avin should be careful as we get close, too."

Tei swallowed and nodded, realising what she implied. For the first time, he found himself wondering about the dangers of the bright world beyond. Though she had spoken of the sun with such reverence, she had also said it wasn't without its evil, clearly knew how to face creatures like the vardra, how to fight and heal herself. The world she had told him of sounded so much brighter at its best... but could it also be worse, in other ways, than the familiar one he knew?

Rakariel had stepped away almost before he noticed she was moving, already checking through the far door for danger. Her lightstone shone brightly into the room beyond, her shadow casting the majority of the one behind her into darkness. Tei quietly walked forward to catch up — and stopped again barely a pace across the room. Looking disbelievingly at the window, he raised one hand to block all sight of Rakariel and her lightstone, staring at the dim grey square he could just barely make out.

"Tei?"

Tei hastily dropped his hand and looked at her, looking over her shoulder at him. He edged silently across to her, and pointed at the window. "Look. It's... it's morning." He could hardly believe it. Had the interminable terror of the palace really gone on through the entire night?

Eyes widening in surprise, Rakariel put her hand over the lightstone, plunging them into darkness. As her eyes slowly began to adapt, she, too, saw what he had: the faintest of grey-lit rectangles in the place of the window. The seventh day had dawned, and she had just one more before her light gave out.

"So it is," was all she said, removing her hand again. "That's good." Though her voice threatened to shake, however slightly, she held it back. "The vardra will be much less likely to see my lightstone in the day."

Realising she was right, he nodded. A little extra light in the grey-lit mist would be much harder to see than a light that shone when all else was dark. "This is the seventh day, isn't it?" he asked softly.

"Yes. So we should keep moving."

She was right, he knew. Afraid though he knew she was of what would happen on that ninth day, seeming convinced that her death would be certain — which it likely would if they were still in the palace when her light finally failed — she still held back her fear, forging onward as if turning back were not even a possibility. Perhaps, for her, it wasn't. Though it scared him, the more he saw of her fears, the more Tei realised the true extent of her strength. Even after the effect the courtyard of bones had had on her, she still pressed on rather than break and run. It gave him the strength to stay with her, made him all the more determined to help for as long as he could.

"Okay."

Rakariel stepped out into the next room, and Tei followed her. Its far door opened into another hallway, which she looked cautiously up and down before turning to the right, following the rough direction he had pointed earlier. A couple of doors further down, she paused again, glancing back at him.

"Show me the way again?"

Tei barely had to wait at all before he sensed Avin pointing, diagonally up and to the left. "That way," he whispered back. "It's up there."

"We'll need to find some stairs we can still climb, then. They'll probably be off one of these halls, rather than a room."

Again, Tei nodded, creeping quietly behind her as she made her way along, almost able to feel Avin's growing impatience. They had to turn away from the direction of the strange person he'd sensed before they found what they were looking for, a hall that ended in a staircase of smooth white stone with an inlaid carpet on its steps, doubtless once finely made, but now ripped and turned an indeterminate brown colour by the endless damp. Near it, the ceiling rose away into the darkness, and Rakariel edged out into the open with her bow aimed high, looking up into the ceiling above whose shadows her lightstone largely banished. Though the painted plaster was scored by the marks of claws, nothing awaited them, and she made her way carefully to the stairs, pausing again before placing her foot on the first. Rather than step on the sodden carpet, she opted to stand on the ancient marble, slow movements preventing her boot from so much as clicking against it. Making her way cautiously up alongside the stone banister, as pale as the stairs she walked on, she turned slowly from side to side as she climbed, though still no danger emerged. Tei followed, five steps behind, trailing his hand along the smooth stone and peering over the edge as he got higher. With Rakariel looking upwards, the floor below was rapidly fading into shadow.

By the time they reached the high landing, there were pockets of near-blackness below, relieved only slightly by reflected light. Though the day outside had grown noticeably brighter, there weren't enough windows to properly illuminate the entire hall. Rakariel looked up the next flight, then along the landing, unsure of her direction.

"This floor or the next?" she whispered. Tei waited only a moment before whispering back.

"This one, he thinks. Along that way somewhere." As he had before, he pointed in the direction he sensed Avin indicating, his arm much more level than it had been on the floor below.

"Right."

Her every step cautious, Rakariel crossed to the wall of the landing, hoping that, at least there, the old floor would hold beneath her weight. The palace's stonework had survived the years, but much of the rest had been damaged more than anything she'd seen outside, and she suspected a part of that was to make it easier for the vardra that now inhabited the place to move around. They could climb walls and quite possibly leap through the holes they'd made between one floor and the next, but she and Tei could not.

Edging along the wall, still looking cautiously in every direction, she came to a corner and paused before stepping sharply around. Once again, the hall beyond was empty, but a gaping hole in its floor proved all too sharply just how dangerous the upper levels could be. Keeping her back to the wall, checking each room for danger before she passed it, Rakariel slowly made her way towards the hole. It was easily wide enough for a vardra to leap through, let alone for her and Tei to fall through, and she could see the marks of their blades all too clearly in the splintered floorboards. She'd have to risk crossing around the edge, though it would put her flat against the wall with little way to defend herself.

"Is there anything below?" she whispered to Tei. Though her sense of direction told her she was almost certainly over one of the rooms they'd passed before, there was no guarantee that it would still be empty now. Tei waited for a moment, then seemed to listen to Avin's silent report.

"Nothing, he says."

Outside, muted by distance and the muffling fog, the vardra's howls began again. Rakariel froze in the middle of a step, her bright and steady light unwavering, and Tei flattened himself to the wall with a gasp of shock. Had they somehow found the trail? Were they hunting fresh prey? Had they mistaken some other poor unfortunate for the traveller who had dared to kill their kin? His blood chilled with fear, he had to force himself to remember to breathe, to remember to listen. All his life, that sound had meant death was imminent, a fate all but inevitable: the cry that presaged the end of someone's life. If he didn't get off the streets before a vardra could travel from wherever that cry had gone up to where he was, it would be his own — but he was no longer on the streets, and there was no safety within the palace.

"How close?"

Rakariel remained almost motionless as she spoke, her arrow aimed down the hall, past the hole in the floor. Her tone, held level by long experience, helped to steady him, forcing him to think. Despite his fear, Tei forced himself to listen to the howls in the distance, judging their strength over the sound of his own racing heart.

"Outside the palace. I think. No, definitely outside. Over the garden. Maybe still where they were when Avin led us around them. I don't — don't think it can be us."

If the situation had been otherwise, Rakariel might have smiled at Tei's referring to the extensive palace grounds as 'the garden', but as it was, she barely noticed. The vardra were claiming another victim, then, and her determination to end it before anyone else fell grew yet stronger. She knew it was almost certainly her fault. They had been so concentrated that anyone anywhere near the area would be bound to fall prey to them. Without the guidance she and Tei had had from Avin, they, too, would have become two more victims all too quickly, but their evasion had left the vardra still searching, and their fury had just found an outlet.

"Then we should keep going," was all she said. "Before they find anyone else."

Realising the truth in her words, realising as she just had that that might not have happened had he and Rakariel not evaded them before, he nodded wordlessly, watching as she carefully began to edge around the hole on the shattered boards that still projected from the wall. They groaned alarmingly under her weight, one dropping several inches with a sharp crack and almost overbalancing her, forcing her to leap the rest of the way and land slightly unstably on the far side, dropping to her knees to keep her balance and staying there for an instant as the floor creaked beneath her.

After a moment in which nothing happened, still poised on hands and knees, she looked over her shoulder at Tei and got to her feet, the lightstone's motion swinging her shadow sharply about the corridor. On the other side, he stepped slowly up to the hole, at the same side she'd used to cross. As he put his foot on the first of the narrow planks, she tucked the arrow she'd been holding back in her quiver and leaned slightly forward, stretching her hand out to him. Back to the wall, Tei took another step, feeling the boards shift beneath his feet and knowing he would never have trusted such an unstable floor in a house. His outstretched right hand met hers at the fingertips, and as he took a third step, bringing him fully within her reach, she grabbed hold. Balanced and somewhat comforted by her strong grip, he made it the rest of the way over faster, and without incident. Thinner and lighter than Rakariel, carrying less, she hadn't expected him to fall where she had not.

Safely on the other side, they continued on once more, Rakariel ready as always, Tei running through the lightning spell again in complete silence. Though the hole was behind them, both still kept close to the walls, with no way of being certain what state the floor beneath their feet was in until they stepped on it. All it would take would be one support that had been broken from below to potentially drop them through it, a sound that would call any vardra in the palace even if they survived unhurt.

They'd passed several more rooms when Tei suddenly froze, whispering fruitlessly into the air. "Avin? Avin!"

"What is it?" Rakariel demanded, turning back to him. Even in a whisper, the commanding urgency in her voice demanded a response. Tei swallowed.

"He's gone."

CHAPTER 16

Waiting for a Saviour

Though she tried to stop herself from showing it too visibly in front of Tei, his words shook her. They were relying on Avin! Much though she'd initially resisted it, she'd begun to trust him, and his guidance was the only thing she was able to rely on within the palace! What had he done — or what had happened to him?

"What happened?" she asked.

"He — he sort of shouted something, and it felt like he ran away. Towards it, like he'd seen something new." He wasn't sure how he knew, but he didn't suspect Avin of willingly abandoning them, or even of having gone all that far. Closing his eyes, he thought, turning slightly in the direction that felt right, the same one that they'd been trying to go in. "I think he went that way."

His pointing finger led onward, through one of the walls, doubtless around a corner she could see not too far ahead. "Where we were headed?"

Tei nodded. "I think so. I think I can find him."

Rakariel let him edge past her, making his way carefully to the corner and peering in all directions before turning left. Just a few paces behind him, she did the same, and stopped dead as he froze, her bow ready, but no danger in sight.

"He's back!" Tei whispered, twisting to look at her. "He's back, and — and he says it's Seivi!"

"*What?*" Rakariel hissed. Seivi? The priestess Avin had known?

"Her ghost. He says it's her ghost."

"Where?" she demanded.

"In the next room. This way!"

Doubtless guided by Avin, Tei led her unerringly to one of the nearer doors, broken open as all the others had been, smashed inward to lie in pieces on the floor. Tei stepped over it without a thought, but Rakariel glanced down as she did. A sturdy lock had been ripped from the frame, and though it was somewhat rusted, she doubted it had been there long when the palace fell, centuries before.

The chamber beyond was large, luxurious, but probably only moderate by the palace's standards. A large bed occupied its centre, splintered and broken now, and paintings ornamented the once fine walls. Some had fallen, others hung at an angle. Though damaged, much of the furniture was relatively intact, diamond-paned glass still present in one window, though the grey-lit fog drifted in through the other. There was no visible sign of anyone being there, but Rakariel hadn't expected to see one. Even though she suspected he'd been growing stronger over the journey, Avin was still too weak to appear, and any other spirit left in the valley would be bound to be in the same state as he had when they first met. Tei's nod to an unheard request, his convulsive shiver as another touch of strength drained away from him, confirmed it in the next moment. Silent, Rakariel gripped his shoulder tightly. It couldn't really help, but it wouldn't hurt.

For the living, a long silence followed, Rakariel standing by Tei with her hand on his shoulder. Eventually, he spoke.

"Avin says... he says Seivi says she's been waiting

for someone. I can hear him talking, but I can't hear her. I guess it's because we're not related, the same way you can't hear him. He's asking what happened to her, what King Sariven did." A pause followed as he listened, looking almost confused. "Now he seems angry about something. He's asking why she didn't come back, then, if she didn't die. ...So you were a prisoner."

Rakariel's mind raced, trying to piece together what was going on from such imperfect information, but how could she? It seemed Avin was barely even talking to Tei, leaving him to pass on what was happening as best he could, and unable to hear Seivi's side of the conversation, he was clearly struggling.

"He's still talking about her being a prisoner," Tei continued. "Now he says something's keeping her here too. He's asking what she means?"

"Get him to tell us what's going on!" Rakariel hissed. The two spirits had been friends long before, and if only their situation had been otherwise she would have allowed them their reunion, but it was taking time that she and Tei didn't have, time that she could feel slipping away from her moment by moment. The vardra could return; the one that had made a kill doubtless would, to leave the remains in that horrific courtyard of bones. There were just two days left before her lightstone gave out: given that on her travels she usually charged it each evening when she made camp, she was halfway through the seventh day already. They couldn't afford to wait, learning nothing from a conversation that they couldn't hear.

"Avin?" Tei prompted, though he had doubtless already heard Rakariel. There was silence for a little while, Tei's expression attentive, as Avin spoke.

"He says that she's been waiting here," he relayed eventually. "That she chose to stay in case she could help somehow. He says she was a prisoner here, but she keeps saying that King Sariven was a good man. I... don't think he believes her."

Rakariel's memory flashed back to what Avin had said before about everyone but him adoring their king, almost too much. Could the same have been true of Seivi? Could she be captured even now by that ancient glamour, whatever it had been?

"What was so good about him?" she asked, testing. The response came only slowly, relayed as it had to be through first Avin, then Tei."

"Uh, she says he cared for his country. He tried to do his best — he got it wrong, but he meant well. Avin says she's trying to tell him not to be angry, or something like that. Uh... now they're arguing."

Rakariel folded her arms and found herself wishing she could see the two spirits to glare at them. They didn't have time for this! The dead might, but she and Tei did not! Schooling herself to calmness, for Seivi, at the least, could have little idea of just how urgent it truly was that they keep moving, she spoke to thin air, addressing them both directly.

"Please. I know a lot has happened, and it's been a long time. But Tei and I don't have much time left. If we haven't done whatever we need to do here by the end of tomorrow..." She trailed off there, but it seemed from Tei's almost immediate response that both spirits had, thankfully, understood.

"Avin says he's sorry," he told her, his eyes flicking to empty air moments after. Was Avin's spirit there? Could he feel it? "No, we can't hear her." He glanced at Rakariel to check, and she shook her head. With no connection to her, neither of them could hear her words. "He says she says she has a lot to tell us — all of us."

Rakariel glanced at the gaping doorway, and sighed. She didn't like staying still, not so close to her lightstone's limit and never in a place like this, where danger could stalk at any turn, but the spirit of the priestess was the best source of knowledge they would ever find. She might know the answers, know what had to be done. However much time it took, they had to listen.

She crossed to the corner furthest from both door and broken window, and leaned against the wall there. Tei followed close behind, standing with his back to the adjacent wall, from where he could see the entrances, her, and the part of the room where he felt Avin stood. He watched as Rakariel got out the lens again, fitting it over her head and flinching slightly as the prismatic colours splintered and broke across her vision. She had to concentrate hard on adjusting it, her fingers jerky on the wheels, and 'missed' the alignment twice, only managing to bring the plane of spirit into full focus on the third attempt. The palace was visible only as a kind of shaped mist, old stonework imbued only with faint memories and microscopic life, not the faded strength of a god's temple. In the centre of the room, however, two clear figures were visible: Avin, relatively strong and bright, and beside him the faded spirit of a young woman in some sort of robe. Both standing more or less at floor level, he was the taller, concern and faint anger visible in his expression where she looked apologetic and largely tired. Finally able to perceive them both, Rakariel spoke.

"Seivi," she began, "what did you want to tell us?"

The lens allowed her to peer into other planes, but it couldn't let her hear. She saw the young woman's mouth move, then Avin's as he relayed her words, and finally heard them spoken in Tei's soft whisper.

"She says she thinks she knows why everything went wrong. She came here to tell King Sariven that, just like she told Avin she was going to. She wanted to tell him what he had to do to set it right, but he thought he had to find another way."

Watching the spirits, Rakariel could see Seivi's sad expression as she spoke and listened to her own words retold. After a moment's hesitation, she turned to Avin, speaking to him; Avin said something back and she replied, the conversation going back and forth with Avin seeming to grow more vehement and anguished while Tei, watching the rough area they were in, could only look confused. Rakariel herself felt equally so. What were they talking about? About to say something, she was cut off by Tei, who'd been trying to put what he heard together.

"Avin's saying something about it being his fault. He wants to know how it can be his fault."

Even as he spoke, Rakariel saw Seivi shake her head, trying again to explain something to Avin in what, for the rest of her audience, could only be silence. Avin reacted at once.

"Now he's saying it's the king's fault. That it doesn't matter *why*, it still is."

Able to see he and Seivi were still speaking to each other, and all too rapidly, Rakariel interrupted them almost as soon as Tei had finished speaking. "Avin! Avin, you have to tell us what she's saying. You *have* to."

Avin slowly looked around at her, nodding after a pause and visibly calming himself a little. The motion set off a faint shimmer around the edges of his head, and Rakariel twitched one of her fingers, still resting on the little wheels of the lens, to adjust the alignment before it drifted any further. She watched him seem to sigh, beginning to speak, pausing in places to wait for Tei to catch up.

"She said that Avin's sacrifice went wrong. That he died for his family, not the king, like you said. That really is why she promised him they'd be safe, because she knew it was true, after the gods accepted his life for it. But because that happened, nobody paid the price for the blessing the priests gave the king. Everything was out of balance."

"So the gods sealed the valley?" Rakariel asked. Seivi shook her head immediately, but it took a little longer for her words to be relayed down the unusual chain of listeners to Rakariel's ears.

"She says no. Uh, because they broke the balance, the priests lost contact with the gods. That might be why Avin is stuck here, too." Even as Tei spoke, the two spirits were already talking to each other again, and a brief pause followed before Avin passed on what they'd been saying once more. "She doesn't know for certain about that, but she thinks the reason he's tied here must have something to do with it, she's always thought that. Particularly since he couldn't be banished." He sighed. "She says the king should have paid the price, and everything would have been all right again. But he didn't. At first, he didn't even know he had to. That's why she left the temple and went to see him, because she'd worked out what had happened and she could feel the whole valley slowly drifting away — I don't know what she means, but that's what Avin said. Anyway, that's why things started to go wrong. But... the king said there had to be another way, and he told her he couldn't let her tell anyone else in case it caused more unrest in the city, so she had to stay here."

Rakariel could see the pain in Avin's eyes, but for once he kept talking, passing Seivi's words on to Tei without immediately acting on them.

"She says King Sariven was kind. He even asked for her advice several times. But everything just kept getting worse. The maid who came every day told her about all the things the king was trying to do to stop what was happening, to stop the monsters — the vardra — to keep the valley from sealing... everything. She didn't think anything he did would work for long, but she hoped she was wrong. She says he was a good man... but he has to be stopped." Tei blinked, whether at that or something else Avin had said to him, and stumbled over his words for a moment before forcing himself to keep going, telling Rakariel what she had to know. He could think on it for himself afterwards, not before. "She says she can't get to him, can't talk to him. She waited here hoping that someone else would come. She... she wants to go now. She's so tired."

They ended there, all three looking at Rakariel.

"Thank you," she said softly. Seivi's explanation had given her much to think about. Absently watching as the two spirits spoke to one another, Tei no longer relaying their words, she considered all she'd heard. It matched with what she, Tei, and Avin had been able to put together before, and she could see no reason for the priestess' tired spirit to lie. If that was the case, if Seivi was right, then the entire fate of the valley hung on one man's life, on the sacrifice Sariven had never made. And if that were true, then as she'd implied at the end, he had to still be alive even now, whether preserved by some artifice of magic or by whatever power kept the vardra going.

"Are you saying he's still alive — that the old king is still alive?" she asked Seivi, her fingers still on the wheels of the lens, adjusting them a fraction occasionally to keep the two spirits in focus. Her response was a nod, clear, direct, and simple.

"How?"

That time, the priestess shrugged, then spoke to Avin, and she could only wait for the words to reach her.

"He says she doesn't know," Tei told her. "She didn't really know what was happening. Since she died, she only saw him two or three times, a long time ago. He was alive then. He made some kind of barrier to block her out."

"So he survived the vardra?"

"At least at first," Tei relayed. "She thinks he must have. They don't go too near the library — that's where he is. She can't go there, either. Even though they live here, they stay away from it, too."

"Why do they live here?" Rakariel asked. "Where did they come from?" Avin's words about their appearance still echoed in her mind, and she had to know. What had warped ordinary people into such terrors?

There was a long pause before the reply came, Seivi looking miserably down past her feet. She said something that shocked Avin, and he questioned her only to receive a sad nod before finally turning back to Tei.

"Avin says... he says she thinks all the curses are blessings that have gone wrong. The king asked for his guardsmen to be blessed, he says, and they were — and Seivi thinks that those were twisted as everything went wrong." He looked up at Rakariel, wide eyes asking if it could really be possible. How could such a thing have happened? How could such a thing have been *allowed* to happen by powers entrusted with the valley's protection?

Rakariel thought before answering him. If she were to choose blessings for soldiers, what would she decide? The answers were all too obvious. Strength, endurance, all the physical attributes so useful in battle that the vardra had in such quantities. The blessing had warped, and the guardsmen with it, but they still bore the same traits.

"It's possible," she was forced to admit, reluctantly. "Strength, speed, endurance, martial skill — those are the sorts of blessings a king would probably choose for his soldiers. Your vardra have them all in one form or another."

Tei swallowed, looking away. She couldn't blame him. Seivi gave a sad nod of agreement, and said something that both Avin and Tei relayed only after a pause.

"So many people have suffered..."

Rakariel could only agree. They had, both then and over the long years since. So many people's lives had been ended or ruined, so many had grown up knowing only darkness and fear. If there was only one more thing she could do, it would be to end it. It had to end.

"We will stop it. Somehow. We'll have to find the king, or whatever's left of him. You said he was in the palace library?"

Seivi nodded, said something.

"As far as she knows, he doesn't ever come out. She doesn't know what's happened to him. Maybe he's some kind of monster, too." A pause followed, and through the lens, Rakariel could see Avin asking a question. He seemed unsurprised by the answer, passing it on to Tei once again. "She says that the tension Avin can sense comes from where he is. She can feel it too. It's all gone on too long."

Resignation touched Rakariel's expression as she thought. So, she would have to fight the valley's former ruler, likely insane at the very least and possibly a worse monstrosity than the vardra that infested the palace. No matter the cost, there was no other option she could take, and she had very little time. The difficulty of talking to Seivi had dragged their meeting out, and it had already been daylight. It would take still longer to skirt all possible danger and make their way to the library, and an unknown length of time to find a way in and deal with the fallen king, sheltering Tei if she possibly could, all with just one day left in her lightstone, if that. The amount of time it gave her was always somewhat variable, and she knew it would grow erratic and dim for a while before the last flicker of its light went out. The only positive thing about it all was that she now, at last, knew what she had to do.

"I'll find him," she said, features unconsciously

settling into a ready, determined cast. "I swear." A thought struck her, and she hesitated, looking at the faded priestess, her spirit weakened by time. "You said that you waited. Can you move on?"

Somewhat to her surprise, her response was another nod, and something that made Avin look surprised and grateful at once, passing her words on to Tei only after a pause.

"She says yes," he said, surprised. "She always could. She's stayed here for a long time to try and help."

Rakariel was impressed by the dead priestess' fortitude. Alone in the monster-haunted palace, the only person she could be sure still lived locked away from her, she had still stayed, unwilling to pass on to whatever afterlife her gods had granted her, all for the sake of a valley she couldn't even know was still inhabited.

"Thank you, Seivi. You have a great strength."

Despite her faded appearance and her clear tiredness, a pleased smile crossed the spirit's face. From what Rakariel knew, spirits, at least the saner ones, were usually little different from the people they had once been, other than having had more time to reflect on their actions, and their death to come to terms with. She wondered for a moment what had killed Seivi, whether the vardra had done it when they finally overran the castle, or she had died alone of dehydration before they broke into the room, unable to escape and with no-one to help. Either way, she had overcome it, and held on.

After a few moments of silence, Seivi turned to Avin and spoke again. Whatever she said, his reaction was one of concern, and he gently touched her shoulder, his spirit dimming slightly as hers correspondingly brightened, lending her a little of the strength he had gained from Tei. A short while longer passed before he turned his head to look at Rakariel and Tei again.

"Avin says she wants to stay here a little longer, in case we need her. She — he says she wishes us luck. She doesn't know what we'll find, but her prayers are with us."

Rakariel smiled. "Thank you."

CHAPTER 17
The Strength of Desperation

Leaving the priestess' spirit behind, Rakariel and Tei left the room and made their cautious way back to the stairs. Though he was invisible with the lens once again tucked into Rakariel's pouch, Tei could sense him, and she trusted he was there. As they turned the last corner and stepped out onto the landing, a sound echoed dimly from somewhere in the palace. Neither could make out clearly what it had been, but both froze at once. Had the vardra returned? Was one hunting them even now?

They couldn't be, Rakariel thought. There was no need for subtlety on their part here, in the heart of the palace that had been their home for centuries. The sound warned of danger somewhere, but that was all. She knew just how much of a beacon her light made her: if it was seen even once, they would become targets impossible to miss, and she couldn't afford to hide it in the dark confines of the palace. If they had seen her, she didn't doubt that they would have attacked. It was no guarantee, however, that they wouldn't.

Looking at Tei, she could see just that fear plain in his eyes, in his tense stance, as though he wanted to run and hide. They had both jumped at every sound, however small, in the ruined palace, but he had even more than she, and she couldn't help but approve of his courage. He was afraid, yes, and rightly so — but he faced it. He went on, as did she.

They crept back down the staircase, staying by the

banister just as they had on the way up, the lightstone's cool light sending shadows creeping across the floor as Rakariel moved. Tei found he was starting to get used to the motion, as smooth as her steps, every shadow moving in perfect time. Only if one of them moved out of sequence, or in the wrong direction, would it mean danger. Avin led them through ruined rooms and halls, echoes of the palace's past splendour still visible in places beyond the destruction and damp. Mist curled in through broken windows, grey-lit still in the light of day, and Rakariel wondered just how much time had passed. Even she was beginning to lose track. She hadn't slept, nor could she now until it was over, and their slow, tense progress was interminable.

Though Rakariel was keeping to as straight a line as she could, they still had to detour in places despite her reluctance, unable to risk alerting the vardra to their presence. The entire palace was a maze of fallen ceilings and long corridors, ruined rooms full of shadow and silence, spectral courtyards to be avoided at all cost, and, though they were widely scattered with most clearly still out in the city, the dark spirits of vardra.

Coming to the end of a corridor that led into what looked to be a vast, open hall, Rakariel leaned back to whisper to Tei.

"What's ahead?"

He waited a moment for Avin to tell him, then answered, his voice all but silent. "We're almost there. There's a vardra up above, but it's high up, three or four floors, he thinks. That's all he can see."

She nodded, stepping quietly forward. Three or four floors seemed likely to be far enough to be safe, at least one set of floorboards between them and it even if the hall ahead was high-ceilinged. As she passed under the archway, Tei's eyes widened in shock, and he grabbed her shoulder, pulling her off-balance with unexpected strength and a whispered cry.

"Wait!"

Before Rakariel could even finish regaining her balance, something large and dark fell before the door with a heavy thud, and she leapt back further, almost colliding with Tei, an arrow ready in an instant. Behind her, Tei stared in horror, unable even to breathe, frozen to the spot with his heartbeat racing in his ears. The dark shape was unquestionably another vardra, picked out in Rakariel's brilliant light, beginning to slowly straighten — and slumping back to the floor even before the arrow shot from Rakariel's bow to bury itself deep in the creature's side. There was no cry, and for a moment, it seemed that the world itself held its breath.

Poised with another arrow ready, Rakariel kept her gaze fixed on it unblinkingly, but the stillness and silence betrayed nothing. Had it died? Fallen because it was already dying, though it looked unharmed? If the landing had killed it, how had it not cried out in pain? *Something* had killed it, though she doubted it was her single arrow. Without relaxing, she gestured behind herself with a twitch of her elbow, only able to hope that Tei would take her meaning correctly. There was no hope of looking to see if he had. Very slowly, she dared to take a half-pace forward, a single, smooth step that didn't permit her aim to waver even a fraction.

It was in that moment that she saw the motion, the faintest, slightest movement traced against the air and the vardra's dark body, and again she leapt back, loosing her arrow and snatching up another without thought. Her arrow buried herself in the motionless black form almost beside its partner, knocking the body sideways slightly as it spent its force upon it, and from somewhere she heard the whisper-thin echo of a voice.

"Nn-!"

She couldn't tell what was happening, and it left her shaken. That had not been the sound of a vardra, if she'd truly heard it at all, but it surely couldn't have been a person unless she herself had let out an involuntary sound without even realising it. It couldn't have been Tei: he was behind her and it had seemed to come from in front. What — who — could it have been? Was it only her own overstressed imagination, seeing an additional darkness in every shadow at this, the worst of all possible times? Though she feared the dark, she had always known her senses to be reliable before, but was the unending darkness taking a greater toll than even she had realised it would? The motion and the sound could maybe, just maybe, have been nothing more than her own internal illusions. She feared the concept almost more than the vardra. They were a real, solid enemy, one that she could fight, but if she couldn't trust her own senses in this place, she would have nothing left.

Moments later, the dull shape moved again, dim, almost invisible outlines against the black of the fallen vardra, and again, she shot without thought.

"Nn-!"

This time, more motion followed it, and that distant, dim voice that seemed to come from so far away sounded again.

"It's dead, I can't see it any more!" she made out,

or thought that she did. What sorcery was this, what trick? The outline blurred into motion, vanishing from her sight, and she whirled in the direction she thought it had gone, pinning Tei in her brilliant light.

"Uh," he managed, fear in his expression, in his voice. "Avin says it's dead. There's nothing there. Are — are you all right?"

"There's something else here with us!" she hissed back. "I saw it move!" There, she stopped, suddenly aware of how she must sound to her young charge. He watched her with a mixture of trepidation and trust, believing in her skills, her experience beyond anything he'd ever know. Even when she seemed to make no sense, he trusted in her, the stranger from beyond the edges of his world. Was she right? Could she be? Could there be something with them even now that Avin could not sense?

"What... what did you see?" he whispered, fighting his nervousness at the thought. Avin's guardianship had protected them, but what would they do if he could no longer warn them?

"I don't know. Something from the corner of my eye. Stay still — don't move unless you have to."

Obedient, Tei waited motionless as she slowly turned her head, sharp eyes scanning the corridor for any trace of whatever it had been. Only as she looked away from him did she finally sight it again, whirling back at once to fix her gaze on a point just beside Tei himself, almost directly over his shoulder.

"There!"

He glanced back, seeing nothing. "Th-that's *me!*"

For the first time, the fear in his voice was one she'd put there with her actions alone, and she couldn't help but wonder for an instant before silencing it: she had to be right, had to trust her instincts, because they were all she had and all she'd ever have, all that had kept her alive through the long years, and when at the last she'd crawled out of the darkness, her strength spent, her companions lost, the only voice she would ever hear in her mind again was her own, the only world she would see the one before her eyes. If that turned against her, with no cause or curse, she would have nothing, and she silenced the thought, ruthlessly barring it from her mind. It was impossible, she had to be right.

"No. Next to you. Move aside!"

Tei did as he was told, edging quickly over to the wall near her and flattening himself against it, close enough that if she turned to face him, her arrow would almost touch his chest. Rakariel ignored his motion completely, keeping her gaze focused on the exact same spot. There was nothing visible there now against the light stone wall, but perhaps that was the key...

She turned her head, slowly, keeping her eyes fixed on the same point. As the light she cast forward faded, something else began to brighten, a barely-visible shape like the inverted silhouette of a person, every line touched with the faintest of whites. There was an almost familiar quality to that oddly human form, but before she could pin it down, it moved again, gone from her sight.

"Did you see it?" she demanded, only just managing to keep her voice to a whisper. "Did you?"

Another voice, dim and distant on the very edge of hearing, made itself heard brief moments before Tei's response.

"She was looking right at me!"

"A-A... Avin says you were staring at *him*."

Rakariel was silent for a moment. Could it be? It would make sense, but she couldn't see how it could have happened: Avin had never been visible to them. He didn't have anything even remotely approaching the strength to make himself so, or certainly hadn't before. Gathering her courage, she raised her hand, grimly covering the lightstone for an instant. As the corridor fell into darkness, she saw the spirit before her, his feet several inches off the floor and leaning towards Tei somewhat more than he could have been had he weighed anything, looking at her warily. The apparition was indistinct and faded, difficult to make out clearly, but she recognised it nonetheless. It was Avin. Their companion spirit had, somehow, become visible. She gestured for Tei to look with her free hand, the one that still held her bow.

"Avin?" he asked, staring disbelievingly at the faded spirit before him.

"You can see me?" the distant voice responded, perplexed. *"But how? I don't — I don't think I —"*

"Did he just ask if we could see him?" Rakariel interrupted. She had to know. Tei nodded at once, looking at her in surprise.

"You heard him?"

Her response, too, was a nod. What had *happened?* How? Either Avin had somehow gained in strength greatly since meeting Seivi's lingering spirit, or something else were forcing it. Could it be something else that was making him visible? She knew from past experience that it wasn't impossible, that both magical and spiritual powers could be used to reveal lingering spirits, whether by forcing them into visibility or by letting the viewer see into the spiritual plane, much as her lens did.

"We can see him," she said, dropping her hand from the lightstone. "We can hear him. Something's happened, but I don't know what, and we don't have time to stand here." She glanced warily back at the dead vardra as she spoke, but it was still, three arrows embedded side by side in its corpse. Satisfied that it would not move again, she crossed to it and yanked them out, noting with relief that none had broken. Every arrow she lost was one less she could use later. "We'll think while we move. Avin, you can't feel anything different, can you?"

As she'd expected, he shook his head, the motion visible as long as she didn't shine her full light on him.

"No, just the same tension. We're close now... it's that way." He pointed ahead, visible on the very edge of her vision, and she nodded. Knowing that the faint motion she could see was Avin reassured her, even if catching sight of it made her instinctively look for danger. Her senses still told the truth.

Stepping carefully over the hulking body of the dead vardra, Rakariel made her way cautiously into the hall beyond. The floor was smooth and polished, little sign of furniture, balconies on the higher levels and a raised dais at one end. It must have been some sort of grand entertaining area, she thought, perhaps a ballroom or something like that. She had little experience of such places; they weren't where mercenaries tended to end up, and certainly not her. The high ceiling was obscured by mist, leaving her unable to tell whether it was windows, the roof, or both that were broken. A dim shape flitted in the darkness of the far corners, small and faint: it had to be Avin, or so she hoped, but she found herself watching it anyway. If it was him, all well and good, but if not...

She found it even harder to trust that which she could only barely see than that which she couldn't see at all. Avin had become a presence, a warning, his companionship, evidenced only in Tei's reactions, growing familiar and even appreciated. The flitting motion in the shadows and on the edges of her vision was a nightmarish distraction, playing as it did on all her worst fears. Anything could be hiding there, anything, the motion possibly Avin's benign presence, possibly something altogether more sinister. Though she knew that he would be likely to sense something living waiting for them even before she would see it, she couldn't entirely quell the fear the motion raised, the additional alertness it forced her into as every flicker of pale motion caught her eye and made her glance towards it.

The only way to deal with it was to pick up the pace, still keeping her footfalls almost silent on the old floor. The faster they could cross the vast hall and leave again, the better. In the enclosed space of the smaller rooms and the corridors between them, Avin would be much less visible, and her fears could rest.

She was a bare few paces from the doorway she'd been heading for when a howl rang out behind her. Tei gasped and she instinctively whirled in the same moment, bow drawn. They had been found at last, her light, her only safety, also a beacon to danger. She had had to weigh that balance many times before, and there had been a time when she could have pushed on in the palace's half-light, waited through the black nights, but she could no longer fight, no longer live without her light close at hand. High up, something moved in the dimly grey fog, dropping to the floor lightly despite its size and proving in the light to be a vardra like those she had seen before as it righted itself, looking toward her and Tei with an unmistakable hatred. It tilted its head back to howl even as two more dropped down with a thud, the eerie cry rippling out into the valley, across the fogbound city — and cut off abruptly as her arrow took it in the throat. The other two took up the cry without a break, the long, endless-seeming howl that she had first heard near the temple, that signified the death of one of their own. Now that they had found the killers, she knew they wouldn't let them get away.

"Tei, go!" she shouted, careless now of her voice: however loud she shouted it could make no difference, all but lost in the vardra's bone-chilling howling. "Follow Avin, run!"

Her words shocked him into motion, and she saw him slip quickly through the arched doorway, vanishing from her sight. Stance blazing defiance, the lightstone burning bright on her brow, she stood her ground before it. If she could buy even a moment's grace, it would be worth the cost. Other vardra outside took up the howl as the two within ceased, and she ran her forefinger up the bow, touching an inset gem, speaking a single word that rang with power as she let her arrow fly. Its speed enhanced far beyond the limitations of her own strength, it punched directly through the leftmost vardra's heavily armoured hide, bowling the creature over, and the other one paused in what looked like shock. Rakariel took a swift step back, feeling her heel hit the wreckage of the broken door. Her bow's battle enchantments didn't hold many charges, a limit to the amount of power that could be stored in the imbued gems no matter the skill of the sorcerer she paid, but the vardra had no way of knowing that. At the least, it might give them pause.

Before the third vardra could gather itself to come after her, she backed quickly through the doorway, loosing an unempowered shot and seeing it hit, knocking its target back with a cry of pain. She doubted it was fatal, but it didn't matter. As she kept backing down the corridor, losing her line of sight on the one she'd shot, she saw another drop down from above, the howling from outside seeming to grow more distant as though it was rippling out through the city. She would be Tei's rearguard, and if they were very, very lucky, they would reach the library and whatever lay within before the vardra overwhelmed her, trading one danger for another unknown.

The creatures hesitated as she began her retreat — only to come charging after her almost as one scant seconds later, though her arrows sang out in a deadly rain. There was only one of her, and many of them. She was limited in strength and speed, and though she had the advantage as long as the corridor remained small and narrow, they were less so. She was running blind, where they knew the area. Her light made her a beacon, where they blended into the shadows. She suspected they knew as well as she did that this time, they had a clear advantage. Quickening her pace, she loosed another arrow that took one in the shoulder as it attempted to duck through the doorway, sent it staggering awkwardly back on legs that were ill-shaped for retreat and felt a moment's grim satisfaction. They could be hurt, they could be killed, and she was not dead yet. Another shouldered the injured one aside, coming down the corridor at her with all the speed it could muster in such an enclosed space; she shot again and a combination of luck and skill saw her arrow take it in the eye, dropping it to the ground. The one behind it was the one she'd shot before, she noted, heightened senses making every moment pass slower than it had any right to; she could see the arrow still lodged in its shoulder, the slightly awkward way it held that arm with the almost dreamlike clarity that sometimes came in such moments. She used the extra speed of thought to aim and shoot as quickly as she dared, taking it in the leg and seeing it stumble to the ground only to start trying to pick itself back up, another vardra looking behind it as she drew her bow and aimed again.

In the same moment, she heard a voice behind her, unexpected enough to shock, intoning rushed, meaningless syllables that held the ring and resonance of magic. All at once, lightning cracked past over her shoulder, so close her shorter hairs stood on end, earthing itself in the face of the injured vardra, which fell back to the floor with an unearthly cry. There was only one person who could have done that: it had to be Tei, standing behind her for all that she'd told him to run. She didn't, couldn't so much as spare him a glance as the next vardra leapt the body of its companion. There wasn't time.

Behind her, Tei stood momentarily still, shocked. He'd felt the magic build for the first time, harsh and sharp, weaving into itself in a way he couldn't describe. He'd felt it snap away from him faster even than one of

Rakariel's arrows, seen and heard the impossible crack of a brilliant light that had left jagged images imprinted into his vision, left him with a smell he could only describe as burnt air, his tousled black hair prickling from its closeness. He'd seen the vardra he'd focused on in desperation fall, unmoving, to the ground, and it was intoxicating and terrifying all at once. He could fight back! He could fight, wielding a power he had never even imagined! He didn't understand it, but he didn't have to, because it was his. Magic sang in his bones as he began the spell again, each syllable falling into place almost naturally, snapping into place as harsh as the light they summoned. Again, that brilliance cracked out before him, passing Rakariel to hit another oncoming vardra that went down with a shriek, the smell of burnt flesh drifting towards him.

"Run!" Rakariel shouted, whirling towards him and already beginning to follow her own command. He hesitated for a single moment, only an instant, but it was all she needed to catch up to him, grab a handful of his tattered clothing and yank him after her, nearly pulling him from his feet.

"But we were fighting them!" His own words almost shocked him, but it was true! They had fallen!

"You killed one," she snapped back. "Killed one and injured another. I don't know how long you can keep that up for, but they'll wear us down by numbers if nothing else! Now keep running!"

"It's not far!" came Avin's indistinct voice, urging them on. *"Just keep going — it's on your right, there's a wall, something — I'll see if I can distract them!"*

He was gone before either Rakariel or Tei had a chance to object, the faintest blur of motion passing them. In one sense it didn't matter: he was a spirit, unlikely to be able to be hurt by the purely physical vardra any more than he had been by the arrows Rakariel suspected she'd shot straight through him earlier. There was a chance that whatever had forced him into visibility would make him more vulnerable as they closed, but all she could do was hope not. He'd made his decision — and they were almost there.

Alone among all the corridors of the palace, the doors to either side were intact. Rakariel stopped at the first one on the right, kicked it open to reveal only a dark and empty room, and whirled to shoot back down the corridor at the hulking black shapes that almost filled it, aiming high to hit those that still stood rather than the fallen at their feet. In the moment she loosed the arrow, she touched another gem, spoke another one-syllable command. As the arrow left her bow, it blazed with magical fire, clinging to the creature it struck and setting it ablaze. Agonised howling filled the confined space of the corridor even as she spun again to run on, and understanding what she was doing, Tei dashed ahead to the next door. He flung it open without thought for caution, and just as quickly jerked it shut once more as something slammed against it from the other side.

"Look out!" he yelled, even his silence finally broken in the desperation and immediacy of the battle to survive. Rakariel raced towards him as fast as she could, passed him as he, too, turned to run and the door shuddered in its frame. They were only just in time, an immense black blade crashing through the ancient wood, reducing it to splinters behind them. Two more strokes made short work of the damaged door, echoing in Rakariel's ears, and she spun again in fatalistic necessity as it raced towards them, already almost on her. She loosed an arrow that took it in the chest, penetrating its natural armour, but not deeply enough; it staggered and howled in pain and rage, but did not fall. A dull shimmer of motion seemed to pass behind the creature as she readied another, paying the faint distraction no heed, and shot again, though she had no clear shot at anywhere vulnerable. Again, the vardra roared, but they were as smart as she had feared, and even injured, it was doing its best to conceal its weaknesses from her. She thought fleetingly of magic while it was still off-balance, shifting her finger up even as it abruptly crouched to try and spring — and fell, crashing to the ground almost at her feet. Revealed behind it, Avin floated, clearly visible now, his hands outstretched in a desperate grabbing motion as though he'd tried to stop it or hold it back, a look of shock on his spectral face. He was stronger again, brighter than he had been before, revealed more clearly in translucent grey-white.

"Run!" he shouted, his voice still distant, but clearer by far than it had been before. Even as she turned once more to race away, Rakariel knew what had to have happened, the answer clear and obvious in her mind. Avin had drawn the vardra's strength from it in his attempt to stop it from reaching her, killing it whether he had meant to or not, just as she had warned Tei that some spirits both could and did... just as some she had faced before had. For all that it had just saved her life, it was an ability that she didn't trust. If Avin chose to turn on her and Tei — she didn't know what reasons he'd have to do so, but it was always possible

that his centuries-long wait could have affected him more than they knew — then she would have only one chance to stop him, and would have to act very quickly indeed.

The thoughts flashed through her mind in the few moments it took her to catch up to Tei, half-turned again as though preparing to try and fight alongside her, but turning back as he saw her run towards him. The wall to their right was unbroken, and then-

"There!" Avin yelled from behind them, his voice sounding closer still. *"The wall's there!"* He shot up beside them with the speed only a spirit, freed from the tethers of the physical world, could have, pointing at a fair-sized door just paces ahead. *"It's on the other side!"*

Rakariel skidded to a halt by the door, gripping the doorhandle in desperate haste, ignoring the sharp tingle of magic beneath her fingers like a static shock. Better an unknown fate at the hands of whatever lay beyond than the certain death that would result if she passed it by, whether at the claws of the vardra or in the dark if she, by some miracle, escaped. Bracing herself, she twisted the handle and threw her weight against the door: it stuck for a moment, then suddenly went, and she almost stumbled through after it. The shock of strong magic jolted through her as she crossed the threshold, but it was only that, a barrier breaking around her as she half-fell through into the room beyond, clutching the doorhandle for balance.

Avin tried to dart after her in the next moment, brought up short by the same invisible barrier, the air seeming to ripple as he pressed against it, but not giving even a fraction of an inch. Beside him, glancing frightened back down the corridor where the agonised howls had finally come to an end, the vardra paused momentarily behind the two most recent corpses but already looking about to spring forward once more, Tei wordlessly held out his hand to him. Avin took it, inasmuch as he could, his all but intangible touch like a chill breeze. Only hoping he could somehow pull Avin through rather than leave him alone and in danger, Tei, too, tried to step through. The barrier of the doorway resisted him at first; he found himself having to push — then, suddenly, he was stumbling on the other side, colliding with Rakariel, and Avin was gone.

CHAPTER 18

Apart from Time and Consequence

Even as she stumbled through the door in desperate haste, Rakariel found herself struck by what lay beyond, slowly straightening up with her hand still gripping the handle. Ahead of her, another wide hall stretched out, filled with aisles of bookshelves taller than a man and untouched by the ravages of time: the repository of a kingdom's knowledge. Somehow, impossibly, it was lit, glass-sided lanterns hanging from brackets at the end of some sections of shelving to provide a warm and flickering light. It was almost ridiculous, out of place and unbelievable, as though one simple move had thrown her centuries into the past. She gathered her wits quickly, but before she could turn to look behind her and check Tei was following, not waiting frozen in the corridor outside, something stumbled into her back, grabbing at her waist.

"S-sorry!"

It was Tei's voice, yet even so, her hands shot instantly to his, only an effort of will preventing her from reflexively spinning and throwing him to the floor as she would any enemy that had attacked from behind. Tei let go of his own accord just moments later, straightening up and turning back to the door, backing away from it. Rakariel turned, too, knowing that the vardra couldn't be far behind. Warm lanternlight pooled in the corridor beyond, its yellow shade washed out by the cool, white glow of the lightstone, neither Avin nor the vardra immediately in sight. Knowing Avin could pass through walls, Rakariel slammed the door quickly shut, for what little protection it would provide without bolt or lock if whatever barrier she and Tei had broken failed to keep them out. A howl of rage came from outside, quickly taken up by an entire chorus of eerie near-voices, the vardra furious at being once again robbed of the prey that they were so determined to catch. Though she stood tense and ready, backing a few paces from the door and prepared to loose another arrow at the slightest provocation, though she could hear movement outside beneath the awful, chilling howling, the door was not so much as challenged. Slowly, very slowly, she began to relax. They were staying out, and the only thing she and Tei would have to face was whatever danger lay within.

"Avin...?" Tei asked, slowly, almost hesitantly as he, too, forced himself to relax a little, recognising the vardra's inability to reach them. If an answer came, Rakariel couldn't hear it, for all that he'd seemed so close before, and she waited, hoping for a response. Had he vanished? Was he trapped on the other side, as Seivi has said? Yet, moments later, Tei relaxed a fraction further.

"I think he's still with us," he said. "It feels strange, but I know he's right here. He almost couldn't get through. I had to help him."

So it was just as Seivi had said, she mused. Whatever ward barred the door likely kept both bodiless spirits and the vardra away, though it had let her and Tei through. Whether it was weakening or not, since Avin had apparently been able to pass through, it seemed the vardra didn't even think to test it. Slowly, the awful sounds began to fade.

"Yes, go away," muttered a strange new voice, cracked and dry, echoing oddly around the library. With a gasp, Tei spun to look for it, a motion almost mirrored by Rakariel. The visible central aisle of the library was empty, but it continued. "You're dismissed. Dismissed. Go. And don't kill anyone. You hear? You don't listen. Insubordination, that's what it is. Not that you have a choice. Not that any of you have a choice." There was a sigh before the stumbling words continued, difficult to make out clearly, let alone to pin down an origin for. "Not that anyone has much of a choice. I haven't found it yet."

"You..." murmured Tei, apparently unconsciously, his voice back to its customary near-whisper. Wary and unsettled by the sheer normality of the library, by the strange voice that echoed around it, and now by Tei's reaction, Rakariel touched a hand to his shoulder, making him start and look up at her with a silent question in his expression.

"What did you say?" she whispered, only to hear him whisper back

"I didn't say anything. What... what was that voice? It sounded like a person..."

Was it true? He wouldn't lie, she was sure of that, not knowingly, and that meant it had to be. But then, what had she heard — or thought she heard? What was happening to her? She'd already been forced to doubt her senses once, and this second time drove fear's needle a little deeper. Unsure, she raised her free hand to the lightstone, taking comfort in its presence, the familiar feel of the smooth, rounded shape that illuminated her surroundings, giving her light. Giving her life.

"I don't know," she said eventually, quietly. "We'll have to find it."

Lowering her hand, she flipped open the pouch that held the lens, pulling it out. Long practice let her tug it over her head one-handed, tipping her head somewhat to keep it in place as she adjusted the loosened strap with one eye closed. Only once it was secure did she risk opening her eye again, flinching at the uncomfortable wash of prismatic colour that splintered across her vision. She took a breath, forcing herself to ignore it and the headache it threatened her with, switching her bow to her right hand to adjust the wheels with her left. Carefully spinning them against one another, she sifted through the colours, slowly shutting out the worst of the confusion as she tuned slowly in to view the world in strong shades of magic.

Her eyes widened in shock as she found her focus, the clashing colours gone, but more woven through the world all around her, through walls, floor, and ceiling, strong and sharp, unsubtle but effective. Preservation's amber shade outlined every stone, every book, even the candles in the lanterns, and the library was filled with wards and barriers, some behind, some ahead. One stretched across between the second row of shelves, not more than ten paces further on, and another beyond it, at least three layers of them lined across her vision in blue and smoky red and sharp, sullen, angry gold like the molten metal at a forge, a blaze of warding and warning. Blue likely meant illusion, concealment; that jagged, arcing gold woven through it was hostility and danger, a coiled whip ready to strike. Red showed solidity, tangibility: the walls were wards of force that might or might not bar their path, their almost frayed patterns suggesting deterioration with age, but their undeniable brilliance speaking of power even now. Hissing through her teeth, Rakariel switched the bow back to her left hand, her fingers brushing across the keyed gems set into it. The motion served as a slight reassurance: she still had greater power yet to wield, and against magic of that strength, she was all too likely to need it. The little she had taught Tei would be such a scant amount as to be almost laughably useless in the face of whoever or whatever had set those barriers, doubtless, she thought grimly, the lost king, whatever he had become.

Gesturing for Tei to stay close behind her, she started cautiously forwards, moving on with a light step that made little sound. Every pace was measured, tested, every sense alert for anything her tread might set off. Passing the first row of shelving, she looked sharply from side to side, but there was nothing more dangerous than dust revealed to either her normal or her magical vision. Many books were missing, or piled on the floor by the shelves; the library had seen much use and little care.

The ward ran between the next set of shelves. Rakariel stopped just short of it, slowly lifting her right hand towards it, and felt a tingle in the air as her fingertips approached the barrier that only her left eye, aided by the lens, could see. She saw the magic thicken slightly ahead of her hand, colours growing more concentrated and opaque, waiting for whatever was drawing near to touch. Rather than risk her own hand testing it, she stepped back and reached over her shoulder for an arrow, drawing one from her rapidly dwindling supply. Holding it loosely, ready to let go in an instant if the ward lashed out, she cautiously stretched out her arm, bringing the arrowhead up to touch the barrier.

A jolt, not of impact, but of magic, ran up her arm as the arrow hit the ward and stopped. Her left eye could see the magic wrapping around the arrowhead as though holding it, testing it, though for what she couldn't have said. Experimentally, she pushed it forward slightly, feeling a couple of seconds of resistance before the spell thinned ahead of the arrow and let it pass, though with a tension that made it feel as though it was moving through water rather than air. The sharp golden arcs that lined the barrier's edges remained quiescent as, daring, she stepped slowly forward and pushed her arrow through almost to the fletching, her hand almost touching the ward. A quick breath, and she leaned slightly further, touching it with the first of her bent fingers. As it had for the arrow, the ward stopped her for a moment, holding her there, and the arcs of gold twitched — then, like the arrow, it let her pass. She stepped through quickly, the feeling akin to walking through a sheet of still, prickly water, and back into the free air of the other side.

No danger showed itself ahead, and glancing from side to side showed her only more ransacked bookshelves, their contents piled haphazardly on the floor. Satisfied, Rakariel turned, beckoning Tei and holding her hand back out through the ward to him. Aware she'd seen something he could not, he took it hesitantly, flinching at the tingle that warned him he was close to it, then gathered himself and stepped forward, letting her draw him through. Like her, he was pinned for a long moment, only to be released to step through.

"What was that?" he whispered, wondering. The invisible barrier was another thing he had never before imagined.

"Magical ward," was Rakariel's short answer. "It didn't think we were a threat. Whatever it was meant to stop, it wasn't us."

Tei nodded, still not sure he understood what it was or even what it meant, but knowing that they had no time for more. Perhaps it was supposed to protect against the vardra; that would make sense. Pushing lingering discomfort and Avin's unusual closeness, something he could almost feel to an extent he hadn't since their contact in the temple's pool, to the back of his mind, he looked forward again. There was no sign of anything ahead, but he hadn't seen the ward he'd just walked through, either. Only Rakariel, with her lens, could see whatever magic lay before them. Freed from looking for it, he couldn't help but gaze at the lanterns that bathed the room in light, struck again by how out of place they were, and yet on some level by how natural it looked. No-one would waste that many candles, certainly not ones so bright. No-one would risk that much light. It was impossible... and yet, there it was.

He noticed Rakariel stepping forwards almost a moment late and followed soundlessly behind her, pulling his eyes from the lanterns to run through the syllables of magic again in his mind. The memory of the spell, of the light that burnt apart the very air and killed, was still fresh, and he knew he could use it again if he needed to. She paused at every set of shelves, glancing from side to side, and Tei paused with her, doing the same. The sight of so many books awed him, even with half of them missing from their shelves, but he remained alert for danger. Though the magical barriers seemed to keep the vardra out, he knew he had to remember that anything could lurk in this strange place, however inhabited it seemed.

They passed another ward, much the same as the first one, another four shelves further in. Again, he watched as Rakariel touched an arrow to empty air, waited for a moment before risking her hand, then took the final step and turned to face him. This time, he gathered himself and stepped through on his own before she could reach out to him, feeling again the uncomfortable pinning sensation that paused him mid-step for a moment before he was released once more. As they both glanced around again, something caught his eye. Was the light slightly stronger, away to the right? He touched Rakariel's arm lightly, lifting his hand to his forehead when she looked at him, and she nodded, covering the lightstone with her hand. Illuminated only by candlelight, the faint difference he had seen grew clearer, and he pointed towards it.

"The light's stronger there. Look."

Rakariel frowned, squinting slightly, her eyes less sensitive than her companion's. She'd grown up under full sunlight, something he had never even known. It took her a few moments to make out the slight difference, but she saw it, and lowered her hand again. Though the hall was lit, she still wanted the lightstone free: magic could easily enough be used to snuff a candle, even within a lantern.

"Well seen," she murmured back to him, edging over to her left so that when they reached it, whatever it was, they would be as far from it as possible. Pausing to adjust the lens again, keeping it focused on the plane of magic, she closed one eye, then the other. The final ward wasn't far from the place the light seemed to be coming from, positioned between the final two shelves, their dusty height concealing the library's corners from view. Anything could wait there in that brighter light — and something with a human voice, she knew, did.

Making her way carefully between the shelves, her slow advance steadily revealed more and more of the hidden corner, until she was almost on the ward. From that angle, she could finally see part of an arched doorway to the right, the door intact and open, the additional light spilling from within. The left corner was dark and empty, the matching door on that side closed. She couldn't see what lay beyond either one, though her left eye hinted at traces of magic around both, unable to look far enough around the shelves without passing through the final barrier. As before, she raised an arrow cautiously to touch it, waited for the resistance to fade, then reached her hand through. It resisted her when her fingers first touched it, just as the other two had, but once again let her pass. Tei edged through behind her even as she turned to the right, ready, and found herself staring into a scene she had not expected.

The room beyond the open door was small, likely intended as a study area of some sort: a scholar's desk sat at its back, strewn with scrolls and books, some piled carelessly with no thought for their value or even integrity, others stacked neatly with strips of paper and fabric sticking from them at odd angles. Lanterns hung on either side of the desk, mounted on the wall, illuminating it with the warm glow of candlelight... light that also fell across a figure slumped before the desk in a simple chair. It was impossible to tell whether it was alive or dead, even male or female, long, uniformly grey hair trailing down its back, once fine clothing faded and worn, concealing its frame. For a moment, she was uncertain of what to do, what to think — and then the choice was lost.

"You!"

It was Tei's voice, but angrier than she had ever heard it, louder than she had thought she would ever hear him speak, even in desperate battle. The bent figure jerked upright stiffly, one arm moving to grope for something before it on the desk, setting it on its head before it slowly stood and turned to face them. The object was a jewelled crown, Rakariel saw, the face beneath it a man's, lined by care but not by age. Her breath caught for an instant as the last doubt was swept away: the valley's king stood before her, the last thing they would have to face. Slowly, he stepped towards the door of his study even as Tei, to her shock, started past her. She stuck out her arm to bar his way, felt him try to push her aside before reluctantly stopping, glaring at the man ahead.

"You seek an audience?" came the voice, the same one that had echoed through the library before, this man — this crowned man, this king — now clearly the speaker. "I'm afraid you're too late. Much too late. Who were you? I don't remember your face." His tone switched from matter-of-fact to commanding and back again, an odd note to it, the words almost faintly slurred like a man in a dream.

"You don't remember my face?!" Tei shouted,

pushing forward strongly enough that Rakariel's arm bent despite herself, forcing her to grab his ragged collar instead as he jerked forward. He pulled against her with a surprising strength, almost not seeming to notice that she was holding him, as if the only thought in his mind was reaching the fallen king. "You killed me!"

Rakariel's mind raced. What was *happening?* Tei was a normal young man, she was certain of it: even if her senses lied to her, the lens couldn't! She'd seen him through it in spirit back at the temple, was seeing him again in magic now; he looked as normal a person as she could expect!

"You killed me and you destroyed the city!" he raged, still straining against her grip. "You killed everyone in the valley!"

Somewhat to her surprise, the tall, regal figure before them sagged, his head bowed.

"I tried," he said softly, the words merging into one another slightly. "I tried to protect you, I'm trying so hard. I haven't found it yet, but there's a way out. There's got to be a way out. Don't tell me there isn't a way out, I won't believe you. I won't. There is a way to end this, I know I just have to find it. There'll be something in here that can give me a clue, I've tried so many things already. I didn't mean for you to die."

"You *asked* me to die!"

He flinched at that, then slowly lifted his head, puzzlement showing in his expression.

"Who are you?"

"My name's Avin!" Tei shouted. "*Now* do you remember me?!"

Tei's collar ripped, and he shot forward, only to

crash into a suddenly-erected ward in the doorway that the man, King Sariven, had keyed into being with a single syllable, commanding the traces of magic Rakariel had seen in the doorframe's stonework to snap together strong and solid. This ward was a barrier, pure and simple, almost a mahogany red to her magical sight, more than strong enough to hold him back. Numb, Rakariel could only stare, her hand still gripping the piece of torn cloth. Tei had said he was Avin. She'd seen Avin gain in strength as they fought, seen him sap it from the monsters in what at least looked like desperation. She'd seen him grow visible enough to be seen in full light... and now, she realised, he was in control. She'd thought that only the most powerful of spirits could do it, but his determination and his connection to Tei must have been enough to let him break the barriers between them. Now, Tei was subsumed beneath Avin's controlling personality, if not gone altogether, and it would be difficult — near impossible, in fact — for her to fight Avin without fatally harming him. There was no way to stop him... only to slow him down.

Sariven was frowning, peering through the distorted air of the ward, bent where it held Tei, or Avin in Tei's body, back.

"Avin," he said, almost musing aloud. "I remember Avin. He gave his life for us, for this valley. He didn't look much like you."

"I gave my life for my *family!*" Avin shot back in Tei's voice. "And this is what you gave them!"

Again, the king flinched. "That's what the girl said. The priestess. I know her. Her name is Seivi. Yes, she came to tell me that. She said I had to die."

"She was *right!*"

He shook his head. "No, no, that's not right, I can't die, I can't!" Sariven turned away from the barrier, began pacing in circles with his head to one side, sounding almost as though he was arguing with himself as much as with Avin. "I can't die, not yet, I have to bring back the light, don't you see? Don't you see? The kingdom will be nothing without someone to protect it! Someone has to stand for it, someone has to watch over it!" His voice had risen to a shout, sharp, choppy gestures with his right hand punctuating his words. "You can't, you're dead, whoever you are! Someone has to watch over it, I have to watch over it, I have to find another way! I know there's another way, there has to be, somewhere!"

Moving slowly, her bow lowered, Rakariel stepped up behind Tei, touching her hand to his shoulder. He jumped, but didn't look around, too focused on the man beyond the ward.

"There is no other way," she said, quietly.

"Of course there is!" Sariven snapped at once. "Don't you see, the kingdom will die!" He paused, looking straight at her, ignoring Tei's furious glare. "Who were you? I never knew you, who were you? Why do you have that light?"

"My name is Rakariel," was her simple, forcedly calm answer. The lost king seemed more than half mad, but a part of him could still be spoken to. She couldn't do anything with a ward that strong in her way, had to convince him to take it down — and she had to find a way to convince Avin to leave Tei. "I'm not dead. I come from outside this valley."

"Of course you're not dead," Sariven grumbled,

flinging his hands in the air. "You would say that, since you're standing here." He paused again, frowning. "But I don't know your name *or* your face. That's new."

She shrugged, repeating herself, lifting the lens from her eye. She knew what magic was there, and couldn't afford to spend her concentration keeping it focused. "I'm not from this valley."

"Well, where are you from, then?" he demanded. "And what are you doing in my library?" He paused, an expression of thought crossing his face, and went on in a strangely altered tone, suddenly measured and thoughtful. "I felt something before, heard it. My guard were tracking something."

"Your *guard?*" This from Tei, or at least in his voice. Rakariel tightened her hand warningly on his shoulder, though she doubted it would do much good.

"I tried to stop them, but it's not possible, you see. I tried so hard before, but all it means is I know what they feel." He shuddered convulsively, haunted by an old horror. "They're broken, but they're still my people. I can feel them all. I just can't tell them. They don't listen. It'd be treason if they knew any better, but they don't, they can't, it's all wrong. All wrong."

"You're talking about the vardra, aren't you." Rakariel said softly. He had to be. "The creatures in the palace."

"The guard," Sariven said. "The Royal Guard, the army, the palace guardsmen. All of them who are left. You killed some of them. I felt them go out." He pressed thumb and forefinger together in an oddly simple, almost childish gesture that sent a moment's chill down her spine as she pictured their spirits no more than candle flames, vanishing in the dark. "I felt them go out." He sighed, shaking his head. "Maybe it's best. But I should be able to save them. They're my people... I have to be able to save them."

Rakariel found herself pitying the man. Driven mad by time and solitude and perhaps what he had done, or even by his own blessings more subtly twisted, in his own mind he still thought he was trying to protect his kingdom. Who knew, perhaps he was. Still holding Tei's shoulder, she studied the arguably pitiful man before them anew, both eyes free to see him as he was. Yes, he stood straight, unbowed by age though his hair was grey; yes, he was physically unharmed, though his face was lined with care and his clothing threadbare with age despite the preservation spells he had doubtless cast on it. Yet his voice was a window to his broken thoughts, changing tone in instants as his mind moved from one to the next, unable even to tell the dead from the living. His words echoed over and over his intent to protect, not harm, his fallen kingdom, to save it from the darkness that had closed about it... even to save the former guardsmen she and Tei had both set aside as monsters, whose death she would have considered a release, whose living redemption not even she would have given a thought. It was impossible.

"I have to save them..."

"You can save them," Avin gritted. "You can save them by dying." Rakariel tightened her grip again in warning, though it was too late — but Sariven didn't seem to care.

"Do you think I don't want to? I can't, don't you see? That's what the young priestess said, but I can't. There isn't anyone, anyone who can protect my people in my place. I have to stand for them. I'll find a way out of this, I've got to. There has to be a way to save them. There has to be a way to save the kingdom."

There was a moment of silence on all sides, but Rakariel could feel Tei tensing under her hand.

"Tei!" she snapped. It was Avin, not him, but she had to try and get through to him somehow, even just to make Avin think about what he was doing. She yanked his shoulder, forcing him to half-turn to face her as the king looked on. "Whatever you were going to do, don't! Be quiet!" She shook him in emphasis, despite his uncharacteristic glare.

"I've waited four hundred years!" Avin snapped back in Tei's voice, though with his own accent and inflection. "Four hundred years trapped in darkness because of him! I lost my family, I've been trapped here, I've watched everything I-"

"-Ever loved go to ruin!" Sariven finished for him, so unexpectedly that even Avin was silenced. "Isn't that how it goes?" He started pacing in his circle again, around a paler track Rakariel realised with shock that he must have worn into the floorboards over years of walking the same path over and over. "Four hundred years, is it? At least part of me knows! That's how long I've been here looking for answers!" He stopped by the ward, jabbed his finger against it where he would have hit Tei's arm if it hadn't been for the magic barring his way. "Trying to save you! I know you're still out there, I don't feel you like my guardsmen, but they know you're there and so do I!"

An idea came to Rakariel then, an almost impossible one, but nonetheless offering a slim, fragile ray of hope. She let go of Tei momentarily to put her bow away: she would have no more use for it here.

Predictably, he whirled back to the ward that barred him from the former king, pressing his hands against it in a futile attempt to break through.

"They're there!" he shouted. "They're there and you're keeping them there! Seivi said you could break the curse any time you chose just by giving yourself up, but you won't! You just want power!"

"I *can't!*" Sariven screamed back, punching his own ward as though it were a wall he could take out his frustration on, the air temporarily seeming to splinter with the shock. "There's no-one to lead them! There's no-one to protect them! They'll be taken over, enslaved, wiped out! In *days!* The kingdom needs a king who can protect it!"

Just like that, there it was, her chance, perhaps her only one. It was her way in, and she had to take it, the fragile ray of hope growing stronger with every word the king spoke.

"There is someone."

Her quiet voice cut through the shouting, forcing them both to silence simply in order to make out her words. She pressed the advantage while she had it, every word freighted with sad certainty. It was possible... and it was true.

"There is someone who can lead them. Someone who has led them." She pulled Avin around to face her, and, taken aback by her interruption, he came unresistingly, looking back at her through Tei's dark eyes. "Avin, let Tei go. Let him go, or will you steal his life for your own ends?"

Avin gaped at her, struck dumb by her words. She'd chosen them deliberately to strike at his heart, at his love for his family, his hatred of what had been done to him. It was the only way she stood a chance of getting through to him, if he could be reached at all, and she went on.

"If you haven't killed him already. Free him, Avin." Though her voice was soft, her words were hard, and she shook him again. "Let him go. He isn't yours. His life isn't yours."

"I- I didn't-" Avin stammered, and gave up, helpless.

"I know," she said gently, though in truth she wasn't even sure. Avin's fury at his king had let him use his link to Tei to take him over, and it was beginning to seem as though he had barely even meant to, but there was no way for her to be certain. She was all but making it up as she went along, desperately reaching for the one distant, impossible glimmer of a chance to end it all without violence. Though she would fight if she had to, she couldn't even say who would win: Sariven's wards might not have had finesse, but they held a lot of raw power, far more than she could ever hope to marshal. But perhaps — just perhaps — there was a chance to avoid fighting at all, and more than that, a chance to truly set things *right*. "Now let him go."

Avin nodded, slowly, almost reluctantly, his eyes still wide and stricken. He staggered, and she moved with him to hold him up, letting him regain his balance in his own time and desperately hoping to see someone else when he lifted his head. Steadying himself after a moment, he looked up, and she saw with boundless relief that his expression was Tei's again.

"What... what happened?" Tei said slowly, in his habitual near-whisper. "I mean, I felt... Avin was shouting, and I was there, but I wasn't, and..."

"Later," she said gently, cutting him off. Taking his shoulders, she turned him around to face the former king, who stood watching with his head cocked to one side, curiosity in his expression. "King Sariven. This is Tei."

"...Uh..." It was all Tei could manage.

"Well," said Sariven into the silence. "I don't remember you, either."

"You wouldn't," Rakariel said. "He's alive, like me. He's one of your people, the ones your guard know are out there." She tightened her left hand slightly, and, taking her cue, Tei nodded, his dark eyes still wide as he stared at the wreckage of the man who had been his people's hero, who had been Avin's indirect killer.

"He comes from a line of mayors," she continued. "They've run the city in your absence almost since the darkness fell. His grandfather leads them now. They're safe, as much as they can be. They protect each other, they work together. That's right, isn't it, Tei?"

Tei nodded, still silent.

"Tell him about them," she prompted.

"Uh," he said quietly, still barely able to speak. "Tell him what?"

"Yes," murmured Sariven, "tell me what?" He fixed his eyes on Tei, gaze keen again, more, Rakariel thought, like the man he had once been. "Tell me about my people, then. Tell me how they live."

"Well..." Tei hesitated, unsure of what to say. "My grandfather is the mayor, like Rakariel said. All my family have been mayors, almost since the beginning. We're better at surviving than just about anyone else, that's why we have the postion. Um... People live far apart from each other, because it's dangerous to be too close together. We make sure the safehouses are kept up, even the ones that don't get used much. Everyone in my family does the long walk when they're old enough, all around the city, so they know everywhere. If anyone has any trouble, they get a message to us, if they can. If they can't, we check on them anyway. ...We go out in the light, not in the dark, it's less dangerous. We try and make sure everyone can stay alive. Mostly they don't need that much help..." He trailed off, unsure of how to go on, and glanced back at Rakariel for help just as the king spoke.

"Mayor, you say? Who appointed you?"

Tei shrugged. "I don't know. People, I guess. They needed someone to lead them. We're good at looking after ourselves, and other people when we need to, so most people generally think we're the best people to do it. We weren't mayors before or anything." He paused again, hesitant. Though he hadn't been able to intervene, he'd been aware of Avin's fury, of his actions. He still was, the spirit as uncomfortably close to his mind as he had been since Tei had tried to pull him through the barrier and he'd disappeared. Despite Avin's presence, he, like Rakariel, couldn't help but feel a little sorry for the fallen king. Though he was clearly no longer sane, it seemed that in his own hopeless way, despite what he'd done, he was trying to do what he thought was best... and that the price had tormented him for centuries. "They... they remember you, you know. Uh... you know, from before the valley closed. They say you tried everything you could think of to stop the darkness, but in the end, you vanished, and the monsters took over the palace." He looked down, then up again as Rakariel's hand tightened slightly on his shoulder.

"Your people remember you as a hero, King Sariven," she said. "But they've found new leaders now. They've had to. You can't protect them and save them at the same time. You must have known that when you warded yourself in here. You had to leave them outside." She paused, brown eyes meeting the king's crazed blue ones. "Lift the curse. Let them go."

For a long moment, all three looked at one another in silence, and she dared, just for a moment, to hope that it had worked.

"I can't," muttered Sariven suddenly, looking down. "You're trying to convince me, but I can't. I'm so close. I have to be."

"You've been looking for four hundred years," she told him gently. "You've done everything you could. If there was a way, you would have found it by now."

He shook his head, his voice barely louder than Tei's. "I can't let you convince me. I have to look after my kingdom. I won't leave it, I can't leave it."

Rakariel looked down for a moment, then up again. She wasn't sure the mad king even really believed she existed, that she wasn't a delusion like the others he had alluded to. "Your majesty, please. Let me through the ward." She had to try, somehow, to prove it to him, but she was gambling everything. If Avin once regained control of Tei's body, it would all be ruined. "I was telling the truth about Tei. He and I have been fighting to save the valley, to save your kingdom." Letting go of Tei's shoulder with her left hand, she reached out to the barrier, touching it lightly. It was strong enough for the air to feel solid, and there was an aggressive prickling under her hand, but no more. "We're here to help. I thought this place was the source of the curse, but now I see what's happened here." She still couldn't be completely sure of it all, but it seemed to make sense, her racing mind tracing around the edges of the shape everyone's tales had made. Though they conflicted in places, they fitted together into a larger whole if she allowed them to overlap, if she simply allowed that the broad events themselves had happened and left the reasons and precise detail to whoever had recounted them, outlining what had to have been a reasonable approximation of the truth. Fearful for his kingdom, King Sariven had sought protection from the gods, thought Avin was agreeing to the same thing; fearful for his family, Avin had died so that they would be cared for by the rewards the king had promised. Each thinking they were doing the right thing, each trying to protect that which they loved, they had unknowingly broken a balance and set events in motion that had plunged the entire valley into darkness.

"I've put my weapons away," she continued softly. "Let us help." Switching hands, she pulled Tei behind her, gripping his arm with all her strength in a silent warning to fight Avin, to say nothing, no matter what happened, to stop him from winning control again. Tei flinched under her hand, but, wonder of wonders, remained silent as she held out her right hand to the crazed king, inviting him to take it.

Looking momentarily bewildered, Sariven hesitated, studying her hand as if unsure of how to react before finally lifting his own in a mirror of the gesture, leaving them separated only by the ward. "You look more like a warrior than a noble lady, my dear. Are you right, I wonder? Well, it's not as though you can really hurt me. I might as well see what you want." He spoke two syllables of magic, and with a wave of his hand, the barrier was gone, keyed back into quiescence in the stones of the wall.

Their hands met, and though there was no spark or shock of contact, no faint buzz of residual power, the king jumped as though someone had stabbed him.

"You're so warm," he said, shocked and wondering.

Awkwardly with both hands occupied, one in front, one behind, Rakariel shrugged. "It's as I said. I'm alive. I've been fighting for your valley. Remember? The — your guardsmen were hunting me."

"And your light," he continued, almost bemused. "I haven't seen a lightstone in years. Centuries." He lifted his free hand towards it, and she instinctively flinched away before she could stop herself. Seeming to respect it, he pulled back. "A very long time. It's been a very long time." He peered past her, at Tei, whose flickering expressions spoke all too clearly of an internal war. "What makes you think you and this boy can protect the valley?"

"I'm a warrior, a traveller," she told him honestly. "I used to be a mercenary... I suppose I still am. It's Tei's people you should look to. Your people. They've had to take care of themselves, these past four centuries. They've even chosen a mayor to lead them. They're good at it, your majesty." Feeling a sudden tension beneath her left hand, she risked looking over her shoulder, saw Tei's changing expressions and internally swore. He and Avin were fighting for dominance, and she had no idea who would win if she left them to it. Stepping to her right, she pulled Tei up beside her so that the three of them formed a lopsided triangle. "Listen to me. I think everyone here... everyone did what they did because they thought it was the right thing to do. Didn't you?"

Tei nodded, or perhaps Avin through him. Looking perplexed by the sudden change of subject, Sariven did the same, as his rambling words had proved he would.

"You thought what you did was right. Nobody brought down this curse on purpose. This isn't the time to blame anyone." She shook Tei's arm slightly. "Avin is responsible too." He reacted with shock, and she watched him for an instant, going on before either Avin or Tei could quite begin to speak. "Avin is responsible because he let everyone believe he was giving up his life for the wrong reasons. You, your majesty, are responsible because you put him in a position where he had to. That's where all of this began. That's why it's the only way that any of it can end." She met the king's shaken blue eyes again, the remnants of his sanity wavering in their depths as understanding, almost acceptance. "Let them go. Please. Your people will be all right. They'll be watched over. They'll be taken care of. You know you're responsible. So does Avin. His spirit is still here because of it. You have to set things right... you have to pay the price for what you were given. *That's* your responsibility now, your majesty. You have to pay the debt you incurred on behalf of your people. You have to set them free from it." She paused, used their linked hands to gently pull him closer; he moved easily, unresisting. "Do you care about them... enough to give your life for them?"

Silent, he nodded, his eyes fixed on hers.

"I know it's difficult," Rakariel went on softly. "You won't be able to see that they're safe. You have to trust that they'll be all right... but they will be. I've seen their strength. I've met the people who lead them in your stead. They believe that you did everything you could to stop the valley from being sealed. Prove them right... and set them free. You can give them the sun again. Not even I can do that." Movements slow and smooth, she lifted their linked hands, bringing them into his field of vision, forcing him to remember that she was present in the flesh and not just in his mind. "They're your people. You care about them... so now you have to let them go."

Slowly, very slowly, Sariven nodded, letting go of her hand. She let him go, still gripping Tei's arm tightly, and followed quietly behind as he knelt in the centre of his little chamber, the place that, together with the library, had been his world for the past four centuries.

"I never meant for this to happen," he murmured, head bent. "I tried to stop it in every way I could. Can my people... will they really be safe? Will they really have a leader?"

Resting her free hand on his shoulder, Rakariel nodded, though he couldn't see it from his position, knelt as he was with his back to her. "Yes," she said. "They will."

The king sighed, unbelievably weary, his shoulders slumped. "I want it to be over. I really do. I want them to be free."

"Then let them," she repeated, her tone still gentle. "Pay your debts, and let them go."

Slowly, the king began to intone the syllables of magic, his voice thin beneath the resonance that imbued it. Rakariel moved to lift her hand from his shoulder, but he caught at it desperately as though seeking the reassurance and comfort of a living touch, and she was forced to leave it be. Tense and strained, she listened as magic far beyond her comprehension built around them, her instincts warning her to leap away and get to safety, far away from whatever effect it could have. She forced them down, knowing the only chance she had of keeping the mad king convinced was to stay with him, and more important even than that, knowing that if he was doing what his words and actions had implied, then her simple touch was the comfort a dying man needed in his last moments. She could not deny him that. She knew that if she'd judged him wrongly, it could mean her death, and probably Tei's along with her, but it was the only way. They were all bound together now, regardless of the outcome, and perhaps, she dared to hope, the wrongs of centuries before were at last being set right.

The spell went on, long and complex, as she and Tei both listened in silence. She felt a faint sense of loss, and realised that magic she hadn't even known was there was fading from the room, its presence in the lens doubtless overwhelmed by all the other, more vivid spells she had seen. One by one, the lanterns in the library began to go out, then those in the study, until finally, all that was left was her lightstone, bathing the room in its cool radiance. The magic she had felt building began to fade as well, and still the king went on. It was an unweaving, she belatedly realised, one incredibly complex. He was undoing all the magic he had left in place, undoing everything, from the preservation of the city to the wards that had shielded him. Her free hand tightened again on Tei's arm. The wards would fall, and all she could do was wait, tense... until the final threads of magic far outside her understanding had faded, and the king had finished.

"I'm sorry," he whispered. "I tried so hard. Forgive me."

Rakariel opened her mouth to speak, but the final word had been his last breath. He slumped forward, slipping from under her hand, and fell limply to the floor.

CHAPTER 19

Though All Things Fade

Though she knew he was dead in the instant that he began to fall from beneath her hand, Rakariel still knelt, after a moment, beside the king's body, releasing Tei's arm. She touched his shoulder again, still warm, but motionless in death. Moving with care, though he couldn't feel her, she turned him to lie on his back, straightening his legs, folding his arms across his chest, even replacing his crown atop his head. Whoever had been closer to being in the right, whoever had made the worst mistakes, he had tried to do what he thought was best, and deserved to be treated with respect in death. Tei watched, silent, and as she stood and turned towards him, she saw a second figure drift disconcertingly apart from him until he and Avin stood and floated beside one another, separate once more with whatever had forced them together released.

"Vardra," she said quietly, reluctant to break the silent peace, yet knowing that she had to. Both Tei and Avin started, Avin looking around, Tei reflexively jumping back to put his back to a wall.

"They're there, but... they're not doing anything," Avin said slowly, puzzled. *"They're... going away. They're not moving around, they're just going away."*

"What do you mean?" she whispered back. Could it be?

"They're going away," he repeated. *"They're getting harder to see, more distant. I... I think they're dying."*

Had she been right? With the king finally gone, had their curse, one he had brought upon them, been released? Gesturing sharply for Tei to stay behind her, she took up her bow once again, making her way quietly back through the darkened library with an arrow at the ready. Once again, her lightstone cast shifting shadows amongst the shelves, the place that had looked so warm and inviting just moments before now empty and dead. At the far end, unbarred by wards, the door still stood, untouched and undamaged. Slowly, almost holding her breath, she took her right hand from the bowstring to touch the doorhandle. Only chill metal met her fingers, no faint prickle of magic left in it to warn or protect, and she hesitated for a moment before suddenly twisting it, jerking the door sharply open and jumping back from it in the same quick move — but her light showed nothing visible outside. Holding an arrow ready once again, she crept up to the doorway, looked from side to side and saw several of the creatures, each with its massive bulk curled against the wall as though in sleep. Though the door had made some noise opening, none of them had noticed her, and didn't so much as stir.

"Alive?" she breathed as Avin drifted past her, stopping near the closest and leaning towards it as though watching for a breath.

"Barely," he said. *"I think it's safe."*

Poised and ready to move in an instant, she stepped out into the corridor. Just as Avin had said, it seemed safe: if the vardra scattered both left and right were even aware of her, they didn't react at all to her presence amongst them. It was strange, unsettling to stand there so completely unnoticed. They had chased her and Tei across the city for days with ruthless determination. Now she stood ignored in their midst as they died.

Stepping up to the closest, she bent slightly much as Avin had, watching it intently as behind her, Tei came up to the doorway, peering through but not quite daring to emerge. At that small distance, she could see the vardra's slow breathing, see it growing slower and more shallow until, after a short time, its movements ended altogether, and the breaths ceased. Rakariel looked down at it for a moment longer before turning back to Tei.

"They're dead," she said quietly, beckoning him. He forced himself to step out and cross to her side, still watching them nervously.

"All of them,?"

"I think so." She turned slowly, looking for Avin, found him standing more or less 'on' the floor with his head back, looking upwards at something she couldn't see. "...Avin?"

"Seivi's here," he said softly, his distant voice a whisper. *"She says we've done it... and I can feel it. Something I've never felt before, something I could never see before. It's calling me... I... I want to go home. I want to go..."*

"The way to the next life," Rakariel said softly. "It must be. It's over now. You're free to move on... both of you." There was nothing else she could think of that it could be, and if they had succeeded, and Avin was free to go, then so was the young priestess who had waited so long, her long struggle to remain finally over. At last, the past had been set right. To her surprise, she realised she could see spectral tears in Avin's eyes.

"It feels so bright."

"Go on, then," she said, her voice still soft. "Go, and be at peace. And... thank you. Both of you. We might not have made it this far without you."

Avin bowed his head. *"Thank **you**,"* he said. *"You saved my family... my home. You're the one who brought it to an end."* He turned to Tei, touched his shoulder one last time, a featherlight brush of cold all that betrayed the contact. *"Live well... all of you. I... I'm sorry for my part in this."* He hesitated, seemed to take a deep breath. *"Goodbye."*

"Goodbye, Avin," Tei managed, his tight voice as quiet as Rakariel's had been, and sadder. Though it had only been for a short time, their close contact had meant that Tei felt he knew him nonetheless. He'd known him, trusted him... and they were family. Now, so soon, Avin's last presence in the world would fade. He would truly be gone.

Rakariel and Tei both watched in silence as Avin's spirit began to fade back into invisibility. In some indefinable way, it felt almost as though he were vanishing into the distance, for all that they could both see him clearly before their eyes. After a few minutes, there was nothing left of him, not even the faint feeling of his unseen presence, and both knew with an instinctive finality that he was gone, never to return.

"Come on," Rakariel said softly after a minute or so. "We need to find our way back out."

Lifting his head, Tei slowly nodded, falling into place behind her. Even if it was safe, he didn't want to stay in the palace any longer than he had to. There would be time to come to terms with Avin's loss, with all that had happened, later.

Though they had seen the vardra lying dead and dying, heard Avin say that they were fading away, neither one of them relaxed as they made their way carefully back through the empty corridors, the vast hall they had passed through as littered with corpses as the corridor outside the library. If they were even once wrong in assuming that there was nothing to fear, both knew that they could, and likely would, still die. Only once it was proven beyond all doubt could they let their guard down, particularly without Avin to guide and warn them.

Navigating their way back through a combination of memory and Rakariel's instinctive sense of direction, they detoured around the grisly courtyard of bones, creeping through the maze of corridors and halls, stairs and fallen ceilings until they eventually reached the room by which they had entered so long before. Fog traced its way through the broken window, hanging in lazy clouds around the room, drifting on currents of air too faint even to feel. All was as they had last seen it, the ruin of ages past picked out in Rakariel's light, the dull grey outside slightly dark in comparison. Looking out at the mists, Tei frowned in thought. Had he grown overly used to the illumination of the lightstone, or was it too dark to be true day? As tired as he felt, could another evening have come? Or even another morning...?

Rakariel crossed to the window, her boots crunching slightly on the broken glass, and looked back at him in silent question when he failed to follow. Realising she hadn't seen what he had, he walked up beside her to answer it.

"It's not light enough," he whispered, pointing out

at the fog, illuminated now by her lightstone as well as the light from above. "It's evening."

Rakariel tugged a fold of her bandanna over the lightstone, brushing a few shards of glass from the windowsill before resting her hands on it to look out. Constant alertness and action of both body and thought had kept exhaustion pushed to the back of her mind, but she could feel it growing, all too easily to overcome her if she once relaxed. It was difficult to tell how long had passed, the hours merging into one another, and she thought back to the windows they had seen, however briefly, on the way back out. They had been dark, too dark.

"I'm not sure," she murmured back. "I think it's morning."

Surprised, Tei looked up at her. "Really?"

She nodded. "We should head back to your home." It was the only thing she knew of that they could do. The price had been paid, the balance restored, Avin's spirit at last free to go. It all indicated that the curse was lifting, and the valley would see the sun once more... but the fog hadn't lifted, and if it didn't, getting Tei to safety was the one final thing she could do for him.

The thought of home boosted Tei's spirits, and he smiled as he scrambled out through the broken window, landing almost silently on the rotten wood and wet soil beyond. As Rakariel followed suit, he walked a few paces further along the wall, looking around. Impossible though it was, they had entered the palace, and come out again alive. All that was left was to go home...

Rakariel came up beside him, tapping his shoulder and pointing out across the decaying gardens in the direction from which they had come. He nodded, and followed her as she crept quietly across the waterlogged soil, heading straight as an arrow for the other side. As they had on the way in, they passed skeletal bushes and trees still draped in places with the black, rotten remnants of leaves, had to detour once again around the wide pond and slip through the wooded area on the other side. The fog around them lightened as they went, proving that it was morning once more, that they had indeed somehow spent two whole days in the ruined palace, searching for answers. Even the simple realisation of how long he'd been awake made Tei feel that much more tired, but as long as Rakariel pushed on, he would follow her.

By the time they reached the wall that separated the palace grounds from the rest of the city, the mist had grown as light as it ever did. Tei stopped by the wall, resting his hands on its upper edge and bowing his head for a moment before trying to boost himself up. They were almost out, almost back to the safety of the world he knew. Relief and weariness mingled as he jumped, and he found his arms suddenly failing to hold his weight, dropping him back to the ground. To his left, Rakariel had climbed up without incident, crouched atop the wall and looking back at him at the faint splat of his feet in the wet soil. She turned, bracing herself with her left hand and reaching her right down to him, and he took it with a certain amount of chagrin, letting her help haul him up beside her.

"Thanks," he whispered, not quite meeting her eyes. Quiet though her voice was, the tone of her response was soft.

"It's all right. You've been awake for two days

now. You must be tired."

Tei sat on the edge of the wall and pushed himself rather ungracefully off, landing lightly on the cobbled street beyond. Rakariel followed, landing beside him a moment later.

"Aren't you tired, too?"

She smiled faintly. "I am. I just can't let myself acknowledge it yet. Not until this is over, and we're safe."

He nodded, slowly. Though she felt the same weariness he did, she had to be better by far at dealing with it, shutting it away until she could rest. The memory of the cellar came back to him, and he wondered just how much of her strength she had to have spent on it, how much she had sacrificed simply to heal him if she could block out the exhaustion of two days' wakefulness so well.

"We could rest nearby today," he said quietly. Though there weren't any safehouses this close to the palace, he knew where the closest was. Though it was rarely used, it was still maintained. Rakariel shook her head even as he was planning out the route.

"No. I'd rather we get as far as we can while it's still light."

For the first time, he realised there was a faint tension still in her voice, belatedly realised that the two days that had passed since they'd slept had to mean this was now her eighth day. On the next, she'd told him, her light would fail.

"But it's over, isn't it? The vardra are dead, and Avin... he could move on."

"I don't trust it," she murmured. "I can't, not until I see the sun again."

If it hasn't worked, if I die, I have to at least get you to safety. She didn't say it out loud. Her fears were not something she would willingly burden him with, and there was little time left. Thankfully, Tei chose not to question her, accepting her words at their face value, and she went on, internally relieved. "Lead the way."

Tei nodded, glanced reflexively around, and slipped across the broad road to the buildings on the other side. Keeping to walls and shadows, cutting through buildings as they had on the way in, he slipped silently through the city in a manner second nature to him, one he didn't even have to think about. He stumbled once, tired feet betraying him on an angled cobble, but caught himself before he could fall and moved on, forcing himself to focus, if not on the length of his journey then simply on the next step, and on the one after, and on what he would find at its end. Behind him, Rakariel followed as quietly as she could, listening to the sounds of the valley. In its eerie silence, the only sounds she could make out were the constant dripping of water and the slight noise of her own passage, strain though she might. If anything were left to stalk them, it made no sound.

They'd been travelling for a short while when Tei noticed something different, strange and unnatural to him, and stopped, staring into the fog to be certain that it hadn't been his own tiredness playing tricks on him. Rakariel paused next to him, peering ahead.

"What is it?" she whispered, almost silently, her bow already in hand and an arrow ready to draw.

"Look," he whispered back, pointing down the street into the mist. "Look at the air. You can feel it, too."

Caught in a gentle breeze, the valley's fog was moving, carried on air that was no longer still. Putting the arrow back in her sadly depleted quiver, Rakariel licked a finger and held it up, feeling the faint brush of air against it.

"It's the wind," she said softly.

"But it's so strong."

She looked at him in some surprise. Did the wind never blow, here in his dark, sealed world? Thinking about it, she realised that she couldn't remember ever noticing it, though she'd ceased to note its absence since first descending into the valley. Even unconsciously, it had reminded her all the more of a cave, another dark, endless, breathless underground, and the conscious realisation was the last thing she needed. She shook her head, pushing the thoughts back.

"This isn't strong to me," she told him. "It's just a breeze."

"What does it mean?"

"I don't know," she replied honestly. "Maybe it's another sign the curse is lifted. I hope so." She paused. "Let's keep going."

Tei nodded, starting forward again after a few moments more. The gentle breeze was completely foreign to him, unnatural: he'd never felt it so strong. The strangeness of it kept him alert, helping to push back the tiredness as he made his way warily on. Rakariel kept pace, moving when he did, stopping where he stopped. Was it her imagination, or was the mist slowly growing lighter, perhaps even thinning out? She desperately hoped so, and that very hope made her doubt herself. She knew her light was running out, knew she didn't have long; adapted to the dimly-lit fog, was she seeing only what she wanted to see?

Whether or not the light's brightening had been illusory, all too soon it began to darken again as they pressed on through the fog-bound streets. More alert than ever to its fading, Rakariel was the first to notice, the recognition of the oncoming night almost as strong as a physical blow.

"Sundown," she murmured. "The light is fading."

Tei nodded, glancing around quickly and pausing before a featureless wall to think. Still nothing pursued them, no sound to be heard beyond their own motions and the endless dripping of water, a background sound so natural and ordinary to him that he would have questioned not being able to hear it. They needed to find a safehouse to rest in for the night.

For her part, Rakariel was rapidly growing ever more uneasy. The curse was broken, she hoped, hoped that the valley would prove to have been unsealed, and the sun would shine again — but if it did not, then she was almost out of time. The beginning of the evening marked the end of the eighth day since her lightstone had last been charged, and sometime through the next it would give up the last of its light. If the sun failed to rise, she would be left in the dark forever.

"Let's keep going," she said quickly, deliberately cutting into Tei's contemplation. Surprised, he looked up at her, and shook his head.

"It's too far. We won't make it before dark." He hesitated. Though he suspected he already knew the answer, concern made him ask anyway. "What's wrong?"

"This is the end of the eighth day," she replied quietly, almost to herself. "My light dies tomorrow."

"But we don't need it now," he said. "It's all over... isn't it? The vardra are dead. It'll be light again tomorrow morning, it won't stay dark forever." A pause, and he added nervously "Will it?" Since Rakariel had arrived in his world, since he had fought alongside her, since he had been possessed by his ancestor's spirit and watched a legend die, anything could be possible.

"No." She shook her head. "At least, I hope not. I don't know why it would. But I need light, if the lightstone goes out, I..." Realising her fear was beginning to escape into her voice, she curbed it sharply, cutting herself off. "Let's just keep going."

Wordlessly, Tei nodded. He didn't, couldn't know what she feared, but her tone told him it was serious indeed. He trusted her word implicitly after all they had done: if she said that they needed the lightstone, then there had to be a reason, even if he couldn't see it. Obeying her words, he went on, still fighting back increasing exhaustion as he picked a path for them through the gathering dusk, battling the instincts of his entire life that demanded he find somewhere to hide and rest, and wait out the night. Their progress grew slower and slower as the fog grew steadily darker, and Rakariel touched his shoulder to bring him to a halt shortly before it became dark enough that even he would struggle to see.

"Are we stopping?" he asked

"No," she murmured. "Not yet." Worn down by two days of wakefulness, by the battles and the shadows, the darker it got the more insistently her own instincts clamoured for her to press on, to escape the darkness before it closed around her forever. They couldn't go on without light, and though her lightstone would be a beacon to danger, that was only if there were any foes left nearby for it to summon. To Tei's surprise, she took out her bow, loosing an arrow high into the air, and listened to the clatter of metal against stone that told of it coming down several streets away. He froze instinctively, but no further sound followed, no eerie hunting call summoning vardra to the chase. Rakariel waited for a few more minutes, giving any unseen foe time to reach the spot where her arrow had fallen, but nothing came. She put her bow carefully away again, then slowly lifted the cloth that covered her lightstone, tucking it back behind the circlet once more. Beside her, his back to the wall just as hers was, Tei drew a near-silent startled breath.

"Look!"

She saw at once what he meant. The moment her light's first rays had pierced the darkness, she had seen the fog was thinner than she'd expected it to be, leaving them able to see further in the city's streets than they ever had before. Despite her fears, she almost smiled.

"The fog is lifting."

It was a good sign in more ways than one. It made her feel better about travelling at night, knowing as she did that though the lightstone's light would be visible from even further, she would also be able to see and shoot true over a far greater range than she had been restricted to before, giving her space to slay anything that came at them long before it came within a range to harm them. Then, like the breeze they had felt, like the vardra that had lain peacefully down to die, it hinted again at the lifting of the curse, as Avin had, finally granted the ability to pass beyond the living realm and into whatever afterlife awaited him. King Sariven's death had ended what Avin's had indirectly begun, four centuries before.

"Do you think it will go away completely?" Tei asked. He couldn't even imagine it, though Rakariel had spoken of a world without fog. He'd never been able to see clearly except indoors, never known a view of anything further away than a few houses down the road, and despite his extensive knowledge of the city, it was all in the most immediate sense, half a street at a time with only an overview of how it all fitted together. He couldn't so much as begin to picture what the city would look like, free of the mist that had concealed it for generations.

"It should do," she told him.

"Wow," was his only comment. With a light push, Rakariel sent him on again, their way lit now by her light. She might have been aware of roughly which direction to head in, but only Tei knew the actual route. Without him, she would have no hope of finding her way back to his family's home.

As they travelled wearily on, Tei's pace slower than ever, the fog continued to lift, blown by the slowly strengthening breeze that was finding its way into the valley for the first time in centuries... and at some unguessable point, the lightstone began to dim. At first, its light faded only slightly slower than the fog was lifting, their field of vision slowly expanding even as the light faded. The illusion of constant illumination meant that not even Rakariel noticed at first, sensitised to it though she was, granting them a temporary gift of illusory time. Only when it abruptly flickered did she stop dead, Tei reflexively flattening himself to the wall and looking to see what had made her, as he thought, cover it for an instant. What he saw shocked him: he'd never seen her face hold such dread as it did then. Moving slowly, she detached the lightstone from its setting on her brow, cradling it in her hands and looking down into it as though she could give it strength through will alone. Even to his dark-adapted eyes, it was no longer as bright as it had been, and he realised with a shock that, just as she'd said, it was going out.

"No..." Rakariel murmured, unaware that she'd even spoken. "Not yet, this can't be..."

Looking at her, Tei realised that she might not withstand her light's disappearance. Though she was a stronger person in many ways than any he had ever known, though she'd faced the vardra without flinching, she was as vulnerable to this fear, whatever it was, as anyone else to theirs. His thoughts raced as he realised that he might have to decide what to do next, to take the decision from her. The creeping dread in her eyes was a match for that of people he'd helped his father to aid before, those less fortunate than him who had seen others close to them vanish in a blur of blackness and bladed claws and a blood-chilling, exultant howl, who had seen for their kin the horrific death that they, by some cruel miracle, had escaped. He had to lead her, even her, if he could, and the realisation was a shock of cold water to his exhausted mind.

Greatly daring, he reached out to take hold of her arm. Her head snapped up at once as though she feared danger, but, seeing his expression, she slowly looked back to her dying light. There was nothing tangible coming, only a danger that, to her, was far, far worse.

"Come on," he said gently, his voice just above a

whisper to let her hear its tone, doing his best to hide his own fear. He didn't even know what it was she was so afraid of, beyond something that might happen when her light went out, but the mere fact that she, impossibly brave and capable though she was, was scared meant that he, too, was unavoidably touched by its shadow. "There's a safehouse two side streets back. We'll go back there." Shoving his free hand into a pocket, he felt for his small collection of candle stubs, reassured by their presence. Maybe their light would help over the rest of the night.

"We have to go on..." Rakariel insisted bleakly, emptiness encroaching in her voice. For once, he shook his head, refusing her.

"We have to get to safety. It'll be safe, and we can move on in the morning, when it's light again." He pulled a candle from his pocket, held it up. "We'll still have light."

Rakariel looked from her lightstone to the pathetically tiny stub of candle and back again, and he gently tugged her around before she could object, setting out for the safehouse he knew awaited them. Thankfully, she let him direct her; he'd never have been able to take her even a single step if she'd resisted. He kept a firm grip on her arm — though not so firm as hers had been in the palace, a hold that had left his own arm aching even now — as he led her there, hearing strained to its limit as he listened for danger, though there was still no sound beyond their own soft footsteps and the dripping of water. It had begun to echo strangely, the sound no longer as flat as it had always been before without the thick fog deadening it, but it was still only water falling to puddles and wet stone.

Listen though he might, there was nothing else.

She was still gazing down at her dimming lightstone as he reached the safehouse, tiredness pushed back again by the burst of adrenaline her fear had sparked, as alert and on edge as he'd ever been. Leaving her to stand, he searched the windows, found a shutter that would swing outwards, and climbed in, leaning back out a moment later to look for her.

"Come on!" he hissed, and Rakariel followed, lowering the lightstone just long enough to climb inside. Tei latched the window shut before turning, taking in the sight of what was evidently once a simple front room, small, but large enough for four or five people to have sat around a table. Rakariel, too, was looking around, and he felt some degree of relief at that. After a few moments, she walked slowly across the room, to sit down against the far wall without removing her packs or even her cloak, staring again at her fading light. As he watched, it brightened slightly, then dimmed again. Slowly, it was fading away.

Tei shook his head and knelt before her, arranging his candles in a small group on the stone floor, glancing up at her several times as he did. For the time being, the lightstone still shone, but from her he, too, had caught a nameless fear of what would happen when it finally went out. Still, it was for her sake and not his own that he had put the candles out between them, that he lit one carefully after a few tries with his battered tinderbox, used it to light a second. That done, he edged around to sit beside her, his back to the wall. She looked up at him as he moved, then down at the little candle stubs set out before her, two of them already alight.

"...Thanks," she said, so softly that someone else

might almost have missed it. He gave her a slight smile despite his trepidation, edged a little closer, watching her still cradling the lightstone.

"Will we be all right?"

She bowed her head again, shook it slowly in uncertainty. "We... we should be. It should last 'til morning. If the sun comes up..."

Tei nodded. Even if it didn't, he'd long since privately resolved to find a way to get her to safety if he could, whatever menace came against them. He wasn't helpless, not any longer. He knew, though, that it wouldn't help her to say that, and instead simply echoed her words of before. They seemed to come from a lifetime ago, though in truth it had only been a few days.

"You should rest, if you can."

To his surprise, she managed a faint smile through the blanket of fear that cloaked her expression and sapped her resolve, still trying to keep up some small pretence of normality.

"Good advice." Still, she stayed in place, seeming an oddly small figure with her knees drawn up, hunched over her lightstone, though she was actually taller than he was, and had always seemed to him taller still. Tei leaned forward, locking his arms around his own knees, his head turned to the side to watch her. The dread in her hollow expression mingled with the exhaustion she was at last letting show, a combination he knew was the worst of all. He couldn't think of anything he could do beyond wait with her, standing guard against whatever it was that she feared.

The remainder of the night passed in uneasy restlessness for both of them. More than once, Tei caught himself starting to fall asleep, forced himself to his feet to walk around the room. For Rakariel's sake, he had to stay awake, at least until they reached safety. The lightstone continued to fade, flickering like a dying fire, and Tei's first candles burned down to nothing, forcing him to light another two, and then another. He was burning through his entire supply of precious candles, leaving himself none in reserve, but it seemed only right. She needed the light, and he rarely needed to use them. They could reach his family's home the next day, without the vardra hunting them to avoid. He wouldn't need the candles then.

Eventually, slowly, morning came. Tei's last candle was burning out, and the lightstone in Rakariel's hands now dimmed and brightened in uneven rhythm like a slow and failing heartbeat, barely giving out any light at all in its darker moments. Each time it faded almost to nothing, he caught her almost holding her breath, only to breathe again as the light returned. Sitting beside Rakariel again, his eyes threatening to close, Tei moved to get up — and stopped. An oddly bright light was slanting in through the cracks in the shutters, unflickering and true as though another lightstone were close just outside. Rubbing his eyes, he peered closer, but the strange sight remained.

"Rakariel," he whispered, pointing at the rays of light, "look!"

Lifting her head with a start, instinctively tense, she focused on his hand before following its line across to the window. All at once, she drew a sharp, involuntary breath, barely daring to hope. Could it be? Could it truly be?

Clutching the lightstone tightly in her left hand,

she got to her feet and made her way slowly across the dim room, stepping over the guttering candle almost as much by luck as intent. Was that light truly daylight, had she once again escaped the darkness at the last? Or was it the cruellest trick of all?

Firming her resolve, pushing the phantasms of nightmare back with all the strength she had, Rakariel clumsily unhooked the latch, pushing the shutter open. All at once, the bright light of dawn flooded in, and she stood transfixed, unable to move or speak. Somewhere in the blue sky she could clearly see through a thin curtain of lingering mist, the sun was rising. At long last, its rays were making their way into the valley that had been all but closed to them for so long.

Watching her as she stood bathed in an incredible light, Tei could only stare until eventually, she shook herself free of her thoughts with an effort and looked back at him, the fear lifted from her face and even replaced with an exhausted elation, her courage returned.

"Come on."

She climbed out of the open window, and he followed, standing beside her on the clear, light-washed street and looking up at the vivid blue, brighter than anything he'd ever seen, so unbelievably far above. The city streets stretched out to either side further than he had ever envisaged, and the valley's sheer walls seemed almost to touch the sky both before and behind. Clear and cloudless, it was a dizzying, impossible dream.

Clipping the lightstone back into place and letting it soak up the brilliant daylight from its position on her forehead, Rakariel quietly took hold of his arm, recognising in his expression an awe and wonder even greater than her own. Together, they stood side by side, watching the sky Tei had never seen grow brighter and brighter still, its blue deeper and deeper, until at last the disc of the sun slowly crept above the edge of the valley, bathing them both in its unparalleled radiance. Eyes closed and head back, Rakariel finally relaxed in its blessed light and warmth as, beside her, Tei mirrored her pose in awe.

"It's the sun..."

— — —

About the Author

I've been writing since I was old enough to arrange words in some semblance of order, and reading from the moment I understood what letters meant. With parents who were avid readers, several younger siblings, and an entire army of pets (over thirty of which were gerbils as a result of an unanticipated population explosion), I was never short of inspiration, or of "willing" victims to try out my latest efforts on. My unusual educational path means that I have full degrees in both maths and physics, but only one A-Level! When not adventuring around other worlds by means of books or games, I spend my time exploring this one, whether through activities from caving and climbing to swordfighting and archery, or by the more considered means of learning to understand as much of our vast universe as possible.

Also by the Same Author

Short Stories:
   Mysteries Unite
   Oranges and Lemons
Web serials:
   The Fused

V. L Bending Online

My Internet presence is centred around my writing blog Distant Realms at https://distantrealms.wordpress.com, and hopefully on my own website, DistantRealms.Net, in the not-too-distant future.

You can also find me on Twitter as @Metalwings. Continuing the theme, my Smashwords author profile is https://www.smashwords.com/profile/view/Metalwings.

Made in the USA
Columbia, SC
31 July 2017